REFRACTION

ANDREW VAN WEY

REFRACTION

THE CLEARWATER CONSPIRACIES

ANDREW VAN WEY

PROLOGUE

A RED DAWN RISES AS THE MERCENARY STEPS PAST THE BULLET-RIDDEN throne and opens the palace window. He finds the view pleasing. This is the height of pineapple season, a time of heat and sugary crispness that clings to the breeze and moistens the tongue. He breathes in the damp valley air. He could lose himself in moments like this; he often does.

Until a distant explosion ends his reverie.

Zade Holloway's vision shifts from the terraced plantations to the royal courtyard below. Men clamoring over fences and pulling down gates. Pickups being flipped over and stripped. Tires burning in piles.

The perfumed wind gives way to an acrid tang of diesel and spent munitions. Celebratory gunfire echoes across the palace grounds, like the firecrackers Zade threw as a child. Simpler times.

"Everything good, boss?"

Zade doesn't have to turn to know who's approaching. After months together, he can tell his men apart by the clatter of their body armor and the width of their gait. Hoffman drags his left foot from a wound in Crimea.

"Everything's perfect," Zade says. "The king is dead. Long live the king."

Their bootsteps fill the cavernous throne room, echoing past the ceremonial armor, the wooden shields hanging on the stucco walls. Hoffman's eyes sweep the doors, the corners. All empty and cleared.

Zade's pacing comes to an end at the throne, this regal chair of marble and gold. He wipes blood from the armrest. Digs a finger into a hole, still warm from the bullets. He steps over the red wetness left by the monarch.

Former monarch, he thinks.

All the while, Hoffman keeps his MK 17 SCAR-H at the ready. Not because he distrusts his commander, but because of where the commands have led. They've jumped from planes, crawled through farmland and jungle. They've rendezvoused with rebels and ducked countless bullets. Adrenaline fades fast, but the battle buzz lingers.

Another explosion, closer now. Zade eyes the dust drifting down from a bank of TVs on the wall. Samsung, 8K QLED displays. For a nation on the edge of starvation, His Majesty had a nice setup. Another reason the monarchy crumbled so fast.

"Word from the rebels is they've taken the airfield and the port," Hoffman says. "Litundi is ours."

"No," Zade says. "Litundi is our employer's."

The TVs are playing a security feed, the end result of a year of political pressure and an agricultural embargo. Starved citizens fed a diet of disinformation. Riots incited outside this very palace. Mix in an incursion of foreign mercenaries—generously funded yet without national backing—and you wind up with this: the gates breeched; the royal guards running away; parliamentarians dragged from Range Rovers, stuffed in old tires, and lit ablaze.

And a king gunned down on his throne just moments ago.

Now comes the celebration and fires and looting. All that tension craving release.

"We have the palace," Zade says. "For now, we are Litundi's

custodians. Have His Majesty photographed and burned." Zade waves a fly away. "How many did we lose?"

Hoffman checks the tablet fastened to his forearm. "Seven wounded, five seriously. We're still awaiting confirmation, but another four dead. Hurwtiz caught a bullet when we breached the inner palace. Yang as well."

"Did you scrub their bodies?"

"I'm told they were."

"Told." Zade turns to him. "You didn't see for yourself?"

Hoffman clears his throat. "I will, sir. See to it, that is."

Zade glances back at the security monitors, where half the royal family now hang from flagpoles, the rebels pelting them with shoes. "Our benefactors want muddied waters. Pull teeth and plant new ones. Get the bone bags from Schneiderman. Clean up with incendiaries."

"Of course, sir."

Once Hoffman is gone, Zade paces the throne room. Past the paintings of the proud royal family. Past all the honorary degrees. Past the framed handshakes with politicians, business leaders, entertainers. So much blood money, and what did it buy?

Nothing.

The king begged and shit himself when Zade pulled the trigger. No different than Aleppo or Juárez or Cabo Delgado.

Zade stops at the window as the post-combat shakes overtake him. He studies the mineral-rich valleys now clouded with smoke. If only the king had shared his benefactor's perspective. If only he'd shared.

Even before the mining companies discovered lanthanum deposits, Litundi was a tinderbox. With half the nation hungry, it didn't take much. A few false convoys of food bound for the palace, intercepted, then spread on social media. Rumors that the royal family dined on caviar while children starved. Hidden caches of medicine uncovered, earmarked for rich politicians, while West Nile ravaged the nation.

At least that's what the videos purported to show.

Soon, even the truth tasted fake. All the royal statements decrying the propaganda fell on deaf ears. All the king's ministers couldn't dampen the anger. The citizens were famished and angry; the fuse was ready to light. Then Zade and his men jumped into the jungle.

The radio squawks, ending another daydream. Damn, he really needs to keep focused. It's just…

What? Something feels off, he thinks. Something's amiss.

"Hoffman here. We secured the king's sister, his nephews and nieces. We're bringing them up. Over."

Zade thumbs the radio. "Copy that." And he thinks, *Now for the spoils of war…*

He passes time counting explosions out the window. Six concussive blasts. Six plumes of dark smoke from distant oil derricks. Tonight, it might rain petrol.

And tomorrow, when the U.N. takes control, a new Litundi will need to be built. New bridges and highways, new statues too. All privately financed, of course. Good business going forward. Perhaps Zade can stick around.

The fly lands on his left arm. There, like a map of his life, are tattoos from Zade's younger days. A pomegranate with a bullet hole for the Battle of Kandahar. A grinning skull for the Second Battle of Fallujah. Each inked in Japanese irezumi, bold colors against gray.

Except one on his wrist. A spiral, like a QR code filled in with flickering static and three alphanumerics: *D22*.

Odd. Zade doesn't remember getting this.

It's just nerves, he tells himself. Even old mercs still get the shivers.

First comes the staccato burst of M4A1s fired in celebration. Then the hooting and hollering follows. At the far end of the throne room: Paxton, Kearl, and McManus, all glistening and grinning. In tow: a mixed group of adults and children. Zade recognizes their faces from the mission briefing, where the word *EXPENDABLE* flashed in red. Here they are, His Majesty's extended family. The remaining royal bloodline of a nation soon to be reborn in democracy's shape.

Or so it believes.

"Please, please, listen to me," the king's younger sister says. "Are you the man in charge, sir?"

Zade raises a hand, palm out, calming and casual. It pains him to see her once colorful clothes now sweat-stained and dirty. Despite three kids, she's kept that strong frame this nation's women are known for. And her voice, laced with that accent from years of studying abroad. Does she know Zade has a thing for the French? She probably does.

"I am that man in charge," he says, stepping across the rug where her brother bled out. "And you are the queen now. So, that makes this all a bit tricky. What do I call you? Mrs. Nazombe? Her Majesty?"

"You may call me whatever you wish as long as you protect my family. My husband here, Emmanuel, he is a good man, a French citizen. He—"

"Oh, we know all about you, Director," Zade says. Nice trick, using her husband's first name, humanizing him. "Monsieur Jett, heir to France's largest importer of corks. You two met in Marseille, yes? And these are your children. What a modern, multicultural family. Hello, little ones."

He squats eye level and offers them a smile. Despite them shrinking away, he has to admit: damn adorable kids. Zade's dad told him never to mix the whites with the colors. But Zade's mother had divorced that old bigot and given Zade a biracial half sister, the best person in his life. So what did the old man really know?

"Sir, I'm afraid I didn't catch your name," the new queen says. "I'm Yewande, and these are our children, Pitir, Stephan—"

"Don't worry your pretty lips. My name doesn't matter."

"You are speaking to the queen-regent," Emmanuel barks. "Who are you to talk to her like this?"

A grin splits Zade's sweaty face. "Monsieur, are you a fan of television? Now, I agree with the general sentiment that it rots the brain. However, here's a show I think we'll both enjoy. Take a peek."

He gestures to the TV monitors on the wall.

At first, they can't figure out what they're seeing, those red lumps dangling from flagpoles. It's only when the security camera pulls out wide that she recognizes the courtyard. Here hang the young princes, all stripped and strung up as rebels pelt them with shoes.

A cry leaves her lips.

"You asked who I was?" Zade spears Emmanuel with his thousand-yard stare. "Well, monsieur, I'm the man guarding that door. My name doesn't matter." Now his eyes shift to Yewande. "What matters is what you'll open to keep those palace doors shut."

Emmanuel balls his fists but Yewande puts a hand to his arm. Gods, she is charming, a woman in charge. Zade can feel himself stiffening.

She asks, "What would you have of us? We can offer you things. Money, cars. My brother kept a vault of a great many valuables. Please, take your pick."

"I already have." Zade can smell her sweat and the distinct heat of fear and… was that a flicker of excitement? Yes, Zade can feel his blood pumping quick now. "Why don't we see what we can work out. I'm told your brother had quite the quarter for his harem—"

"You son of a bitch!"

Emmanuel is fast and angry, facts Zade counted on. The first strike is wide, sloppy, and he easily dodges. The second slides off his ear, rings it soft like a concierge bell.

There is no third strike.

An inward snap and Zade has Emmanuel by the wrist in a *kotegaeshoi* lock. A sharp twist and Zade feels the ligaments tear in his grasp. Emmanuel hits the ground, shrieking. Then Zade's men have their guns raised and ready, one word away from pruning this whole royal branch.

"Please, please," Yewande begs, stepping between the guns and her mewling man. All her husband's old money in France and it can't help them here.

"Your move, my queen." Zade motions to a set of doors beyond the throne. "Join me in the back. Or join the rebels out front."

Moments later, he's closing the door and watching Yewande shiver as the lock slides into place.

The great room is spacious, filled with trinkets and art. He makes note to return for a few souvenirs. For now, its leather sofas will suffice.

On the far wall hangs a painting: the former king staring down from six feet of canvas and gilded frame. All those medals and ranks on his chest and what had they earned? He cried as Zade's men raised their guns. Begged and crawled and—

A flicker of light races down the marble floor. Wincing, Zade rubs his eyes. Bad time for a migraine.

"Go ahead and take off your clothes. No need to be coy." He begins unfastening his body armor. A clack as his ballistic plates hit the floor. Next come his shoes and his belt. "Your majesty, I said start getting undressed."

Yewande's back is to him, giving Zade a perfect view of her curves and that colorful dress. But she doesn't move.

So, defiance it is. Zade enjoys a bit of foreplay: the biting, the scratching, the screams. Yes, he can feel himself getting light-headed.

"I said take off your—"

"I think it's time to wake the subject up, yes?"

Zade swallows. Yewande's accent has vanished. *How?* And the colors of her clothes, the reds and yellows and greens that form dancing patterns, they are—impossibly—fading to gray. Her skin, that dusty caramel that he covets, now swims with flecks of silver and white, iridescent fish within water.

No, he realizes. Like static.

Her skin glistens with interwoven threads. A dead radio signal, buzzing. An empty TV station, crackling. A strange voice, saying, "Neural oscillations in sync."

Queen Yewande turns around. Only she isn't the queen or Yewande but just a featureless shade. Eyes of flickering mist and lips that drip whispers right into his mind.

The palace walls fall away like cards.

Zade stumbles back. Yet there is no back. No away. No out. The gilded ceiling, the marble floor, the windows looking out onto the revolution of their making, all fall apart.

Only a void remains, a landscape of electrical snow. And Zade, here among it, senses that he is witness to *everything*, to all of the universe at once.

His mind simply shatters.

"Subject D22, it's time to wake up." The words wriggle inside his skull. "Your target is a man in his mid-seventies. Five feet eleven inches. Caucasian. Bald. Visual incoming… now."

Zade's gaze is pulled to the painting. No dead king looks down from that gilded frame. Instead, here looms a man Zade senses he's seen in newspapers, on CNN, in the background of federal hearings.

Zade tries to avert his eyes, yet the picture follows. He shakes his head but it stays, locked to the center of his vision. He buries his face in his hands. Still it persists, the ever-present frame and the man he simply cannot escape.

"Your blind site is a house, two stories, surrounded by oaks. The address is 3350 Larchmont Way. The driveway is gravel. You will see a BMW 5 series pull up shortly, license plate 4SOC642."

With each word, details bloom from the static. First the roof, asphalt shingles floating above nothing. Next the black shutters. Then a driveway unfurling like a rolled carpet. Reeds rise among yard lights as mossy oaks stretch out and groan.

It all slams into view, assaulting Zade's senses. The dark house pushes forth from the void. The yard lamps upturn to illuminate the address: *3350* in quaint, cursive script.

And Zade, unable to look away. Unable to scream or cry out. Only able to think, *Why? Why is this happening?*

Now the calm voice pours into his ears and suffuses his mind. "Do we have your attention? Good. Now let us begin."

And now he is there.

[PART 1]

"You can lose your way groping among the shadows of the past."

— Louise-Ferdinand Celine,
Journey to the End of the Night

DAHLONEGA, LUMPKIN COUNTY, GA

8:45 PM EST

THE CRICKETS HUSH AS JUDGE MABERRY TURNS INTO HIS DRIVEWAY and shuts off the car's engine. He gives himself a moment to collect his thoughts. Far off, a coyote howls from the safety of the hills. No others answer.

Alone. Alone is a good thing. Especially after the past several days and all that it brought. The bitter salt in the fog. The murmuring sea. From several hundred feet above, the waves hummed louder than the helicopter that brought him there, to that facility, to the edge of the world.

And what he saw in those flickering halls…

He shudders. *No. Put that out of your mind.*

The judge lets the summer breeze wash over him. Home. Sanctuary. And yet so much to do and undo.

"Frank?"

At the warm porch stands Cheryl, his wife, his partner in life and best friend for fifty-some years. Every now and then, when the light catches her at a curious slant, he can still see the young woman that stepped into his study group, back when the world felt larger, its problems smaller, and everything seemed solvable.

"I thought that was you. Come in before you catch cold."

The judge takes the old steps one at a time, careful of the slick the mist brings. Cheryl gives him a kiss. "And welcome home, dear."

Inside his home office, the judge lets the Eames chair embrace him. He waits until Cheryl is out of earshot before opening his desk. After the bypass, he promised her he'd cut back on liquor. And he had. No more golf course cocktails, no more social martinis. But tonight, he'll be damned if he won't drink after what he's seen.

So, Pappy Van Winkle it is. A bottle of twenty-three-year-old Family Reserve, hidden behind printer cartridges. He pours two fingers into a squared glass and knocks it all back. Now two more.

On a chemical level, the judge knows the bourbon warming his gut has sent signals to his brain, suppressing glutamate while letting the dopamine flow. And at his age, it does the trick quick. One sip for courage. A second to wash away the stink of salt water. Now a gulp to dull the memory of machine-threaded flesh.

Shit, he's out again. Better pour another.

The phone vibrates, spiking his heart rate. A message: *Meeting ID Incoming.*

The computer before him was sent and set up for one purpose: to answer these calls. It's a cumbersome thing, black and red and with all the personality of a toaster. He misses his colorful iMac, the stickers his granddaughter covered it with. Around this device, he treads lightly. And that webcam with its wide field of view. He senses it's always on, always watching.

Another vibration. The code: *Pleasant Gargoyle.* He types that into the two-factor authentication box.

Green lights.

CONNECTING...

The screen splits into three boxes. At the top: himself, in letterbox format. Below, to the left: Congresswoman Chatterjee. To the right: Senator Marks.

The congresswoman looks exhausted, fresh off the debates where she'd been decrying the president's call for cutting health care. The senior senator from Kentucky smiles, his toad-like jowls stretching taut. It's a curious mix: a congressional democrat, a Kentucky Christian on his third wife, and this textualist judge appointed two presidents ago. Three lives here onscreen, here for the sake of the nation's safety.

And tied to a clandestine agency they founded over a decade ago.

Until I cut the strings, Judge Maberry thinks.

"Well, don't keep us waiting, Frank," the congresswoman says. "Now that you've seen it up close, is there any hope of salvaging this project?"

Another sip to buy him some time. The judge stares deep into that plane of pixels connecting Georgia, Kentucky, and D.C. How many millions had they redirected each funding cycle? And how to close it down before they're all shackled inside?

"Give it to us straight," the senator croaks. "What's your inclination on the longevity of Day's Bane?"

"I have deep concerns," the judge says. "The project has made strides, this much is true. It's also taken liberties. We're exposed here, all of us, to a very high degree of risk. To be honest, I'm still processing it."

"But what gives you pause?" the senator asks. "You can speak freely, Frank. We're in this swamp together."

The judge clears his throat. Where to start? "With the funding coming through us, that's one liability. And the test subjects, they're Americans—"

"No one who'll be missed," the senator adds. "Bad hombres, the lot of them. Worst of the worst is what we signed off on."

"But Americans nonetheless," the judge says. "When that pool's overfished, then what happens?"

The others say nothing. He tries to gauge their expressions. Disappointment. Or perhaps fear. Fear is good. It means they know the blowback. Christ, it'd make Abu Ghraib look like a kid's show.

He continues, "The security costs, the infrastructure. Electrical alone is in the millions."

The judge wipes his brow. At some point he'd started sweating. It's always hottest when you're holding the torch.

Senator Marks steeples his fingers. "So it's the fiscal and legal entanglements. Fair enough. What else?"

A creak behind him. Frank turns around. Damn, he'd left the door ajar. Well, no matter. Cheryl's upstairs; he can hear the sink running.

"What else? Morale is low, especially with the researchers. They've had resignations, concerns of ethics. We're tracking informational leaks on the dark web."

The congresswoman leans in. "You don't think Coordinator Nox can handle it?"

"No one can." Frank sucks in air through his teeth. Tries to let the liquor lighten his words. *God grant me the strength…*

"This program, if it achieves full viability, is going to reshape the very nature of conflict. No one would be safe. Heck, all you'd need is a video feed and a willing body and you could kill with impunity. No. We need to bury this. Cut all funding, sink the findings, torch and scorch from top to bottom, just like the major general did in '92. We have one chance to make the hard choice. Otherwise, that choice will be made for us, and when it does, history will tear us to shreds."

Silence. The implications are simply too heavy, too shattering. He prays they feel the weight of his words.

The congresswoman sighs, lowers her head. The senator's tongue circles his teeth. The judge listens to the stillness of the night. To the crickets once again growing silent.

"Frank, I'm glad we see eye to eye," the senator says. "About the transformative nature of Day's Bane. And about its implications. We've got tough roads in front of us, my friend. Thanks for being candid. Now, you give Cheryl our best, you hear?"

"Goodbye, Frank," the congresswoman says.

It's just a glance, a quick flick of their eyes off camera. Yet it says everything. And Judge Frank Maberry understands on an instinctual level why the crickets have stopped singing. Why the humid air has cooled.

First comes the flickering of lights. The same on-off, on-off that made his stay aboard the facility play hell on his eyes. Then comes the low pulse. Quantum displacement, the technicians had called it. Something arriving from a higher dimension.

With a groan, the old study door closes. A rectangle of light, shrinking, shrinking, shrinking. Oozing shadows now, and a single night-light, winking.

When the eyes open, the judge finds the scream that starts in his throat leaves his lips as a dry gurgle. Two pupils of cold fire bloom before him, eyes of winter fury. And now, staring at one of the *things* he saw on that fog-soaked lab, Judge Frank Maberry realizes why the crickets had been wise.

They had kept their songs to themselves.

The grip seizes him, compressing the breath from his lungs and squeezing the blood from his heart. Frigid fingers wrack his mind as time slips down a distant chute. The judge has one final thought before his world dims forever.

It's all on him now, the only man who can stop it. The one who set this nightmare in motion.

LIGHT BEHAVES STRANGE ONE HUNDRED AND FORTY FEET BELOW THE water's surface.

Red fades first, followed by orange, then yellow. These fish should be vibrant pastels and pure blacks. Instead, they are muted blues and greens, scaly forms weaving through the two halves of the shipwreck before him.

Michaels checks his dive watch. Less than twenty-eight minutes of oxygen at this depth. That's assuming no temperature changes, no surprises, no panicked gasps. Bold assumptions to make.

So he swims carefully. Tries not to disturb the seabed and sparse kelp. His rebreather sends bubbles up to the surface marker buoy where the boat rocks on ribbons of light.

One figure-eight lap around the shipwreck and he's certain: this has to be it.

How the hell did she survive?

The odds are staggering. What the kelp and coral and a decade of decay have left are cleaved pieces of the boat scattered along sandy ridges. Swimming alongside the ruins, he can see the bent mast, the shattered cabin, some box that might have been a refrigerator once, now covered in rusticles and starfish.

Another pass and a prickle of doubt; he has to be sure. Closer now, careful not to disturb the silt. Beneath paint-chewed lichen, beneath a decade of decay, beneath the very light that bleaches color over the years, there hangs an etched metal frame, its bolts long rotted, save for one.

Michaels stretches a hand out and wipes off the sediment. There it is, the name of her boat: *Argent Tomorrow.*

Twenty minutes later, Michaels surfaces with a quarter tank and hoists himself onto the boat's launch. He removes the dive weights and takes in the breeze. He measures his thoughts. When they set sail from Mauritius in Caitlyn's Beneteau Oceanis 473, he was just another vacation diver learning to scuba. In the six months since, he's become something of a pro.

This is a problem.

The mind overestimates its own skill, tricks itself with false bravado. A mental mirage, shortening the true chasm between amateur and expert. It's why new investors with weeks of experience blow their savings on sure bets. It's why Everest is littered with corpses.

Today's scuba dive is over, not because Michaels doubts his ability to swim inside the shipwreck.

But because he thinks that he can.

"So tell me what you saw?" Caitlyn asks, climbing out of the cabin and joining him on deck.

Almost a year of sun has drawn the freckles to her cheeks' surface and lightened her hair. Her tattoos, so vibrant beneath the gray light of San Francisco, are now hints upon sun-kissed skin.

And her eyes…

A deep blue-green suffuses them now, as intense as any of the waters they've sailed.

She asks, "Have we really found it?"

"Yeah, Cait, we found it." He holds out the dive camera. Onscreen: the name of the old sailboat in rusty metal, *Argent Tomorrow.* Another swipe brings up a top-down view of the wreck.

"I need to be sure." She pops the camera out of the protective case and plugs it into the cockpit's monitor. She flips down the sunshade. Doesn't think to hand Michaels a towel.

Of course not, he realizes. This is it, the end result of months scouring the seabed. Simulating drift patterns and currents off the warm Kenyan coast. Back plotting her parents' route.

When he caught up with her in Mauritius, this moment was the distant future. Now here it is, her past in the present.

"What did the inside look like?" she asks, tapping the image of the kelp-covered hatch. "Could you see any signs of fire, or—"

"I couldn't get inside."

"What? Why not?"

A squeak as he tugs off his fins. "Because there's over a decade of coral and rot. Plus the sediment. One nudge and I'd stir it up, end up blind and feeling my way through."

Caitlyn squints at the pictures. "That's how I made it out during the accident."

"You were damn lucky. You also had your trick. It's different down there now. The whole boat is ready to collapse."

She continues swiping through the photos. After months together, he's learned to read her fierce gaze. Here it is, focused on the screen: the end of her adolescence. She climbed aboard the boat as the daughter of two expats, just some third-culture kid raised in the classroom of the world.

And what came out of the water? The daughter of two fugitives, two government subjects. Herself, formerly blind, formerly captured, a genetic accident formed by two decoherent minds and decades of lies.

Yes, he can see her thoughts forming, her face hardening, an action impending.

She asks, "What's the depth?"

"One forty even."

Caitlyn is on her feet now, opening the dive cabinet. There are extra weights and belts and wet suits, all organized in the weeks prior to departure. But what there isn't are an additional four tanks.

"Cait, let's talk about this."

"I'm just going to take a quick look."

"If you're going inside, I'm coming down to support. We'll need time to set up reels and guidelines. Lights too. It's dark—"

"We don't have enough tanks for that."

"Not on us, no. But the dive shop will."

"That's two days there, two back. What about the compressor? It won't take more than an hour."

"It would, if we had full batteries. But we're on solar, barely charging. We used up our juice this morning."

"So I'll go down to scout and tomorrow you can lay lines."

He can see where this is going. "No, no way. If you run into trouble, then I have to dive on half a tank? That's not safe. Two full tanks each."

He steps across the cockpit and checks her work. She's connecting valves quickly, hands trembling too much to thread them.

"Cait, listen—"

"No, you listen." She spins, turning those bright eyes on him. "That's my home down there, okay? I need this. I need to know what happened."

"And I'm here for that, okay? Any answers you want, we'll find them. But we need to be safe. And don't tell me you won't swim inside when you're down there, because we both know that you will. We wait, fill the tanks, string some guidelines and lights. We do this the right way."

He takes her hand, runs his thumb across her wrist to feel her pulse. It's racing.

"What if I say no?" she says. "That I want to go down there now. What then?"

Michaels studies her face. The way her jawline tightens, tensing for a fight. There have been a lot of those lately. Little room for privacy on a forty-seven-foot boat. Ample chances to get in each other's way.

When they set sail from Mauritius, it felt like the start of a new adventure, perhaps a new life together. And for a while it was. Their hearts raced with the winds in the sails, the tilt of the yacht. They filled the nights with long talks and laughter and passion beneath infinite stars.

Now, most days they can't make it to lunch without awkward silences, a sense that they speak the same language yet their words carry different meanings.

"What then?" Caitlyn repeats, the wind blowing her hair in her face.

"I guess I'd have to let you."

"Let me?" Her eyes narrow. "This is my boat."

"It is."

"I saved your life."

"You saved many lives. And I covered your escape. Cait, ask yourself, would your parents want you to risk this? Come all this way just to throw caution to the wind?"

A pause. Her eyes study the cockpit as if the answer is close. Something softens. "No, you're right. I'm not going to put us in danger. That would be silly."

A sigh. "Thank you."

He squeezes past her and checks the battery. Some quick math. They've got enough juice to get through the evening. If he fires up the genny, they can run the compressor past sundown. He'll have to stay up with it, but okay. He can even cook some red snapper.

Tomorrow they'll dive at first light.

"Cait, so listen…"

But she's gone, descending into the cabin.

$$[\ 3\ ]$$

CAITLYN TAKES THE LADDER TWO STEPS AT A TIME. DIM LIGHT DOWN here, the afternoon sun through the portholes and glass hatches. When it was just her family in a Cal 40 sailboat, the clutter felt endless, the walls impossibly cramped.

Here, Caitlyn's Beneteau Oceanis 473 is spacious and sleek. Despite its age, everything is integrated into little compartments. One thing she learned going blind was the joy of minimalism. Not every shelf and drawer needs to be stuffed.

It also helps to be romantically entangled with an obsessive-compulsive.

Michaels…

A coppery tinge whenever she clenches her jaw. She knows he's right. About the dive, about her parents, about everything. She knows he's just being safe.

And yet…

A glance back to the cockpit. He's adjusting the compressor while the grill warms up. He'll have his hands full for a while. Now, if she can just clear her mind.

It has been quite a while.

Caitlyn takes a cushion from the master bed and lays it on the floor. She crosses her legs. Feels the click of her cartilage, the shift of the boat in these soft African waters.

Next, she closes her eyes.

When Michaels pulled her from the pod at Clearwater, he told her how to escape. The exact route out the back and which turns to take.

And he told her the truth.

"You're not blind, not quite. Your brain is lesioning to keep its systems in balance. If you stop blinking, there's a chance the lesions will shrink."

So that's what she did. She spent the summer in Argentina, staying with Tiago under a false name. She stepped off the plane with a folding cane and near-total doubt. She put her trust in the process, the hardest thing she'd ever done.

Then, one day, it happened.

First a flicker, little fingers at the edge of her vision. Hands made of static, tugging the persistent curtain of shadows.

Week one: just flashes.

Month one: entire landscapes swam behind a milky haze.

And then came the faces, and gods how she missed them. The smiles and frowns, the lines and the wrinkles that stretched out from the corners of eyes or creased foreheads and cheeks.

Six months after she lay in a Clearwater pod and blinked her mental body to Iowa, Caitlyn finally saw her own face in the mirror.

So why is she doing this now?

Because it needs to be done. Just like Teddy and Mrs. Jensen, when Caitlyn guided the gun in the old woman's hand. *Because I need to be the one to do this.*

Caitlyn focuses on the camera's viewfinder. A dozen photos and a video. More than enough to assemble her blind site. Another deep breath. Now count down from ten. See the blue-green sea bottom. See the coral growing from the old boat. The tracts of sand, little dunes and valleys beneath barnacled rocks.

It all blooms out from the camera display. A pixelated wave

crashing into the bedroom. Water, then coral, then the full weight of the sea in one simple blink.

And now she is there.

Caitlyn opens and closes her luminous fingers. She brushes aside drifting sea particles. Clenches her toes. Feels sand shifting beneath her, little clouds swirling at her ankles. *Interesting…*

Caitlyn has long suspected something changed at Clearwater. In those cold rooms, something awakened in her mind. Silly to think it was gone after so many months. Like riding a bike after years off the seat, the decoherent mind picks up where it left off.

Focus on the boat. That's why you're here.

A cool voice whispers, "We're down here."

Caitlyn turns around, scaring off a school of curious fish. She studies the empty seabed.

No one else.

It's not the first time her senses have distorted while blinking. Technically, she's not even hearing with ears. And yet…

She follows the silty seabed, taking it all in. Here it is, her old home for so many years. What her mom called the traveling classroom.

Now look at it, this wreck. Two sad halves devoured by coral and kelp, homes to countless fish. An eel gives Caitlyn a silent snarl and slithers through a porthole.

When the fisherman found her adrift, she was covered in sunburns. But she had sworn there were other burns too. A propane tank. Diesel gas. The burning of plastic and fiberglass.

Walking around the shattered hull now, she finds no signs of fire, no scorch marks, no charring. There is only this twisted vessel, splayed outward, as if sundered by some terrible expansion.

Go inside. See for yourself.

So she focuses on the nearest half. She blinks. And now she is there.

Inside, she recognizes the layout of the master bedroom, but the years have been cruel. Her parents' bed is a mound of decay.

Just a frame of rust and frayed plastic, slick ribbons like infinite hairs. There it is, above, the hatch she escaped from, forever open. Her own boat, *Dionysus*, floats 140 feet up.

Anemones sway as she crosses the sandy floor, little tentacles opening and closing. A school of minnows darts past. Further, where the sediment meets the collapsed hall that once connected the V-berth to the kitchen, an octopus squeezes beneath a tangle of pipes and planks. The way forward is blocked.

Michaels was right. Swimming in here is suicide. Damn him for always being clearheaded. Why does she push him away?

Because you're allergic to happiness. Just look at you now. Seeking out what you already know.

Caitlyn visualizes the cabin beyond the murky depths. She blinks. And now she is there.

Potted herbs rest in the sunbeam, her mother's favorite basil and thyme. A mini Persian rug covers the floor. Here is the cork board that catalogs their voyage, from Italy to Greece, then Turkey and down off the Egyptian coast. There is the pinned photo, young Caitlyn and her mother making funny faces in the shadow of the Sphinx.

No. It's all gone. The herb shelf is splintered, the porthole long shattered. Nothing but lichen where the corkboard once hung. The floor is carpeted in rot and ruin, the whole structure tilting to the right. Even the mast beam—the spine of the boat—is crooked and buckled.

Caitlyn takes it all in, this place where she had woken to find the sea surging forth. They had fought that night, hadn't they? A real Grey family blowout before going to bed. And what had she said?

"You keep making us leave just when I start making friends. I hate you for that."

There was no fire. Caitlyn can see that now. No explosion of gas and flame. No collision. She can see the very shadow of time, right here on the wall: the old brass clock with its cracked glass, hands forever still at 8:17.

And there it is, the very source of the blast.

It was her nook. Her bunk. Where she slept every night.

A glimmer catches her eye. Near twisted stairs to nowhere lies a sandy mound reclaiming the steps. But not all of it. The sun has threaded its way down here, through 140 feet of water, colors sloughing one by one.

Yet the beam of light strikes half-buried metal, twinkling like a fire's last ember. Caitlyn focuses, uses all her concentration to scoop the errant glimmer from the seabed.

She opens her hand and a silent cry leaves her lips.

[4]

ONE HUNDRED AND FORTY FEET ABOVE THE RUINS OF THE GREY family boat, Michaels lowers the gas on the marine grill, savoring the smell of sizzling red snapper steaks. He savors the crimson dusk bleeding across the sky and the sea. He checks the rumbling compressor.

He does not hear the splash to his left. Still, he senses the change, a low-frequency pulse and a feeling he hasn't sensed in a year. An instinctual bristling as a cool gaze passes over him.

He turns to the bow. No one there. Yet from the corner of his eyes… Was that a shape climbing aboard?

Michaels ducks under the boom and follows the rail to the bow. There is water, a lump of gray sand settling on the deck. And a rusty necklace with a medallion on a loop. *What the hell?*

When Caitlyn squeezes past him and scoops it up, the answer clicks into place.

"Oh no, Cait. No, you didn't…"

"I had to see for myself."

"You could've waited."

"I saved us the trip. And the oxygen."

"Yeah, but not the risk."

Necklace in hand, she heads back to the cabin, back to where the light won't burn her eyes.

"Hey, look at me." He takes her hand, and she turns, giving him a sidelong glance. Or tries to. Hard to see through the tears in her eyes. One wipe and her hand is a burgundy smear. "I'll get the medkit."

Five minutes later the bleeding has stopped, yet iron still clings to the world. Her left eye, a burst vessel staining the whites. Her right, vibrant and defiant. Michaels dabs the last of the liquid trickling from her tear duct.

"How many fingers am I holding up?"

"None, you're making a fist."

"How about now?"

"You're giving me the finger."

He draws the blinds. Wincing, she lays her head on his lap.

She says, "I know what you're going to say: 'It was stupid and I'm probably going to have a stroke.'"

"Technically, you might have."

"Gods, I forgot how hungry it makes me. Can you—thanks."

He's already opening an energy bar for her. In five bites, she devours the whole thing. "Did you at least set a timer?"

She nods. "Thirty minutes."

"Well, you burnt a few thousand calories." He glances back at the cockpit. "And I burnt the fish."

She gives him a weak smile. Little crescents where her cheeks rise to her eyes. He finds her smile so beautiful it sometimes brings his thoughts to a halt.

"I'm having trouble focusing. When I close my left eye, it's like I'm still blinking. Weird."

He holds up the chain, the silver medallion cool to the touch. "This is Ganesh." He thumbs the Sanskrit around the edge of the medallion where the elephant-headed deity dances atop a rat. "It's for good luck, right?"

"Ganesha," she corrects. "I got it for my mom, for her birthday before we left Chennai."

He turns it over. "It's real silver, barely tarnished."

"When we lived in India, every time we'd take an auto rickshaw, the drivers would clock me for some rich American kid, which I suppose I was. I could never just catch a ride. They'd take me to their cousin's rug store or their brother's boutique or... wherever."

Closing her eyes now, she can almost see the diesel fumes and golden light, the parade of traffic. Cars and mopeds, bicycles and the occasional cow, all jostling for space among the dusty air tinted copper by time.

"Anyways, I was out with some friends, shopping for my mom's birthday. The driver brought us by this little boutique off Marina Beach. You could tell the owner was an artisan 'cause he had these hands like soft leather. Everything was way out of my price range. But there was this medallion." She runs a finger around the edges. "It was the only thing without a price. When I asked him how much, he held up his hand."

Caitlyn spreads her fingers.

"Five?" Michaels asks.

"Five hundred rupees. Which was exactly how much I had in my wallet. Ganesha doesn't just provide good luck. He is Ekadanta, the one-tusked, remover of obstacles. His ears symbolize patient listening. He provides safe travels. And he did... until I killed my parents."

"No, Cait, you didn't."

"I checked the boat. The clock was cracked at 8:17, after I went to bed. There's no burn marks, no signs of collision or explosion."

"Yeah, because it's been underwater for over ten years."

"But there'd be evidence, right? You're an investigator—"

"A field agent. *Former* field agent."

"So follow the clues. You saw the wreck. It's like something built up inside, some pressure. I was that pressure. What happened in there, that's on me. No different than if I lit a candle, fell asleep, and burnt down my home."

"No, it's not on you," Michaels says. "It's on your parents."

She tilts her head, eyes refocusing on him, hardening. Damn, this is a minefield of memories. Best to step softly.

"What I mean is that your parents..." He swallows. "They suspected you had this ability, right? They took you on the run—on a boat—for years. They didn't teach you about it or how to control it, nothing. Look, my point is, those were some questionable choices."

"Questionable?"

A deep breath. "Not the best choice of words, but yes, questionable. I mean, they're knocking off CIA bank boxes while you're bouncing around international schools. What was their endgame?"

Her eyes darken. "Oh, I don't know, maybe a normal life? Retirement? Not having to look over their shoulders."

"Yet they chose to go on the lam. That's my point."

"Because if they hadn't, they'd have been rounded back up, like the rest of the Clearwater cohort. How'd that turn out when you brought them in?"

Michaels tenses, his hand beginning to twitch. Despite the findings that said otherwise, he blames himself for all the deaths at Clearwater. Sometimes he wakes up to their echoing screams. And yet, to hear that from Caitlyn...

Before he can stop himself, he says, "Yeah, well, Tae Hwan and Zara's choice didn't work out much better."

Caitlyn opens her mouth, but nothing comes out. She never knew them by their old names, their birth names. To her, they were just Jason and Terry, her father and mother.

Her eyes harden, two rosy shards. She gets up. Doesn't care if the blood rushing to her head turns her blind once again and all of her brain tumors burst.

Michaels holds up a hand. "I didn't mean it to come out like that. I'm sorry. Come, sit—"

"Don't tell me what to do."

"Stand then, fine. I'm not... My point is, I'm not condemning your parents' choice. They made what they thought was the best decision. But I'm not condoning it either. It can be both, you know?"

Caitlyn fumes. In the past month, how many blowouts have they had? Five? Six? One thing is for certain: they've grown more frequent.

As she looked down the dock that windy day when Michaels found her, her first thought was joy. Her second was to wonder how long this might last.

But things had felt good. The excitement of new horizons. The meals of fresh fruit and caught fish. The evenings sleeping in the hammock, cocooned by a sea of sparkling black glass.

And now this: her beating heart, the taste of metal on her tongue. And yes, she thinks—no, she knows—he is right. Logically, he is right.

And a dark part of her hates him for this.

She turns. Walks to the bedroom. There is a jump cut—a flash of blackness—and now she is behind the closed door. Pacing and thinking, *This boat is too small. This boat is too small.*

Outside, Michaels stands frozen, ignoring the burning red snapper, trying to rewind the events: what he'd meant to say, what he'd said, and the vast chasm in between. Why can't they ever converge? Mostly, he thinks of what he just saw.

Caitlyn said she needed some space. The bedroom door slammed.

But her hands never touched it.

[5]

LOCATION: REDACTED, THE GULF OF ALASKA

NOON

FROM THE PLATFORM'S NORTH DECK AT TWO HUNDRED FEET ABOVE sea level, he can still taste the salt water. It clings to his skin and rattles his teeth. On a clear day, he can almost see Clarke's Landing thirty miles to the south. Reedy hills and sharp rocks, hard scraps of earth all swaddled in fog. Day's Bane to the old whalers and mariners whose boats broke on its reefs. To the west, the fog offers dim views of the wind farm, colossal spires where shadowed blades turn in the haze.

Bitter winds for bitter deeds, he thinks.

Doctor Robert Chase, a man who spent years in the cold halls of Clearwater, now steadies himself against the damp railing. He told himself to treasure the isolation this facility would bring to his research. Told himself the alliance would be worth it.

Yet here, now, he finds each day longer than the last. He turned sixty-eight this morning. For the first time in years, he doubts he will make another lap of the sun.

Leaning over the railing, he watches the waves crash against the legs of the platform. All that holds this rig in place are the great chains tethered to the seabed. All that holds Chase is this railing. And if he falls, would anybody know?

"Doctor Chase?" The libretto tone of young vocal cords.

"Good afternoon, Anders," he says, turning to face the junior researcher.

At thirty-two, Morgan Anders has a sharp mind yet a body softened by long hours in the lab. He is pale and soggy, an oily sheen to his shaggy hair. He has lips a little too pink and the righteous fire of the perpetually underestimated.

He reminds Chase of himself at that age.

"The coordinator requested your presence." Anders glances at the edge of the deck, where Chase's crutches lean against the railing. High above, a lone albatross circles. "Oh, and happy birthday, boss."

They ride the lift down to the fourth level, salty air giving way to the stale tang of filtration. Millions upon millions of dollars and it tastes like an airplane. Anders holds the door, metal rattling as they step into artificial daylight.

It is one hundred meters of right turns and lefts. Past servers and climate control systems all humming and flashing. Past offices where X-rays and next-gen MEG scans fill ever-flashing screens. Past medical suites, where Tyvek-suited technicians dissolve muscle fibers and unravel nerve cords like tender threads from a loom.

Chase has seen all this and more. Seen enough to go numb and count his horrors at night. Yet there is one thing here that still tightens his body.

A door marked COORDINATOR - AUTHORIZED ENTRY ONLY.

"Doctor Chase, come on in," says the man from the other side of the desk. "Close it behind us, Anders."

Coordinator Nox rises behind his steel desk to greet Chase with a firm shake and a smile as precise as a scalpel. His turquoise eyes, two jewels in an unreadable face. His fashion unremarkable. He is a man forgotten by most, a man passed and never remembered.

Except by those who know him.

Nox waits until the metal door slides closed. One drawback

with staging a lab on a decommissioned oil rig: everything takes longer. The opening of windows, the closing of drawers. Even the sinks and toilets have a delay that lets it be known: this structure is built not for convenience but to stand against the very might of the sea.

"Anders looks up to you," Nox says, settling back into his chair.

Chase grunts and takes in the view behind the coordinator. Triple-paned glass that looks out onto a plain of gray waves and wind that can whip over two hundred knots.

"His teams have hit all their metrics," Chase says.

"Exceeded them. According to my reports."

Chase nods. In his experience, it's best to let his employer steer the conversation.

"And he speaks highly of you, too. I think your colleague considers you something of a mentor."

Colleague, Chase thinks. *There it is, a curious word.*

He's never been sure what to call his benefactor. Not "Mr. Nox." Of course not. Nor "sir," since the man is easily two decades younger. But "coordinator"? It gives him too much distance, too much room to maneuver. To Chase, there's still an echo of partnership, even if echoes always fade.

"Something on your mind, Dr. Chase?"

Like always, Nox has read him like a children's book. Nothing to do but push forward.

Chase opens his tablet to the test logs and swipes to *SUBJECT D22*. He sorts the tests by *MOST RECENT*, filters by *AUTHO-RIZATIONS*. His name, Anders's, a few others. And then something curious. Five days ago, no data, just asterisks in every field.

*SUBJECT D22. AUTHORIZATION: *******

"Someone's taken our subject on another joy ride," Chase says. "I was told I was the only one with super user access. These logs say otherwise."

Nox gives the screen a cursory glance, then back to his guest. For a moment, he seems truly human. He even takes a deep breath. "Dr. Chase, how happy are you with this facility? With this arrangement? Do you have everything you need?"

"You've been generous with your resources."

"And your shore leave, you have several weeks coming up. Are you looking forward to seeing your niece?"

Chase nods. He is. Dry earth beneath his feet. No salty fog. And an unsettling fact: he hadn't told any colleagues about his niece's visit. Just the facility's counselor on his required bi-weekly visit.

Nox folds his hands. "Then I encourage you not to worry about glitches. We'll have IT see that it's fixed. Something to be worked out, not worked up over."

It's Chase's turn to center himself. "I understand. However, this is still a lab. And a lab's duty is to science, the pursuit of truth, yes? If there is a glitch, as you say, and this glitch continues… our data could take us down false halls."

Nox's face is a placid mask, nodding at every point Chase makes. And yet the doctor wonders if the man isn't already five conversations ahead.

Chase pushes on. "We're measuring results down to the neuron. Any hidden variables, any test subjects pushed beyond documented conditions, these could corrupt the results we both seek. Worse, it could cause another cascade, like at Clearwater."

"That's an important consideration, Dr. Chase. I appreciate you bringing this to my attention."

"I'm sure it's nothing—"

"I have a helicopter to catch." Nox smooths his jacket as he rises. "Walk with me."

Instead of taking the lift up to the helipad, Nox turns right at the southern stairs, and a shiver slides down Chase's spine. He grips his crutches tight, following the silent path of the man before him.

There are two ways to get to the fifth deck. One is through a secure checkpoint outside the central lift. A checkpoint that only admits Chase and his team during approved clinical trials.

The other way is down the stairs, accompanied by the coordinator or pre-authorized Foundation personnel. Chase has never been on that list.

And that is a good thing, he thinks, as the metallic scent of the fourth fades behind a pressure change on the fifth.

In an unclean and mostly closed environment, microbial growth is exponential. Sailors and submariners know this. And so do the medical staff on deck five. Part of this wing is a sterile lab, like a contaminant-free burn ward.

After all, the subjects within are open wounds.

Beyond the cool glass where Nox stops, five bodies hang in suspension harnesses. On first viewing, one might think of meat in a great freezer. Judge Frank Maberry certainly did.

Even now, after months of induced catatonia, Chase still shudders when he sees them: four men and one woman. Their ears and eyes are swaddled in sound-blocking headphones and goggles. There are no straps or bands but surgical screws tightened into bone. The rest of their heads simply do not exist. Jigsawed plastic and SQUID sensors meet engorged folds of brain. Hair-thin IV nets act as meninges, enclosing the cerebrum and infusing it with oxygenated blood. Behind each subject, their spines open, fibrous nerves joining silicon and charged glass like the pressed roots of slumbering trees.

The control room screens chart neuronal connections in vibrant fractals, the full map of the mind. Recently, Anders's team deployed machine learning to visualize the subjects' subconscious in real time. Although the video feed is fuzzy and prone to distortion, Chase knows it'll quickly improve. It always does.

"In nine months your teams shattered every milestone and metric thrown your way," Nox says. "We provided the minds. You mapped the mechanisms of decoherence. We kept our side of the agreement. Tell me, do you feel you've lived up to yours?"

In the sterile room, Tyvek-clad workers carefully remove goggles, open eyelids, and flash lights into dry pupils. No dilation.

Chase can sense his appetite fading. He's lost forty pounds since coming to Day's Bane. "Progress comes in waves. We've replicated the Jensen-Grey phenomena five times and counting."

Jensen. The name tastes sour on his tongue.

Teddy Jensen was Chase's prized pupil back when the program was fumbling blindly at the end of the Cold War. Different times and different rules. In the years after, Teddy's body collapsed in on itself like a dying star. But his mind crystalized, becoming so potent it cost him his waking world. In the end, Teddy became a vengeful revenant guided by his mother's voice and thirty years of fury. He was a *dhimoni*, the God's Breath Killer.

Chase promised himself he'd never repeat that mistake.

Yet here he is, looking in on those comatose bodies, connected to systems like Teddy's, machines that keep them alive.

"Replicated," Nox repeats. "Anyone can dismantle a clock and copy the pieces. But have you improved it? Have you stabilized it and truly made it your own?"

"The mind can endure only so much before the body collapses. Anatomy has its limits."

"And you're certain we've found those… limits?"

"We found them thirty years ago."

Nox's eyes flicker. "Anders thinks differently."

Christ, now it makes sense. Anders wasn't carrying Nox's summons; he was pleading his case before the coordinator left. The smug kid went over Chase's head. *Keep calm, Robert. Diplomatic.*

"With respect to Morgan Anders," Chase says, "he's basing his hypothesis on two points of data, both outliers. I won't authorize such barbaric methods to find out if he's right. It's not good science. It's not good research."

"And I respect your position, Dr. Chase. That's why I made the call. I've given him only two subjects, the ones at the end."

Chase eyes the sterile room, realizing now why the coordinator brought him here. Why there are more physicians than normal. They're not checking the subjects per routine. They're prepping for surgery.

"Removing their eyes won't replicate the circumstances behind Caitlyn's ability." A wave of nausea hits Chase as the technicians lay out the instruments: the forceps and scalpels, the clamps and the scoops. "Anders's theory is built on brain scans he can hardly understand. She was a genetic fluke."

"And if she isn't? If the Jensen-Grey phenomenon holds the key to sustained decoherence?"

"Their bodies will reject the procedure. In time, their minds will revolt."

"Anders claims his team can maintain stable comas."

"I'm sure that he has. But if these subjects achieve metacognition, all bets are off."

"We have safeguards in place."

"So did Clearwater."

Nox tilts his head. "Dr. Chase, to an impartial observer, it might seem like you're steering the research."

"Only because I've found a few cliffs. I've analyzed every ounce of brain matter from the Clearwater cohort. I knew their minds to the tumors and folds. Should we induce gambling habits and substance abuse just because our subjects did?"

It's a clumsy distraction. Chase knows it. Nox doesn't take the bait.

"Some of your team think this procedure could hasten your progress."

Chase squeezes his crutch. Wonders if he could stop this surgery. Maybe. Perhaps he could throw a chair through the window…

No, too heavy. And he is old, tired, worn down from a lifetime of choices that brought him here. All he can do in this moment is turn away as the surgeons go to work.

"My team?" Chase scoffs. "These are biohackers and dropouts. They're opening doors in the mind they don't understand. My team died back in Clearwater."

[6]

Chase finds Anders wearing a smile and waiting at the edge of the research manager's bullpen. It is five o'clock and the teams are off the clock, Alaskan microbrews in hand. Sometimes the whole place feels like a startup, especially in the hours after Nox leaves.

"Boss, listen, I just want to clear the air," Anders says. "I know it feels like it, but I didn't go over your head. I mean, it wasn't intentional." He offers Chase a beer, but the senior researcher declines.

Chase searches for a path that will get him through the room quickly. Not a straight line, which would give Anders fifty meters to walk beside him. And not the wide way, into the orbit of the security team, who always have new protocols Chase needs to be updated on. Like his years advising biotech companies, Chase finds half the job is fighting for time.

"But what I'm trying to say, boss, is that Nox knew about our divergent conclusions. He read all the proposals, even the drafts you didn't sign off on."

Crutches clattering on the metal floor, Chase says, "How fortunate that you were ready to brief him on your theory. I'm sure the surgically blinded subjects will understand it wasn't *intentional*. Excuse me."

Chase squeezes past Janet, one of the junior lab techs. Spotting Anders, she clears space, backing against the espresso machine. Almost to the exit now. After that it's upstairs to the privacy of his suite.

Then Anders does the unpredictable. He steps in front of Chase, puts his hand on the wall, blocking the way. Dr. Robert Chase, PhD, MD, beholden to Beyond Top Secret clearances, now boxed in by this cocky young kid. It takes every ounce of his willpower not to beat him with his crutch.

"I feel like you're not letting me clear the air, Bob."

A deep breath. Chase offers Anders a smile. "Enjoy this moment, Morgan. You got what you wanted."

"Thank you." Anders offers a sarcastic bow.

"But did you ever stop to think that if you had played this diplomatically, you could have had a whole lab for yourself? Not just a shift but a project and teams?"

A chink in Anders's pallid facade. His eyes narrow.

"Anders, my boy, some advice from an old wolf to a pup. Half this job is getting results, yes. But equally important is moving the right pieces into play. Your colleagues placate you socially, but how many respect your research, your methods? Ah, you've seen them recoil in your presence, yes? You've heard their whispers. You come to them during happy hour. But do they come to you on their own? No, I didn't think so. And when they learn what you've done to the subjects in your care… Congratulate yourself. You've dumped long-term collaboration for immediate gain."

"You're suppressing her results," Anders hisses. "Everything from the Clearwater cascade. How to prime their minds. If you would just share your core data, I'd have something to improve."

Chase straightens. "A poor craftsman blames his tools."

"I'm not…" Anders stammers. "If we could replicate Ms. Grey's exact mental state, we could take this to the next phase."

"And yet you can't. Not even when you have all that you need."

Anders can't find the words. He's received Chase's praise

plenty of times, but never his wrath. Now he's knocked off balance and reeling.

"You want to blow your own face off, you build your own sandbox and bring your own firecrackers. This lab, this research, and these people in it, they're my responsibility."

Anders swallows. "You're right, boss. They are. For now."

CHASE DOESN'T WAIT to see Nox's helicopter off. No need for goodbyes with every hall under surveillance, every frame of video algorithmically scraped. Even if this suite is private—as IT promised him it was—he knows his communications are not. Data has only one way off the platform: the satellite uplink. Every email, every internet search, every keystroke, all stored on those black servers down on deck four.

Last week, before Judge Maberry's visit, a mistake cost the facility a twelve-hour data purge. It was just a picture of the sunset at sea, the distant islands, and the words *Wish You Were Here*. It was shared by an operations technician to his fiancée's social media page. Embedded in the photo's EXIF data were the camera model, exposure, and F-stop. Worse: the geolocation. A simple mistake, yes, one that cost the op tech his job.

And hopefully not more, Chase thinks as he sits down at his desk.

So, to the internet now. Time to reach the outside world without leaving tracks.

He opens his browser, signs into his Amazon account. Types out his search: *SMART MICROWAVE.*

The loneliest places on the internet are the second pages of search results. It takes Chase until Amazon's twenty-third page to find what he needs.

Here it is, an Amazon Basics microwave. The right combination of words. *No turning back.* He saves the product to a wish list: *NIECE HOUSEWARMING.*

Another lengthy search, another item goes on the wish list. And then another.

When Chase closes his browser, his hands are shaking.

It was all true, Chase muses, what both Anders and Nox said about his direction. He truly has been steering the research. Not because of a cliff or a dead end, but because of a promise he made in Reno one year ago, to a woman with eyes of bright dawn.

[7]

KILIFI, KENYA

THIRTY MILES NORTH OF MOMBASA, COCONUT PALMS AND LOAMY sands meet the teal river and sea. This is the sleepy marina of Kilifi. Here, dozens of flags fly from the masts of moored boats. It is sunset, magic hour, and Michaels is motoring into an amber blast, cloud-smeared skies softening in twilight, the first stars just starting to wink.

He guides the *Dionysus* through the shallows, between the concrete twin pillars of the Kilifi bridge. Above, the buzz of mopeds and pickups. Below, the purr of water taxis and fishing boats returning to harbor. He readies the rope. They have the mooring reserved for another eight weeks.

And yet, as they tie up to it and take down the sails, Michaels senses what's coming next. Has sensed it for days.

"So," Caitlyn says. She is wearing her sunglasses. In part because of the post-blink distortions. But also, he suspects, because of what she's going to say next. "Michaels, listen—"

"It's okay," he says. "You don't need to explain. I know what—"

"Please, don't interrupt me."

He swallows. "I'm sorry. It's just... I can read the signs. I figured I'd save you the trouble."

She crosses her arms. This was easier when they had the whole journey ahead. "The trouble?"

"Of this. Whatever this is. But first, I need to say something and then I'll go. Is that okay?"

A boom drifts across the marina. One of the waterside resorts is starting up its evening festivities. Jimmy Buffett over a tinny sound system, buzzing across the sparkling water. Drunk Europeans and the occasional Aussie. Michaels wishes he could mute the whole world.

"Fine. Go ahead."

He clears his throat. "First, I can honestly say you are the most unique and original person I know. Cait, there's no one else like you. But it's also a battle, one I can see you fighting." He taps his temple. "It's lonely in my head. Must be lonely in yours. Now, I know you're going to say something about how, 'It's not me, it's you. You need space to figure things out.' You were practicing this in your sleep. So, can we just skip that?"

"Okay."

"Yes, I am difficult, risk-averse, and stubborn. I'm sorry you discovered that on this trip. If it's any consolation, you hog all the blankets."

She just stares. Doesn't smile. Damn, he'd hoped for at minimum a smirk. His fingers twitch and his words rattle like stones in his throat. *Tell her, you idiot. Tell her you love her.*

"I… *care* about you, Cait. But I can't let you blame yourself for something that wasn't your fault. You didn't put that boat in the water. You were a kid and that wreck wasn't your fault. That's all the past is, just the good and the bad. But it's how we meet tomorrow that matters. I guess I still see a future together. I hope I'm not the only one. Tell me I'm not."

The water taxi drops Michaels off at the dock. With a grunt, the porter makes a half-hearted effort to help him unload his backpack and duffel, his satchel and daypack. Michaels soaks up the last of the sun, the waning light warming his cheeks. Takes in the distant music, the laughter. Out across the estuary is her boat, moored and dark against the golden waters.

He starts his long walk down the pier.

So, what to do now?

For the first time in months, he can't envision his next move. Not since he left his condo in St. Louis and caught up to Caitlyn's cold trail in Argentina. Not since he tracked her to that beach at the western edge of Mauritius. Not since they set out together in search of her past.

Now it's just him, his thoughts, and his twitching left hand. The worst company he knows.

"Need a place to stay, friend?" asks a thin Kenyan with a bright smile. "Backpacker's hotel, right down the way. Good price, clean rooms. I can drive you there."

Michaels considers the man. "You have a car?"

"Of course. Uber, Little Cab, what you need?"

A strong drink, he thinks. However, Kilifi is a port town. The last thing he needs is to get sauced in view of her boat. The whole coast feels too small for the two of them now.

"Take me to Mombasa," he says.

The man's eyes light up. Mombasa. Good fare. Now he's taking Michaels's duffel, leading him to the parking lot, where a dusty Hyundai awaits.

"Where you go in Mombasa?"

"Whatever hotel has the best bar."

Caitlyn turns the cockpit light off and descends below deck. She doesn't watch him go. If she wanted, she could be there just by closing her eyes. No. She needs him as far away as possible.

Not because she is angry with him—which she isn't—but because of what she is.

If she could destroy her family's boat in her sleep, the last place she should be is beside the man that she's started to…

No. She pushes that word away. Like everything and everyone else. Like Mrs. Bakshi and the neighbors and all the others who made a place for her in their lives.

Look at yourself. One year ago she couldn't leave her front door. Now what does she have? A new name, alone, on the run. No more connections than ten years before. No closer to finding home.

Caitlyn lies down on the bed and stretches out. All these blankets to herself now. All this space. And yet it feels… what?

A little less comfortable, yes. A little too big. Has her boat always been this noisy? The scraping of a loose chain. The groan of a rusty drawer. The deep hum of distant motors, echoing off the hull.

Caitlyn sits up, woozy. Without her glasses, the berth is a quiltwork of shadows. Her vision has improved since she blinked, true, but not as fast as she'd hoped. Slow going for the next couple of days.

And beyond that?

Caitlyn doesn't have to close her eyes to see further ahead. There are two paths, both luminous threads, interwoven through potential tomorrows.

In one of them, she finds a quiet place, far away from others. And then she rebuilds. She shuts this ability away, trains herself to forget it. Chase was right: her mind is a weapon. But perhaps that weapon can be locked in a safe. Perhaps it can even be disassembled.

And if not?

Then she follows that other thread, a future coming to a quick end. She carried herself out of a collapsing boat. Carried herself out of Clearwater. She fought to keep her physical body safe and alive. Perhaps she could do the reverse.

If she could sink one boat, could she sink another?

[8]

MOMBASA, KENYA

8:00 P.M. EAT

THE HOTEL MZURI HAS AN EXCELLENT BAR INDEED, AND CHARLES mixes some mighty fine drinks. Cleaned up and shaven, Michaels hardly recognizes the reflection below the shelves of liquor and glasses. Six months of equatorial sun has turned his skin a deep shade of chestnut. His dark hair has taken on an auburn sheen, curly in places. Even his tired eyes sparkle. Oddly, he looks both ten years older and younger.

And drunk, he thinks. He looks properly sauced.

"Another dawa, sir?" Charles asks.

Michaels studies the glass before him. Lime, honey, white sugar, and ice. Splash in some vodka and you've made the perfect refreshment for this climate. He closes one eye. Then the other. Two drinks become one. Another dawa is probably a bad idea, but—

"Sure." Michaels taps his finger on the bar. "Why not, Charles?"

It's a quiet night, a weeknight, a Wednesday. On TV, the BBC buzzes out the latest unrest in Litundi, another election postponed. In the U.S., politicians are honoring a federal judge after a murder-suicide at the hands of his wife. The markets are mixed.

As Charles shakes the cocktail, a warm body slides into an empty seat down the bar.

"Where are you from?" the woman asks. "I can't quite place your accent."

Moments ago Michaels had been at the edge of seeing double. Now a cold instinct sets his nervous tic in motion. He puts his left hand in his lap.

"Canadian. But I grew up all over the U.S." He nods to her. "South African, right?"

She smiles. "Jo'burg. But I grew up all over, like you. Mind if I…?" She glances two seats closer. She's good on the eyes, and she knows it. Skin as dark and smooth as the wood that makes up the bar. A smile that whispers mischief.

But something about her feels off. Is it the watch? A Patek Philippe paired with a dress that screams sex. She's over-perfumed. Like she dressed in a hurry and isn't used to this look. A working girl still wobbly on those heels? No, that doesn't fit.

"Sorry, it's hard to hear you over the cricket game." She scoots over with her newspaper, her purse, her drink. "I'm Nandipha. Friends call me Nandi."

No, you aren't. No, they don't. Michaels finds himself sobering up fast. Nandipha… That name left her lips clumsy and unpracticed.

"Name's Jeremy," he says.

She squints. "Jeremy, really?"

He nods. Jeremy Vedder is the identity he created when he set out to find Caitlyn. Jeremy, the name of his favorite song as a kid. Eddie Vedder, the musician who sang it. Aliases need to come quick to the tongue.

"Nandipha" did not.

Another sobering thought: he isn't the only one here trained to listen for hesitation.

She says, "I ask because my brother had a mate named Jeremy. He was from Vancouver. You aren't from Vancouver, are you?"

"Quebec, I'm afraid."

"Really? What part?"

Interesting. Nandi, or whoever she is, is leaning into his bluff. It forces the liar to double down. It also risks unsettling them. A nervous liar is likely to overexplain. To improvise details to counter their own doubt.

Then a third worry: if she's working him, perhaps she isn't alone. Maybe she's trying to keep him here, keep him distracted, keep him—

"Your drink, sir." Charles places the cold dawa on a napkin. Michaels peels off some cash and lays it on the bar. Heart beating, he uses the moment to rewind his mind. When was the last time he'd been to Quebec? Another concern: he hadn't kept his eyes on the bartender. Instead, he'd been distracted when Nandi struck up conversation.

Or maybe—yes, maybe—you're being too paranoid?

Months sailing up and down the Kenyan coast. The only inter-action: the occasional trips into port. And one night with some German sailors, boats tied while they cooked fish and smoked hash. Had the sea turned him even more socially feral?

No, there's something off here. He can sense its presence, like he sensed the dhimoni on the first corpse he saw.

"I'm from Sherbrooke originally. Just moved to Mirabel, west of Montreal. You ever been there?"

"To Canada? Afraid not. Maybe someday." She swirls a finger in her drink and gives it a lingering suck. Switching tactics and playing to her looks. Which are, he has to admit, striking in their features. Sharp chin, full lips. Hair worn up in rows to expose her bare, muscular shoulders. The old battle line between the body and mind.

She catches his glance, smiles. "So, Jeremy, what brings you to Mombasa? Business, or something else?"

Time for a new move. Best to be unpredictable now. Michaels holds up a hand, shushing her. He whispers, "I'm here on a secret government assignment, just like you."

This really throws her off. She covers with a blink and a scowl, but her eyes betray the mock confusion. She's a half second too slow. "I'm sorry?"

"Not as sorry as I am if I'm wrong about this."

Then he winks, stands up, and heads for the bathroom. Doesn't need to turn to see her confusion; he catches it off the mirror. He adds an extra stumble to sell the performance.

The door is barely closed and locked and he's at the toilet, one finger down his throat. How many dawas did he drink? Three. So six ounces of vodka. Time to empty the bilge.

A quick flick and up come the cocktails. Another tickle, another purge. By the third retch, it's bilious, just knots in his side. If the drink was spiked with GHB, the euphoric effects should begin in ten minutes. He sets his watch timer. Fifty-fifty. Those are the odds he gives himself that he's overreacting. Flip a coin.

So, time to test this theory.

He lies down on the floor. Peers through the gap between the tiles and the door.

Shit. Two shadows, high heels coming to a stop inches away from the other side. Okay, so the odds just tilted closer to ninety. Nandi is listening in.

Slowly, he rises. Flushes the toilet. Turns on the sink, then kicks the stall door. Hopefully she heard that.

Then he opens the window.

Rooney almost catches herself cursing as the bartender fumbles with the keys. Charles is his name—not his real name—but his name for this play. Had to grab local talent and whip up fake names. The whole thing came together too bloody fast.

Nandipha… what a mouthful. He'd clocked it in an instant.

"C'mon, I think he fell over," Rooney says.

"They don't keep the keys labeled," Charles grumbles. Another key, another. Then a proper click.

When the door opens, she's greeted by two things: water pouring down the sink and the open window.

Sloshing across the bathroom, she peers outside. Down below, where the outdoor lounge overlooks the waterfront, their target lies collapsed on the patio. Not a long fall, but the poor bastard must have clipped his head on the jump.

"Close up shop," she tells Charles, still fumbling with the keys. "And prep for extraction. I'll fetch this idiot and call it in."

Downstairs, the steps play hell on her ankles. The worst part of this honeytrap are the pumps. She clutches the handrail, walking past the disapproving glare of the concierge, eyes on her tight skirt. *Let them think whatever they want.* She knows her real job.

And the bounty will make it worth every blister.

Outside, the night is warm and the breeze a sweet breath. With the influx of Chinese investment, the whole marina has remade itself in the vibrant palette of LED lights. Lavender and pastels paint the way past cafes and closed storefronts to her target, face-down by the empty waterfront tables.

Stupid drunk. Weren't these guys supposed to be the best?

She takes out her phone, dials. "Yeah, it's Rooney. I'm standing over the target. Bring the ambulance to the marina cafes. Yes, he's breathing. Yes, of course I'm going to check him—"

It happens so fast. The target—Jeremy or Michaels or what-ever—springs up, driving the back of his head—the hardest part of the skull—into her chin, slamming her jaw and muting her words. A flash and a crackling deep in her sinuses. Suddenly, he's twisting and sweeping her legs from beneath like two flimsy sticks.

Rooney hits the ground hard, a pump flying loose. In less than a second they've switched positions. Him atop, her on the ground and nursing her face. Everything sparkles and throbs.

"Who's on the other end?" He holds up her phone. "Nandi, Rooney, whoever. Who is on the other end of this call?"

Focus returns to her eyes. Then fear. She twists, turns, struggles, but he puts a hand on her wrist, has the leverage to hold her down.

"Hey! Last chance. Who is—"

Her knee catches him in the small of his back, hard enough to jostle his weight. It's just the twist she needs to free her left hand and make a tight fist.

The first blow catches him right in the crotch. So does the second. Air leaves his lips in a violent wheeze. Gasping, coughing, his knees buckle. Then he's crawling on all fours, vomiting for the fourth time tonight.

Rooney springs to her feet, aims a kick at his face that he barely deflects. Somewhere, far off, the ambulance wails. *They better hurry.*

"You *bwoke* my *noze*," she hisses.

He clutches his gut, his groin, keeps a hand out to fend off further attacks.

She kicks off her other pump, lets her bare feet dig in, left leg one step forward, right foot back and on the ball. She raises her open hands, palms outward. His eyes widen as he recognizes her classic Krav Maga fighting stance. Good. This man's mostly lean muscle, more of a jogger than a brawler.

But not Rooney.

She's had years of training, every inch of her quivering for this moment. And hey, the bounty was for a live extraction; it didn't forbid a few broken bones.

Rooney is right in her assessment: Michaels is not a good fighter.

But he's not a predictable one either.

Head down to deflect her blows, he runs forward. Drives himself right into her. Keeps driving through her as she rains down blow after blow. In any ring he'd be disqualified. Here, he just needs some distance to build up momentum, a fact she senses too late.

In a tangle of limbs, he pushes right up against the marina's chain railing. Her punches turn to a desperate grab. Her legs pinwheel and rise. It's fifteen feet from the edge of the deck. Then the warm waters engulf her, the moon shimmering above and the pastel lights blinding off the surface.

It is minutes before Rooney finds the marina ladder, climbs up to the café at the deck's edge, soaked and cussing, searching for her target as the guests giggle and point.

[9]

FOUR BLOCKS AWAY FROM THE HOTEL MZURI, MICHAELS FLINGS HIS smartphone in the back of a passing pickup and cuts through an alleyway. Adrenaline is sobering him up quick. He takes seven deep breaths and listens to orient himself. The persistent buzz of mopeds. A distant siren. Laughter, the kind infused with booze and good company. Mombasa is a major port city, and ports always have an expat community. Closer now, and he can make out the language: Russian.

Michaels rounds the corner to find a small yet lively bar. Minimally staffed, just as he'd hoped. A few locals, but mostly boisterous Russians in bright tropical shirts and the occasional flat cap. All eyes on him as he enters and limps up to the bar.

In the mirror, his left eye is beginning to swell. Blood rings his right nostril. Damn, she really did a number on him.

"You all right?" the bartender growls.

"Got mugged," Michaels says. "You should have seen the other woman."

A chuckle, and the bartender slides him a bowl of peanuts. Michaels nods his thanks.

This dive bar is his best chance to lie low and gather his thoughts. But first he needs to earn local trust. He peels off a few thousand Kenyan shillings, enough to make the bartender raise an eyebrow.

"For a few rounds of drinks." Michaels gestures to the Russians. "You keep the change. But I need to borrow that computer, okay?"

"Ya, no problem." The bartender passes Michaels the sticky house laptop. Money doesn't buy everything, but it smooths out a few cracks. When the round of cold Tuskers hit the Russians' table, they explode in cheer.

"*Vashee zdaróvye,*" Michaels says and presses an ice water to his cheek.

Okay, think. You've got a computer and the goodwill of this bar. You've bought some time. Now find out what you've lost.

He rewinds the past day. The drive down from Kilifi, the hotel paid in cash. His passport is clean; he'd checked in under an identity with no agency connection.

A shower and a nap before dinner. An evening stroll along the marina followed by drinks at the bar, where Charles had taken the other bartender's place.

It's a safe bet his hotel room is being ransacked. His luggage and his tablet are all gone. He's still got some cash, prepaid ATM cards, and plenty of crypto.

What else? Rooney called it an extraction and it seemed staged in a hurry. So who are they? If they found him in Mombasa, they'd clearly been waiting. Perhaps she was a freelancer, Charles a local asset. He knew a hundred agencies that could do this, but only one that would try.

So, if this was Foundation-sanctioned, then why? He'd left on neutral terms, all things considered. He hadn't broken any NDAs.

None of it sits right. Time to check some old tripwires.

Michaels slides the laptop to the quiet end of the bar. He opens it facing the wall, folds a napkin, then slips it over the webcam.

The web browser is a year's worth of updates behind. He navigates to an old GitHub repository that holds a sandboxed browser, single-serving web access through double VPNs. Secure browsing but slow. *Loading… Loading…*

Outside, the alley hums with vendors hawking *mishkaki*, spiced meats on skewers and cooked to perfection. A street cat leaps onto a wall separating the bar from a small petrol station. He catalogs his options.

Before the Clearwater case wrapped up, before the Foundation bureaucracy tried to pin Reno on him, Michaels set up safeguards, anticipating the worst and hoping to be wrong. The last time he interviewed Dr. Chase, the man echoed Caitlyn's warning: "Be worthy of this."

It's this memory that sets his fingers twitching. Michaels is not autistic—not according to his psyche profile and a dozen specialists—yet he feels a kinship toward certain traits. He finds prime numbers and consistent fabrics comforting. Back home in St. Louis, he has a wardrobe with twenty-three identical bespoke suits. When he's stressed, invisible ants wriggle beneath the skin of his left hand. And now, pulling up the website, he lets his fingers tap free.

Robert Chase maintains a public wish list on Amazon, gifts for his niece. The last time Michaels checked, it was empty. If all went to plan, it would stay that way forever.

Instead, five items are now listed, all added last week.

Michaels borrows a pen from the bartender and more cocktail napkins. He clicks the first item on the wish list. An Amazon Basics internet-connected microwave. Seven hundred watts, 0.7 cubic feet, Alexa-integrated. He scrolls to the description.

They say full-featured microwaves can't come at a low price, but we disagree. With Amazon Basics, even entry level is…

Michaels writes down a word: THEY.

He clicks the next item on the list, a set of six hundred thread count bedsheets.

You work hard every day. But are you getting the sleep you deserve? Discover the very definition of comfort…

Another word on the napkin: ARE. Two out of five. A noun, a

state of being verb. If he's wrong, the third won't be a verb. If he's right…

Shit. There it is, COMING. Two more to go.

He scrolls through the final two product descriptions. The cipher they codeveloped is far from perfect; its core weakness is its unidirectionality. To respond, he'll need time. Which is exactly what he doesn't have, now that the message clicks into place. Ballpoint ink spreads in the cheap fibers of the napkin, five little blue words:

THEY ARE COMING FOR HER.

[10]

KILIFI, KENYA

11:00 P.M. EAT

Cool air above water creates a temperature gradient that changes the shape of sound as it travels. It's why there are few secrets by a lake.

And none in a harbor.

Caitlyn slumbers in the dark comfort of her boat. The closest she's found to the comfort of blinking. Sounds swaddle her here in the deep. The low plop of a shorebird that slips underwater. The swish of kelp. Condensation dripping down the mini greenhouse.

Now the crackle of feet upon the deck.

Caitlyn opens her eyes. Some days, she still feels out blindly upon waking, searching for the edges of the Clearwater pod. Or the headboard of her bed in San Francisco. Though she no longer needs to feel her way through the world, the instinct runs deep. Here, Caitlyn waits until the shadows take shape.

The V-berth, lit by the low moon. The cabin door and the hatch, both open. There is someone on her boat. They could come in, right above her. What can she do?

Quietly, she swings her legs out from the sheets. A deep breath. She feels the cool floor beneath her toes. Tells herself, *Drop down, careful, not too fast. Good. Now listen.*

"This vessel is a noisy girl," the old sailor warned her. "She likes to chatter."

Now Caitlyn can hear every word. The drip of a recently used oar. The groan of weight shifting over the bathroom. The swish of shoes near the cockpit. There are two people, one at each end.

And here she is, pinned in the middle.

Caitlyn pauses at the threshold of the kitchen. Her glasses, damn. They're back by her bed.

She is mid-turn when a hand shoots out from the bathroom, covers her mouth, rotates her to face the mirror. She almost doesn't recognize him through the bruising. Michaels, here in the shadows, pressing a finger to his split lip. *Shh…*

He gestures: *Two intruders, upstairs. One at each end.*

I know, she mouths. *Why?*

He points to her chest. No. To her.

For me, she realizes. Fear turns to fury, what she had hoped would never come to pass. She lets out a little gasp.

Quiet, Michaels mouths. Another groan of old wood beneath heavy feet. Someone's descending the ladder, trying to be silent without knowing where to step. Another squeak, closer.

First comes the gun in the shadows. Then the arm holding it. The good news is that they're not assassins; they're not here to kill her.

The bad news is the quarter-million volts in the Kenyan man's grip. Those are police-grade Tasers. No room for mistakes.

Michaels ropes a towel between his hands, makes a choking gesture. Caitlyn nods and maps out every inch of the boat in her mind. A Beneteau Oceanis, forty-seven feet of glass-reinforced polyester and teak woodwork. Ten small steps from the bathroom through the saloon to the ladder. Two, maybe three seconds?

Two simulations clash in her head. In the first, Michaels leaps out, goes for the man in the kitchen, gets two charged prongs in his chest or his back. In the second, he drops the towel over the passing intruder's neck and holds on as they both thrash off the walls.

Neither optimal tactics.

A third option, then.

A low hum and a flicker of the night-light. Then a blast from behind that sends the forward intruder stumbling into the bedroom.

It happens so fast. A muffled gasp, the Taser wrenched from his hand. Then he's knocked onto the bed, knocked out entirely.

A face from above peers down through the V-berth hatch. Another Kenyan, short hair and clean shaven. He raises the Taser, aims it at… At what? There is no one else there, just his unconscious partner.

Then a shimmer sweeps through the moonlit room. Two hundred pounds of trained muscle, yet he's never trained for this. A bright-eyed silhouette with hands like vises yanks him down through the hatch. He hits the mattress. Then a blast knocks him back. Lights out. All in mere seconds.

Michaels turns to Caitlyn. She's sitting on the toilet, pupils dilating as her eyes flutter open. "You didn't."

"I did," she says, "what needed to be done. Make sure they're down for the count."

"That's all of them?"

"All of them here."

She can tell he's angry. He wants to yell, to tell her she was stupid for putting her mind at risk. But instead he just kisses her on the forehead and says, "Thank you."

MORE THAN ANYTHING ELSE, a boat is a floating house under perpetual assault from the elements. As such, a boat is always in a state of repair. The *Dionysus* is stocked with endless ropes and strings, clips and zip ties, all useful in securing things to shelving or pipes.

Or binding the hands of two Kenyan men who just crept aboard.

Michaels lays the Tasers in the saloon, pats the men down and turns out their pockets.

"No wallets or ID. They're not packing heat, so they didn't want to wake the neighbors." He finds handcuffs and blindfolds in their bag. A ball gag as well. The barest equipment to execute a capture.

Caitlyn asks, "Are they from your agency?"

"Doubtful. The Foundation would send specialists, not local greenhorns."

Another thought. They didn't use the harbor patrol, which means this is only part of a team. They'd need transportation waiting dockside, like the ambulance at the Hotel Mzuri.

"We need to fire up the engine," Michaels says. "Can you do that quietly?"

"It's a loud-ass engine." Caitlyn pinches her temple. "I'll do my best."

While she starts up the boat, he gags the intruders, binds their wrists to each other. The short-haired man mumbles, eyes widening as he discovers he's on the wrong side of a Taser.

"Let's keep this friendly, okay?" Michaels says. "Nod once if you agree."

The man nods and tugs at the rope, but it just tightens.

"You're both Kenyan, yes? NPS or NIS?"

The younger man squints, mumbles something. Michaels tilts the Taser. "Ah, I was unclear. Nod once for National Police Service, twice for National Intelligence Service."

Two slow nods.

"And your buzz-cut friend behind you? NIS as well? I see. Here comes the big question, and it's critical that I believe you. How many others are waiting for you? Blink the numbers out."

He blinks three times.

"And they're in the parking lot? No? Are they waiting for you to call? Good. I assume this operation is off the books, not a state-sanctioned job, yes?"

The man doesn't even need to nod or blink; his body tells all.

The slumping shoulders, the tired eyes. A policeman's salary only stretches so far. Looks like this is some after-hours job to pad the coffers.

"You've been most helpful. Thank you."

The pillowcases go over their heads, fast. They struggle, twisting and moaning, but fully trussed, there's little resistance. Michaels leaves them in the V-berth to their fears.

Up top, Caitlyn retracts the mooring line from the buoy. A plop as the rope dips into the water. She stays low and silent, stifling her fury. After all she had done for them. After Reno. After saving Chase. Saving them all when Teddy Jensen was tearing through them like claws through wet paper. She will show them. When she finds where Chase is, she will pay him a visit.

No. Why did she think that? That's the darkness and fear. She doesn't live there anymore.

"You've always lived here, my girl," a familiar voice says from over her shoulder.

She senses a presence just past the boom and the scent of forgotten cologne.

"Dad?"

Michaels climbs out of the cabin, whispering, "C'mon, we need to leave."

She switches places as he takes the helm. A glance back, her eyes scanning the deck past the boom. No time-lost whisper or scent. No glimpse of her father.

A Yanmar 75 is a workhorse of an engine, capable of spinning 3200 times a minute at full throttle, strong enough to get the *Dionysus* cruising. For now, they hold back. The engine purrs beneath the bass of the shorefront restaurants, the buzz of mopeds, the ambient harbor noise whispering, *All is ordinary. All is fine.*

To the team of NIS officers waiting several blocks away in a brown paneled van, the *Dionysus* might as well be a murmur in a storm. Most of these men are new to off-the-clock gigs. Most are distracted, minds wandering to the promised bounty and what delights it could buy.

It is forty-five minutes before they grow nervous and call the extractionists' phone, which is now sitting at the bottom of the harbor. It is an hour before they figure out the boat is missing. Not wanting the local police involved, they alert the harbormaster, who calls the police anyway.

By sunrise it's a full clusterfuck, the Kenyan coast guard on high alert, searching for a suspicious vessel with two missing NIS officers aboard. The whole cover story is unraveling fast.

"If you thought they were drug smugglers, why didn't you open a case?" their supervisor asks as morning becomes midday. "Either you're in on the job or you're too stupid to stop it."

None of the shamed officers bother to tell him the truth: it's a bit of both.

That afternoon they find the *Dionysus* anchored thirty miles up the coast. They storm the vessel, guns drawn and ready for a fight. Instead, they find their missing officers inside, tied up, treated well, left with enough food and water for days.

They do not find the man and woman, the owner of the boat, supposed drug smugglers Jeremey Vedder, a Canadian, and Myra James, an American with visible tattoos.

Nor do they find the inflatable dinghy resting upon white sand, two miles to the north.

[11]

WASHINGTON D.C.

5:00 P.M. EST

THE RESTAURANT STANDS AT THE END OF A NARROW GEORGETOWN alley, fifteen minutes by taxi from the Capitol building. Within, antique china clinks beneath fine silverware held by fingers soft and precise. Spacious tables are lit by lanterns stained red, white, and blue like the ideologies they serve. In the leathered booths, enemies trade whispers and favors, safe from reporters and cameras and curious aides.

The Dancing Spaniel is by invitation only, a fine-dining club founded at the apex of the gilded age when its first members feared civilization was tottering toward ruin. It is a sentiment still echoed from brandied lips over rosewood tables, a sentiment that keeps its members leery of new faces.

Like the man in the corner booth, seated across from the senior senator from Kentucky.

The powerful and the subtle, they sneak occasional glances. On an instinctual level, they know not to stop by.

"Dig in, son," Senator Marks says through a mouthful of mashed potatoes. "And please, give this brisket a try."

Nox pokes at his Shepherd's pie and savors the taste. Damn good indeed. Just the right balance of Worcestershire and herbs.

But he's not here for culinary inducement. Food is for

consumption; this meeting is for coordination. Confuse the two and you get this: a Kentucky senator on his third bourbon, mind softened and cheeks flushed. *The man truly looks like a frog,* Nox muses.

Senator Marks wipes his lips. "Now, tell me something, Holland. How long've we been friends? Close to a decade, I reckon?"

Nox feels a spike of frustration at being addressed by his first name. "Eleven years since we all signed the MOU."

"The memorandum of understanding." The senator licks sauce off his fingers. "Yes, that's when we got in bed together. But how long have we been chums?"

"I hesitate to describe our relationship as chummy."

"Well now, you came to my wedding."

"So did half the Republican party."

The senator laughs. "And plenty of Democrats too. Which, I suppose, brings me to my point. Now I am a political servant, and I serve the people of my great state. Most of 'em—bless their hearts—just vote straight party ticket 'cause of that letter next to my name. Blind faith can make a fellow go soft. But not us. There's value in spanning the partisan divide—even bending rules at times—all in service of those who trust us. You, me, the congresswoman, we understand the higher calling that comes with this service. And when there's a threat to our service, well, isn't there a duty to defend it?"

Nox's lips rise to a pencil-thin grin, near-flat, but for him, that's as high as it goes. He leans forward, close enough to smell the senator's halitosis. "That was a lot of air just to talk about Judge Maberry."

Another polite chuckle. "Son, you do know me well. Sometimes a man has to speak his way around things. That's the campaign trail rubbing off on me, you'll have to forgive."

"I'll save you the performance, Senator. You saw the result. Full decoherence with targeted elimination."

"May the good Lord embrace the Maberry family." The

senator raises his glass. "I hope you don't blame yourself. It was… unavoidable."

The senator waits but Nox doesn't fill in the silence. Better to let the bourbon-plied man do it himself. Politics truly is team sports for the ugly.

"Hell, sometimes people you saddle up with don't turn out to be in it for the long haul. You did what needed to be done. For the safety of our nation."

"We did," Nox corrects. He doesn't like the senator's distancing language. Best to keep the man roped in.

"Yes, *we* did, son. You and me and our Democrat compatriot. Which reminds me: why wasn't Chatterjee able to make this little powwow?"

"She has a debate in Seattle. First one against Senator Drogan."

The waiter clears the table, smooth and efficient. While the plates are stacked, the senator orders dessert and picks at his teeth.

"Dave Drogan," he says. "Now there's an interesting fellow. You ever had the pleasure of meeting him?"

Nox shakes his head. Still, he knows all about Drogan, the junior senator from Kentucky. The man is young, classic hand-some, and well spoken. Four years ago Drogan took a stab at running for president and ended up nearly contesting the primary. Dave Drogan, Brave Dave, a decorated veteran, an inde-pendent, an outspoken critic of politics as usual. His supporters are often called Drogan's Bros or Dave's Babes, depending on which gender is being smeared. Firebrand populists demanding government expansion in social programs and deep military cutbacks.

Sure, Drogan lost the primary to a milquetoast boomer from Florida, but he won the popularity contest. New blood and new money and a prestigious assignment to the National Threat Assessment and Strategic Defense subcommittee.

Senator Marks wipes his lips as the waiter returns with another bourbon. "Well, I have served with Dave on a number of committees, and let me tell you that man is a bloodhound. His little wet nose has started sniffing in our direction. Now, Dave says it's all about overturning the military-industrial complex. I think he believes it, and it plays well with the kids. There is fat to be trimmed."

"But you're concerned we're the fat." Nox notes the way the senator squirms.

"What concerns me is our ability to focus. To, uh, fly under the radar. I see storm clouds, I check the weathervane. That's just how I am."

The senator smiles as his dessert arrives, creme brûlée with a snifter of brandy. A terrible pairing, Nox thinks.

"I can see you counting the eggs now, Holland. Sussing it all out. Dave Drogan, poking around and pulling purse strings. Less funding for our little endeavors. Or an audit perhaps, top to bottom." He points his spoon at Nox. "Now, I suppose I could fence him in. I've got colleagues on that subcommittee. But he's got eyes on the Oval Office and the poll numbers to take it. And we know the truth about bloodhounds, don't we? They never lose the scent. Fortunate for us, Dave Drogan ain't a problem out of our hands yet. Or rather, he ain't a problem out of our reach."

The senator offers Nox a smile, custard yellowing his lips.

The Washington, D.C., sanctorum is a humble apartment at the western edge of Dupont Circle. It has good ventilation, an excellent view, and a safer data connection than the Presidential Emergency Operations Center beneath the White House.

Nox locks the door behind him. He knows the video conferencing equipment is tracking him since he's entered. He lets it track him all the way to the sink, where he scrubs dinner's filth from his skin.

Hands clean, he sits at the desk and takes six measured breaths to organize his mind.

Project CZ-93, nicknamed Day's Bane, this child of Clearwater.

It was to be his contribution to the nation's safety. A clichéd sentiment, yes, he admits, but a mandate he believes in, one he's dedicated his life to pursuing.

No need to risk soldiers when you can strike from a blind site. No need to rain Hellfire from drones. No need to waste twenty years, trillions of dollars, and all those American lives. If something like this existed back when Nox's older brother was in Afghanistan, perhaps he would have made it home.

Day's Bane, the potential to bring nothing to a gunfight and win every time. And now the senator's fingers are growing clumsy, leaving sticky prints on this once-simple design.

A text message appears on his tablet from Senator Marks's burner account. *To make things a bit easier.*

It's all here: the travel itinerary for the next week of Dave Drogan's rallies. The details from the Secret Service threat assessments. Building heights and floor plans. Where agents will be stationed. Even the color of park benches and plaza fences. Nox can see it in his mind's eye.

Which means they can as well.

It takes him a few moments to prep the mission brief. Onscreen, the video conference begins as seven thousand miles of protected data synchronizes. Then a crystal-clear connection. The cool gray of the facility's false light. Anders, his face filling the frame.

"Coordinator. How's the road treating you?"

"Like a den of snakes when you kick over a rock. How are the subjects responding to your adjustments?"

Anders hesitates, swallows. "We've had… complications. We lost one a few days ago. The other's fighting off sepsis. We're running some tests, seeing how her mind adjusts."

Annoyance tightens Nox's shoulders. Perhaps he'd given the young upstart too much leash. There are things about Anders that Nox finds unsettling. An eager energy that lands in the uncanny valley. His lack of work-life balance. Perhaps it's a discomforting reflection, like hearing your own voice recorded and played back.

Nox waves off the thought. "That subject you lost cost millions to procure. These aren't lab rats or chimps."

"Yes, I realize that, sir. We've already harvested some groundbreaking data. Sometimes knowing what doesn't work is equally vital."

"And Dr. Chase?"

Anders glances down. "Dr. Chase has competing theories."

The biometric polygraph running on Nox's screen spikes. Anders is holding back.

So, the supervisor and his protégé continue to diverge. If this keeps up, Nox senses a hard choice ahead. Anders has drive, no doubt, and the fortitude to do what others will not. He also has the hubris of youth. Anders might push the program to new heights.

Or he might bring about its collapse.

On the other hand, Chase has stalled out. It was only with Anders's promotion that new results were discovered. Nox has his own suspicions beyond the doctor's advanced age. But suspicions aren't proof.

So, what to do?

"Chase believes their minds and bodies failed to synch up," Anders continues. "Post-surgery, the subject rejected his mens corpus. His body mounted a subconscious response, like—"

"Like a mental infection."

Anders nods. "Correct, sir."

The mens corpus—the mental body. God, Nox hates that thought. That right now his mind is bound to his body through a synchronized reality. That with targeted neurostimulation and choice surgery, that tether can be stretched or frayed.

"What's your read on the situation?"

"Inconclusive. My read, sir, is that we need more data. I'd like to run an A/B test."

A potential solution. Good. Nox swipes his tablet, sending the mission brief across seven thousand miles. A second later,

Anders's glasses reflect its arrival onscreen. The target and description, the strike times and location.

Nox asks, "How confident are you in their ability to board a moving target?"

Anders clears his throat. "Confident, sir. Very confident."

The biometric polygraph on Nox's screen says otherwise. Closer to a coin flip.

"Good. Use one subject from each group. Let's put these competing theories to the test."

Before Anders can respond, Nox ends the connection.

[12]

DAY'S BANE, ALASKA

WITH THE VIDEO CONFERENCE OVER, ANDERS IS LEFT STARING AT HIS reflection in the black screen. The shaggy hair, the stubble. He knows he's gone soggy since moving to this platform. He feels it with each breath. More than that, he feels the weight of tomorrow.

Now if only he could get there.

The digital dossier before him tells a story of four-dimensional space: longitude, latitude, elevation, and time. The flight plan: a cross-country red-eye. The plane, the pilot, the entire description right down to the trim of the chairs.

And the target, Jesus…

This is more than a house in rural Georgia. This is hitting one bullet with another and doing it blind. Perhaps he oversold himself.

Still, Anders knows it's conceptually possible. Teddy Jensen achieved such power. They've got his brain in the lab, every fold mapped to the neuron. But they still need Caitlyn's.

So, double down time.

On the walk to deck five, Anders issues the command to his off-the-books team. There is Yuri Roskov, who calibrates neurostimulation. Bethany Clemson, the nutritionist, an essential position after the first batch of subjects developed ketoacidosis and chewed off their tongues. And Janet O'Farrell handling electrical systems, most crucial of all. The knowledge that stabilized decoherence requires a well of deep energy.

Anders learned much from surviving Clearwater and found much to improve. No Cold War electric systems, no knob and tube and patchwork aluminum wiring. Here, the facility is charged by wind turbines, stabilized by batteries that take up entire floors. Day's Bane can run for days on its own.

Crossing through the secure checkpoint, Anders finds his team waiting.

"Couldn't let us have a day off, eh?" Yuri asks in his Ukrainian accent.

"Didn't you get the memo?" Bethany says. "Anders never sleeps."

At the far station, where the glass looks into the sterile lab, Janet cues up the scans. Next-gen magnetoencephalography—MEG-II—displays dormant minds in a sea of black pixels. "Yeah, he just drinks the blood of young interns, isn't that right?" She gives Anders a wink.

"Ah, so it's true," Yuri says. "That's why he takes the late shifts."

Anders soaks in the banter, even at his expense. At least they're in good spirits. Easier to work with on these full dark assignments.

"You know, Anders, I don't care what everyone else says about you," Janet says. "I think you're an okay fellow."

"At the minimum I am a pro-social psychopath," Anders says. "That's why we all get along."

"Yeah," Janet says. "At the minimum."

Anders locks the control room. A dozen workstation screens reflect in his glasses. They can do anything here: sedate the subjects, rouse them, bring their brains into twilight consciousness.

Yuri swipes his screen. "Initiating test log."

"Cancel that," Anders says. "Use my secure folder. Mark it for our read/write only."

"Chase is going to love that," Bethany says.

Anders ignores it. Of the four subjects in suspension, three still have their eyes. Anders swipes across the screen, activating one from each pool, Chase's and his own.

"Okay, go time. Target's current elevation is thirty-five thousand feet. Coordinates incoming. Let's use subjects K14 and F31."

A sidelong glance from Yuri. "Dual test, huh?"

"Our benefactor wants to pump the gas."

"Risky move," Janet says. "Two decoherents on a moving target, that's a cascade if things get sloppy."

"Then let's not get sloppy."

"Your show, Anders." She raises the safety cover on the emergency disconnection switch.

Yuri says, "That's why they pay him the big bucks."

"Wait, you guys are getting paid?" Bethany grins. "Okay, bringing the subjects to REM stage."

On Bethany's screen, a real-time readout from implanted lab-on-chip sensors. Everything from blood glucose to thyroid functions, bilirubin levels and thrombosis warnings. The Foundation even intercepted Neurolink's latest implantable and were pleased to discover their own designs were generations ahead.

"Beautiful numbers across the board," Bethany says. "They're a picture of health."

A grim chuckle from Yuri. "Ya, for a bunch of houseplants."

"That's enough." Janet dims the lab lights to a cool glow. There is a moment of awe, always, as the shadows part to reveal what hangs before them.

To Anders, it is like seeing the Grand Canyon at dawn. No matter how many times the lights bloom across nerve-wound wires, no matter how this dismantled flesh breathes and twitches, he still finds himself awestruck by the human body.

And how it can be transformed.

At death, Theodore Jensen weighed fifty-four pounds. His

biological systems existed to fuel his mens corpus—what they called the dhimoni. Through surgery and select amputation, Anders's team has achieved a similar result.

"System check," he says, studying the reflection of his full body off the glass, and the husks beyond.

"Subject K14 and F31 are both peacefully dreaming." Janet taps the MEG-II scans at low-level rest. Cool blues and deep greens and a flicker of violet.

"Well then," Anders says. "Let's give them a challenge."

The scans transform. A single river of colors becomes several, then dozens. Like an old television searching for stations, the algorithm begins visualizing their neural activity onscreen. Anders holds his breath. More intimate than a childhood shame or the most fearsome act of lovemaking are these deepest secrets of the mind now unfolding before him.

[13]

Iliana Kennedy, a haggard thirty-five, glances over her shoulder so fast the world teeters. There was a voice, a whisper. Yet as she searches her house, she finds only the open window, the breeze through a curtain, and the distant shouts of new recruits jogging off breakfast.

That's right, she thinks. *I was in the middle of breakfast.*

She turns her attention back to the kitchen table, to the four hot meals and three seats before them. Well, two seats and a booster. And if she is being pedantic, one seat is now empty.

The man on the floor shudders, tries to crawl across the floor. He stretches a hand out, fingers digging at the cool tiles. A grunt as he inches forward, wormlike and weak.

Then he collapses.

Iliana soaks in the quiet, so rare in this house. As a dual military couple, she has grown used to the noise. The shouting, the stress, the late-night drinking with her husband's Army pals. She had grown numb to it too.

For a while.

Today, she made their favorite: pancakes. The key is to separate the yolk from the egg and beat only the whites. Let the batter rest for a moment. Flip each pancake once and only once.

The fentanyl lacing them was her husband's hidden contribution. All those little plastic baggies smuggled in from China by way of Taipei.

"If Uncle Sam won't let us make ends meet, we'll do it ourselves." Bruce's words, when he showed her the first shipment and told her his plan.

She'd protested, hadn't she? And he'd ignored every word.

So here he lies now, his own product fed to him, suppressing respiration, cognition, consciousness. What is he thinking as he crawls across the floor? Does he know what's truly going on? At some level, he must. Why else push the broken plate away and keep inching forth?

"It's okay. Daddy's just tired." She strokes her daughter's blonde hair. That precious face lying in the oatmeal, bubbles no longer rising. "Daddy's had a long week. We all have."

Iliana pauses, sensing a curious warmth on her face and a buzz like the brightening of lights. Is she back in the interview room? Are the MPIs laying out their case against Bruce and his trips to Taiwan?

No. That had been last week, in October. Today is the first Tuesday of November. She told them she needed time to consider their offer: turn evidence against Bruce, or join him in court-martial.

Now, here is her answer: Bruce curls up by the fridge and gives up the struggle. Here is her family, forever free of his schemes.

Wind rattles the leaves on their lawn. Iliana basks in the breeze. When she decided to poison her family, it arrived with a certainty purer than she ever felt. No plea bargain. No noncompliant accessory to article 112A. Today is her brave rejection.

Her spoon is ready. The pancakes and oatmeal are still warm. A few bites and it's over. So why can't she swallow this meal?

Because…

She touches her lips to find them flaky and dry. She opens her mouth, probing fingers into the damp cavity that should hold her tongue.

Instead, she finds an odd blockage mid-mouth. There are tubes and cords, a braided ribbon of wires. She tries to cry out, realizing she can't make a sound with her throat fully numb.

The crackling breeze picks up, fluttering the curtain now. Filling her home with the hint of cold metal and salt.

Mind reeling, First Sergeant Iliana Kennedy, mother of two, stumbles to the mirror to behold her ruined reflection. Her lips hang parted by thick tubes. Twisting hoses penetrate her nostrils. Her hair is not shaved or slicked back but entirely missing. Where blonde locks once hung there are circuits and wires, a transparent cap housing tumors and skull.

It is her eyes, however, that spike terror deep into her heart. Eyes that cause Iliana to mewl and gasp and claw at her intubated throat.

Her eyes are gone.

Two sutured flaps peer back, lids freshly sewn shut.

Trembling, she fingers the soft hollows. There is nothing, no form or warm ocular sphere beneath. Only emptiness.

How? her mind screams out. *How can this be?*

Crying through a dry throat, Iliana scrambles away from it all. But there is no away.

First, the kitchen tiles fall out under her feet, squares tumbling into a chasm of static, *tickity tick tick*. Then the walls slide back, like movie props coming down after wrap. And still the wind whips up, a great ocean of leaves, rustling and hissing, a storm in her mind.

"Please remain calm," a voice says. It comes from her daughter, her young face dripping with oatmeal. Five-year-old lips move, but that's no child's voice from her throat.

"Focus, Iliana," speaks the thing with dead lips. "Your target is on an airplane, registration N443ED. Current altitude: thirty-five thousand feet traveling west over Lake Michigan."

The oatmeal-soaked lips describe every detail: the trim of the seats, the silver paint of the wings, the woven layers of fabric and wires, the metal fuselage. It all blooms into view, a narrow cabin and several chairs where men sleep beneath dim lights as the earth passes below.

And Iliana Kennedy, her hands liminal and hazy, knows with cold certainty that the voice in her mind is not her daughter's; it never could be.

That life passed long ago.

"Good. Now let us begin."

[14]

WHILE HIS AIDES REST, THE SENIOR SENATOR FROM KENTUCKY relaxes in the moonlit cabin, his body still warmed by the brisket and bourbon. His thoughts turn to tomorrow's speech in Las Vegas. He'll need to get his condolences out quick, of course. Nothing unites the chambers of governance like an untimely death. Perhaps he can even read on the floor of the Senate. Yes, that will play well to the cameras.

He takes out his pen and scribbles a few lines.

He was a daring man. He put his people above party, above policies, above the petty fray of D.C. rhetoric. Most of all, Dave Drogan dared to believe in America. And Americans dared to believe in him.

Yes, that has a nice ring to it. And perhaps he—

A vibration passes through the cabin, rattles the ice cubes and sends a jagged scribble up the page. A new thought emerges: *Is the jet speeding up? And banking?*

With a ding, the seat belt sign blinks on. Odd. The pilots always tell him before turbulence.

Senator Marks rises, steadies himself on the armrest. Like most things, the seat belt sign is a suggestion. Rules don't apply to men like him. Knees cracking, he shuffles past his aides. Gives the cockpit door his usual *tappity tap* before opening it.

First, the chill hits him. Next, the taste. This air is charged, a forming tornado both humid and cool. Then comes the feeling: there are too many people for such a small space. At an instinctual level, the senator knows they're no longer alone, him and the pilots.

"Uh, sir, you need to strap yourself in," the captain says, fumbling with the yoke and pushing buttons.

"Everything hunky-dory up here, Todd?" The senator studies the buttons and knobs, and how a few are moving on their own.

"Sir, return to your seat, now!" the co-pilot shouts.

"Now listen, fellas, there's no need to take that tone—"

The turbulence hits him with a breath-stealing crunch, sends him ten feet back and onto his ass. So fast he hardly notices his shirt torn on the door. Three hundred dollars, right down the drain.

What the senator does notice—only when he's back in his seat —is the pain in his ear, a low-pressure hum. It's as if the plane itself is breathing, expanding in a furious whir.

The cockpit door swings shut, open, shut again, then open. Glimpses assault him. The captain fighting, tugging back on the yoke just to have it snap forward. The co-pilot's desperate fingers, twisting dials left only to have them turn right. Something breaking on the instrument panel as the engines roar, faster and faster.

The senator's aides are all awake now. One is screaming. Another is taking a crash position. And a third—bless her heart— is calling out for God's mercy, begging the Lord to protect them.

God's not here, the senator from Kentucky thinks. *But something else is. Something our wickedness made.*

It is the last clear thought to crash through his terrified mind. But not the last thing. That is the cold water and shattering metal, a wall of churning fury that obliterates all his fear and deeds and ambitions.

[15]

MOMBASA, KENYA

DOWN A NARROW ROAD THAT ENDS NEAR A PILE OF SCRAP METAL AND tires hangs a sign that reads, *Jambo! Cyber Cafe*. Inside, the cafe days are over. Its once-proud Italian espresso machine is a dusty husk, a prop for selfies and kids skipping school. The caffeine comes from the refrigerator now, where canned coffee is poured over ice. The customers do not care. They are here for the high-speed internet and the latest online games.

At one workstation, two foreigners lean in and whisper.

"There." Michaels points to a line of red text in a sea of blue code. "That's how they found us."

"What do you mean 'they'?" Caitlyn squints at the screen. "I don't understand."

"They've red-listed us." Michaels enlarges the text. "Before I resigned, I left a keystone script running on a page the Foundation uses to transfer scraped data. It's a fake repository for queries: phone numbers, social security, biometrics."

"You're losing me."

"A waiter takes an order and heads to the kitchen. This intercepts that order, copies it, and passes the original on. If no one's searching for us, this page stays empty. If a search is ordered, it starts filling up the log. I call it a canary, like—"

"A canary in a coal mine," Caitlyn says. "Yeah, I get that. What I don't get is how they found us."

As Michaels scrolls, patterns emerge among the logs. Dates and times beginning weeks ago. "See here? That's a query for known facial patterns within ninety percent confidence. There's the date it returned a hit, eleven days ago."

"That's impossible. We were at sea."

Michaels highlights the URL that triggered the match. Just an IP address and a hexadecimal link. He opens a new tab.

"Yeah, we were at sea. Those German friends we made? Not so much. What do people do when they return from vacation?"

Caitlyn nods as the page finishes loading. "They share their photos."

An Instagram post, two sailboats rafted together in calm waters. The caption: *Zwei Boote. Eine Welt. Glückliche Erinnerungen.*

"Two boats," Caitlyn says. "One world. Happy memories."

There they are, the friendly Germans: Reinhard, early fifties and as tanned as a clay pot; Elsa, smiling proud as she hoists the red snapper she caught. Michaels cleaned it, cut it, and they ate like kings for a day. They insisted he and Caitlyn take ten kilos for their freezer. Reinhard played guitar and the greedy gulls circled above, crying out into the dusk. The next morning they sailed their own way.

It wasn't the memory that triggered the hit. It was Caitlyn's face. There she is, in the background on the *Dionysus*, just off to the right yet clearly in focus.

"But I'm not on social media," she says. "Reinhard, he couldn't tag me."

"He didn't need to. Any pictures of you—your passport, high school yearbook, headshots from your travel agency—they train the algorithms. He uploaded it two weeks ago and it took a few days to find a hit. Now that it knows where to look, it's going to get faster. See this, right there?" Michaels taps several hyperlinks below. Another new window. "Someone's TikTok picked me up at the harbor."

It's an unremarkable video, a teenage Thai girl walking down the beach, narrating her vacation on camera for her friends back home. She passes a man on a bicycle selling green coconut water. A tourist lathering sunscreen on a squirming youngster. Two Kenyan youths, smoking cigarettes and waving to this cute girl talking to her internet audience. Michaels can almost see the little boxes around objects detected as faces, as license plates, as street signs with names in bold text upon uniform color.

The Viola-Jones object detection framework forms the core of facial recognition. It maps common properties across humans: eyes are darker than cheeks and positioned above; a horizontal line always runs under the nose; and unless surgery botches it, the bottom lip is bigger. These are the patterns humans are hardwired to notice but machines need to discover.

Facebook used DeepFace to scrape user uploads. Perceptics has been reading license plates at the U.S. border for decades. Clearview AI trawls the Internet and sells its results to law enforcement.

And the Foundation can access it all.

"That's you," Caitlyn says as the TikTok video pans. Sure enough, there he is dockside, carrying his backpack and duffel bag away from the boat. "You look like a sulking puppy."

"Yeah, well, you're welcome." He closes the video. "I came back."

"Yes, you did. Thank you."

She squeezes his hand. It feels nice. Feels like these past weeks might have been a speed bump and not a cliff.

"Anyway, these queries started three weeks ago," he says. "The Germans were the first hit. But others are coming, especially onshore."

"So how bad is this?"

Michaels struggles with the words. "The Foundation is using every social media network, smartphone, and security feed to find us. They had teams ready within hours when we came ashore.

There are few places this algorithm won't reach. And it's only going to get smarter."

Caitlyn removes her glasses and rubs her eyes. "This shouldn't even be possible."

"We've landed probes on comets and split atoms to the boson. Anyone who thinks a webcam can't watch them without a green light is in denial of our species. And that's not to mention your game-changing trick. That's what they're after."

"How can you tell?"

"Because we're still here. The teams had capture and contain orders. This is a quiet operation, probably unsanctioned."

"So what do we do? To make them stop, I mean."

"I don't think they will."

Caitlyn straightens up. "Then we fight back. Go public. Blow the lid off this thing."

"Much easier said than done."

A month after he was detained by the Foundation and later killed by the God's Breath Killer, Sam Stephens leaked many of Clearwater's secrets via his lawyer to an audience of millions. Containing that and the fallout from his investigation had cost Michaels his job. There had been hundreds of false flags and a slew of disinformation that muddied the waters. Even his dead partner's daughter didn't know what her mother died to protect.

Michaels lets his fears wander his mind, groping for direction. Nearby, the tapping of caffeinated teenage fingers against keyboards. Pixel-dazed kids and the dopamine flow of hyperconnected games. Beyond them, the wall displays the hourly price of PC access: 120 Kenyan shillings. But if you're a member of the Monthly Club, you get premier access to…

His fingers twitch. An idea. Or just the seed.

"There's a white file," Michaels says. "Like a VIP list. Any metadata on that file gets ignored, no matter the requests."

"That's good, right? Let's put ourselves on it."

"We'd need a Foundation connection. Even if I still had credentials, I couldn't get into a sanctorum."

"But I can."

"No. Three times in a week and you'll give yourself a stroke."

"Not if you guide me. We can make it quick."

"Even if I agreed to, the sanctorums are EMI-shielded, basically Faraday cages in all but name. *If* you could blink your way inside, and *if* you could use the keyboard, there's biometrics to unlock it. Heck, the closest one is in Cairo."

"Cairo," Caitlyn repeats.

Michaels lets his fingers do their two-three-five prime number tap. No, the idea is a stretch. It's—

"Dammit, why do you always do this?" she asks. "Just tell me what you're thinking."

"I don't know what I'm thinking. It's… Okay, you know that feeling when you need to sneeze but can't? That's what it's like, up here." He taps his head. "Sometimes it's an idea. Sometimes it's nothing. The only way to tell is to give it some space."

Her gaze falls to his twitching fingers. He covers his hand, squeezing. "I'm sorry. That must be exhausting."

"We don't always get to pick between a good choice and a bad one. Sometimes all options are suboptimal."

A police car speeds past, sirens blaring. Funny how different they sound overseas. And the interlude is just what he needs to loosen a brick in the wall of his mind.

"Okay, this is a long shot but…"

"But?"

"I have an asset in Spain, someone who owes me. If they can meet us in Cairo and get me into the sanctorum, I can add us to the white file."

"So we're going to Egypt. Won't there be cameras at the airport?"

"We'll need another way in."

He loads up Google Maps, searches *Driving Directions, Mombasa, Kenya, to Cairo, Egypt*. The result: 5626 kilometers. Nearly 3500 miles.

"One hundred and ten hours," Caitlyn says. "And that's crossing how many borders?"

"Ethiopia, Uganda, Sudan, Egypt. Each one a roll of the dice. Might as well just sail there."

He runs his hands through his hair. A year ago the Foundation was using this same system to search for Zara Eisler, a member of Project Clearwater that had vanished. Now, he's sitting next to Zara's daughter, the algorithmic lenses pointed at them. Not a good feeling, this high-level paranoia. The kind that might make a person fake their own death.

"A boat," Caitlyn says. "Michaels, that's actually a good idea. A container ship."

He tilts his head.

"Mombasa is on a shipping lane to Egypt," she says. "If we can get a room on a cargo ship to Port Suez, that'll take us within ninety miles of Cairo."

"You're serious?"

"One of my clients was a novelist who took cargo ships around the world. Three meals a day, tons of privacy, spotty internet so there's no distraction. Cheaper and less obnoxious than a cruise. Michaels, this is what I do. I built my travel agency from nothing but photos and promises."

"And your ability to blink."

She nods. "I bet I could find us one within a day."

It turns out Caitlyn is wrong. She doesn't find one ship but three, all within hours. She arranges the trip using a booking ID recycled from her travel company. She weaves a story about two tech entrepreneurs turned flashpackers, a pair with deep wallets and humble lifestyles. And it's not a lie, not entirely. A quick chat with a rep through a web-based relay service, and they're booked on the *Shen Hai Long Obregón*, a container ship sailing under a Panamanian flag of convenience.

"And we're good to go." She closes out the chat box. "Officially, we are ex-techies helping budget-minded millennials see the world. The ship has limited internet, though they do have a lot of DVDs."

"I'll bring a book."

"You'll bring several. Last time you ran out of reading material, you got on my nerves."

A moped buzzes by the window. Three computers down, two Kenyan friends raise their phones and smile for a selfie. Michaels and Caitlyn quickly turn away.

[PART 2]

"Give not thyself up, then, to fire, lest it invert thee, deaden thee, as for the time it did me. There is wisdom that is woe; but there is woe that is madness."

—Herman Melville,
Moby Dick

[16]

THE JOURNAL OF TEDDY JENSEN

PROPERTY: CZ-93 "DAY'S BANE"

AUGUST 9TH

Happy birthday to me! To celebrate, Mother bought me this diary and a handmade leather cover. Aren't they lovely?

Twenty-five. A whole quarter of a century. I wonder what the next quarter century will bring. Good things, I'm sure.

I have promised my neurologist I will journal regularly. She believes it will help with my recovery. Isn't it peculiar how I have to recover from this? Like my mind is a healing wound and I need to keep myself from scratching or picking the stitches.

It's not fair. It's not a wound but a gift.

They say that they're worried it will hurt me, but you know what I think?

I think they're worried I might hurt someone else. I would never do that, of course not. But that's why they're worried. I saw how they looked when I signed their forms.

They stayed far away.

November 21st

Thanksgiving is almost here, my favorite holiday. Do you know why? Because I am always thankful for all that God has given me. I am healthy and happy. I can go places in my mind. And I can help. I am blessed with duties here at the farm—even if they're duties I sometimes fail.

Yesterday, Mother sold Mr. Hopfwood ten chickens for his restaurant. I was tasked with processing them. I broke their necks as I'd been taught—quickly and with mercy. And yet I found my mind wandering. I thought of Claudia, my old school friend (Mother doesn't approve of the word "girlfriend") and I wondered what she was up to. I heard she moved to the city.

So, I did it. I imagined Des Moines. I imagined her house.

I went to see her, but she screamed so I quickly went home.

There were dead chickens everywhere. I must have wrung fifty necks.

I gave the ten chickens to Mr. Hopfwood. Then I buried the rest behind the old barn. Tomorrow I will tell Mother, but for now I must be more careful.

Dr. Chase once warned me that my daydreams could be dangerous.

March 2ND

Headaches, headaches, be gone with thyself!

Sometimes, I envision taking a drill to my skull. Sometimes a bolt gun. Then I remind myself of Elijah or Job and all that they endured for God. One of my favorite verses from First Peter:

> *"For this is a gracious thing, when,*
> *mindful of God, one endures sorrows*
> *while suffering unjustly."*

So I endure!

Oh, I saw the boy again, this morning.

I was stacking wood by the back porch. He came from a sunbeam and watched me for minutes. He mimicked my breathing.

When I approached the boy, he grew translucent and dim at his edges. The closer I stepped, the further he receded.

Yet he never moved. It was as if he was always there, always fixed at some unreachable distance.

I called out and he called back in a frozen voice that rattled my skull.

So I chased him away. I chased him all the way down the driveway until I could no longer see him. When I looked back at the house, I could see myself there, still stacking up wood.

And my eyes were still open.

August 20th

Two men came to visit this morning. They said they represented the government. They didn't say who they were with but I didn't have to ask.

Clearwater.

They left a check for one hundred thousand dollars. I've never seen that many zeroes at the end of a number. There will be more checks, they said. More zeroes as well, if I agree to sign more of their forms.

I told them I needed Mother to lend me her wisdom. They insisted no others could be party to this agreement or these terms.

So, I signed it.

I asked if they'll talk to Dr. Chase about the headaches and the gaps in my memory. They promised me they would.

I don't believe them.

Tomorrow, I'll take the check to the bank and deposit it. This is a great blessing. It will be enough to pay off the remainder of Mother's mortgage. Perhaps she can start the horse sanctuary she's been talking about.

She will be so happy.

May 27th

I bumped into Claudia at the grocery store. She nearly screamed when our carts collided but then she gave me a hug. She said it was so great to see me. It had been a long time and she'd been meaning to visit.

There was a ring on her finger, all big and sparkly that shined like the heavens.

I watched her load groceries into a pickup. A handsome man asked who she was talking to. I closed my eyes and heard their words beside me. No one special, she said. Just an old childhood friend. No one at all.

[17]

DAY'S BANE, ALASKA

GRAY WAVES CRASH AGAINST THE LEGS OF THE PLATFORM, FOAM spattering and sliding down the forty-foot marker. Chase ignores the swaying horizon. After months here, he knows this storm will soon pass, like all others.

What comes after is what has his attention. Much to do and be done with. And much to undo.

First, he turns on his computer. Even bolted to the desk, the monitor arm vibrates with the storm. A cursory scan of his emails: a receipt for his flight to Seattle, his Daily Stoic message with calm thoughts from Marcus Aurelius, a handful of cold offers for consulting work. He deletes every one.

This year has taught him that his instinct is right: his work here at Day's Bane will be the last of his career. He knows too much to be let go.

So it's no surprise what he finds on the news.

There, on *The New York Times*, is the top story on politics: *Investigation into Senator's Fatal Flight Deepens; NTSB Eyes Co-Pilot's Actions.*

Christ, the pressure is building.

But Chase isn't here for the news. He's here for the comments. One user in particular: *SanguineMoon2242.*

He finds the user profile and sorts comments by *new*. Five in total, all in the past twenty-four hours. Good, the message got through. Now time to decrypt it.

Long ago, when the Cold War was at its most vitriolic and the Iron Curtain its thickest, Robert Chase, a specialist stationed near Heidelberg, spent a year listening in on Soviet officer chatter. Their cryptography was simple, just two points of contact, shared ciphers, and a dozen dull conversations about "mothers going to stores" and "ships sailing through storms."

Listening in, Chase had been charmed by the banality of coded talk.

Mothers were munitions, he eventually learned. Storms were conflicts abroad.

But these weren't for his ears alone, he learned. The KGB was also eavesdropping. If every conversation became mundane, there was nothing extraordinary to report. If bland chatter could be laced with hidden meaning, then it confused the whole system. Russians, ever the masters of bleak novels and subtle connections, simply overwhelmed unauthorized ears.

It was a lesson Chase shared with Michaels last summer, in the waning days of the God's Breath Killer investigation and Caitlyn's disappearance. A lesson Michaels understood instinctively. And here, now, is proof that lesson had worked.

>SanguineMoon2242: *Copy her all you want but Billie Eilish has more style in her pinky than your entire ancestry.*

There, the first word: *Copy*. Chase scrolls down. Another post, two sentences long.

>SanguineMoon2242: *Another commie owned by the facts. One who refuses to see the flaws of socialism.*

Chase marks the second word of the second sentence in his mind. *Who*. More scrolling now, passing the posts by chronology, knowing that, like the Soviets he spied on, it is the syntax that makes the message. Simple once known yet nearly impossible to detect.

>SanguineMoon2242: *Wow! Such a cute dog. What breed is it?*

Three sentences, three words in: *Is.* Chase adds it to the mental list, searches for the fourth.

In five minutes he has the message in his mind, a few mental adjustments made for the lack of punctuation.

Copy. Who is the enemy? Why her? How to stop?

A deep breath. Outside, it's midday at the edge of the world. The storm clouds have softened, the wind turbines shadows among fog. A few birds circle the loading cranes that hang over the platform.

So, how to send out a bottled message under near-total surveillance?

Chase cues up his Amazon wish list. Another browser tab and he finds the first item. Five minutes later, a second item. Then a third.

A half hour of browsing, clicking, adding items to that wish list, and he's done. The easy part's over. Knees cracking, he stands up and studies his left arm.

Now comes the challenge.

He picks up the phone and dials the medical bay. He can almost see it in his mind: the subjects in their twilight sedation. Anders, poring over the results. Bethany, still elbow deep in an autopsy. And a phone, now ringing on the wall.

"Medical," Bethany says.

Chase bites his knuckle, cries out. "Beth, it's Bob. Bob Chase. I've had an accident. I need you to send the on-call to my suite."

Then he hangs up. They're on the way now. No turning back.

Chase opens up a filing cabinet and tests the weight. Heavy, good. He gives the lower drawer a tug, loosening the rollers, back and forth, back and forth. It's a monstrous thing, filled with reams of reports detailing this quarter's achievements. Not perfect, but it'll do.

Using his crutch's left forearm brace, Chase leans against the filing cabinet. Two feet of space where the frame meets the extended drawer. He puts his left arm in the gap. He waits, feeling the might of the ocean, the sway of the waves. Heaving momentum and—

He slams the drawer on his arm. A sickening crunch and his legs buckle, sweat blooming instantly across his body and his world collapsing beneath a tempest of flames.

[18]

WHITTIER HARBOR, ALASKA

THE SCENT OF WET DEATH AND ICE FILLS HIS NOSTRILS AND TIGHTENS his bowels. Rubber-gloved hands grab transport baskets, nets burping forth mounds of fish, soon to be gutted and stuffed into ice and shipped off to all corners of the world.

As he disembarks the ferry, Robert Chase scratches the cast on his left arm. He is grateful he gave up meat long ago. This fish market catapults him back to the depths of Clearwater, where wet subjects slipped from sensory deprivation pods. Where salt crystals sparkled between lubricated latex and briny skin. Like a fish frying in its grease, the decoherent mind burns its own body as fuel.

Chase shrugs off the thought. A container of salmon on ice to his right. A pair of fishmongers to his left. He adjusts his cast against his forearm brace to steady his sea legs. He starts down the long dock.

One hundred yards of hobbling and a shape breaks from the disembarking tourists. "Dr. Chase," says a woman, gruff and formal. He knows the tone before he sees the badge. Immigration and Customs Enforcement. "Please come with us."

Glancing back, he's not surprised to see two other ICE agents, windbreakers flapping in the breeze. Stony faces say they're not asking twice.

Chase is led through a door labeled *FOR MARKET USE ONLY* and down a series of halls. He notes the twists and turns. The color-coded pipes, not unlike the labyrinthian corridors of his darkest work.

Very well. If this is it, then let it be fast. A cold barrel to the base of his skull, a silent puff. That would be best.

And yet, too much work remains to be finished.

"Have a seat at the table," the female ICE agent says. "Hope you don't mind if we take a look at that arm."

"My arm?" Chase raises his left hand, gives his thumb a weak wiggle. The cast rattles against his watch, plaster and gold.

"Lay it on the table please. There you go."

The female agent takes his cast and removes his watch. He senses movement behind him: the door being locked, a clatter of something hoisted from a case, then the click of a battery pack sliding into place.

"I sure hope you know how to use that," Chase says as the large ICE agent hoists the surgical saw. "It's a delicate machine."

A tightening on his wrist. The woman has a strong grip. He could probably pull away, yes, but what then? Hobble for the door? The last time he went without his crutches, Teddy Jensen had been in pursuit. It'd taken months for Chase's weak knees to heal.

No choice but to endure.

The worst part about getting old isn't having to piss three times a night. Nor the persistent aches: the tendons and teeth and the new click in his elbow. It isn't even the fact that sometimes he doesn't recognize his lined face in the mirror. It is, simply, that he is becoming an invisible man.

"I assure you, this isn't necessary. They searched me before I left."

Of course, they ignore him.

"Try to stay still, sir." The woman tightens her grasp on his arm. "The sensors detect skin, but not if you fidget."

A cold smirk. The saw whirs and whines and whistles, chewing into the soft cast and spitting plaster fibers.

Heat. A tickle at the edge of his skin. Warmer now, hotter and—

Like shucking corn, the agents crack open the cast. There it is, Chase's arm, bruised and purple, sticky with a week's worth of mildew and sweat.

Stoney-eyed, the agents turn the cast over, peeling layers and pulling fibers.

"There's nothing here," the agent with the saw says. "He's clean."

"Well of course I'm clean," Chase says. "I already told you that."

They ignore him, conferring. He takes out a spare thermoplastic cast from his bag. A wince as he tightens the Velcro straps.

From the corners, one of the ICE agents taps his phone, eyeing Chase occasionally. Then it comes: a flash on his screen, the pop of a message. The agent nods.

"He's free to go."

Chase adjusts his hearing aid, turns to the man. "Come again?"

"You're free to leave, sir," the woman says, unlocking the door. "Welcome to the U.S."

The SFO arrival terminal greets weary travelers with beige walls and a rug the color of lumpy custard. After nine hours, one layover, and twenty-four hundred miles, Robert Chase is happy to put his crutches upon each hideous inch. With a bloom of light, the automatic doors open and a smile breaks his face.

"Hey, Uncle!" his niece shouts from the far side of the rope barrier.

"Katherine." Chase wraps her in a soft embrace, the first he's felt in months. "It's wonderful to see you."

He takes a moment to study her. At twenty-five, Katherine is more his sister's reflection by the year. He can spot the fierce blue in those eyes. And the shadow of his brother-in-law in her jawline, wide and strong.

"Uncle Bob, what happened to your arm?"

"Old age and a bit of clumsiness with a sticky drawer."

"Really? Why do I sense there's more to the story?"

A narrowing of her eyes as she takes his rolling suitcase. She's not buying it. And perhaps she never has. For all of his failings in life—both professional and personal—Chase is comforted that there's one person who can see through to his core, to his very intentions, which have always been good.

Or so he tells himself.

"Katherine my dear, it's a bit soon for the inquisition. So how's my niece doing?"

She smiles. Goodness, how it shines. "I'm doing well. Great, actually. Oh, and I got the job, thank you very much."

"No, no need for thanks. Just a smart young woman with a bright future."

"Brighter now. Your introduction certainly opened the door."

"Not as much as it used to, I'm afraid. And don't sell yourself short. You stepped through on your own."

Chase leans against the escalator. Down below, the baggage carousel buzzes, the first suitcases sliding out. He knows his will be near the end, a little TSA flyer inside: *NOTICE OF BAGGAGE INSPECTION.*

"What about you?" Katherine turns those kind eyes on him. "Keeping busy on another one of your top-secret projects?"

A chuckle from the doctor. "It's never that dramatic, I'm afraid."

At the bottom of the escalator, he spots a man with a green baseball cap talking on his phone. When Chase passes, the man turns the cap backward, the number 237 on the back.

Chase gives Katherine's shoulder a polite squeeze. "If you'll excuse me, dear, I need to visit the men's room."

Inside, Chase closes the stall door and waits until the sound of running sinks and flushing urinals subsides. There is a rhythm to airports, and a rhythm to their bathrooms. Quiet time now.

Lowering the toilet seat, he lays several pieces of tissue on the lid. A tug on his left ear loosens the canal. Then comes the slim-tip earpiece, the tube, and the hearing aid itself. Only a few grams of plastic and battery.

Carefully, he lays the hearing aid on the toilet paper. A deep breath to steady his shaking fingers and a count down from sixty.

For twenty-four hours he's waited with this damn thing in his ear. Waited on helicopters and ferries. Waited as hands tore apart his cast. He can wait now until his heart settles down.

Forty-five.

Chase has sensed his employer's fading faith in his work for months. Anders's promotion, the edited test logs. He knows how to read the room.

Thirty seconds.

And he knows when to drop a false tip. Just an anonymous message to Day's Bane security: a disgruntled employee will be smuggling data off the platform. If the Russians or the Chinese catch a whiff of what's being built, they'll pay any price.

So while the agents were sawing his cast open, he'd been tilting his ear toward them. Playing his hand right in front of their eyes.

Three… Two… One.

Now his fingers are steady.

Pulling, twisting, he gives the hearing aid battery compartment a tug. It releases a chamber no larger than a pebble. A tilt and out it comes. He holds the aerogel up to the light. Five little chambers, each filled to the brim.

Outside, Chase finds the long-term luggage locker area and activates the rental kiosk. He punches in locker 237, then enters the pin. When it unlocks, he peers inside.

There, sitting in the locker, is a green baseball cap. Above it is a blue Post-it note with an address written in black marker.

Chase takes the note and quickly folds it. He leaves the hearing aid next to the hat, so small in the shadows. And he thinks size doesn't matter when your evidence is molecular. A mountain looks mighty until you realize it's made up of rocks. Now, to start an avalanche with a pebble.

19

PORT TAWFIQ, EGYPT

CONSIDERED THE GREATEST ENGINEERING FEAT OF THE NINETEENTH century, the first waterway dug by human hands to split a continent. Here, the Suez Canal stretches out, sand and stone lining its banks. Almost a hundred ships pass through daily, an artery of commerce visible from space.

With the sunrise in her eyes and the wind in her face, Caitlyn surveys the smoggy horizon from the monkey island of the *Shen Hai Long Obregón*. Up here, nearly sixty meters high, is like gliding along a blue railway between vast sandy smears. Below her sits the bridge and the accommodation deck, their home for the past fourteen days. Further down, stacked containers fill the deck of the ship.

And it's all just a blur.

Sighing, Caitlyn puts on her glasses, the strongest pair they brought. Focus returns. Hard lines here and there. Still, it's a dusty veil.

"Good news," Michaels says, clanging up the stairs from the bridge. "Our paperwork pre-cleared customs and immigration. We'll disembark the moment we hit Port Suez. There's a taxi waiting, then a two-hour ride to Cairo."

"Easy peasy," she says. "Why do I sense there's bad news as well?"

In the morning light, it's hard to see him. For a moment, there are two. One standing before her and another still clanging up the steps. A blink, and they've merged.

"Well, it's more of a fashion suggestion. You've got tattoos and a face as unique as the Mona Lisa. Our best strategy is discretion."

"You want me to cover my arms?"

He gestures to his head, then on down. "The covering I'm thinking of is more… traditional. If some wide-eyed teenager gets a look at your ink and snaps a picture, game over."

"How dare you." She narrows her eyes. "Patriarchal oppressor and most certainly *un*-woke."

"Hey, call me a barbarian if it gets us into the sanctorum without getting spotted."

Grinning, she takes his hand and gives it a squeeze. "Relax, I spent a semester at a Malaysian prep school. I can rock a kick-ass hijab."

He slides in behind her. With his chin resting on her shoulder, they take in the daybreak. These past two weeks have been good. More room than on the *Dionysus*. The Filipino crew cooked excellent meals and left them alone. Enough privacy to rediscover some intimacy.

Funny, she thinks, how their personalities can complement or clash. Here is a man that lives half a life in his head. Always searching for one perfect word when several will do. And here is a woman who lived for so long outside her own body. No wonder the words they exchange often mean different things.

"Do you remember what I said in San Francisco?" she asks. "When I walked into the lobby after your top-secret meeting?"

Michaels considers it. "That you're one stubborn cunt?"

"Besides that." She nudges his side. "What I said was that I'm blind, not stupid. You're still hiding things from me."

Michaels breathes in the warm harbor air. Down below, the

tugboat guides the container ship in, sending up rooster tails of brown water. "Nothing, it's—"

"Bzzt. Try again. You're leaving something out. It's the asset, isn't it?"

He narrows his eyes. "You listened in."

She scoffs. "If I did, I wouldn't have to ask. You were chewing your toothpicks and pacing the deck counterclockwise after the call. You usually walk clockwise."

She's right. He prefers the ocean to his left. Funny what a decade working for a shadowy agency does to the mind.

"Yeah," he says. "It's the asset."

"They fell through, didn't they?"

"No, they didn't. They're on their way to Cairo right now. They just don't know why."

20

BAB AL-LOUQ, CAIRO, EGYPT

5:00 P.M. EET

ON HIS THIRTY-FIRST BIRTHDAY, BYUNG-SOO "BRAD" LEE, FORMERLY of the California Bureau of Investigation, celebrated the milestone with a cupcake and a candle and lights out at 9:30. His field agent trainer, a brick wall named Omara, congratulated him on surviving another lap around the sun. Then he scolded Brad for bringing junk food into the training center. He gave Brad an extra ten minutes to eat the cupcake and study a map of Foundation sanctorums, over one hundred covert locations, CONUS, OCONUS, and overseas. Pop quiz incoming.

Now an associate field agent nine months later, Brad Lee senses his training paying off.

Here is Cairo, this tawny metropolis, home to nine million souls. As a member of the global community of Americans abroad, Brad has spent the past several months hiking the Camino de Santiago, just another expat with a backpack.

Or so his fellow travelers believe.

Brad is part of a small detachment attempting to locate disappearing backpackers along a hundred-mile stretch of Pyrenees footpaths. Four missing, their phones and IDs dumped in the same church basement. The same cryptic message sent to their families about noises at night and stairs to ascension.

Whatever the hell that meant.

Still, he continues the search.

Service. Development. Initiative. These are the three pillars of Foundation ascension. Brad serves the Mediterranean coordinator through weekly reports. He is developing new skills: threat detection, HUMINT, anomaly investigation. And he demonstrates initiative by following the odd leads, wherever they take him.

Such as this forlorn hotel at the western edge of the Bab al-Louq neighborhood.

"Are you sure this is it?" Brad asks as the driver brings the taxi to a stop. "The Nobellese Hotel?"

The driver studies the tablet Brad passes him. Compares the digital photo to the fire-gutted wreck before them. A group of kids kicks a soccer ball past a rusted Mercedes.

"Yes, is that." The driver points to the sideways letters—*elle*—in faded flaked paints. Once a six-floor marvel of mid-century optimism, now a charred husk. At least the entrance is unchained.

"Well, can you wait here?" Brad instantly regrets his choice of words. A field agent *never* asks. They issue subtle commands since there's nothing to discuss. Dammit, he's acting sloppy.

"You pay, I wait," the driver says, adding, "Be very safe, my friend."

Old hinges groan as Brad opens the charred double doors and steps into the lobby. A high atrium rises, all dust and smoked glass. The singed dreams of tourist dollars now teeming with tetanus.

A distant clatter in an elevator shaft. Brad's hand goes for the Glock holstered in his waist band at a fifteen-degree cant. Training stops his fingers. Clumsy force on foreign soil means a mess to clean up. Keep steady and calm.

A bottle rolls down the dusty stairs, going *plinkity, plinkity, plink*.

Instinct pushes Brad away from the atrium, away from the stairs and elevator and into the shadows. An icy feeling and a memory: a foggy night last spring on stakeout. Watching the dark windows of a blind woman's apartment. And sensing that she was watching him back.

"Caitlyn?" He searches the musty lobby, feeling silly as her name echoes.

"She sends her regards, Agent Lee," says a voice from the end of his old life and the beginning of this new one.

Michaels stands by the door, a shade of the man Brad last saw. Maybe it's the sun-lightened hair. Or perhaps it's the khakis and polo. Brad has never seen him without his olive-green three-piece suit.

Mostly, it's the suspicion Brad had that there was more to this meeting than a clandestine powwow with an Interpol agent who knew Foundation secrets.

"So," Brad says, "there's no snuff film black market here, is there?"

"Not that I'm aware of." Michaels wipes dust off a bannister.

"And those anonymous tips about a Chinese mole in the Foundation? Those were you."

"They wouldn't be anonymous if I said that they were."

Brad shakes his head. "I should've been more careful."

"I just played to your profile. That's what they still teach at Kray Mesa, right?"

"Yeah. Now come here so I can cuff you."

A pause. Brad studies his mentor, wonders, *Could I take him?* Brad's hardened up, lost some of those handles. But Michaels is the smartest man he's ever met. If Brad is simulating three moves ahead, Michaels is at ten.

Instead, Brad does what he knew he'd do since the moment he saw him. He smiles, reaches out, and gives Michaels a hug.

Fifteen minutes and the past year evaporates into familiar banter. Strolling through the ruins, two spooks brief each other while keeping their cards close to their chests. They stop at an old pool, the water mostly turgid puddles.

"Cruising the seas, living off the waters," Brad says. "Never pegged you for a hippy, but I have to say, it's like the life."

"Yeah, it was. Until they come knocking."

"They," Brad repeats. "They being the ones you got me a job with."

"You earned it. You blew the Tae Hwan case open, connected it to—"

"Caitlyn, right. So, how's she taking it?"

"How would you if you learned your childhood was a lie? That your parents weren't who they said they were and your head was full of Dr. Chase's mistakes?"

Brad clears his throat. "That well, huh?"

"She had a good thing going, a truce. And someone broke it. I need to find out why, but not on the Foundation's terms. On hers."

"Maybe Chase wants to bring her in as a consultant."

Michaels shakes his head. "It's not Chase."

"How do you know? Last I heard, he was incommunicado."

"Trust me. I know."

A smirk tugs at Brad's smooth face. "I always get the feeling you've got more angles than a Picasso. So, if it isn't Chase, who?"

"Nox," Michaels says. "Or maybe others cleaning house."

Brad's smile fades. "Cleaning house?"

"Judge Maberry and Senator Marks from the hearing. They're both dead."

Michaels hands him a printout of the crime scene report from Judge Maberry's house. Highlights dance before Brad's eyes. Inconsistencies most would overlook.

Unless they knew where to look.

Brad whispers, "You think they were assassinated?"

"The judge and his wife were college sweethearts, married for fifty-plus years. She booked two weeks in Florence for their anniversary, first-class tickets, opera, the works. A woman with no history of mental illness or jealousy and she snaps, murder-suicide with an extra helping of arson? Think about it."

"People snap all the time."

"Country club grandmothers aren't in the husband-killing, home-torching demographic. Check that autopsy report and tell me those fractures make sense."

Brad hesitates, tongue circling his teeth as he studies the chart. Major blunt force trauma to the neck and chest cavity. Broken fingers indicating defensive wounding. An obvious struggle. Could Maberry's wife really cause such damage, a woman six inches and ninety pounds smaller? All before shooting him in the back of the head?

"These wounds are familiar."

"Like God's Breath." Michaels points to another page. "And Senator Marks. The pilot's suicide note in his email, all those crashes logged on his home flight simulator? Too convenient."

"Just because you're paranoid doesn't mean it's a conspiracy."

"Except when you've been a part of it."

Sighing, Brad takes a seat at the edge of the pool. "You didn't have me fly to Cairo just to shit in my Corn Flakes. You need something, don't you?"

Michaels nods. "And it's a big ask."

"Then let's hear it. Can't be any worse than what I've just learned."

So he tells him.

"Oh Christ, why did I ask? Smuggling you into a sanctorum, that's what, treason, right?"

"It depends. But not if you were forced into this under threat of great bodily harm. That this wasn't your choice."

Brad squints. "Threat?"

A pop of glass as an old bottle breaks at the edge of the pool. Then a splash as the tepid water ripples. A ribbonlike shimmer skims to his left. Then a voice right beside him.

"Hey, Agent Lee," Caitlyn says. "Long time no see."

Hand to his heart, Brad breathes deep to steady his nerves. *Inhale, count to five, exhale.* Just as they taught him. Every last hair on his neck stands at attention.

"Hi, Caitlyn. Wow. You've certainly improved."

There is a faint wind and golden eyes at the edge of his vision. The slender shape of a sun-kissed woman, hair floating as if underwater. He turns and she's gone. Just an empty patch of swimming pool tiles. It takes most of his focus just to keep from pissing himself.

Michaels says, "The Foundation maintains seventy-two sanctorums across the globe. I need access to the Cairo site."

"Ninety-eight," Brad corrects. "My fiancée and I helped bring Madrid online. But if your biometrics are red-listed, they've shut you out. Bounties with local friendlies on speed dial, like in Kenya."

"Right. So if you helped set up a secure site, you know its weakness. Think about it."

Brad retraces his months in Spain: the FLAG Europe-Asia submarine cable with its tapped landing point in Estepona; the encrypted connection, piggybacking to Madrid on fiber funded by NGOs and development bonds; the hardware—cameras and biometric scanners, server blades running software every hour, every second.

Sanctorums, his project coordinator had told him, forked off from the hidden dens of fraternal organizations scattered across Europe and North America at the dawn of the Scientific Revolution. Refuges in plain sight marked with symbols only members knew how to spot. An inn with a left-facing rooster. A paintbrush and a compass at a university plaza. Or a youth hostel with two candles and a flower behind a leaded glass window.

Now that Brad has learned what to look for, he sees hidden messages everywhere.

But he doesn't see a single path into the Cairo sanctorum.

"I give up," he says. "I just made associate agent. Barely. You're asking me to run before I've learned how to crawl."

"What's the Foundation's mandate?"

"ICC. Investigate. Contain. Control."

"No, that's a field agent. C'mon, how'd you get your wings without knowing the agency's goal?"

"To preserve stability," Brad recites, closing his eyes. Over this past year he's read more dossiers and taken more quizzes than he has in his life. Some days, his brain actually feels heavier. "'Civilization collapses without a stable foundation of assured security.'"

"Right, so what happens if the power goes out? Does a sanctorum collapse?"

"No, of course not. They have a buffering system—*oooooh.*"

A slow nod and the hint of a smile on Michaels's lips. God, Brad has missed this. The way his mentor tested him, took his thoughts and stretched them to the edge of his skill. He can almost taste the dopamine.

"Every secure site is meant to work if it loses power," Brad says. "If there's an outgoing message and the whole city goes dark, that data queues up until the connection's restored."

"Which is what? Ninety minutes of battery and buffer time, right?"

"Maybe at the new ones. But Cairo, this is old. Probably fifteen, twenty minutes of low-power mode before it goes to standby."

Brad can see it in his head. The equipment is nothing special, off-the-shelf hardware, time-tested and agency-approved. The Foundation poaches the occasional toys from DARPA, the DIA, even the National Science Foundation, but their backbone is like NASA: no frills and total stability. Their one consistent weakness is that sanctorums exist within the society they're surveilling. A hidden room behind a bookshelf is still dependent on the house.

Now, if they can just pull a few levers...

"This is the Pension Ramses II." Michaels opens up a notebook —an actual notebook with grid-lined pages and thread binding. "It's a backpacker hotel a stone's throw from the museums."

On the left page, a map scratched out in ballpoint pen of a six-story building. Brad's impressed. Michaels has a hint of talent.

"First floor, lobby and cafe." Michaels runs his fingers along the ink. "Second through six are guest rooms, with two exceptions. Here, the owner's suite on five. And at the far end of four, there's this: the only room with barred windows and no balcony."

He taps the corner room, 432, a stairwell beside it. No accident that it's not listed on the pension's website. An island sealed off from all other rooms.

"How'd you get this?" Brad asks. "You shouldn't be within a mile of this place."

"He wasn't." Caitlyn's voice echoes from every angle like thunder.

"I swear to God I'm going to have a heart attack." Brad takes several deep breaths.

"I'll try not to pace." A shimmer to his left. At the edge of the bench, a shape sits down, crossing her legs.

"Yes, please do that." Brad mouths to Michaels, *What the fuck?*

"This electrical junction," Michaels says, turning a page. "It powers the pension. And here's a parallel box that feeds the sanctorum. If we throw the hotel's power, it won't work."

A curious thought scratches at Brad's mind. "What about the whole block?"

"There you go," Michaels says. Another warm flash. Brad's actually doing this. Actually keeping up with his teacher.

"And that's why I'm here," Caitlyn says. "It's a three-person job. Two inside, one outside."

Michaels nods. "While you were tracking down Tae Hwan in Korea, Caitlyn and Teddy took out a chunk of Reno's power grid. She'll do the same thing tonight."

Brad whitens. "Hold up. Tonight? You want to do this now?"

"Not now but in two hours."

The dopamine vanishes, chased off by a metallic surge: fear. Brad's shaking his head before he knows it. "That's too soon. I haven't even figured out how this works."

"The sanctorum drops to low-power mode," Michaels says. "It buffers outgoing communications to nine-minute batches. You get me in, I upload revised biometrics to the white list. The computer hashes it, syncs with Kray Mesa's cloud. In and out, all under nine minutes."

"That simple? Why do I feel like there's more to it?"

"Because you're smart. Basic tenet of our trade: know only what's necessary."

Brad scoffs. "That'll comfort me when we're sharing a cell."

"A cell? No, there's no cell for this. Just a helicopter ride offshore and two empty seats coming back."

The road in Brad's mind stretches back, from this derelict hotel to a case file that fell into his lap over a year ago. He can still see Professor Karl Moore's murder. Can hear Kembo Mlotshwa's eyewitness account. A simple word, *dhimoni,* and then the twisting path that brought him from the CBI to this moment, on the cusp of betraying the very agency he'd started to serve.

"I'd probably be playing Xbox right now," he says. "I never should have taken that case."

"Yeah, maybe." Michaels closes his notebook and offers Brad a hand up. "But think of how much you'd miss out."

[21]

CAFE AL-HARASSI, CAIRO, EGYPT

THE VIOLET SKY HANGS OVER CAIRO, A CITY NOW ROUSING ITSELF into nighttime delights. Downtown, this crossroad of cultures and tongues, all stretching back to humanity's dawn. Here are gap-year backpackers mingling and drinking. There are hawkers plying their wares to wide-eyed tourists. Mopeds meep and bicycles clatter beneath electrical lines as tangled as the ancient streets.

These electrical lines have her attention.

To the passersby, this veiled woman at the cafe is the picture of modest decorum. Her shoulders and arms are covered in a simple thin shawl giving mere hints of her sharp features: the soft eyes and freckled cheeks, the neck and collarbone that seems sunken, as if she has recently lost weight. Her razor-cut hair, black-blonde and shaved on the left, is hidden beneath a muted scarf.

Sipping her bold milk tea, Caitlyn wipes her eyes. When her vision returned, she loved how they looked, fierce and brown, a tiger's latent gaze. After repeated blinks, her world now swims in dull focus. She should have brought her thickest glasses, she supposes. Too late for that now.

Her earpiece buzzes as the line opens. Michaels and Brad nearby, the same pattern of traffic that makes up her immediate soundscape. "Okay," Michaels says. "Here we go."

Despite what sighted people occasionally believe, the blind don't innately gain boosted sense. Some, like Caitlyn, have trained themselves to cross-check their assumptions against secondary senses. The spices of the nearby kofta kebabs. The fruity shisha on the wind. The squeak of chairs and the pattern of the cafe's laughter.

"We're crossing the street now," Michaels says, and she can sense it without looking. An audio split, the traffic slowing down as two men weave between beeping mopeds and taxis. "We're at the pension."

"Copy that." She savors the last sip of her tea.

The cafe is a thing of old wood, ochre walls, and copper chandeliers. Gray-haired men laugh and bellow while teenage couples whisper in dark corners, bodies close. If it wasn't kitty-corner to the Pension Ramses II, she might spend a whole day here, soaking up the culture.

But there's work to be done.

While they're busy checking in, she begins checking out. Busy street, time to go quiet. She activates her earbud's noise cancellation and lets the audio curtain fall.

Ten, nine, eight…

"We've checked in," Michaels says, his voice a candle in the darkness.

Seven, six, five…

In her mind's eye, she can see the pension's lobby. Chipped walls. Ceiling fans circling. The corkboard with local activities and pinned flyers for rideshares. A few more seconds of quiet and she can join in.

"On you, Cait. Throw the power when you're ready."

Four, three, two… Now time to step out.

"Hey." A voice at the edge of the curtain. The heat of someone standing opposite her table. "Hey, you."

Caitlyn opens her eyes to find four faces looking back. Short hair and skin still smooth and oily with youth. Three guys and a girl, all close to twenty. All looking at her.

"You're American, yes?" the woman says. She has sharp eyes, mischievous lips. The husky young man to her right is nearly six inches taller, yet Caitlyn senses this young woman runs the group. "Me and my friends, we're taking bets. They think you're Canadian. Amit here, he's betting Kiwi. Me? I think you're from the US of A."

Caitlyn spots a patch on their backpacks. The Star of David and two blue lines on a patch of white. Israelis. One of the few nations where every youth gets conscripted. A quick assessment of the group before her: thirty months of serving the IDF, guarding buses and being alert. Then here, at the other end, a meager paycheck and a pat on the back. It takes the human mind a long time to unwind.

And alcohol doesn't always help.

"You're right," Caitlyn says. "I am American. From San Francisco originally. I'm sorry, I'm a bit busy—"

"Oh! No way!" says Amit, the shortest one. "I'm from Cupertino. Mind if we sit?"

Caitlyn eyes the smartphone in the husky one's hand, his thumbs typing quick. And the phone's camera tightens her shoulders.

She says, "I'm afraid I'm waiting for someone."

They sit anyway. A boozy whiff, the hops of Stella and the burn of Auld Stag whiskey. They've been partying all day.

The myth of the ugly American abroad is just that: a myth. Wherever tourist dollars bring cultures together, there are always a few assholes. For every Texas frat boy taking up an elderly seat on a Japanese subway, there is an illegally parked Chinese tour bus blocking ambulances or a Russian sexpat prowling Cambodia's brothels. No country or culture has a monopoly on bad behavior abroad. These four Israelis, Caitlyn reminds herself, are kids away from home, away from base, away from the structure that defined much of their lives.

But they're still a liability she needs to shake.

"Do you want a sip?" The husky one asks, holding out a flask.

Caitlyn shakes her head. "No thank you."

"I'm going to have a sip." He takes a deep swig. "Oh, s'good. You sure you don't want some?"

"She's not interested in you," the woman says. "Stop being a creep."

"I can't help it. She's got pretty eyes."

The tall one takes a chair, turns it around backward and sits. "Yeah, she really does."

A quick scan of the cafe patrons. Nervous glances at her table. Yet no one's making a move toward them. It's Friday night, downtown. Probably best to keep to themselves.

"Caitlyn?" Michaels buzzes in her ear. "Waiting on you. Over."

She sighs. "Look, I get it. You probably spent the past six months at a West Bank checkpoint. You're used to base level of friction, right? Makes you feel alive. And now you're bored on vacation and feeling tough with some booze in your belly."

Amit grins, holds up a finger, and then belches. Caitlyn clenches her toes. This youthful rudeness. And the woman with them, she should know better. So much for sisterhood.

"Well then, that's a goodnight from me."

Nothing good will come with sticking around. So she gets up and heads off, around the corner, down the street, and down the walkway. Here, she can regroup and listen in peace. Here, she can—

"Hey, wait up!" It's Amit, calling out. His friends, the tall one, the husky one, the woman, all trailing behind. "Hey, I thought you were waiting for someone. Come back."

Enough. In their stupor, they don't see the flicker, a few bulbs glowing brighter than usual. Now Caitlyn's crossing the street, weaving between the mopeds, a thumb pressed to her ear.

"Caitlyn? Hello? Cait, is everything all right?"

No, it's not all right. She has one job and she's fumbling it. These drunk idiots are fixated on her. If she can just get inside, somewhere cool with a fan to let off the heat.

A hand falls on Caitlyn's shoulder. Then comes the voice, soapy and hot and laughing. "Hey, we just want to hang out."

Caitlyn blinks and the world splits in two.

From her left eye she's four floors above. Looking down on a woman flanked by drunk Israelis, weaving through the human traffic. Trying to find quiet. That woman is her.

From her right eye she sees herself, three feet behind and zooming closer. There's the girl and Amit, the husky one and the tall one, all laughing and leering and closing in on her space.

"I said back off," Caitlyn shouts.

But not in her voice.

Sharp harmonics rattle the edge of her vision. The sound hits the Israelis, stops them in their tracks and widens their eyes.

But it's the push that sends them scrambling back.

Caitlyn, both inside her body and beyond it, feels something rise from the bicameral depths of her mind.

To her left eye, a young woman just trying to walk alone.

To her right, a shimmering vapor, black ribbons stretching out and shoving the Israelis backward.

Then it's gone. The two perspectives merge, jarring and unruly. A forgotten voice whispers, "That's my girl."

"Dad?"

No answer. Just the Israelis, bottles clattering to the pavement as they scamper off. Numbness washes over Caitlyn. The lights of Cairo dim behind a thickening curtain and her vision softens.

You can do this, Caitlyn tells herself, feet coming to a stop at a busy street corner. She wipes away ruby tears. *Go try again. Find a dark place and count down from ten.*

[22]

PENSION RAMSES II, CAIRO, EGYPT

Four floors above the bathroom Caitlyn is entering, Michaels and Brad wait in the dim stairwell and listen to radio silence.

"Caitlyn?" Michaels whispers. "We're waiting on you. Cait?"

Nothing. Brad peers down the hall. There's room 432 lit up and locked at the far end. And perhaps it's also the end of his time with the Foundation. A quick glance at Michaels, and Brad realizes this is the first time he's seen worry on his mentor's face.

Then a deep click as dozens of breakers pop all at once. The smell of burned metal and circuits pushed to their limit. The hallway falls to darkness.

"Okay, that's the power," Caitlyn says, out of breath over the radio. "Your turn now."

Michaels sets his timer to eight minutes. More than enough if all goes to plan. And if not, it might be the last night of his life.

A nod to Brad. Now they're both running, down the hall, Brad taking the lead. Michaels hangs back to avoid the fish-eye lens built into the door. Brad taps the keypad, puts his finger on the sensor. Waits…

Click. Green means go.

They hit the room fast, one after the other. Just a standard sanctorum, the workstation set up in the corner near blackout curtains. The web camera array, always on, always watching, always ready to call home.

Except when its connection is severed.

For now, every second of this raid is being recorded on the server blade, queued up to go out the moment the internet is restored. Michaels knows there's not enough time to clean the video *and* revise the white list.

Which means that Brad cannot be appearing to help.

Michaels seizes him from behind. Gives him a shove forward and a hard smack in the back of the head. A bit too hard, perhaps.

"What the hell?" Brad hisses.

"Quiet," Michaels whispers, blocking his lips from the camera. "This is me saving your job."

Another shove, and he's got Brad by the collar now, flex-cuffing his hands and pushing him facedown onto the bed. The camera takes it all in through dispassionate glass. A performance for a paused audience.

Seven minutes now. Michaels logs into the workstation under Brad's account. No internet connection, but that's just what he wants. Cloud computing has made document synching a breeze but not without a few key vulnerabilities. A Man-in-the-Cloud Attack hijacks a user's token to convince cloud servers that third-party files are authentic. Like kidnapping the postman to peek at the mail.

It takes Michaels less than a minute to find the hashed biometric logs stored locally. Another thirty seconds of aiming his phone's camera at the screen as the code scrolls past. The human eye can only perceive so much data at once. The human mind becomes saturated at several hundred words per minute.

A camera has much higher limits.

With the proper sideloaded apps, Michaels's jailbroken phone identifies the subsections of code pertaining to him and Caitlyn. There they are: *Active Trace e242, GIDEON, Michaels C.;* and *Active Trace e243, GREY, Caitlyn M.*

Dozens of known identifiers: skin tone and eye color, the slope of the nose and the average width of the smile. Ninety-four scraping parameters and that's just for their faces. There are gigs of cloud data here on Michaels and Caitlyn. Rings and tattoos, gaits and inflections, all culled from as much media as the world feeds it and constantly evolving.

Five minutes now.

A new choice before him. Deleting it all buys them some time. But like debt, it only delays the collection. So he takes a page from the Foundation's tactics. Time to muddy the waters.

In two minutes his smartphone uploads seventy-six new biometric profiles. Faces culled from Shutterstock, Instagram, corporate websites and more; body profiles from fashion magazines; scans of jet-setting celebrities and even a former vice president. It's all loaded into hashed files and tagged as *Active Trace e242* and *e243*.

God help the support technicians at Kray Mesa that have to unravel this mess.

Three minutes. Now to test it. Moment of truth.

With the new batch synchronizing, he reactivates the facial-recognition software. His face fills the screen, dozens of boxes and dots tracing his unique geometry.

Name: MICHAELS, Gideon Carris

Height: 5′11″

Citizenship: Dual USA / Canada

Clearance: REDACTED

Search Strings: ALL PUBLIC AND PRIVATE

Biometric Records: 14,742

Beneath the fields, in green: STATUS CLEAR.

Bingo.

He logs off, hoists Brad up by the collar and cuffed wrists, and whispers, "Sorry, it had to look real."

Heading out, Brad says, "Your first is Gideon?"

Michaels winces. "Don't be silly. No one would give their kid such a horrible name."

Out in the hall, the home stretch. Michaels thumbs his mic.

"Caitlyn, go ahead and throw the switch. We're out." Then, to Brad, "Here, let me uncuff you."

Before he finishes, a figure steps out of the stairwell and stops in her tracks.

It has been nine months since Michaels met Dr. Dana Park outside the closed-door hearing that heralded his resignation from the Foundation. He knew her by agency reputation and her public-facing persona, that of a tenured professor of forensic anthropology at Busan University. And he knew her real name— Field Agent Olivia Moon—from a few key reports, always thorough, always precise.

And here she is now, eyes widening as her stare meets Michaels, with Brad still flex-cuffed at his wrist.

"Oh hey, honey," Brad says. "So yeah, this isn't what it looks like."

The power outage. The sanctorum door closing with a deep clunk. A quick snap of her hand into her blazer and she has her Glock leveled at them both. "Put your hands up. Do it now, Michaels!"

"Afraid I can't do that, Olivia," Michaels says, ducking behind Brad. "But it's nice to see you again. We're going to take the stairs, nice and slow."

"No, you're going to lay down by the count of five or I hobble you both. One!" Her aim drops to their legs.

"Whoa, babe, hold up for a second—"

"Two!"

Michaels bobs behind Brad, fumbles in his coat pocket. Brad is a thicker target, more soft mass to hide behind. But Michaels is taller, has to duck just to keep his head level. And he knows field agents aren't trained to fire on five. That's just what they tell perps. Always pull the trigger on three.

So Michaels raises his own weapon, a flashlight featuring six hundred lumens of blinding whiteness. He lights up her face. She spreads her hand, struggling to blot out the beam.

"Babe, uh, you're supposed to be in Yemen," Brad shouts.

"I was, until you left Spain," Olivia says. "And don't call me babe."

"Olivia, listen," Michaels says. "This is a misunderstanding. It's not what you think."

"Yeah? 'Cause it looks like you just used a grid drop to execute a Man-in-the-Cloud."

Michaels swallows. Well, maybe it is.

"So here's what's going to happen, *civilian*. You're going to release Associate Agent Lee—who I may kneecap anyway. You're going to raise your hands. And we're going to talk this all out—"

Click. A buzz as power returns and the lights flicker back on. The dim hallway, now bathed in brightness. His flashlight is no longer blinding. If she wants to take the shot, now is the time. Michaels knows this.

And so does Brad. He says, "Sorry, babe."

"I said don't call me—"

Brad breaks free from Michaels's grip and rushes Olivia, weaving left, right, left. Twenty feet in five seconds, and then he's upon her, throwing himself head-down, shoulder-first, 180 pounds against 110.

A tangle of limbs provides a gap. Michaels pivots and slides into the stairwell, then springs over the bannister, coming down hard on the steps with a grunt. Two more flights and he's limping out, through the lobby, searching for Caitlyn at the cafe across the street.

Only an empty chair at the table.

"Cait?" Michaels fumbles with the mic. "Cait, are you—"

"Behind you." He almost doesn't recognize the woman in the brown chiffon scarf, little webs of burst vessels reddening her sclera.

With his arm hooked in her elbow, they try not to draw any attention. Just two tourists out on a lively Cairo night.

She asks, "How'd it go?"

"Sloppy, but it worked."

"Mine too."

With the power back on, it's playtime in the backpacker district. A nearby stereo booms *mahraganat*, Egypt's distinct urban dance music. An orange juice vendor passes glistening cups to thirsty teenagers. Just down the sidewalk are the four Israelis.

And a pair of cops they're talking to.

"Oh, lovely," she says. "They found reinforcements."

"They?" Michaels catches a sidelong glance of white uniforms and a lazy demeanor. Tourist police. "Who are they?"

"Drunk kids that couldn't take no for an answer."

When the Israelis spot Caitlyn, they turn and point.

"Hey!" A shout from across the street. Michaels spots the reflection off a car window: the tourist police are weaving through traffic. "Hey! You!"

Michaels and Caitlyn make a break for it. Turning past the cafe, they duck down a tight squeeze between buildings too close for fire code. Another quick glance back. The cops are shadows stretching against the streetlights, merging with traffic. A whistle disperses the wall of mopeds.

Rounding the corner, Caitlyn pulls Michaels into an alcove. They can't outrun them so they'll have to outsmart them.

She pulls off her scarf and throws it to the ground. "Give me your jacket."

"What for?"

"A distraction." She dumps his jacket by the scarf and picks up an empty beer bottle. "This is going to feel weird. Now shut up and kiss me and don't you dare stop."

He pulls her in close and kisses her deep. She shuts her eyes and takes a deep breath.

Clubs at the ready, the policemen round the corner and squeeze down the alley. Dirty walls here. Dark nooks where drunks toss their rubbish and piss out their drinks. Hossam pauses and catches his breath while his young partner blows past.

This is not how he should be spending Friday night. He

should be hitting up tourists for baksheesh, not putting a stitch in his side.

Ah, but the suspects. He sucks in air and hurries on. The American girl, it's probably nothing. And yet, what the Israelis had said… *No, too strange.* Then why did they flee? Guilty hearts never run.

Lumbering, Hossam resumes the chase. Feet pounding, he passes a young couple necking in a doorway, a beer in her hand and her shoulders exposed. He might even return to fine her, but—

Movement at the far end.

"Akram! Over there!" Hossam points with his baton. Just a brief shadow, a form threading the darkness past piles of recycling. A shape in a jacket.

Akram doubles back and takes a hard corner. Damn he runs fast. It takes Hossam thirty seconds to catch up where the alley ends in a chain-link fence. Here is Akram and there is the suspect. Nowhere to run.

And yet Akram is frozen, his arm pointing and trembling.

"Hossam, look!" Akram says, as if Hossam could do anything else. "Her legs… Where are her legs?"

Where the fence meets the wall in a flickering, dirty corner, something is crouching. Something wrapped in a jacket and a brown chiffon scarf. Something that seems to be crawling backward into the shadows.

And looking out with two cindering eyes.

Twin sunsets, Hossam thinks. *Like dusk on the Nile.*

A low pulse rumbles. Hossam feels it in his sinuses. Then comes the chill as every light buzzes and winks. It's hard to tell who screams first, Akram or Hossam.

It takes them a minute to work up the courage, to stop swearing at each other, blaming each other, telling the other one to go first. Finally, the elder cop shouts, "Idiot! Give me your light!"

There, where the chain-link fence meets the shadowed corner, where trash and cardboard lie strewn in a heap, there is… nothing. Just a scarf and an empty jacket that he knows—impossibly—once held a dark feminine form.

[23]

Two miles from the Pension Ramses II, they check into a four-star hotel under different names. A quick elevator ride to their suite and then Caitlyn pushes Michaels onto the cotton threaded bed, tears his shirt open, and sends buttons rolling. Their hands touch and tug and peel free the last of each other's clothes. Then she's atop him, grabbing his shoulders, pushing him down, reaching down, and guiding him in.

It has been days since they've been intimate, weeks since they've made love, but months since they've *fucked*.

In the afterglow of adrenaline and the long tail of fear, they find each other's rhythms, strength and submission, tension and tenderness. In this building ferocity, they find each other's speed. Wrapping her legs around his hips, squeezing him in as her eyes shut and his toes curl, and now it hits her: the great release of all future worries. They are here, here only in this moment, here only for each other.

Exhausted, they lie against each other, her mind a white canvas, his counting the rotations of the ceiling fan. All smiles and deep sighs.

Caitlyn says, "Why does it take having our backs against the wall for us to stop fighting and focus?"

Michaels turns to her. "What do you mean?"

"We had the whole ocean and we just kept stepping on each other's toes. I drove you nuts."

"Nuts is a bit hyperbolic."

"God, I hate that word." Caitlyn sits up, eyes unfocused. He runs a hand down her back. "Maybe it's pathological, you know? Maybe I need a sense of discovery or danger. Like I can't be happy without struggle."

"Or maybe," he says, "it's because every time you saw me on that boat, I reminded you of the investigation."

She hesitates. "You all laughed at my story."

"I never laughed."

"Not outwardly."

"And I'm glad I was wrong." He leans his head against her back, counting the freckles that trace her spine.

A long silence falls between them.

"Something's changing in me," she whispers. "I can feel it, like a storm forming just past the horizon. Something up here." She taps her left eye.

"Your vision's degrading."

"No. Something behind it, something deeper, ever since Clearwater." She rolls over, onto her side to face him. Caitlyn has thirteen freckles on her face and neck, a prime number. To fall asleep at sea, he often counted them. "I'm having trouble finding the curtain."

Puzzlement narrows his eyes.

"When I was blind, I visualized this black curtain between reality and blinking. I could count down, get calm, and push it aside. When my vision started returning, the curtain thinned, like the fabric was fraying. But the thing is, I could still *feel* it. I could reach out and touch it and there it was, thick and heavy, a barrier between body and mind."

Harmony, Michaels thinks. That's what Chase had called it. Caitlyn's system in perfect alignment. One sense stepping aside for the other.

She reaches out, traces a space in the air between them, an invisible divide. "All I feel now are cobwebs and threads."

Michaels sighs. "We shouldn't have done this. We need to be smarter. Tonight, there had to be another way."

"There wasn't. We did the math: two inside, one outside."

"My point is, you can't keep blinking."

She leans in, lips next to his ear. What she says raises every hair on his neck.

Because her lips never move.

"I don't think I can stop."

[24]

WHILE TWO EGYPTIAN COPS ARE STRUGGLING TO EXPLAIN HOW A woman vanished into thin air, and while Associate Field Agent Brad Lee is apologizing to his furious fiancée, a thirteen-gigabyte biometric packet is synchronizing across dozens of hidden global servers.

Seven thousand four hundred miles to the west, the packet completes its journey. A simple green blinking light on a server heralds its arrival at Kray Mesa, the Foundation's cradle of operations.

Here, where the long halls and colored walls separate departments like state borders, countless servers sift through the world's data. From known terrorists with kill records to nation's leaders whose habits have flagged algorithmic concern. Most packets settle in quiet, inactive data kept for future referral and rarely noticed.

But not this packet.

Within seconds of the packet's arrival, computer screens in the operations bullpen light up, forcing trainee Diego Mendoza to pause his conversation, mute the support call, and wave his supervisor over. Within minutes the worry has spread.

Two floors above sits a ringing black phone. The woman who

answers it checks her screen to confirm what she's hearing: a fresh hit on a high-priority target.

And he's here on home soil.

Hoping to impress the chief coordinator—who is thankfully off-site—she authorizes the operation: a high-visibility daylight takedown.

Nine hundred and fourteen miles northwest of Kray Mesa, Nox stands in line at World Foods. The cashier scans the wine and cheese, the fresh dates and raw Ahi tuna. He offers the woman a flat smile. To pass the time, he counts the security cameras: five at the store's ceiling with poor line of sight, and one here at the credit card reader. In the parking lot, he passes three Teslas.

When his phone rings, he places the groceries in the passenger seat and waits until the connection encrypts. He has a feeling it's good news.

"Sir, sorry to bother you, but a priority target just lit up the bullpen. We've got teams en route. I figured you'd want to be aware."

Nox settles in behind the wheel. "Thank you, Donna. Just feed me the highlights as they come."

Then he clicks off.

Ten minutes later the first update hits his phone and appears on the dashboard display. He considers pulling over. But no, he's been away for too long and he enjoys cooking dinner. Besides, it's a beautiful day for a drive.

>*Target is mobile. Air and ground teams deployed.*

Nox taps the steering wheel. It's a pity about Michaels and Caitlyn. But did they really think they could stay neutral forever? The world changes fast and they'll need to change with it.

Another text.

>*Target sighted, will keep you updated.*

Nox weaves around a slow-moving truck and glances at a traffic camera. He almost gives it a wink. Poor Michaels never stood a chance.

Then a helicopter roars overhead.

The engine shakes his car and the downwash sends freeway debris into the air. That was too low for the state cops.

Nox eyes his rearview mirror. Are those sirens and lights coming up on him?

A pang of anger straightens his back. No. No way. A new text lights up his dashboard.

>*Target vehicle being immobilized. Will update ASAP.*

The standard practice for vehicle immobilization is the Pursuit Intervention Technique—a PIT maneuver. The pursuing vehicle lines its front bumper with the offender's trunk and merges into the vehicle. Nox sees it coming a second too late. He is too busy dialing Kray Mesa, about to tell them to stop, that there's been a mistake.

Michaels, he curses, pumping the brakes as his tires squeal and the freeway slides into a spin. His groceries tumble over. The wine rolls to the floor and takes the raw Ahi tuna with it.

And Nox, one of the most powerful men on the planet, finds himself staring at a dozen Tasers and guns held by keyed-up police who don't know who he is.

[PART 3]

"Life is going forth; death is returning home."

—Lao Tzu

[25]

AIR EGYPT 787-400

FIRST CLASS

FROM FORTY-FIVE THOUSAND FEET, THE WAVES SHIMMER PINK AND violet, dawn speckling off the vast Atlantic. Michaels lowers the shade and takes stock of his thoughts. Home on the horizon, the little plane on the inflight map one hour from arrival. American soil, untouched in almost ten months.

And what now?

The Foundation is searching for him and Caitlyn; that much he gleaned in Kenya and confirmed in Cairo. They want them taken alive.

Which means there are still moves left to make.

For all its tricks, the Foundation is not without budgetary constraints. Black ops extractions and bounties paid to cooperating agencies in Kenya aren't cheap. One angle of attack: hit them in the pocketbook, again and again.

But first, they need to get past the gate.

The stewardess offers Michaels a practiced smile, passing out customs declaration forms and taking final calls for duty-free. A dozen pens click across first class. Michaels reaches into his pocket.

It is a remarkable document, the American passport, one held by only a third of its citizens. And it's a pity, Michaels thinks, that those who often harbor strong opinions about the world see so little of it.

The most complicated component of a passport is its pages, where florescent particles react to ultraviolet light and unique fibers wind into keystone threads. Thermochromic ink contains details down to the micron. Even the font is a state secret, little inconsistencies deliberately randomized to fool forgers.

Ironically, one of its least secure features is the most high-tech: the RFID chip. All that keeps the RFID from being read is a clever piece of magnetic tape buried in the cover.

Unless the passport is open.

Like when weary passengers are filling out forms.

It takes a glance for Michaels to identify a target. Ever since they took off, the bearded man in 3C has been nothing but trouble. He complained about the food ("Too much Middle Eastern crap."), the in-flight Wi-Fi ("If they can build a plane, then why can't they keep the internet on?"), and the fact that the first officer was a woman ("Well, let's hope they can fly better than they can drive, am I right?").

Now, as the tired stewardess walks down the aisle, the man in 3C leans out to take a long look at her ass. When he catches Michaels's glance, he gives him a wink.

"Mmm, how long was I out?" Caitlyn lifts the eye mask to reveal a glassy gaze, one pupil dilating faster than the other.

"Most of the flight." He gestures to the bag hanging from the handle of her suite. "Here, I saved you some snacks."

Caitlyn tears into the cinnamon roll, peeling sticky chunks and licking her finger. She chases it with an orange soda.

"Don't forget to breathe." He gives her a kiss on the top of her head, then takes a pen from her tray.

Wiping crumbs from her lip, she asks, "Where are you going?"

Michaels smirks. "Fishing."

Squeezing past a hot towel tray and up a row, he gives the bearded man in 3C a nod. Then he lets his eyes dart downward. A quick bend of the knee, a fake scoop, and he lifts a pen up and hands it to the man.

"You dropped this."

"Hmm? No, mine's right here." The man taps the magazine rack, pulls out another pen. Doesn't notice Michaels's left hand and how he waves his phone over the open passport. Nor does he hear the phone's vibration over the thrum of the engine.

"Well, now you have two." Michaels gives him a wink.

In the bathroom, Michaels checks his phone. *RFID UPLOAD COMPLETE.*

Officer Danny Tran of Customs and Immigration rubs his eyes to buy himself a moment's rest before waving over the next arrival. For the past seven hours, he'd been dealing with one emergency after the next. A coworker called in sick and he drew her booth at morning assignment. After weather delays, three long-haul flights arrived all at once: Singaporeans, Emiratis, and Egyptians, all hungry and impatient and mixed in together. And now, a new software update loads on his screen: *10%... 20%... 30%...*

His eyes drift to the television, where the news is a parade of Washington's driest. A silver-haired former VP acting pious on the campaign trail. A loudmouth pundit talking over him in a grab for attention.

And then the camera cuts to Dave Drogan, arriving in a convoy of electric pickups, American-made and painted red, white, and blue. The window rolls down, and there he is, behind the wheel, waving and smiling.

50%... 60%... 70%...

Danny Tran likes what he sees. A man who served his country, killed a few terrorists, yet isn't afraid to cry at a speech. It doesn't hurt that Drogan's nice on the eyes. But Dave has his babes and rallies packed full of fans. Danny Tran has his computer and clearance stamps. Still, can't a boy dream?

90%… 100%… Software Update Complete.

"Folks, next up!"

A pair queue up and shuffle over. Backpackers, Danny suspects.

"I didn't know if we should come together or separate," the young woman says. "He said separate, but you said next up and waved, so—"

"You're married?" Danny asks, eyeing the tan man behind her.

"Him? No, never seen him before in my life." She smiles, leaning closer to the booth. A whiff of lilac and sweat. Tattoos take up nearly her whole left arm. *Such a waste of nice skin.*

"Angie, you're annoying the poor man. Let him do his job." The man slides his passport over as well. "Isn't lying to an immigration officer a felony?"

Angie blanches. "I'm sure Officer Tran has a sense of humor. Unlike some of us, James."

Danny sighs, takes her passport, and presses it against the scanner. Here it is, her travel history. Argentina to India to Mauritius, then on to Egypt. Another glance at the woman, this modern-day hippy. Probably trust-funded by Bank of the Dad. And the husband, Danny clocks him for a leech. But hey, if you've hitched a good ride, it's hard to let go.

Processing…

Processing…

Processing…

Odd. It doesn't usually take the computer so long.

"Do we have to declare our phone if we got it repaired overseas?" the man asks. "I just want to be sure I didn't miss anything."

Danny lets the script fly from his lips with little thought. "All new or altered items must be declared upon reentry to the United States."

The man smirks at his wife. "Aren't you glad *I* filled out the forms?"

She returns it with a dim gaze. "Anything to keep you occupied, love."

Her gaze, her gaze… What is it about this woman's thick glasses and those amber pools? Danny has a passing sensation of looking upon two faces. One soft and sun-kissed, a dampened smile on her cheeks. The other beneath, a tempest of shadows and light.

He is about to ask the couple additional questions when a commotion interrupts him. Two booths down, a bearded man is raising his voice.

"And I told you, I've never been to Kenya in my life. This is insane!"

Officer Brown gives a quick wave to Officers Mayfield and Hart, on patrol with Bowser the beagle. The bearded passenger is growing unruly, cheeks reddening as he points to the screen. "Yes, I said that's my passport, but that is *not* my travel history!"

"Sir, keep your hands away from me, sir." Poor Sandra Brown, she's doing her best until the cavalry arrives. Mayfield and Hart surround the large man, gesturing to the additional inspection area. Even Bowser gets in on the action, tail swinging as he circles and barks, circles and barks.

Typical. The long summer rush always shortens the tempers. Danny turns his attention back to his screen. *Processing Complete.*

He hands the woman back her passport. "Welcome home, Mrs. Frost."

THEY DUMP their clothes in the bathrooms, trading sandals, scruffy T-shirts, and three-quarter-length cargo pants for innocuous active wear: Lululemon and Athleta and Brooks running shoes, all pre-delivered to an Amazon Hub Locker. Michaels insists they dump their phones and tablets too, in case the Foundation's algorithms are cross-referencing active electronics in both Cairo and the U.S.

In the food court of the JFK airport, he plugs in the new

phones, jailbreaks them, and sideloads his latest apps using Tor browser.

"I feel like I overacted," Caitlyn says, returning in yoga pants and a hoodie. "I was worried he'd see right through me but it went just like you said."

"You sold it perfectly. The less you tell someone, the more they fill in on their own. Our brains are wired to take lazy shortcuts. Especially bureaucrats."

He hands Caitlyn her phone and a GoDark bag. She squints at the mesh pouch. "What's this?"

"It's a Faraday pouch. Kills all incoming and outgoing signals. Our phones go in there when we're not using them."

She slips her phone into the black pouch while he customizes his apps. She studies the families, the businessmen and women, the hustle and bustle of travelers rolling suitcases, pushing carts, weaving past one another. A thousand stories going in a thousand directions. "It's odd to be back. Like we're fish who ended up outside the bowl."

"Well, it looks like we need to swim west."

He shows his phone to her. The message from Chase's wish list is cryptic, just a pair of VIP tickets and an image beneath bright text:

OUR REVOLUTION IS LIVE - RALLY IN CHICAGO!
WEDNESDAY 5PM

Caitlyn squints, studying the screen. "Who the heck is Dave Drogan?"

[26]

ALDER GLEN FOOTHILLS

SANTA CLARA COUNTY, CA

With a sharp upward jerk of his hairy arm, the electrician throws the switch to the *on* position. "There you go. You're officially wired up, off the grid and on battery."

Robert Chase gives the wall of white boxes an approving nod. Eight 13.5-kilowatt-hour batteries, fed by rooftop solar, warm and near-silent with stored energy. Lights. Microwaves. Electrical heating. Twenty-seven hundred square feet powered without drawing from PG&E.

"Or if you want to sell some back, make a few bucks, just press this button here, see?" The electrician taps Chase's smartphone, the little diagram switches to show electricity leaving the house in cartoon bolts.

"Are you happy, Uncle?" Katherine asks. "It's pretty neat, isn't it?"

"Indeed," Chase says. "And convenient too."

"It'll get you through a zombie apocalypse. Go stand beside it for a photo. Hashtag: Green Energy."

"Oh, I prefer not. Too many creeps on the internet."

Packing up, the electrician grins. "Wise words, my friend. Can't be too careful."

Thirty minutes later and Katherine brings the broth to a

simmer, pours it onto the noodles and savors the aroma. Garden-fresh ginger and onion, charred and mixed with cinnamon and star anise. Add some thin brisket and mung beans and there's nothing quite like it.

As usual, she finds her uncle in his study, a magnifying glass to his eye and a finger tracing papers on the desk. She waits for him to notice. Uncle Bob, the family's black sheep. Distant and erratic, demanding and cold. Except to her.

Yet lately, something has felt off, hasn't it? A rattling in the engine of her thoughts.

"Come in, dear," he says. He always knows when she's at the door. As a kid, her brother joked that Uncle Bob had an eye in the back of his head. A single cycloptic orb, just beneath his hair. As an adult, she sometimes wonders if his senses aren't more attuned. "Put the soup by the computer, would you? Goodness, it smells delightful."

"Brisket pho, your favorite." She places the tray on the desk, careful not to disturb his stack of papers. To his right, the floor-to-ceiling bookshelf takes up the entire wall. She's seen it a thousand times and still it humbles her, these shelves and their wisdom. How could a mind contain even a tenth of this knowledge?

Her eyes drift from the holes on the bookshelf to the road atlases on his desk. "Uncle Bob, are you taking a trip?"

"I am," he says and turns around to face her. A blue Post-it note and a long list of handwritten directions across California and Oregon.

"You know, there's Google for that."

"I know. It's like you kids say, I'm going old school."

"I'm twenty-five. Hardly a kid."

"No, of course not, dear, though I suppose that makes me an old man now. Funny, isn't it? How we never think of ourselves as such."

She squeezes his shoulder. "You'll always be Uncle Bob. Even if you're a hundred."

For decades his reputation loomed, the eccentric builder

etching the family name upon companies that change humanity's direction. Robert Chase, the innovator. Here, now, she seems to be catching him in a new angle of light. Something tired, nostalgic, and spent.

"You don't have cancer or something, do you?"

"Goodness, no. I'm the picture of good health. My employer sees to that." He taps his fingers on his desk, closes the map. "What I meant was, simply, that you are young. I don't say that dismissively, just as a statement of fact. To the young, life is a long hallway, many rooms and many doors to be opened. When you reach my age, you discover that few doors remain. Your father and I... Well, I wasn't the brother he needed. I let him drift away."

"You cast a long shadow, Uncle Bob."

"Mmm. And that shadow cost me my family, my marriage. My lineage is a cul-de-sac. Some might find that discomforting, but not I. You know why?"

She shakes her head. Words seem heavy in his gravity. Often, her thoughts feel nebulous and come out like clouds without boundaries.

"Because you can still do more good for this world than I ever did. You already have."

She finds her voice, finds herself shaking her head a second time. "You're kidding, right? You've helped kids walk, literally. Bloomberg just did a profile on Biotronika. They gave away hundreds of patents—*your* patents—and they said you insisted. People without hands are playing instruments because of your work."

"Yes, my work." He closes his eyes, leans back in the leather chair, letting that image sink in. A curious epiphany suffuses her. The long months away, the missed family reunions. *My God, does he not see himself clearly?*

"Uncle Bob, do you... Do you think you're a failure?"

Deep quiet inside while the sun paints the afternoon golden and the motes twinkle and sparkle. Robert Chase, this man of limitless ambition, turns his attention back to his notepad and maps. The silence seems endless.

"No, Katherine. I don't think I'm a failure. But I wish that I had."

Again, Katherine finds herself without words. He must sense her shock. Immediately, a smile creases his face and he waves off the sentiment.

"Ignore my musings, dear. A tired mind lets the wrong words past the lips. Tonight is a time for celebration. I have something for you." He opens the great oaken desk, withdraws a manilla envelope, and passes it to her. "Please, open it."

So she does. And the floor nearly falls out from beneath her.

"Uncle Bob, I…" The words catch in her throat. Her vision grows misty.

"Perhaps this will cause a family fuss, but it's beyond my concern. I have many nephews and nieces, but you are the closest I've ever had to a daughter. This is my way of thanks for allowing me a small glimpse of that life."

"But… it's your house. You just built it."

"That trust names you the beneficiary. From the moment they broke ground, this house has been yours. Now, it's merely official. I—"

Before he can finish she wraps her arms around him and squeezes. Gone is the long worry of finding a home near her work. A place to live in a market that only favors the rich. Gone is that nagging voice that whispered, *You don't belong here; you never will.* And gone is a great weight she didn't realize she carried. In this new void, she feels only gratitude.

"Thank you."

He squeezes her hand. "It is the least I can do for bringing me such joy over the years."

Then he rises, his hand searching out his crutches. Like always, she has them before he knew he was reaching.

"Now, follow me, dear. I'm afraid there's one favor I must ask."

An hour later Chase sits in his car, in the driveway, the warm house in the rearview mirror. Home. Paid for by a legacy of bad choices. A sanctuary founded on screams.

No more.

He confirms the route on the legal pad taped to his console. He turns the key. He spends a moment tuning stations and is pleased to find the Scorpions singing a tune from half a lifetime ago. A hymn of revolution and changing winds, when the world's end seemed one nuke strike away. Chase finds his eyes heavy, the music catapulting him to simpler times.

Deep in the heart of Clearwater, the same song played through the rec room television. He had pulled strings that Christmas, hadn't he? Argued with the brass to get the subjects a new television and a cable connection. He even paid for MTV out of his own pocket. Martin Peck connected the coaxial cords. Sam Stephens tuned the cable box to the right channel without touching the dial.

But it was Teddy who sat there, transfixed, as the fuzzy lines clarified into images and sound. Tanks rolling down streets. The Kremlin and the Red Square. The Scorpions, in all their eighties glory, playing soft rock before an audience of thousands in Moscow.

And Teddy looked up at Chase, his eyes sparkling, and said, "I think that's where I'll go next."

The song ends and Chase opens his eyes. He is here, the founder and final member, alone in his car with only the quiet of night and the tangled deeds of his past.

He presses the accelerator, the house fading behind him, dark roads ahead.

[27]

THE JOURNAL OF TEDDY JENSEN
PROPERTY CZ-93 "DAY'S BANE"

APRIL 3^(RD)

I have a confession I'm ashamed to admit. I think you already know. It has been quite a while since I wrote in your pages. Will you forgive me, old friend?

I had almost forgotten about you until I was cleaning my closet and you fell from the old shoebox. For a while, I just stared at your pages. All these words feel so light and so distant, somehow written by different fingers. Wasn't my penmanship beautiful back then?

So what happened?

Oh, you know what happened, don't you? Yes, you know.

Stop it. Stop it now.

I've had great trouble sleeping lately. My dreams have turned dark and stretch on forever. Sometimes I don't know when I'll wake up. Sometimes I think I don't want to.

I see him often now, my dark partner. That's what I call him. I once told myself he was a trick of the light. Perhaps some young boy from a neighboring farm.

But you know who I am.

He never leaves. He just watches and waits and slowly creeps closer. Sometimes when I step out of myself, he tries to step in.

And sometimes… Sometimes I let him.

I must contact Dr. Chase.

SEPTEMBER 13TH

Today, I was visited by a lawyer. Then I was visited by several federal agents. They didn't identify themselves, but I knew.

We knew.

They said I was in violation of the contract I signed. I needed to stop sending him letters. I told them I just needed Dr. Chase's help. That's all that I'd asked. I told them my mind feels like old wallpaper that's coming undone, all peely and brittle. If I could just talk to the doctor, perhaps he could offer me some advice.

They told me no, he would never see the letters. If I wrote any more, there would be consequences.

All the while, my dark partner whispered, *Show them what their silence will bring. Let's show them what we can become.*

Outside, the days are growing shorter and cooler. I think summer is finally ending.

JANUARY 22ND

I saw Claudia today while visiting the post office in town. She bought her parents' old house and moved in with her husband. She's been here for several years.

I smiled and nodded and I wished them my best. I invited them to visit the farm. I joked that we could climb the tree like we used to. I didn't mean to start crying.

She asked me if I was okay. She said that I'd lost so much weight I looked like a scarecrow. I told her I was fine, that I was so happy for her blessings. I had to excuse myself when my headache returned for fear I might puke on her shoes.

I don't remember getting into the car. Nor driving down the highway. I must have blacked out.

And then I was home and Mother was hysterical. Something happened in my room while I was gone.

All my yearbooks were open and strewn about. My elementary school, my middle school, my high school, dozens of pages ripped out and reduced to little shreds of old paper. I didn't understand why until later when I put one back together.

Every torn page was a picture of Claudia.

[28]

CLACKAMAS COUNTY, OREGON

7:00 P.M. PST

AFTER EIGHT HUNDRED MILES, SEVEN REST AREA BATHROOMS, AND one truck stop shower, Dr. Robert Chase pulls up to the darkened cul-de-sac of Rock Creek Court. He rolls down the window, taking in the spring air, cool off the Cascades. Happy Valley, Oregon.

He shakes his wobbly legs, squeezes the circulation back into his knees. A deep breath. The house is lit up, its residents home. Good. Two sedans sit parked in the driveway near a fence for a dog. A child's bicycle leans against a hedge, pink streamers dangling from the handlebars. Down the way, a neighbor is grilling some steak.

Chase checks the blue Post-it note and his list of directions. This is the place. It cost him every favor he was owed to find this address.

He opens the glove box, stuffs the directions in, and removes the Colt 1911. Hand-cut 30 LPI checkered front and rears with a beavertail grip safety and ivory stocks. A heritage pistol worthy of being passed down.

If only he didn't have plans for it now.

• • •

NADIA TILTS the tablet toward her father and beams. "Look, Daddy!"

"Wow, that's pretty neat," he says, playing the part of the surprised father. "So, let me guess. This is our house." He taps the lilac and white rectangle that makes up their home. "This is Daddy Tony." Another tap on the scribble that forms himself. "Okay, that's Boomer, right?" A jagged tangle of yellow that could only be their goldendoodle. "And here's Daddy Holland." There he stands at the edge of the screen, all dark blue shapes and formal, more statue than living subject.

Most interesting, Tony muses, is the composition itself. Children rarely render a scene with elements existing past canvas. Not at four. But Nadia has included the neighbor's fence, a sense of layered depth, even a variety of clouds. They might have a little Van Gogh on their hands.

"Our f-f-family," she says, struggling with the F-sound but finding it quick.

"That's right, kiddo. Now tell me: what's this over here? Are those fireflies?"

She shakes her head. "That's Mister Whispers."

"Mister Whispers, huh?"

She leans in. "He lives in the old chair."

"He does? Do you tell him to go away? Is he grumpy and ugly with long fingers like these?"

Tony digs into her armpits, tickling her. Squealing, she flops over and rolls in his lap until her cheeks are pink.

"No, silly," she says. "He's sad and he smells like the beach."

"Not yummy like Daddy Holland's cooking?" He gestures toward the kitchen, where steam leaves the stovetop in herb-laced waves.

"Pee-eww," she says and covers her nose.

"Pee-eww, indeed."

"Hey, I heard that," his partner of twelve years shouts from the kitchen. "Mocking the chef has its consequences."

"What are con-se-quence-es?"

"Results of actions," his partner shouts, and there is a clattering of pots. "Tony, where's the pasta strainer?"

"In the island, dum-dum," Tony says, sharing a wink with the little girl upside down in his lap. *Dum-dum*, Nadia mouths with a giggle. *Dum-dum*.

A chime at the door. Then the television switches to the doorbell camera. A wide-angle view of their porch. And a man upon it.

"Are you expecting company?" Tony asks. He does not like the man on the other side of the walnut door. No, he does not sense anything good about him here, on a Tuesday night. "Holland? Hello?"

In the kitchen, the chef studies his smartphone, which displays the same feed. Dr. Robert Chase, here on his doorstep. Holland Nox feels his stomach sour and his shoulders constrict. For a second, the world recedes to a narrow keyhole. So, work has followed him home. Implications that follow: Chase is here to catch him off guard. But why? A dozen possibilities. Top of the list: he knows he's being pushed out; he's losing control. So how did he find him? Doesn't matter. Just deal with this threat because that's what this is.

"Holland, honey?"

Nox forces a rare smile to his lips. "It's a friend from work." He uses the walk to the entryway to organize his thoughts. "He's in town and it slipped my mind. Sorry."

Two turns of the lock and Nox opens the front door. Here, backlit by the streetlamp and misty evening, stands Dr. Robert Chase.

In a quick sniff, Nox takes it all in: bad interstate food, the salty musk of a long drive, the red eyes from the road and summer pollens. A shower cleaned Chase up but didn't conceal it. To Nox's senses, here stands a man on a ledge, a hand in his coat pocket. Time to disarm him with words.

"Robert, so glad you can join us for supper."

There is a pause on Chase's face, a near-silent stutter. Nox swings the door wider so Chase can see straight inside. There is

Tony and Nadia, and Boomer wagging his tail in the playroom past the baby gate. A straight view, all the way to the dining room and the kitchen and the stove steaming and warm.

"Please, come into our home."

"Are you sure you won't have some wine?" Nox asks as Chase places his fork on the plate. Nox offers a pour of the bottle but Chase shakes his head.

"Well, I'll take another," Tony says, draining his glass and holding it out. "Wow, generous. Is it Friday already?"

Nox gives him two fingers more than he usually pours, but tonight he needs Tony at a distance, happy and chatty and comfortably dumb.

Nadia slurps up some spaghetti. "So you work with daddy?"

Chase gives the girl a short nod. "Yes, dear, I do."

"And so, are you Daddy's boss?"

"No dear, but your father is mine."

"Oh," Nadia says. "But aren't you *older*?"

"Nadia," Tony says. "What did we discuss about assumptions?"

Her eyes light up. "Assume means to… to make us… to be an A-S-S." She nods, proud.

Tony chuckles. "Well, close enough." He sips his wine and takes in their guest across the table. The sunken cheeks and tired eyes. "So, tell us, Robert, what secrets of the universe are you unlocking? I always try to pry some details from Holland, but you know how private he is."

"I do." Chase lets the agreement hang over the dinner table while a cartoon echoes from the playroom. "The truth is, there's little we do at work that's as interesting as what we come home to. We are, after all, much more than our jobs."

"Well said, Bob," Nox says and refills his sparkling water. "So, what has your interest lately?"

"My retirement," Chase says. "I'm in town to negotiate my exit. I feel it's something best done in person."

"But why in person?" Nadia asks, and for once Nox feels a genuine smile. He picks Nadia up and puts her on his lap.

He says, "Well, sweetie, that's because Dr. Chase is a man of his word. When you have bad news, you tell people to their face."

"But *why*?"

"She's in the interrogation phase," Tony says and ruffles her copper hair. "Every sentence ends in a question mark."

"It's a marvel, isn't it?" Chase says. "How a child's mind scours the world for logic and structure. All those neural paths forming connections will last a lifetime and define their reality. The pursuit of knowledge for the pure joy of understanding. I envy it."

Nox says nothing, only listens and meets Chase's gaze with a flat reflection.

"Yes, well, certainly." Tony clears his throat. "And retirement, how exciting. All the days to fill without the pressure of saving the planet or whatever it is you spooks do."

"Is a spook a ghost?" Nadia asks. "Like Casper?"

"No, dear." Nox hoists her off his lap and back into her seat. "A spook is someone who solves complicated problems."

"Like a calculator?"

"Sure. Like a calculator."

She puts her thumb on her chin, pinches it in a gesture of mock contemplation. "So, what is twenty times twenty?"

"Four hundred," Chase says, his voice like smokey logs in a hearth.

"And what is, uh, fifty hundred times eleventy one?"

Tony laughs. "Sweetie, there's no such thing as eleventy—"

"Five hundred and fifty-five thousand," Chase says. "If you meant one hundred and eleven."

"And what is—"

"Okay, dear, you've drilled our poor guest enough," Nox says. "Time to go with Tony-dad."

"But why?"

"Exhibit A, your honor," Tony says, scooping Nadia into his arms. "Robert, can I get you some coffee and dessert?"

Chase turns to Nox. "I don't mean to intrude on your evening."

"Evening?" Tony laughs. "It's the edge of chaos around here. I'm just glad Holland finally brought someone home from work. For a while I thought he might be an assassin. Okay, bugaboo, let's fetch the coffee and pastries."

Nadia in hand, Tony leads her out through the hall and into the kitchen with its marble counters and hanging copper pots. The dining chair creaks as Nox rises. In measured steps, he walks to the stereo, finds a CD, and puts it in the tray. Daniel Barenboim delicately performing Bach's "The Well-Tempered Clavier." Just loud enough to hang some piano between the two rooms.

Nox lets his heart settle as he sits down. The past hour has taken him a dozen mental tricks. Timed breathing. Visualization. Mostly, it has been about letting the old man feel in control.

"Tell me something, Robert. At what point did you decide against using the gun in your coat?"

A flicker from Chase's eye betrays his surprise. He folds his napkin, lays it upon the table. Simple trick, Nox thinks, and easily spotted.

"I suppose I haven't decided," Chase says. "But seeing your daughter has tilted the scales in your favor."

"Lucky for me."

"And for her. No child should grow up without both parents."

"As a child of divorce, I couldn't agree more. Would you?" Nox gestures to the bread. "Thank you." *Butter the roll, Holland, and guard your fury. He came here to be heard, so give him space for his moves.*

"Children are challenging at Nadia's age. I remember taking my niece for a week and dropping her off exhausted. It does end."

"So I've been told. Truthfully, I don't spend much time home.

These visits are refreshing… and refreshingly brief. Perhaps that's the trick."

"You don't worry she'll grow up missing you?"

"I have many concerns. But, in the grand scheme, no." He dips the bread into a saucer of garlic and olive oil, then chews. The psyche profile at Day's Bane on Chase listed a tilt toward the dramatic, a fact Nox uses to simulate potential outcomes. One trajectory traces a green path, from a handshake over this table to a porch-side farewell. Another is red and ends with multiple bodies here in the shadow of Mount Hood. Neither acceptable.

The doctor's next words come as little surprise.

"So, I'm out," he says. "I owe it to tell you. I'm resigning the project."

Nox gives Chase a moment to continue. He does not.

"With respect, Dr. Chase, you built Clearwater from scattered data and dreams. Now look at what you've accomplished. I find it hard to believe you're walking away."

"You certainly might. But it's happening. Our arrangement has come to its logical end. A friendly one, I hope, seeing as we're still negotiating." A blink, from his jacket pocket and back up to Nox. And an understanding: this could still turn for the worse.

"Yes, we are," Nox says. "But humor me. What would you do with an employee that hasn't fulfilled their end of a bargain? Someone who requested funding and resources. Someone who stalled while you provided what all they required. Would you let them terminate their obligation while you upheld your own? And if they showed up at your lovely new home—found your young niece Katherine—and asked for a favor wrapped in a threat, well, what then?"

Silence between them as Tony returns with two cups of coffee and a plate of pastries on bone china. Nadia follows, taking measured steps to carry a pitcher of cream and a dish of sugar cubes.

"Thank you, dear," Chase says and helps her place it on the table. "You are most considerate indeed."

"Tony?" Nox says. "Why don't you and Nadia go watch *Sesame Street*?"

A flicker in Tony's eye. Fear, deeper than Nox has ever seen. *Damn the price of this moment.* Then Tony smiles and takes Nadia's hand. "Let's go see Big Bird and get ready for bed."

"But I'm not tired," she whines and seizes Dr. Chase's sleeve. "Want to see my new dance?"

"Not tonight, sweetie," Tony says. "Do the nighty-night shuffle, okay? Say goodnight to Dr. Chase."

"Goodnight to Dr. Chase." She feigns marching and gives them a little salute.

"Goodnight, dear heart," Chase says. "May your sleep be restful and the morning soon greet you."

She blinks. "Okay…"

And then she's off, skipping into the playroom. Tony turns his soft eyes on the doctor. "Will you be in town for a while?"

"Unlikely, I'm afraid. My business seems to be mostly concluded."

"Well, it was a pleasure meeting you."

With an affectionate pat on Nox's head, Tony leaves the men to the soft notes of Bach. Nox pours two cups of coffee, passes one to Chase, who eyes it with uncertainty.

Nox says, "If I wanted to poison you, it would have already happened."

"One doesn't live to my age on assurances alone." Chase waits until Nox takes a sip. Now his turn. Just two men drinking coffee in the quiet that follows a good meal.

"I admire the bold move. Coming here, you must have felt your back was to the wall."

"We all have our Achilles' heels, Coordinator. Such attachments keep us human."

"And humble," Nox adds. "Earlier, you used the word 'negotiate,' which begs the question: what do you have to bargain with?"

Chase stirs cream into the coffee. "My assurance policy."

Nox stares, unblinking.

"You have my assurance that certain facts of the project don't make their way to curious journalists and politicians interested in unsanctioned endeavors. Not the mad ramblings of Sam Stephens, but specifics. Blueprints and patents and operating manuals. Things impossible to ignore or suppress, even with the Foundation's advanced tactics."

Nox reads the elder man's eyes. The looseness of the jaw, the unwrinkled forehead. This isn't a bluff but a bomb he's strapped to them both.

"In my time in the private sector," Chase continues, "I have sought funding from those far outside our own cultural... *sensitivities*. Those who might see family as a pressure point. This assurance policy—a treaty, it could be thought of—ensures that such vulnerabilities need not be exploited. Peace, true peace, is always preferable."

A short, hot burst of air from Nox's nose. He balls his feet, feels the hardwood floor beneath, yet keeps his eyes focused on Chase. So, the old man laid out his cards and this is his game. Total disruption, at a time when Nox and his family had settled into their forever home. When the Foundation is most vulnerable to political theater. When Day's Bane is still in its infancy. He hates to admit it, but Chase has him on the back foot.

And yet, the precedent this would set...

Best-case scenario: the payouts end in promises of silence, the subcommittee hearings buried in rooms no one can find, more funding rubber-stamped by friendly politicians.

The worst possible case: Day's Bane and its data in adversarial hands. Foreign governments and third-party actors all fighting for scraps. Almost unthinkable.

"I'm sorry it's come to this, Robert," Nox says. "Truly. But if you can no longer perform your duty—if it's retirement you seek —I won't stand in your way. I'll see any personal effects are released. Pending security, of course. Deal?"

He holds out a hand. Chase studies it. Just five fingers and a palm above a blue lacquered Piaget watch curiously worn on his right hand.

And they shake on it, Chase's palm like a damp dishtowel. Nox wipes his hand on his jeans and leads Chase toward the entryway. Through the window, the sky is that gold and magenta that Nox loves, Mount Hood lit up in the east.

Stopping near the door, Nox glances at the old chair beneath the grandfather clock. Perhaps Chase senses it too. Yes, time to linger here for a moment.

Nox raises his smartphone and centers the camera on his guest. A swipe, and Chase catches a glimpse of the word *ENABLED*.

"One last thing, Dr. Chase," Nox says and turns toward the empty chair. "Something to consider after threatening my family. Someone to meet, actually. My daughter calls him Mister Whispers. But, well… you know him as subject N77."

There is a groan as the chair cushions shift, the wrinkles and indentations release. Nox feels the displacement, the cool breath that comes with their *other* guest's movement. It passes him, stopping at the door and the man who stands beside it, frozen and wide-eyed. *Clunk* go the footsteps. *Clunk, clunk, clunk.*

Subject N77—legal name Raymond Flay—is unrecognizable to the man that helped forge his new form. In Day's Bane, his limbs have been removed to reduce caloric load and his head reduced to a hollow of plastic and glass. Here, he is more than mere flesh.

First come the eyes, two orbs of frost. Then the cold unfolding of space. A blue face. A muscular body. Dendritic legs and arms of white lightning.

"My God," Chase says to the low buzz that signals decoherence. Here it is, something beyond Clearwater, beyond Caitlyn and Teddy, beyond all he thought possible. A post-human form, consciousness manifested and boundless and cruel.

"Thank you for your contributions," Nox says. "But as you can see, we're taking the project in a different direction. Goodbye, Dr. Chase."

A hiss of wind and a cry. These are the last clear sounds to leave the lips of Robert Chase. Harsh fingers seize him and squeeze, squeeze, squeeze.

Nox turns up the music. Barenboim is into "Prelude No. 6 in D Minor" and he's really tickling the ivories. Such precision of touch.

Opening the door, Nox lets the evening wash over him. The first stars of the night and the distant rumble of a train. His neighbors down the street—the Parsons—laughing over beers as they fire up their new grill. Ken Parson cooks a hell of a tri-trip.

Nox puts the phone to his ear. "Operator, Coordinator Nox badge ID four one nine tango alpha. Thank you. I need an immediate clean team at my current location. One adult, male." He spots Chase's car parked by the mailbox. "And one car. Thank you."

He hangs up and breathes in that fresh Oregon air. He's going to miss this.

Inside, he steps past his guest on the floor, still husking and wheezing. Still trying to pry impossible fingers from his throat. "Pardon me, Robert."

Nox peeks into the playroom. There's Tony and Nadia, their noise-cancelling headphones on as they cuddle in the beanbags and watch *Sesame Street*, together and safe. Big Bird and Snuffleupagus are arguing whether to play tag or hide-and-seek.

Tony gives Nox a weary glance, lifts an ear cup. "Everything okay?"

"All taken care of," Nox says, adding, "Just give us some time to clean up."

Tony nods. Beyond his sight, past the edge of the hall, Chase crawls across the floor. A hollow cracking, and he's yanked back into the foyer. Tony winces, slides his headphones back on, and turns up the volume. Big Bird and Snuffleupagus sing a little louder, and soon Nadia joins in.

CREDIT UNION ONE ARENA
CHICAGO, ILLINOIS

A SEA OF FLICKERING SCREENS. NINE THOUSAND ATTENDEES, ALL armed with smartphones, many raised and recording and live-streaming this rally. Michaels observes them, wondering, *If a tree falls in the forest without five hundred* likes, *did it actually happen?*

"This doesn't feel like politics," Caitlyn says over the chanting crowd. "More like a rock concert or a protest."

"Yeah, it's kind of all of the above." Michaels gestures to a shirtless man with a red Dr. Suess hat and a digital sign: *MAKE THE OLIGARCHY HEADLESS AGAIN!*

Squeezing through the crowd, Michaels keeps a tight hand on Caitlyn. A friendly pat on the shoulder of a bongo drummer and the man lets them pass. A gentle shoulder forward, and they split a conversation between a group of students. The air is thick with sweat and patchouli and the occasional cloud of vaporized weed. Onstage ahead, a bluegrass band finishes their set as signs rise and cheers make all conversation impossible.

Closer now. Closer to the backstage entrance, the security detail all neck and chest, arms like crossed logs. Michaels catches the nearest guard's eye.

"We're here to meet Dr. Charles Munson," Michaels says. "He's expecting us."

"Charles Manson?"

"Mun-son. He's… *there*. That's him."

A man takes the stage, smiling from the podium and waving to the crowd. It's the same man Michaels last saw in Boston. A man who pointed a camera down at the dissected corpse of Roger Fenton and said, "This man didn't jump to his death from that window. This man was thrown."

In the year since, Dr. Charles Munson, a medical examiner from Santa Rosa, earned the nickname the Death Detective for his involvement in the case of the God's Breath Killer. His once-obscure podcast—a pet project called *Veritas Ex Mortis*—shot to the top of the charts. Michaels listened to a few episodes, and he had to admit, the man is a natural. Every Tuesday Munson and his co-host would analyze a forensic mystery in a straightforward manner, a pair of macabre Neil deGrasse Tysons. And he's classically handsome in his late fifties. One of those rare men who can sport a mustache and make it all work.

He also happens to be one of Michaels's off-the-book assets.

"Thank you, Chicago," Munson says, smiling as the applause dies down. "What a warm welcome, thank you. As a board member for the National Association of Medical Examiners—and a pathologist myself—I have seen the casualties of our opioid epidemic. I've traced the scars of gang violence. Held the hands of parents as they've identified their dead sons and daughters. I've seen failed policies burn community trust and felt the embers of fear stoked by divisive lies and the D.C. elite, many of whom turn their back on science, on medicine, on facts. Compared to most politicians, my cadavers have more life in their bones."

Laughter, applause, and a sudden raising of signs. The rally hall booms with the energy of youth. And yet, as the guard escorts them through to the VIP area, Michaels wonders, *How many will show up to vote?*

Backstage, event coordinators bark into their mics and choreograph orders. A buzz, and the backdoor security ushers the candidate through. Here he is, in from Kentucky, Senator Dave Drogan.

Michaels and Caitlyn watch as he strolls through the crowd of VIPs, offering fist bumps and back slaps. He hoists an excited kid up onto his shoulder. A buxom volunteer with a cap reading *DAVE'S BABES - LOUD AND PROUD!* squeezes in for a group selfie. Drogan and the kid both give her a high five.

"What do people see in this?" Caitlyn asks as the candidate makes his way to the far side of the curtain. "It's just pageantry and promises and a whole lot of blame."

"It is," Michaels says. "And it makes people feel like they're being heard. Never underestimate a scorned American. They'll believe anyone who says it's not their fault. Here we go."

From the other side of the curtain, Munson's voice: "And now, I'm pleased to introduce a man who believes in building a better tomorrow, our next president, Senator Dave Drogan."

In a flurry of gestures, aides peel Drogan away from his backstage fans and over to a parting black curtain. Beyond: a sea of signs, blue and red and white, all bouncing above waves of applause.

A faint displacement as hands silently clap. Caitlyn pushes her glasses up tight on her nose. Blinks. The signs, like flickering static, like pixels behind a shifting veil. The black curtain, like that division deep in her mind.

Another blink. There are two curtains now. One, where she is watching the candidate pass through to muted applause. Another, where she is standing onstage, watching him stroll out to the podium, all smiles to the band. Now, he is shaking Dr. Munson's hand and the pathologist is heading offstage, back through the veil.

The audience melts to undulating shadows, an ocean at night. Two shapes drift through the inky-black crowd.

Her parents.

"Mom? Dad?"

Weaving among the dark masses, her father's luminous form holds her mother's glimmering hand. There they are, Jason and Terry, two runaway lovers with fingers entwined.

Terry's free hand reaches up to her throat where her finger touches empty, bare skin. *The silver medallion,* Caitlyn realizes. *Her neck looks naked without it.*

"Mom, wait, I have…"

Caitlyn's words catch in her throat. She never noticed their sopping footprints. Nor the kelp clinging to her parents' clothes. With a rotten crack and a puff of loose sediment, her father turns his drowned gaze toward Caitlyn. Her mother tilts her head and smiles, an eel wriggling forth from her mouth.

"Cait, focus up," Michaels says, his voice both intimate and distant.

Suddenly, she is backstage, back here at the rally. Munson's handler is pointing them out.

And yet, if she closes her eyes, she can almost see them again, the shades of her past.

"—introduce you to my colleague, Myra," Michaels says. A tug ends her bifurcated vision, and now Dr. Munson is before her. "You didn't meet her, but Myra consulted on the God's Breath case."

"Right, of course," Munson says, his eyes hawklike and suspicious. Then back to Michaels. "I was sorry to hear about your other colleague, Carruthers. She seemed like a good one."

"One of the best," Michaels says. "Can we go somewhere private for a moment?"

Another weary glance at Caitlyn. "Yes, I think that's for the best."

The emergency access door creaks shut, dampening the rally and buying some quiet. Just the cool breeze of the alleyway here. A pair of cameras swing toward them, reporters grumbling when it's not a shot of the candidate. Secret Service agents and scattered journalists linger by the distant limos.

Michaels, Munson, and Caitlyn find a quiet spot by a recycling bin. A glance back, and it's all clear.

Munson says, "To be frank, you're the last person I thought I'd see again. I never got much closure after that mess last year. When we matched the beta burns on the victims in San Francisco to those men in Boston, I knew the God's Breath Killer wasn't done. Then things went quiet and the gag orders followed. Tell me you got him."

"She did." Michaels tilts his head toward Caitlyn. "Unofficially, of course."

"Of course. I've had a run of good fortune this year. The less I know about who's pulling strings, the better."

"It's best to keep the pieces separated and safe."

"Safe, huh?" Munson flashes a Colgate grin. "Well, what I'm getting at is that you aren't the only ghost of Christmas past who's reached into my present. This was couriered to my lab by a mutual friend."

He turns on his smartphone and hands it to Michaels. A photo of a circular object, no larger than a jelly bean.

Michaels squints. "Is that frozen smoke?"

"Yeah, aerogel. You've seen it?"

"Space probes use it to catch comet dust. Neat stuff."

"This is custom-molded graphene aerogel. They're starting to use it for biomedical sensors. According to a colleague, only a dozen places can fabricate it with this precision. Notice anything?"

Munson zooms in. It's not Michaels but Caitlyn who spots it first. "Are those pockets?"

"Right, pockets," Munson says. "Sharp eyes. It had five cylinders cut into it. Whole thing was shaped like a zinc-air cell battery, like—"

"For a hearing aid," Michaels says.

"Exactly. There's a name and a set of numbers around the edge, see?"

"Day's Bane," Caitlyn says. "Sounds like an herb."

"Those are GPS coordinates," Michaels adds. "What about the pockets?"

"They contained hair, nail clippings, tissue samples," Munson says. "We had to dissolve the aerogel to extract them, hence the photo. We sequenced the DNA and got five unique genetic profiles. I'll send them to you now, if you give me permission."

Michaels swipes up on his phone, enabling *DISCOVERY* mode, and accepts the file transfer. Five distinct DNA profiles in simple text format. The sum total of a human's unique lineage in four little letters: A, C, G, and T. At twelve-point font, it would take over a hundred thousand pages to print.

For each one of them.

"You said those are coordinates," Caitlyn says. "So what's there?"

Munson shrugs. "Just some house in California. Maybe you'll find something more useful. Here…" He sends them the coordinates, eyeing Caitlyn's Faraday pouch as she pulls out her phone. While she searches, they continue conferring.

"Maybe I'm missing the big picture," Munson says, lowering his voice, "but why not send this straight to you? Or have a known lab process it?"

"Because our mutual acquaintance is being watched," Michaels says. "You're a pathologist. I'm an investigator. That's two parts to this puzzle."

"Then the question becomes, who's watching him? And what's Chase's angle?"

"Guys, I'm not sure he has any angles," Caitlyn says. "Not anymore."

She shows them her smartphone. At the top of Lovelace Biotronika's website, where the company's latest news scrolls past, is the following:

IN MEMORIAM: Dr. Robert Chase, *innovator, entrepreneur, advisor, and friend.*
In a career that began in the military applied sciences and branched out to pharmacology, biotechnology, transhumanist futures, and a love for the mind, our former advisor and friend

Dr. Robert Chase embodied the bold visions that are foundational to Lovelace Biotronika. We mourn his passing and celebrate his rich life. In lieu of flowers…

Five browser tabs and as many articles later, Michaels switches off his phone and shakes his head. "This has Foundation tactics all over it."

Caitlyn asks, "How can you tell?"

"Simultaneous press releases, all within hours? No way companies would sync up. This was fed to them. PR just rewrote it."

Munson studies his own phone, displeased. "And the Portland medical examiner listed myocardial infarction in the report. Who rushes an autopsy on a sixty-eight-year-old male? This should take weeks, and that's if the death were suspicious."

"Because they're getting in front of it," Michaels says. "Make the news first, and you make the news whatever you want. They've probably cremated already."

Caitlyn says, "If this was his last act, Chase wanted these samples in our hands. So the next question is, who are they?"

"We'll need to check them to known databases," Michaels says. "NDIS, CODIS, GEDmatch. My credentials are all cut."

Munson sighs. "I think it's clear why the late Dr. Chase wanted us together." He hands his rental car keys to Michaels. "Drive us, please. I have a colleague at the University of Chicago, and I need to press her for a favor."

[30]

DOWNTOWN, CHICAGO

THIS CITY OF IRON AND GLASS HAS LONG LIVED IN CAITLYN'S imagination, built up to a thing of abstract splendor. Here it is now, moving past, too fast to touch. No time today to visit the Cloud Gate. No time for the culinary tour she once planned. All this history and industry passes her by. She can only crack the window and let the winds off Lake Michigan fill her mind with visions of gray waves.

The Crime Sciences Lab at the University of Chicago is on the sixteenth floor of an Art Deco tower in the heart of downtown. The entrance is vintage brass, the lobby white marble. Patinated motifs give the elevators tasteful accents, cherubs and vines and olives, all aged for a century. Upstairs, the halls are as austere as the machines that they house.

Arms crossed, Dr. Tanya Lopez stands in the lobby. A medical examiner, a scholar, and the co-host of *Veritas ex Mortis*, winner of this year's Ambie Podcast Award. At an instinctual level, Michaels senses her hesitancy and leaves the introductions to Munson.

"You didn't say anything about bringing friends, Chuck," she says and leads them down the hall. "Let me guess: you figured you'd just hold out until you got here in person?"

"Something like that," Munson says. "Tanya, this is Myra and—"

"I don't want to know," Lopez says. "Know why? It's so I don't have to lie if there's a HIPPA hearing."

"Fair enough," Munson says. They squeeze past a group of students congregated by a printer.

"You send me DNA and tell me it's for a project. I can spin that. Cool. You show up with discount Agent Smith and the Girl with the Dragon Tattoo, my bullshit meter overloads."

"Also fair enough," Munson says.

Caitlyn elbows Michaels, mouthing, *Discount Agent Smith.*

A turn at an empty lounge. Lopez badges her way into a suboffice. Narrow walls now and lots of machines.

"You're keeping busy," Munson says. "That's a new arc spark spectrometer."

"Don't flatter me with distractions, Chuck. You know what burns me the most? You're in Chicago for a Drogan rally and you didn't invite me. You know the man's single."

"I didn't peg you for his policies, Tanya. Sorry."

"Policies? Have you seen him in swim trunks? I'd hold my tongue for a meet-cute. Okay, here we are."

Another swipe of the badge on a door marked *Dr. Tanya Lopez, Senior Researcher.* In the corner is an L-shaped dissection table repurposed into a standing desk. The volume of books and files stacked upon it weighs more than most corpses. Yet Lopez navigates it all quickly, pulling pages from the printer and passing them to Dr. Munson.

"Here's the first three matches. The others are coming in now."

"Matches?" Munson asks, sharing the pages with Michaels. "Plural?"

"Five sample sets, five hits. Two came from the DoD Serum Repository."

"These are military?" Michaels asks.

"Whoa, it speaks," Lopez says. "*Were* military, past tense. We're still testing the system but it casts a wide net. We've been using it to identify sex traffickers on both sides of the southern border. And reunite a few scattered families. Remember how our teachers told us something would go on our permanent record? Well, this is it."

"So who were they?" Munson asks, studying the list.

Lopez daps the top of the second page. "First one is Zade Holloway. Army discharged him for some bad business in Iraq. After that, he went full mercenary. Ran a small unit out of West Africa."

"Zade," Michaels says. "Why's that name familiar?"

"He made the news a few years ago. Part of that coup in Litundi that slaughtered the royal family."

"That was him?" Caitlyn asks.

"Probably depends on who you ask," Michaels says. "Last I read, they're still pointing fingers. Even the mining companies didn't want in after that bloodbath."

"Here's another," Lopez says. "Sergeant Iliana Kennedy. She and her husband got caught smuggling Chinese fentanyl in a few years ago. She poisoned her whole family: him, their kids, even the dog."

"Yeah, I remember that," Munson says. "Dr. Phil did a special episode on stress in military families."

"They carried out her sentence in December. First military execution in years. Here's the rest of it. I've seen too much already."

She hands Munson the stack of warm paper and opens the door, the hallway a wall of light into this dark den of study.

"Look, it's obvious you're kicking over some serious rocks. In my experience, that's when the snakes start lashing out. Good luck, but you didn't get this from me."

Downstairs, in the shade of the Art Deco tower, Munson rubber bands the files. "Five names, five death sentences. Maybe that answers why our late mutual acquaintance wanted us together. Maybe not. But Tanya has good instincts so I'm bowing out as well."

"Dr. Munson, we need you," Caitlyn says. "Chase put his trust in you."

"Maybe he did, but he's gone now. Which means this is a deadly path."

Caitlyn holds her tongue. In her right eye, she can see Munson for what he is: a man out of his depths, scared and trying to hold on to all he gained in the past year. And from her left eye, she's back in Lopez's lab, watching to be sure the doctor doesn't pick up the phone.

With a tight squint and a pinch of her nose, the split vision fades.

"Look, I'm sorry. I'd love to help," Munson says. "But one thing my career has taught me is that death is never cheap. If someone's offed Chase to keep this from leaking, well..." He shrugs. "I've had a run of good luck after I kept quiet about Boston. Too good. I don't want that run to come to an end."

[31]

DAY'S BANE, ALASKA

In the cool deep of the level-five labs, three minds are at work.

The first mind is long dead. Its neurons are mapped, its synaptic paths digitally reconstructed in terabytes of code. What physically remains of Teddy Jensen's brain and nervous system floats in cloudy preservatives, the bullet his mother put in it buried too deep to extract.

The second mind is alive but missing in action. Hers is a series of videos compiled from MEG-II scans, the final burst of data that was Clearwater's death rattle. A picture of equilibrium in vibrant webworks of thought. Caitlyn Grey, when her consciousness was first recorded leaving her body.

The third mind—the one observing the other two—feels something frustrating and rare, akin to the first time he fell in love.

Lonnie Tarpin, Anders thinks. *Yes, that was her name.*

A wave of humbling fear tightens his toes. Lonnie Tarpin, who rejected his first kiss. Who laughed at his acne. Now look at her. Three kids pushed out before thirty and a stillborn career. Would Anders still feel those butterflies if he met her today? Of course not.

So why does he feel such bashful awe when he studies Caitlyn's charts?

Because she got away, Anders thinks. *That which eludes us is what we covet.*

He scrolls through the videos. The Clearwater cohort brain scans measure like dim candles. And then Caitlyn's, like the surface of the sun. So strong they needed new scales on the charts. Sometimes, he can even tell what she's thinking by the colors onscreen.

Here, in cool blues and greens, is when the test first began. But what gave her thoughts such perfect form?

There, beneath ribbons of deep purple and copper, is the result of traveling a great distance. A flawless score on the calibration exam.

Anders touches the screen's surface, tracing the folds of her brain. If he could just harvest her thoughts in real time, he might find the elusive balance, the key Chase locked away without sharing.

A heavy clunk interrupts his reverie. Like an adolescent caught with pornography, Anders swipes the touchpad, clearing Caitlyn's scans from the screen.

"Don't bother knocking." He recognizes the tang of sweat and spray-on deodorant barely covering it up. Junior Researcher Jason Freeman, fresh from the gym.

What surprises Anders is the retinue behind him. Stretching out into the narrow hall is the majority of his team, eight colleagues and not a single smile.

"Your presence is required," Freeman says. "Meeting in the conference room, now."

Curious terms, Anders thinks. And on his only day off. He's certain there are no all-hands scheduled today. So, a new fire to extinguish.

Three hundred feet later, each step thick with silence, and he arrives at the conference room with a view to the foggy south. He takes a seat at the round table. No head here. That had been the great Robert Chase's command. A true Arthurian.

And it turns out that's why they're all here. After ten minutes of accusations ranging from treason to murder, the chorus hardens against him.

"Anders, the bottom line is that it's over," Freeman says. "We've met. We've discussed it. Consensus has been reached. This is not what we signed up for. Without Dr. Chase, we're through."

A few grunts of approval and plenty of nods. Even Wendall in the back bellows out, "Here, here."

"You need to read this." Freeman slides a document across the table. "Don't speak. Just bite your tongue and let it sink in before you start weaseling your way out."

Anders takes the document. He long ago taught himself to speed-read using the Tracker-and-Pacer method. In seconds he's scanned the whole letter, even found a few typos and spliced commas. Still, he gives the team a show and pretends to study it while reading the room.

Rule one in a coup d'état: numbers don't matter. Key players are needed, as well as a structural advantage. A glance around the table and Anders stifles a grin. All replaceable here.

Rule number two: never show your cards early. Nox taught him that.

Anders runs his finger down the list of grievances. Violations of medical ethics. Breaches of law. They've even nicknamed his group the Frankenstein unit. He gives it all a nod.

"Yes, this list is accurate and fair. I admit, we've made tough decisions. Gone down some dark halls in search of improvement."

"Improvement?" Freeman scoffs. "We've mutilated our subjects. Betrayed our oaths as scientists, as doctors, as humans. And now Robert Chase is gone, dead, and don't pretend you didn't have something to do with it."

Anders sucks in air between his teeth. He's never been a good liar and has no intention of starting now. So he glances at the document again. There are twelve names and signatures at the bottom, all affirming the statement. The bulk of the team.

But there isn't Yuri, Anders thinks. Or Bethany. Or Janet. Because they'd all seen this coming.

Freeman taps the table. "Our involvement ends here, now. That's our resignation."

"Dr. Freeman—Jason—I want to propose a thought experiment," Anders says. "You're a history buff, so help me frame the hypothesis. A man finds an old tree, sick and withering. He tears from it some branches, uses those sticks to make fire. You're following? Good. With that fire comes warm food and safety and the searing pain of the flame. Heat that leads to forges and metals, steel and swords, and all those killed by the blade. Where should that man stop? With the first little burned finger or the first scorched village? The first knife that cuts meat or the first sword that kills? Where do you draw the line, Doctor?"

"Here, Anders," Freeman says. "We draw the line here."

Anders points. "Not we. You."

Then he takes the paper and crumples it. Just gives it a toss to the trash can and misses. No matter. He's already scored a slam dunk and the rest haven't caught up.

Freeman's nostrils flare as heads shake around the table. Someone mutters, "Told you."

"And that's why you need me," Anders says. "To push you past some arbitrary line. To help you reach your potential." Anders swipes his tablet and brings up the teleconferencing app. "And that's fine. We all need motivation from time to time."

With a swipe like a conductor, Anders brings up a dual view on the conference room TV.

On one side of the screen: a live feed of this room from the cameras in the corners. Nine curious faces looking back at themselves. The Foundation's biometric software identifies each face with a little blue box. There beside them: everything from age to net worth to credit score. Nine data-rich lives all on display.

Freeman smirks. "What's this?"

On the other side of the screen: the darkened, sterile lab, where four decoherents hang in twilight suspension. Exposed lungs breathe in acrylic housing. Machines spin, cleaning dark blood and pumping in nutrients. Faces forever masked behind goggles and headphones.

"Bethany, do me a favor," Anders says, and there's Bethany, screens lighting her face in the shadowed control room. "Go ahead and power down our Faraday shielding, would you? Thanks."

Gasps around the table. *It's the little things*, Anders muses, *that people often overlook*. Like the fact that Day's Bane is protected by the same lightning arrestors SpaceX uses for Falcon 9 launches. Four metal towers that can be disabled with the press of a button.

"I have your attention now, good," Anders says. "But it's their attention that should concern you, Dr. Freeman—Jason—my friend. Let's see where you draw that righteous line. Let's see if our subjects have similar compunctions."

"Anders, wait—"

Another swipe of the tablet, and the blue box around Freeman's face onscreen turns red. On the other screen:

Subject: 91D.

Status: ACTIVE.

Target: NEURAL VIDEO INPUT.

Everyone seated near Freeman immediately scoots away. Eight chairs squeaking, falling over, and now he's all by himself.

Anders says, "I seem to remember other names on that paper. Nick, I think you were there."

Another swipe on the tablet. Now it's Dr. Nick Baker's face in the red box onscreen. Bodies scramble away. Hannah actually shoves him away.

"Now, we can't forget Cathy," Anders says. "After all, we must be inclusive." Another swipe, and now the red box is on Dr. Cathy Millicent, who simply covers her face and cowers behind a chair.

"Fair point, Cathy, thank you. Friends, this is why alternatives are important."

Another swipe. Onscreen, the video feed switches, no longer live but prerecorded. A suburban park, where a man in his late thirties pushes a little girl in a swing. The girl's hair, the same shade of blonde as her mother, now crouching behind the chair and pleading.

It takes the software less than a blink to identify her husband, Alan Millicent, thirty-eight, and their daughter, Arya Millicent, four. Location: Cypress Green Park. Two blocks from her house.

The prompt: *INITIATE?*

Onscreen, the father and daughter are all playground smiles and laughter. In this room, near-total hysterics. From the cool lab, Bethany stifles a grin.

Freeman says, "Christ, Anders, you've lost it."

"I'm hurt by that, Jason, truly. Because as I see it, I'm the only one in this room with my eye on the future. But there are others. The Russians, the Chinese, they've all caught wind of Clearwater's achievements. This is an arms race, folks. The final arms race. And there's no prize for second place. All of us here, we're either a finger on a button or a face on a screen."

Sweat beads on Anders's back. At some point, he'd gotten so worked up he'd stood up and started pacing. He takes a focused breath, zips his hoodie, and lets his words linger. Now, back to business.

"Bethany, go ahead and reactivate the Faraday shield."

"Copy that."

Anders shuts off the lab feed but leaves the video of Cathy's family onscreen.

"What… what do you want from us?"

He is delighted to see that it's Jason Freeman, all diplomacy now. "Your very best. I want you to map every thought, every memory, every last synapse in those heads until you find what Dr. Chase kept hidden from us. I want results. Stable and reproducible results."

"We've tried…"

"Try harder. A blind girl and a vegetable were able to achieve more than we have."

"It took them *years.*"

Anders pats Freeman on the shoulder. "Have some faith in yourself, Dr. Freeman. Ten minutes ago you were ready to quit. Imagine where you could be in another ten days." He pauses by the door to take in the conference room, the air thick with sweat. "Greatness awaits!"

Then he is off, down the hall, a spring to his step now that that unpleasant business is behind him. He finds himself whistling as he strolls back to his office. It's a beautiful day outside beyond these cool halls. The seas are calm, the sky a deep gray. The wind turbines slowly spin. And the horizon, a near-invisible line, limitless like all things ahead.

[32]

THIRTY MILES EAST OF ARIZONA'S GEOLOGIC PROMONTORY KNOWN AS
the Boundary Cone, there stands another natural landmark, one
known to the indigenous peoples as Kray Mesa. It is a squat
plateau at the edge of the Black Mountains, smoothed by erosion
on its western side, chewed by volcanic collapse on the east.

To most, the plateau merits no further attention. It is a land-
scape already desolate and barren. To the nearby pilots, it is
Special Use Airspace P-212 R-781, both prohibited and restricted.
No flyovers lower than fifteen thousand feet.

To the Foundation, it is home.

Overlooking forlorn housing developments reclaimed by
desert sage looms a sprawling office park of corridors and rooms.
Within, labyrinthian halls chatter with more daily data than the
Pentagon sees in a year. The average employee age is twenty-
seven. The average salary just north of two hundred grand.

Like the Silicon Valley companies who unknowingly carry its
code, the Foundation is a thing of sleek mystery, knowledge siloed
by departments and halls. Some believe themselves to be white
hat hackers, hired to stress-test the cameras and microphones
consumers bring into their homes. Others believe they're digital
praetorians, fending off the Russians, the Chinese, the North

Koreans. Those who have ascended the ranks have come to terms with their part in the machinery, edge pieces in a great puzzle few will assemble.

In a slate office without windows or a view, five people gather around a mirror-black table.

On the administrative side are Coordinator Lennox Thompson, Assistant Coordinator Ron Fig, Chief of Security Brian Skinnell, and Kari Mendoza, a beady-eyed woman from legal who is chewing her pen.

On the other side sits Associate Agent Brad Lee. He's been holding his breath for what feels like an hour.

"There, did you see that?" Skinnell asks, his hand tapping the remote and rewinding the video on TV. "He could have stopped him, but he didn't. That's textbook collusion."

Onscreen, Brad is flex-cuffed, laid out on the sanctorum bed. Michaels, in the foreground, operates the computer. The label reads *CAIRO*.

"You expected Field Agent Lee to initiate a counterassault against someone who just used a drop-grid attack and a Man-in-the-Cloud to circumvent our security? All while zip-tied and stripped of his firearm? There's nothing textbook about this."

The statement comes from Fig, who never seems more than a bad day from resigning. Brad pegged him for more of a yes-man than a defender. Yet here he is, scoffing and shaking his head.

"Agent Lee had no moves to make," Fig adds.

"*Associate* Field Agent Lee," Thompson corrects, turning his stare back on Brad. "And how is it that the assailant was granted access again? Your report has more holes in it than my teenager's excuses."

Brad clears his throat and organizes his words. He'd done as they told him. First Michaels, who put him into this mess. Then his fiancée, who told him how to get out. The best lie is the one that's cloaked in the truth.

So that's what he says.

"Well, he got in because I let him in."

Silence, not unfamiliar to these sound-dampened rooms. Yet the pause hangs heavy, a cloud of doubt.

Skinnell repeats it slowly. "You let him in?"

Brad nods. "Field Agent—sorry, *former* Field Agent—Michaels indicated that he was the target of an ongoing extraction. And that he was in possession of an experimental weapon. Which—if you read my report—you'll note its type and classification are beyond this committee's clearance. I'm the only one in this room who has seen the effects of this… weapon." The word sticks to his tongue, sour and wrong. "When Michaels made contact, my goal was to bring him into the fold, peacefully. To avoid an incident, like last year in Reno."

More silence at the mention of that time and place. For all its secrets, the Foundation isn't a vacuum. What happened in Reno quickly became rumor and myth, and myths always grow in the absence of fact. That Brad had been recruited shortly after was a card he rarely played.

Unless he's pinned to the wall.

Chair squeaking, Fig leans in. "You've encountered this weapon before?"

Another nod from Brad.

"And you thought you could bring him in… how?"

"You catch more flies with honey than vinegar. Agent Michaels regarded me as a friend due to our… previous involvement."

A few curious stares down at his file. He has them now, just like his fiancée told him. Time to press the offensive.

"Look, I made a mistake. But it bought us actionable intel. We know Michaels and the other target are cooperating. After months off-grid, we know they're rejoining society. Otherwise, why bother purging the biometrics? And we discovered how a former employee could bypass our security. The penetration testers can thank me." He turns his stare onto the chief of security. "At the beginning of this hearing, you asked me if I had anything to say for myself. Well, I do, sir. 'You're welcome.'"

He folds his hands. Fifty-fifty odds. That's what he gives

himself that in another ten minutes he'll have a job and not a black bag over his head.

WHEN THE CONFERENCE DOOR CLOSES, Brad stifles his grin. A dismissal, no record in his file. Even better than he'd hoped for or deserved.

Now, to get back to profiling those missing backpackers in Spain.

"Agent Lee, hold up."

Olivia—his fiancée—finds him in the long corridor between Administrative and Data Analytics. Her heels clack off the stone floor. Not one for smiles or displays of affection, she keeps the distance professional as they walk down the hall.

Officially, the Foundation does not have an anti-fraternization policy; it's neither condoned nor condemned. Unofficially, it is accepted that the long hours, high stress, and social isolation breeds a need for intimacy. More than once Brad has walked in on stairwell gropings and the occasional bathroom fling. Now, in the aftermath of the hearing, he's drawn to Olivia and how good she looks in a suit. It has been a while...

"Stop looking at me like that," she says.

"Like what?"

"Like you're fourteen and just saw your first tit. And quit grinning."

"Jokes on you. I was sixteen."

"Wasn't that kind of your sister?"

He tries to match her pace but she walks fast and with purpose. In another day he'll be on European soil, backpack on, researching hostels and albergues along the Camino de Santiago. For now, he just wants to savor this small victory.

"I said everything, just like you told me to. And it went just as you said. Babe, you'd be proud."

"First off, of course it did. Second, stop calling me babe. Third, congratulations, you crash-landed the plane after setting it on fire. And fourth, now we're both in the jungle."

Brad glances back. They should have taken a left at the junction. Instead, she's walking down a new corridor, the stripes on the walls a deep green and past his clearance.

"Uh, the bullpen is back there."

"You're not going back to your desk and neither am I. We've been reassigned."

Shoes squeaking, Brad stops. "What about my missing backpackers?" He hurries between her, blocking the way. "Wait, my cases, they're—hey!"

"*Our* cases, Agent Lee. And yes, they're no longer ours. Now, we need to hurry."

Brad winces. "Hold up. Who the hell reassigned us? What do they think they're doing?"

"They?" Her face hardens. "You still don't get this, do you? The only reason you're still badged is because I traded us up. This was a package deal. My supervision, your connection. You don't like it? Take it up with our new coordinator."

"New coordinator?"

Brad studies Olivia. Those calculating eyes. That ferocious independence. She is four years his senior, five years further into her Foundation career. She'll make assistant coordinator soon. Yet sometimes the canyons between them seems so vast he can't see the far side. Sometimes he wonders how he will look then. Will he even recognize himself?

Her face softens. The shadow of that smile he's come to love.

He says, "I'm sorry, I just… Sometimes it feels like I've been dropped into one of those Japanese game shows and all the rules are in hieroglyphics."

Her eyes sparkle. "You're not exactly wrong. Here we are."

They stop before the last door in the hall, unmarked except for a small security card reader. She takes a moment to straighten his tie and brush some hair from his jacket.

Then she taps her phone to the reader. The screen beeps. *HOST HAS BEEN NOTIFIED. PLEASE WAIT.*

He asks, "Should I be nervous?"

"Always."

"Does it ever go away?"

She doesn't answer. Just a little puff of air, her nostrils flaring, her jaw tensing. She reaches out and gives his hand a soft squeeze.

The door beeps and opens, and her hand drops away. Brightness bathes them from within, the afternoon light off the Black Mountains. This is the only suite he's ever seen with a view.

Which means one thing.

"Agents Moon and Lee, come in please."

Blown out by the daylight, the man does not rise but gestures to the empty chairs before a desk stacked with folders. His turquoise eyes glisten as he studies the tablet laid out before him. A knot tightens deep in Brad's gut.

He has met this man twice in his life. Once, on an encrypted connection from a back room in Busan with Olivia doing the talking. Again, when he summarized his role at the Clearwater hearings. Both times he could remember every detail, down to the time of the day.

Chief Coordinator Holland Nox's stare sweeps over them, razor blades against Brad's soft gaze. He wants to look away, every instinct crying out. Instead, he gives him a subtle nod.

"It's been a while, hasn't it?" Nox says. "We've got a lot to catch up on, so pull up a seat and let's get up to speed."

[33]
SOUTH SIDE, CHICAGO, IL
1:00 P.M.

IT IS FIVE FLIGHTS OF PISS-STAINED STAIRS AND GRAFFITI-COVERED walls to the top floor of Buena Vista Gardens. There are no gardens here, just concrete and urban decay. Inside the apartment, the view is far from good. At the window, Caitlyn squints, focusing on a shirtless man in the building across the courtyard, a crying baby in one arm as he hangs wet laundry out his window.

"You're the first person come around asking about my brother in months," Beverly Holloway says. She brings in sweetened tea on a tray and places it on the coffee table. A crinkling from the plastic wrap as she sits on the couch.

"First I thought maybe you was another one of them reporters," she continues, "trying to dig up more dirt on my family. Like, 'How could we raise someone to do what he done?' Maybe see if we had, like, pit bull fights and all kinds of nastiness. But we ain't. Zade came from BVG, same as me."

"BVG?" Caitlyn asks.

"The Gardens," Beverly says. "Buena Vista. Some of the kids still call this the Dens, like they hardcore baby gangstas and this is the nineties. No one takes 'em seriously. Sure, things are tough, but we've got more high school grads than convicts these days."

"That's your doing," Michaels says. "We've seen the numbers. What your charity's accomplished is impressive."

And it was. At the height of the Great Recession, when homes were being foreclosed and opioids were taking hold, when her older brother had been on his second tour of duty, Beverly began her own war against illiteracy. The Full Circle Club was founded in this building's community center, a place where at-risk youth could read and get free tutoring instead of prowling the ramshackle streets and housing projects.

Now, a decade and a half later, the Full Circle Club is a South Side institution. Proud photos line the cracked walls: Beverly with the mayor and the governor, with Al Sharpton and Jay Z.

"We make our own luck," Beverly says. "And in spite of my brother's bad press, we been fortunate. Enrollment is rising." She turns her brown eyes on Caitlyn. "What's your story, sister? You look like you've had quite the journey."

"My story?" Caitlyn considers it. "I suppose I'm still writing it."

"Good girl. And don't be afraid of a little revision. Men, they get to have their mid-life crises, their comeback tours and shiny sports cars. Us girls? We gotta stay in our lanes. Least, that what they try to tell us." She winks at Caitlyn.

"I've never had much patience for rules."

"Then there's a place in history for you too, God willing." She turns her stare back on Michaels. "And you? What gets your bones out of bed in the morning?"

"Justice," he says.

Beverly takes a long sip of the iced sweet tea, studying these two on her couch. Michaels can hear an echo of Carruthers telling him to mirror her movements, build subconscious empathy. So he drinks the sweet tea. Despite his aversion to sugar, he has to admit, it's damn delicious.

Beverly must sense it. Her eyes light up. "My meemaw was a Southerner, and she insisted we always keep some at the ready. It's good, isn't it? Even if it's just liquid diabetes."

"My mom made a ferocious Thai iced tea," Caitlyn says. "I'll leave you with the recipe."

"I'd appreciate that, dear, and you be sure to give her my gratitude."

Caitlyn's eyes crinkle in a forced smile.

Michaels says, "Beverly, I was hoping you could tell us more about your brother. Maybe any stuff the media overlooked."

"How long you got?" she laughs. "Media overlooked a lot, always does. That horror in Litundi—calling him the Butcher of Bakango Bay—that's the only story they peddled. What they don't say is who gave him those skills. Who benefited before he went free market. Zade, he used to sit right where you are when he'd visit, telling me 'bout those old generals begging for peace on TV and paying him to start insurrections. How convenient it was to have soldiers like him. Heck, y'all must think I'm a crackpot."

"Not at all," Caitlyn says. "Quite the opposite, actually."

Beverly stirs her tea, gaze hardening. "My brother was no saint. What he did to that poor royal family, there's no justification. Zade, he's answering to God. What I am saying is, you train a dog to tear flesh, you can't act surprised when it bites."

Michaels asks, "When was the last time you heard from your brother?"

Beverly's tongue circles her lips. "Night before his execution. So, what… Eleven months back? They gave him one call and it cut out. That was it, our long-distance goodbye."

"Did they ever return his body?"

"Why you asking?"

Because his DNA turned up with four others, Michaels thinks. Instead, he says, "We're just checking timelines."

Beverly shakes her head. "The Swiss embassy, they arranged the cremation."

"Why the Swiss?" Caitlyn asks.

"There's no U.S. embassy there," Michaels says. "No diplomatic presence."

Beverly nods. "Well, the Swiss must've gotten tired of me so they stopped returning my calls. I would've liked to see my brother resting here, where his family is, even if it's just his ashes. When we was little, he'd sit here, playing his video games, talking 'bout how he was gonna get outta BVG. I s'pose he did. Got himself all the way to the far side of the world." That same melancholy smile splits her face, eyes focusing not on the rug but something beyond, backward in time.

"I'm sorry," Caitlyn says. "We can't choose our family, but we can still miss them. Even if they hurt us."

"I was just thinking of the last thing he said." Beverly waves it off. "No, never mind."

Michaels leans forward. "What was it?"

"It's nothing. Just something that didn't sit right."

"Actually, that's what we're looking for," Michaels says. "Anything that was left out, maybe overlooked. The news sold a violent coup, but what did they miss?"

"On the phone, at the end, he said, 'I've found a way out of this mess.' Those were his words. He said that his death was gonna bring us some good. Then the call dropped."

"What did he mean?" Caitlyn asks.

"First I thought it was the money or maybe denial of his situation. 'Cept that ain't Zade's style, you know? He was clever. Not long-term smart but *cunning*. And for a man about to hang, he was talking like his best years were ahead."

A glance passes between Michaels and Caitlyn. This is taking a detour into the uncanny. Often, that means they've wandered too far. But sometimes… Sometimes it means the truth is dangerously close.

"Beverly, you mentioned money," Michaels says. "Did Zade leave some behind?"

"Sure enough, when they closed his estate, I got a ping on my phone. Bank transfer. I thought it was some sort of mistake. Now, I ain't saying how much it was, but you cut a million in half and you're mostly there. Full Circle's lawyers dug into it, and it was all proper. Zade's executor wired it through."

Caitlyn shifts on the couch. Shades of her father, the uncle she'd never known. And the blind trust fund that kept her afloat all those years after the accident. Medical bills made easy by her family's careful planning. Savings that feathered her nest in San Francisco until the curtain grew heavy and daylight turned dark.

"So you see," Beverly says, "there was a bit of good to come out of all the bad my brother done. That gift he sent us, that's helping a dozen kids go to college. More tickets outta the Gardens."

Downstairs, they make their way past cracked glass and spray-painted walls, scrawled phone numbers offering good times. They squeeze past a group of youths on the landing, paint pens in hands, fresh tags on the bricks.

"Damn, girl," one of the boys says as Caitlyn passes. "You got some wicked-fine ink on your skin."

Caitlyn gives him a nod. *You know it.* A cool breeze chills their spines.

Outside, they find shade beneath a lone tree. Laughter at the playground as girls push each other on rusty swings. The squeak of sneakers as boys play basketball, all elbows and talk. High above, that shirtless man watches Caitlyn, who watches him back, a blurry blob still hanging his laundry.

"We need to follow the money," Michaels says. "Give me a moment."

Michaels works his smartphone, searching. His left hand flaps every few seconds. Caitlyn has learned the signals, the way his mind works. And she has learned when to give him some space.

For now, she lets facts of the case ramble and roll about her mind, all discordant and odd. Five sets of DNA, all deceased within the last year. The man who unlocked decoherence, now dead as well. GPS coordinates for some house in California, laser-etched into aerogel. How the hell does this all connect?

Or does it?

Paranoia claws at her thoughts.

Months on a boat with an ex-government spook. A lifetime of lies passed down from her parents. And now, when she closes her eyes, she finds a second perspective, a split just past the edge of perception.

Was this how Sam Stephens felt? Or Jamal Munday? All those from Clearwater whose fractured consciousness nurtured this power inside her mind?

Michaels's hand stops flapping when the call connects. "Yes, hello, this is Donald Kovak calling on behalf of the Internal Revenue Service for a Mr. Elmore Kennedy. Is this him speaking? Ah, good." He gives Caitlyn a nod and a finger. *Wait.* His eyes brighten, a missile locked onto target. "Mr. Kennedy, yes, we're trying to reconcile a bank transfer we have on record. As you know, any amount over ten thousand dollars has to be declared and we're just... What's that? Yes, that's correct. For the current tax year. Ah, that's what we're seeing on our end."

He says nothing but his eyes say it all. Bingo. His pen moves quick. *$500k to Father's bank account. Who paid?*

Earlier, while Michaels drove, Caitlyn put on her thickest glasses and reviewed Iliana Kennedy's file. Her husband, an Army transportation management coordinator, caught smuggling fentanyl into the U.S. And the prosecutor's case claiming Iliana was in on the cut. Two choices before her: turn evidence against her husband or spend a decade in Leavenworth.

When the neighbors found them, her family was already dead. The paramedics revived her, saved her life and sealed her fate. Murder-suicide didn't play well to a military court. Nor the base community where her husband's product had claimed a few lives.

On August 21, while a bleary-eyed Caitlyn was drinking a Singapore Sling on her flight to Mauritius, Iliana Kennedy consumed a cocktail of her own. She was the second female federal inmate to be executed in nearly six decades.

"No, sir, you've been most helpful," Michaels says and circles a page in his notebook. "I'm sure there's nothing to worry about.

In the meantime, if you have any questions, don't hesitate to reach out."

He gives Iliana's father a name pulled off the IRS directory. Then he hangs up, eyes gleaming. Caitlyn can almost see the strings starting to connect.

"Let me guess: Zade isn't the only one to come into money before he died?"

"No, not before but after," Michaels says. "Iliana's estate transferred half a million to her father. I bet it's the same song if we check the others. Five sets of DNA, five deaths, five infusions of cash."

"Five deaths," Caitlyn repeats. "Are we sure about that?"

GEORGIA DIAGNOSTIC AND CLASSIFICATION STATE PRISON

JACKSON, GEORGIA, 4:00 P.M.

THE DEAD MAN RUNS HIS HANDS OVER THE METAL TABLE, CARESSING the dents and dings formed over countless conversations. All the family and friends, all the clergy promising God's final salvation. How many midnight miracles had been prayed for at this table? How many souls supposedly saved?

But not today.

"Are you listening?" the attorney asks. "What I'm telling you is, we've run out of options. The courts have been clear—"

"You've run out of options," the dead man says. "Say what it is: you've bungled your job."

The attorney clears his throat. "Mr. Sawyer, the appeals process is specific; it's not a menu to pick and choose. Federal judges need persuasion. Courts need reason. We've tried everything—"

"Everything you wanted," Sawyer says. He's a big man, wide in the shoulders with a slouch that hides extra inches. Prison has given him that swollen strength he could never hold on to outside. Here, even on death row, an hour of gym time and weights is an hour of distraction.

Until it all comes to an end.

On most days, Sawyer might stand up, tower over this little

man and put some fear into his skin. Today, he's too tired to rise. "What about that juror?" Sawyer asks. "The one who talked to the press?"

The lawyer's already shaking his head. Damn, he really does look like a stoat. "The court declined that appeal. They felt—"

"And the prosecutor, you never followed up on his connection to Judge Maberry. They're golfing chums—"

"Respectfully, all United States attorneys have a relationship with the bench. It doesn't poison the case—"

"And that search warrant?" Sawyer rubs his index finger against the dent in the table. Perhaps some other inmate felt their counsel needed motivation. Helped them change their smile where metal met teeth. Or maybe it was their own knuckles, dug in with despair. "They never did find that stolen car, even though that's what the warrant was for. What they *claimed* it was for. That's a… what'd you call it? A Trojan horse. They was fishing."

"Be that as it may, Mr. Sawyer, everything that can be done has been done." The lawyer starts closing his briefcase, *click, click, click.* Can't even look his client in the eyes. "I am sorry, truly. But it's the end of the line for us."

"No, not for us both."

A deep breath and an odd thought: no more tables in his future. He'd hoped to build one someday. Learn carpentry, how to measure and cut. Learn how to make something instead of just taking. He'd even bought a book. In a few hours, he'll have his last meal right here. No more tables after tonight. No more tomorrows.

The lawyer is standing now, looking down at him.

"Well, this is it then," Sawyer says. "Don't suppose I'll see you for the midnight goodbye?"

"The execute…" The lawyer hesitates. All these years and he never spoke that lumpy word, just danced around it. "No, no, I'm afraid not."

A tap on the door and a click of the locks. The lawyer hesitates. "Mr. Sawyer, we really gave it our best."

"Yep. One of us did."

Then the lawyer shuffles off, just a cheap gray suit down brown halls and out of this prison. Free to see tomorrow and all those that follow.

Fuckin' hell.

So this is what it feels like. Aiden Sawyer, a grifter, a getaway driver, and occasional muscle for hire. He can see it all now, the toppled dominos of his past that brought him to this end. The bad decisions and the junk in his veins. The wrong crew to run with and the wrong bank to hit.

And the dead…

That federal officer, the bank manager, and a schoolteacher, what a plumb fuckup. Did the fed feel this same fear when he went for his gun? Did the manager know it was a death sentence when he hit the alarm? Did that teacher mean to get in the way?

No. Their mistakes had played out in seconds. Sawyer has had years to wallow in his.

The clanging of locks breaks his reverie. There is another visitor now, a middle-aged man in a suit that screams custom-sewn. He is barrel-chested, eyes glinting in the institutional light, hungry and sharp. One glance and Sawyer feels that precise fear gleaned from a lifetime around criminals. Here is a man who has killed.

"Mr. Aiden Blane Sawyer," the man says and hoists a leather bag onto the table. With precise pulls on the zipper, the bag opens like a traveling toiletry kit. "Do you recognize this bottle to the left? Your left."

"Who… the fuck are you?" Sawyer studies the man, his no-bullshit expression. Can't quite meet that dominant gaze. "What is this?"

"Just answer the question please."

He looks at the glass vials before him. Green-capped to the left. "Pan… pan-coo-ro—"

"Pancuronium bromide. Do you know what this does?"

Sawyer cocks his head. "What are you, some kind of medical salesman?"

"Yes, Mr. Sawyer. That's exactly what I am, a salesman of sorts. In fact, I would like to sell you on a proposition. Consider it an off-ramp at the end of this road you call a life."

Sawyer blinks. He doesn't like this man, doesn't trust his formal locution. Try as he might, he never fully buried his Appalachian accent. And people never stopped reminding him about it.

"I've offended you, Mr. Sawyer," the man says. "Forgive me. What I meant, simply, is that I'm here to pitch you an idea. Would you permit me to continue?"

Sawyer takes the two other vials and rotates them in his fingers. Damn doctors and their long words. Potassium chloride, that's the second one. There's something familiar, an itch that persists.

"Shit, this's the cocktail, isn't it? The lethal injection. It's what they're gonna put in me tonight."

"Yes, well done, Mr. Sawyer. Pancuronium bromide will paralyze you. The potassium chloride will stop your heart. That sodium thiopental there in your hand, that will render you unconscious—a palliative sedation—like end-of-life care."

"Is that what this is? Like a tutorial or something?"

A smile crosses the doctor's face. Something infected in it, something sick. Any other day and Sawyer might reach across and smack it right off. But he's so tired. That's the thing they never tell you about death row. All the changes, the appeals, the last-minute reprieves, it's all so exhausting. Sawyer used to read five books a week. Now, he can hardly read the final goodbyes.

Christ, this is really happening.

"Mr. Sawyer, I'm here to make you an offer. Seeing as how limited the time is, I will not repeat myself. You have something that is of great value to the scientific community, a certain combination of traits. You—"

"I do?"

The man holds up a finger. "Please, do not interrupt."

Sawyer's toes clench. His fingers tighten. He once knocked a fellow's teeth down his throat for doing the same thing. But hell, he's worn down like an old saddle.

"Mr. Sawyer, you've indicated you wish to be cremated immediately after your execution. A noble endeavor. However, there is another option. Have you heard of Henrietta Lacks?"

"Who?"

"Henrietta Lacks was a tobacco farmer and a housewife. In 1951 she had a rare tumor. Her cancer cells, it turned out, reproduced at exceptional rates. Even today, long after Henrietta passed, her cells are still kept alive. You see, they've helped us understand cancer, AIDS, even toxic substances. The world owes Henrietta and her body a great debt."

"So, what, I've got some of them special cells?"

"You have an entire body, Mr. Sawyer. Should you choose to sell it—to assist in the research my organization represents—we are willing to pay the following sum to the recipient of your choosing."

The man turns his phone toward Sawyer. The number is high, high enough for him to scoff. Hell, now that he adds it all up, that's more than the total of all his robberies and scams. Which means that's what this is.

"Bullshit."

"You've spent your life around liars and thieves. Look into my eyes and tell me I'm being dishonest."

Sawyer searches the dark pools on the man's placid face. "What d'you need my permission for? Couldn't you just take it?"

"It works better for everyone when our subjects are willing."

"Subjects?"

"Mr. Sawyer, ask yourself, is there someone whose life could be changed by this infusion of wealth?"

God damn, he really does sound like one of those Wall Street suits. And yeah, Sawyer thinks, there is someone. It's the first name to come to his lips, the only name that means anything good in his life.

"Mariangela."

The man smiles. "When all else forsakes a father, a daughter's love is resolute. Mariangela could be back in college now. The first in your family. But those loans… I'm afraid it's expensive funding her father's defense."

"Look, I don't need your attitude." Sawyer squeezes his knees together. This man, this *con* man with his condescension. Yet how does he know where to squeeze? Mariangela, the one good thing he'd made with his life. And yeah, it stings to admit it, but the man's right: Sawyer'd gummed that up too. Sold Mariangela on the big lie, the one he told everyone, including himself.

That he was innocent.

That he was just the fall guy.

That he really hadn't pulled the trigger.

But the truth was that he'd done it. He'd shot that fed and the bank manager both because—fuck it—they'd made a move when he'd said to stay still. Simple as that.

"So, you're telling me, what, if I donate my kidneys and stuff, that money there, it'll be Mariangela's?"

"The funds are in escrow, Mr. Sawyer. It could be hers within days. But a minor correction. Not donate, *sell*. This transaction is for everything, from the hairs on your head to the skin under your toes."

"And you think it's special? Like, uh, Henrietta?"

"We believe there is great knowledge in all the locked places." He slides a tablet to Sawyer. "The transfer is pending. Check the account, the social security. Is everything in order?"

Sawyer scans the screen. Sure enough, that's her name, her address, date of birth and social. Even the Lincoln County Bank and Trust with her account and routing filled in. Mariangela had bought him so much in the joint, from toothpaste and internet credits to that lousy attorney and all those billable hours. Now, like a miracle, he can finally pay it back, and with interest.

"That's change-her-life money, Mr. Sawyer. Pressing *send* constitutes an acceptance of this agreement. You will forfeit all rights to your body, beginning at 12:01 tonight."

"All right," Sawyer says. A tap on the screen and it asks to confirm. *Transfer $500,000 to SAWYER, MARIANGELA?* He taps *YES*.

"You've made a generous choice, Mr. Sawyer. One I hope brings you solace in these final hours. Your daughter's future is secured."

The man collects his little bottles, his phone. Clasps the bag in a practiced motion, not one wasted gesture.

"The guards do have you on death watch, Mr. Sawyer. Please ensure you hold up your side of this deal."

"And yours?" Sawyer asks. "How will I know you ain't stiffed me?"

The man rises. "When you see me again, you'll know that I haven't. Godspeed, Mr. Sawyer."

With a clang, the door closes behind the odd man. Freedom in one direction, the end of the line in the other. And Sawyer here, in limbo, but only for the next several hours.

"Damn bastard skimped out," Sawyer mumbles as the clock passes one minute after midnight. As the drugs scald his veins, throbbing and caustic.

Sawyer can't see if his daughter is there, somewhere on the other side of the mirror. Can't see anything beyond the bright reflection, his body strapped to the gurney like Christ on the cross.

And those tubes. He watches the liquid flow in. In this final moment, he tells himself she'll be all right. Perhaps Daddy's built some good from all of the bad. But his tongue's heavy now. His throat's closing in. The lights are beginning to dim.

It is not painless, he thinks as his chest tightens and his veins expand. But it's not painful either. Just odd and uncomfortable, like cats inside him, all scratching to get out.

Aiden Sawyer, convicted killer of three, feels cool panic as he realizes he can no longer lick his dry lips. He can no longer blink. Can no longer breathe.

All he can do is stare at his own reflection in the window. Stare at the crawl of the clock hand, each second slower than the last. Stare as it all stretches out to a corridor of vast white.

And then, at the edge, a man steps forth from the fog, presses his stethoscope to Sawyer's chest and checks the EKG. It's the man Sawyer knows, the man who sold hope from a far-distant place. And Sawyer smiles inwardly. Yes, he had traded something to this man. Something so valuable it followed his thoughts to his very last breath.

The man steps back, his white coat gleaming with snow. He turns to the warden and the viewers beyond. The words leave his lips, solemn and slow.

"Mr. Aiden Sawyer is now deceased."

The sliding curtain falls, sealing the mirrored glass. Sawyer thinks of his daughter, her name heavy and wet. Mariangela, yes? *Sweetie, don't cry. Daddy's gone but he's left you a gift.*

And then comes a new thought, impossible yet known deep in his bones. *No, Daddy's not gone. He's not gone at all.*

[35]

RURAL KENTUCKY

MIDNIGHT

"Read it back to me," Michaels says and stifles a yawn.

Through the windshield, Interstate 65 is a void, double yellow lines winding through shadows as bugs cloud the rental car's headlights. The occasional glare of other nocturnal drivers. This is Hart County, the names on passing signs stirring Caitlyn's imagination. Tanyard Hollow. Munfordville. Cave City, Kentucky, its offramp proclaiming, *Ancient Adventures Await at Dinosaur World!*

"Cait?" Michaels asks. "The company trace. Read it back to me."

Caitlyn has to concentrate to focus on the tablet. "Omni Medical Solutions, LLC. It's listed out of an office in Delaware. They're a registered vendor for the Federal Bureau of Prisons."

"And who's it registered to? There's a button by the advanced search tab, here…"

He reaches over, fumbling for the screen. The car drifts across the rumble strips, *bump bump bump.*

"I got it, thank you. Focus on the road."

Caitlyn taps the button and waits. Like so many things about Michaels, his tablet is a fastidious enigma, every screen and app organized by codewords. She watched him sideload cryptic apps:

AirCrack-NG, Network Spoofer, Hackode, and more. When she asked what they did, he said they kept them safe.

At the top right, the result returns, the same name they've seen four other times. "West Vector Holdings."

"Companies within companies," he says. "It's like finding the same car at the scene of five accidents. Statistically improbable."

"And the same driver too," Caitlyn says. "Doctor Dennis Walker."

The web searches have done little. Just some physician floating around the federal prison system. Michaels drums his fingers on the wheel. Outside, a large bug hits the hood and leaves a long smear.

From the image searches, Dennis Walker could pass for anyone. His broad shoulders and large frame, that half smile and dark stare. He almost looks designed to be so neutral his visage eludes memory. He reminds Caitlyn of those she's met from the Foundation. He reminds her of Michaels.

"Five deaths, five money transfers," Michaels says. "I don't like where this goes. Steer for me."

Caitlyn takes the wheel while Michaels opens the pouch and powers on his phone. A ring over the speakers as the call goes out. Caitlyn keeps her eyes on the yellow center line to the left, the shoulder to her right.

And every few hundred feet, a different perspective. The dark highway becomes a dark hall underground. The overhead lights become the patterned bulbs of Clearwater, luminous pearls among concrete and metal.

Stop it, she tells herself. *Focus.*

Dr. Munson's voice fills the car, groggy. "Who is this? Do you know what time it is?"

"Doctor Munson, it's Michaels."

A sigh and the clattering of plastic and wood. Caitlyn envisions him fumbling for his glasses at a bedside table, turning on the light. "I thought we agreed to go our separate ways."

"We did. We will. But the paths are still tangled."

"Lucky me."

Michaels gestures to her: *Hold up the tablet.* With a series of swipes and taps, he brings up a map and multiple dots:

Munson's iPhone. Range: 452 miles. Status: Standby (89% Charging).

Munson's iMac. Range: 1821 miles. Status: Off.

Munson's MacBook Pro. Range: 452 miles. Status: Sleep (100% Charged).

"Check your laptop," Michaels says. "There's something I need you to see."

"How do you… never mind."

The groan of a bed and the shuffling of feet on hotel carpeting. Another click. On the little map, the laptop turns *Active.* It has occurred to Caitlyn that she and Michaels are similar in some ways. Two outsiders with means to see beyond reach. And little reason to draw back.

Munson's voice fills the car. "So, I'm looking at four death certificates and a consular death report. Lethal injection, lethal injection… What am I looking for?"

"Just keep reading."

Munson grumbles. Then, "Wait… This can't be correct."

"Assume that they are," Michaels says. "What jumps out at you?"

"The certifying physician, Dr. Walker. It's the same name on all."

"And that's odd?"

"Odd would be a dog with two tails. This is unprecedented. Except in rare cases, capital executions are handled by the state, including the physician. Hold on." A series of taps in the background. Michaels's tablet reads, *Munson Laptop > New App Active > Google Chrome > Multiple tabs.* "This Dr. Walker, I can't find any real record. No conferences, no presentations, nothing. It's a small field, too small not to leave tracks."

But not if you have the Foundation sweeping them up, Caitlyn thinks. She tilts the wheel left, bringing it back into center. At the edge of the dark highway, the bright lights of civilization. A town with gas stations and rest stops.

Munson continues, "This Walker guy is turning up in unusual places. Not a lot of clean money to be made this close to death."

"What about the unclean kind?" Michaels asks. A distinct clink of glass against glass followed by the burble of liquid. "Doctor Munson?"

"I'm having a nightcap for my nightcap. Only way your little mysteries won't give me nightmares." A sip and the sucking of air. "Okay, if we're speculating—a word I tell my junior pathologists to erase from their lexicon—I'd say you're looking at organ harvesting. Kidneys can go for as high as a hundred grand. Livers as well, though they're regenerative. Corneas, ligaments, even skin are all valuable. The organ trade is a multibillion-dollar business that rubs up against everything from medicine and life extension to beauty and biohacking. I'd be lying if I claimed I hadn't been approached a few times over the years."

"But there's got to be safeguards," Caitlyn finds herself saying. "A process, something."

"You've got me on speakerphone, lovely." Another clink of glass against glass. Another pour followed by a sip. "Of course there are safeguards and systems. But that doesn't mean they can't be bent or broken or erased altogether. Just ask the man sitting beside you. Ask him what happened to that fellow in Boston. That's your answer, Michaels. Maybe it's just too close for you to see clearly."

[36]

THE JOURNAL OF TEDDY JENSEN
PROPERTY CZ-93 "DAY'S BANE"

OCTOBER 8ᵀᴴ

I had a seizure at lunch; Mother said it wasn't my first. There are gaps in my memory, yet I still find it odd: how can I forget such disruptive events? I must try harder to recall…

Recall what?

Recall what I was doing, yes. I was writing to myself in this journal. I seem to have filled so many pages. Yet like the seizures, I don't recall writing half of these words. Some of them I don't even know.

Outside, autumn has finally arrived and the leaves are beginning to fall.

My favorite season.

Goodness, I'm so very tired.

February 9ᵗʰ

Most people would be grateful to shed their holiday weight, but not me. I've lost fifteen pounds since Christmas. Mother says I'm all skin and bone and that I need to eat more.

So that's what I do.

And yet, where does it all go?

I've been struggling to get out of bed lately. I've found myself dreaming I'm anchored down and drifting through time. I can see myself, so young and so strong.

And I can see myself now, from above, all sickly and infirm. A piece of rotting meat balanced on the sharp edge of a knife. Perhaps I'll slip one way or the other.

Or perhaps I'll simply split down the middle.

Yesterday, I made it to the feed store. I saw Claudia there and I met her son Isaac. She took over the family business. Everyone seemed to know her and chatted as they entered and left. I lingered by the rakes, nervous and quiet. I forgot why I'd even come.

Her son is charming, well spoken, and he's already five.

Where have the years gone?

May 1ˢᵗ

Another seizure, last week. This time while driving to the post office. I woke up off the road, the fire already spreading and coming up through the hood.

I'm blessed to have been thrown clear and come out uninjured.

The truck is totaled, of course, and Mother is worried. Already, I can see her taking on more of my tasks around the farm. Sometimes, she talks to me slower, as if I might not understand her simple commands.

Sometimes I don't.

She says I keep too many secrets. Perhaps one day I'll let her read my journal. Perhaps one day, someone will understand.

It's like I've been out of my body and my dark partner has stepped in. Like coming home to find the fireplace full of embers and my bed already warm.

I heard terrible news this morning at church. Claudia's son, Isaac, fell from his bunkbed at night. They said she heard a terrible crash and the boy's poor neck was bent. They say God called back one of his angels. And they said we should pray for them, so I did.

Sometime in August

Remember when I was young and I wrote in this journal?

My thirty-eighth birthday, today. I found this old thing while cleaning my drawers. And I thought I had lost something, yes, lost something important. A thing I cannot remember.

And it scares me because it's one of two things. I've lost my body again or I've lost my own mind.

I need to think logically. If I am in here, then my dark partner is out there.

But if he is out there, then who is here, standing beside me and helping me write?

Have I done some terrible thing?

I can't even close my eyes now; I see him inside.

I don't know what is real anymore. I can't remember or think clearly.

Clear…

Clearwater.

Remember, yes, I think that's the key. I need to remember.

Remember that moment when Dr. Chase beckoned me into the pod and I said I was scared of the shadows. What did he say? He told me a secret, that it's always inside me: the key and the anchor. The key is to build a house in my mind and anchor it with good memories, the strongest I could find.

So that's what I did.

I built it deep in my mind—not a house but a church—and I filled it with song.

When I climbed out of the pod, I felt like a god. Dr. Chase said my numbers were off the charts. And he said to be careful, to never forget my anchor and key.

Tomorrow is Sunday.

I will go to our church down the road. Tomorrow, I will sing and repent for my sins.

But today, I must remember, just like Dr. Chase once taught me.

I will return to that church I built deep in my mind.

NO FURTHER ENTRIES

[37]

WHITLEY COUNTY, KENTUCKY

1:00 A.M.

THE CANDLELIGHT INN HAS NEITHER CANDLES NOR AMPLE LIGHTING. It squats in pooling darkness, tucked between a lonely truck stop and a diner that served its last pancake a decade ago. More weeds than vehicles in this grotty lot.

But it's the only place to get some rest, which is exactly what Michaels isn't doing.

"Look at this." He pulls the tablet close to them both. Caitlyn crosses her legs, the lumpy bed squeaking. "Dr. Walker's traveled to at least five executions in the past nine months. Before that, he was overseas. Litundi, China, Iran. You know Iran actually has a legal market for organ peddling?"

Caitlyn studies the doctor's travel history as it scrolls past. It's the same pattern at each location. An execution, then a private flight out the next morning. "Lovely."

She takes off her glasses and rubs her tired eyes. Years ago, when her vision was in its death throes, she moved to San Francisco to take part in a corneal stem cell injection trial. It hadn't worked. Because the very thing that was blinding her wasn't her eyes.

It was the lesions her brain produced whenever she blinked.

Now, she thinks of those stem cells. Were they ethically

sourced, lab-grown, or scraped from the DNA of willing donors? She hadn't asked. She hadn't thought to.

Michaels says, "His business card has been active today. He had a five-star dinner at the Capital Grille in Atlanta." He swipes down the screen, zooms in on *RECENT ACTIVITY*. "Then he filled up his gas tank outside Jackson. There's a prison there."

"Are there any scheduled executions?"

"Less than an hour ago. My guess is he's there to pick up a body. If we can intercept him in the morning, we can find out what he's up to."

"You want to interrogate him?"

"I want some alone time to ask him some questions."

Caitlyn smiles. "Walker's ex-military, built like a bulldozer, and trafficking dead bodies. You want to race to Atlanta so you can intimidate him on a few hours of sleep?"

Michaels considers it. "They would be pointed questions, but I see what you mean. I'm tired, not thinking tactically. We should get some shuteye before I do something clumsy."

A new line of text at the top of the *RECENT ACTIVITY* screen catches her eye. "What's that charge, Platinum Tigers?"

Michaels googles the name. The screen fills with silhouetted women, all hips and chest. A gentlemen's club, where a trio of buxom ladies offer cigars and snifters of brandy. The website design is aiming for elegance but landing on gaudy, all cheap sparkle and sleaze.

"Looks like our man Walker is stopping off at the old skin rodeo."

Caitlyn's eyes drink in the images, the velvet chairs and brass poles, the very shape of the rooms. She says, "Funny. I just realized something."

Michaels turns off the tablet and slides it into the mesh bag. Yawning, he asks, "What's that?"

"Nothing." She turns off the light.

And she thinks, *I've never been to a strip club before.*

[38]

PLATINUM TIGERS GENTLEMEN'S CLUB, ATLANTA, GA

1:00 A.M.

Dr. Dennis Walker, fifty-one, treasures life's finer indulgences: the nutty spice of cigars, the purr of a fast car, the crystalline chill of good vodka. Each spring he flies to Hong Kong to have new suits custom made at the Armoury. He is a collector, yes, and in this line of work, a man must collect many rare things. Tonight, he's celebrating the close of one such procurement.

The murderer's body has been prepped, transport arranged. Poor idiot. The next time he opens his eyes, it'll be someone else's concern. The Foundation's to do, well, *whatever*. Walker didn't get to this rarefied air by asking messy questions.

Time to celebrate now. Time for dessert.

And what better way than a fine Asian girl who reminds him of his neighbor's daughter? The one that casts him those glances in church, flirtatious perhaps. He can't have her, of course; he's no kiddie diddler. And besides, her dad's his dentist and a pretty swell guy. But tonight, he can take a little trip in his mind.

"Your name is Suyin," he says.

The stripper hesitates, a plucked eyebrow rising. Then he flashes a wad of hundred-dollar bills. She nods, getting the drift. Money doesn't buy manners, but it does make it easier to tolerate a man of his proclivities. That's real power, he thinks as Suyin bends over before him, ninety pounds of ballet tightness.

"Suyin, okay," she says, a coy smile as she collects the bills off the VIP room floor. "I can be Suyin for you, mister."

Walker knows her smile is as fake as her tits. But who cares? He wasn't blessed with good looks or good genes, and chivalry only gets you so far. Cash is his ticket to this parade of young skin.

"Tell me, Suyin, what do I get for another three hundred bucks?" He peels the bills from his shirt pocket, holds them out like bait.

"Oh, you can get whatever you want." She reaches for the green, but he pulls them away.

"Call me daddy," he says and lays the bills on the ground. "Oh, and lose the accent."

She tilts her head. "I don't have an accent."

Damn she's cute. All of nineteen and still so naive. Yeah, he likes a bit of role-play, so what? If she wants his money, they'll both have to act.

"Lose the American accent."

Suyin hesitates, connecting the dots. The trick, he's discovered, is to ease them into his kink. Don't front-load the girls or they easily frighten.

"Indulge me."

Like flipping a switch, she surprises him and becomes a new girl. "Oh, Daddy, look at those green American dollars."

Yes, he thinks. Far from the Cantonese of his favorite Wan Chai brothels. But when in Atlanta…

"Mmm, go on, take it." He holds out another hundred, growls when she snatches it, laughs when she recoils.

"Oh, you big A-mer-i-can man. You scary. You protect me, how?"

How? Is this a question or a challenge? Walker winces as the mood shifts.

"Daddy, I need more money for schoolbooks and supplies."

And now she's rubbing up against him, her dental floss thong and glistening hips. He could grab her, hold her down with one arm, have his way with her and no one would care. *Well, no one who matters.*

But no, not now.

The real fun isn't in taking by force. The fun comes when someone realizes they've sold themselves for so little. Like the murderer now in his chemical coma. Like Suyin soon.

"Oh, Daddy, so much money. If you spoil me, I be naughty." Another hundred tossed onto the floor. Another gyrating bend.

"Then you'll just have to get punished."

He reaches for the champagne. Twelve hundred bucks for this bottled crap. But hey, it bought him this room. He pours himself a glass.

Then he pours more onto the floor.

"Daddy, you spill."

He shakes his head, neck jiggling, grin growing, and he taps his shoe in the bubbly puddle. "Drink. My glass. And yours."

For a beat, her hips lose rhythm. She furrows her thin brow. This man, he can't actually be serious?

But he is.

Another pour splashes the floor. "Suyin, you're wasting champagne."

These American women, Walker thinks. *All so fucking soft.*

In his trips collecting, he's seen unspeakable things done for a glimpse of the money Suyin holds in her thong. He's learned everyone has a price and a line they dread to step over. Tonight, his entertainment isn't Suyin's tight body. It's helping her find that line.

And then making her cross it.

"Go on. Use your tongue. Down on all fours. There you go."

As she lowers her lips to the floor, he glances at the camera in the high corner. He slipped the manager a thousand bucks for this video. Another memento for his growing collection.

Hesitating, she looks up at him from the wet floor. The champagne's lost its bubbles. And her eyes, are those tears misting in the corners? *Yes, this is it*, he thinks. The first of several lines she'll have to cross.

"Suyin," he says, wagging a finger. "No licky, no money."

A sharp knock at the door. Dammit, he paid good money and that included a promise: no interruptions.

Another knock. Suyin, on all fours, so close to drinking off the floor. Now Suyin is breaking character and opening the door. "George, what the hell—"

There is a low, concussive hum and the flicker of lights. Then Suyin is yanked right out the door, just like that.

Blood rushing to his head, Walker rises to see a thin glimmer beyond, like fire refracted through glass. A luminous woman, carrying Suyin across the back room, raising a finger to her shimmering lips. *Shh…*

And then it's before him in a blink. The door slams; the lock drives home. Dennis Walker, on his feet, two hundred and forty pounds of shuddering fear. He reaches for the door but the handle snaps off. Brass and steel, broken just like that.

"Naughty man," comes a cold whisper from every direction.

So Walker does all he can think of, the most basic response.

He screams.

Or rather, he tries to. The hand comes fast, unfolding from emptiness before him. A vise on his jaw. He can see her just at the edge of his vision, hair of luminous ribbons, her skin a shifting mosaic of tattoos and static.

He cannot cry out, so he simply lets the champagne pour from his bladder. And now he is thrown, back into his velvet chair. The assailant's full form blooms before him.

The human brain orients itself in reality by using the past to predict the present. Water is wet, fire always burns, and what goes up usually comes down. With no prior knowledge of decoherence and mens corpuses, the wet machinery of Dennis Walker's mind simply gums up. He falls back on his Sunday school whispers.

"Oh God help me, oh sweet Jesus—"

"No God here," the voice says. "Just you and me, Dr. Walker. And I want answers. What happened to Zade Holloway after his execution? What did you do to these people?"

He opens his mouth but finds his tongue dry, like he's been sucking on pennies. This thing—this woman before him—how does she know?

"Answer me!"

A blur, and the chair is torn out from beneath him. She is behind him, above him. He's fallen onto the wet floor, and now it's his turn to crawl to the door, to the corner and the camera, high up and silent. He waves his hands at the dark lens. "Help! Help!"

Then the camera caves in on itself. She is there—upside down—prying it free from the ceiling. Then she is gone and the crushed lens hits the floor, all smoldering circuits.

"What… are you?"

"Answers!" Her voice envelopes him. He spins, catching glimpses of sun-threaded flesh and veins made of auroras. Two eyes smoldering gold. "Zade Holloway. Iliana Kennedy. Raymond Flay. That man executed tonight. You signed their death certificates. What did you do with them after they died? Why were they paid millions?"

"Oh Christ, they'll kill me." Walker breaks for the door once again. The champagne puddle stops him. With a squeak, his feet slide out, and he smacks the corner, desperate and shaking.

"What did you do?"

"What the client requested," he mewls. "What was instructed. They… the subjects have to agree, you see? The mind resists. It's a subconscious defense… Oh Jesus, I'm dead, I'm dead—"

"What did they agree to?"

Pounding on the door and voices beyond coming in to save him. *Hurry! Please help!*

The woman-thing returns, hands on his ankles, and now—somehow—he is hoisted up to the ceiling, upside down.

It's a curious thing, this twist in perspective. Gravity doesn't apply to her.

But it does to him.

Twelve feet and he is pressed against the ceiling tiles, his limbs dangling. She's eye to eye with him. Blue eyes. Green eyes. Flickering static spreading in every direction.

There is a place beyond terror, a place of base fear where the body takes control to maximize survival. Dennis Walker had long thought it a place of subservience. A place his fetishes could probe on his terms alone.

Now, upside down, held by a hand that should not be able to keep him pinned to the ceiling, he realizes humans are made of such delicate parts. True fear is a void. And from that dimming well of his consciousness he can only watch.

"WHAT DID THEY AGREE TO?"

"They sold their bodies after the execution. They signed themselves over for medical use."

"And what use is that?"

"They never said and I never asked. But the subjects couldn't be brain dead. That was the clause. They had to be conscious and they had to agree. We had less than an hour to smuggle them out. So we put them under, stopped their heart and revived them. I signed the forms… Oh God, please don't—"

"Where did they go?"

"I just called the number… They coordinated the rest."

"Show me!"

"I… I can't—"

The drop is sudden. His stomach has only a half second to leap against his screaming lungs as the floor races toward him and…

And now he is yanked back up, pressed into the ceiling once more.

"Show me," she repeats. He can see her. God help him, he can see her when he looks down. A sunburnt specter, hair billowing, youthful arm glistening with impossible colors. *How is she hovering six feet off the ground?* "Show me the number or you fall all the way."

"Phone… pocket…"

The phone whips out of his pocket and is turned to his face. The sensor unlocks. He fumbles with the floating screen, swiping, opening folders with shaking fingers.

"They took delivery at different airports but I never saw anyone—" Another tumble and his teeth chatter as she catches him, hoists him up. "Okay! Okay! Here's the number. It all went through that switchboard. Take it!"

The descent blasts his stomach into the back of his throat. The floor rushes him. He closes his eyes, crying out.

A loud, wet crack. And that's it, he thinks. Lights out. The end.

Until hands fall upon him—not luminous but human, faces he knows. The bouncer George, the strippers. He wants to tell them to run, to get far, far away. But his words only come out in sputtering cries.

THE CANDLELIGHT INN

WHITLEY COUNTY, KENTUCKY

THE ACRID SMELL OF BURNING ELECTRONICS IS UNLIKE ANY OTHER. A warm whiff of melting plastic and an undercurrent of ozone and dust. It is this scent that pulls Michaels from his dreams.

In one world he is back in Clearwater, looking down from the control room at an audience of dead scientists and test subjects. With mute lips, he begs their forgiveness.

In another, he is tasting smoke and waking to a motel room with yellowed walls and dim corners. And a shut bathroom door where lights flicker beyond.

"Caitlyn?"

No answer from the bed space beside him. He reaches out. No body either.

Please no, he thinks, feet carrying him across the crusty rug to the bathroom door. "Caitlyn? Are you okay?"

No answer.

He steps back and studies the door. Old, probably hollow, so he won't want to hit center mass. He takes a deep breath.

Then he kicks in the door.

In the corner, past the toilet, Caitlyn tugs out her noise-cancelling earbuds. "What the hell?"

Michaels studies the setup: her phone on the floor, the strip club's address mapped out, her legs in a lazy half lotus.

And her eyes, two wet orbs, the whites blooming to plum as rusty tears streak her face. "No, Cait, please tell me you didn't."

She swallows. "Atlanta's six hundred miles away. I saved us some time."

He wipes the blood from her cheeks. "Yeah, you did." He kisses her warm forehead. "But you just blew our cover."

Outside, the crickets sing while a distant freight train rumbles down rusty tracks. Michaels loads the bags into the trunk and leaves the room key in the drop box. To her eyes, he looks pinned between exhaustion and frustration.

"I don't understand," Caitlyn says, limping into the passenger side. "I did us a favor. How was that blowing our cover?"

Michaels starts the ignition, then pauses to collect his thoughts. Five minutes ago, he'd been hoping what he'd seen in the bathroom was still a dream. Now, the cool Kentucky night stretches out around them, infinite shadows and infinite fears.

"Michaels? Dammit, I'm not getting in until you tell me why."

He sighs. "You said you went after Walker, right? How'd you find him?"

Caitlyn studies him. "I told you. I blinked and I asked him some questions. He gave me the number he contacts to transport the dead. Which aren't dead, by the way. How messed up is that?"

"Right. And you did great, thank you. But how did you find him? Take me through it, step by step."

"I… looked up the strip club. I went to the site. I got photos from Google Maps. I—"

"Did you use any sort of VPN? Did you cover your tracks, incognito mode, anything?"

Caitlyn hesitates. "No."

"Did you kill him?"

"Of course not."

"But you interrogated him?"

"I asked him pointed questions."

"A man working for an organization that erases itself from all records. Who do you think he's calling right now?"

He watches it play out on her face, the very chain of awareness. "Shit. I left breadcrumbs, didn't I?"

"When they find out—which they will at any moment—they'll retrace every incoming web query for that strip club. Every visitor to that site. Every Google and image search and street view and Yelp review. How many sources did you use to build your blind site?"

Her shoulders slump as the sigh leaves her mouth. "All of the above."

"Which means it's a matter of minutes until they link your IP address to the cell towers in this area. Instead of our biometrics popping up in Florence and Frankfurt, they'll know we're in rural Kentucky."

"How do you know this?"

"Because it's what I would do. Foundation playbook: cast a net around the surrounding five counties and work my way in."

She nods. "We need to get out of here, now."

"We needed to get out of here five minutes ago. Will you please get in the car?"

[40]

It happens like Michaels predicted.

Mostly.

At 2:14 a.m., a phone call hits a local Atlanta cell tower and is passed off to a mobile telephone switching office. The MTSO assigns a rarely used frequency, pairing the connection via the public switched telephone network, which in turn passes the call off to a network of dark wire and satellite relays. The call—now classified Beyond Top Secret—connects to a phone in a cubicle farm at the edge of the Black Mountains.

Field Agent Trainee Diego Mendoza, starting his shift in operations support, recognizes the code paired with the incoming number. This is past his credentials. Even if he wanted to answer, his clearance prevents him. Last year, a penetration tester bypassed Kray Mesa's security by convincing a fresh operator to connect them directly with the chief coordinator.

Which is where this call is now headed.

Fingers shaking, Diego presses the button and logs the location. The caller is coming from a cell tower in Atlanta. The chief coordinator's location is redacted, always.

A flash of Abuelito Mendoza's advice. "Beware of old men in a profession where most people die young."

And though he knows the chief coordinator is not old, he also knows time flows different in the Foundation. An hour can feel like a year, and a year can pass like an hour.

Which is why when his terminal lights up five minutes later, each second grows heavy. A direct call. The name onscreen: *CHIEF COORDINATOR NOX.*

"Uh, yes, sir," the trainee says, his voice cracking as he reaches for a pen. "How can I help you?"

"We have a situation."

WHAT NEITHER MICHAELS nor Nox anticipates is the chain of events unfolding sixty miles off the coast of Alaska. In a dark room, Morgan Anders is rewinding the last scans from Clearwater before the cascade ruined the readings. He's studying the delta brainwaves from Subject 13, Caitlyn Grey. He likes what he sees.

Dr. Freeman's imaging translation software gives her brain scans vague shape. Anders can see trace objects: waves and clouds, swirling waters and vibrant light. Perhaps even a boat. Just a glimpse, enough for his eye to recognize before it's subsumed by vibrant static and mad fractals.

But software can only go so far. Anders needs more. More data to cross-reference, more input. Chase had done more than just oversee Clearwater. He'd worked with the subjects one on one. Christ, he'd even taught them how to think.

How to visualize the world all at once.

How to anchor their bodies.

And how to balance their minds.

If only Chase hadn't been so stubborn. If only he'd shared his techniques, they might have it now, stable decoherence, a way to keep the mind from devouring itself.

They'll need more than old brain scans, he realizes. They'll need a record of her thoughts.

Good luck getting that.

Anders is not religious, not really. Still, he believes in the occasional miracle. More than that, he believes in ample preparation.

Which is why he likes the words before him, now blinking onscreen. An alert from his contact deep within Kray Mesa.

>*SEARCH TARGET LOCATED.*

>*FIELD AGENTS REROUTED.*

>*MORE INFO FORTHCOMING.*

Anders logs off and takes his tablet with him. He considers assembling his team. It's not a work night, of course, and he last saw Janet drinking beers with Suresh from engineering. No, let them have their fun.

Tonight, he'll have some of his own.

[41]

DR. TANYA LOPEZ'S CONDO
CHICAGO, IL

BRAD HAS TO ADMIT, IT'S SOMETIMES SCARY TO WATCH HER AT WORK. For the past fifteen minutes, Olivia has broken through every one of this researcher's lies.

The researcher said she was at home between the hours of 5:00 and 6:30. Her university key card said otherwise.

The researcher claimed she was watching Netflix at 6:00. The logs on the DNA databases said her user ID was downloading records.

She insisted it was a mistake; no one was in her office. The lab's laser printer contained her workstation's previous commands, five different printouts sent from her PC.

Now, as the feisty researcher crosses her arms and hardens her glare, Brad finds he is holding his breath. Olivia rarely smiles without purpose. Yet here it is, the corner of her lips rising, a slight tilt to her head.

"Dr. Lopez, if you're about to say you were alone tonight, please stop. The building's camera recorded three visitors, all to your floor. Besides, we both know the elevator requires an access code after hours."

Lopez doesn't return the smile. Her eyes drift past Olivia, past Brad and the living room they've spent the past thirty minutes in.

Her gaze falls on the window with its view down West Washington. Something hardens in them.

"Well, you already know the answers then," she says. "So what's the point of this conversation?"

"With respect, Dr. Lopez, there's always more to be learned. After you matched the DNA to those profiles, Dr. Munson and his guests must have indicated a direction they were headed. Further questions. A destination, perhaps?"

Lopez sucks in a little air. It's almost like this impending betrayal hurts her, Brad thinks. But it's really a lifeline. The Foundation has infinite ways to apply pressure, from the overt to the insidious. He can see Olivia working her way to it, Lopez's defenses falling one at a time.

"I never should have answered the call."

Olivia scoots closer. A tilt of her head, an empathetic nod. "But you did, Dr. Lopez. You used a private database to pass on medical information to unauthorized individuals, two of whom are currently persons of interest in an ongoing multinational investigation. If this breach puts American lives at risk, well, I hate to imagine the blowback. Your crime lab receives federal funding, correct?"

He can see it on Lopez's face, the taste of that favor fast turning sour. He wants to throw her some hope, but he's learned how important silence is at a moment like this.

Then his phone rings.

Johnny Rivers's banger from '66, "Secret Agent Man," fills the condo with its playful guitar licks and chorus.

Brad can't silence his phone fast enough. Excusing himself, he hurries out into the hall, Olivia's glare burning holes in the back of his neck. What moves him is not the shame. It is that only one number has that ringtone: a call from Kray Mesa.

He answers, providing his badge ID and following the new onscreen passcode. While the connection encrypts, he finds a quiet spot by the vending machines and squeezes his toes.

Then, the voice he dreads.

"Agent Lee," Nox says. "I take it your other half is still working that researcher?"

"Uh, yes, sir. Coordinator, sir. She should be done any moment."

"I don't doubt it. It's good to work close with those we care about, isn't it?"

"Yes, sir."

When Nox had briefed them on their new assignment, Brad had felt a pang of confusion. Why him? But the more Nox talked, the more it made sense. Michaels's psyche profile suggested he viewed Brad as a mentee.

And that relationship could be exploited.

Still, it all feels a little grotesque.

"We've had another sighting," Nox says. "As you've discovered, Michaels has a way of getting under one's skin and wriggling around. It's what made him so effective when he played for the good guys."

"Yes, sir. Of course, sir." Brad doesn't like the way Nox used the past tense.

"And our mutual acquaintance has put us in a predicament. They're in possession of information—Foundation intellectual property—that could cause a certain amount of stickiness should it get out."

Interesting. Olivia and Brad hadn't updated the case file with what they just learned. Still, Nox somehow knew. Lopez's smart fridge, her smart speakers, even their agency-issued phones, all potential ways for the Foundation to listen.

"You're talking about the DNA they searched?"

"I'm talking about the misconceptions its release could lead to. We are a nation at a crossroads, Agent Lee. Cracks are forming and enemies gather in the shadows. It's the Foundation's silent mandate to maintain the stability of civil society. I presume our ideologies are aligned?"

"They are, sir, absolutely."

"Because of your history, Michaels trusts you. This affords you a unique chance to demonstrate your commitment to this organization. A chance to erase any blemishes and secure your future."

A hesitation. Brad finds his smile fading.

"Sir, what are you asking?"

It's just as Nox told him. The courier is waiting in a dark town car at the corner of Clark and Washington, hazards on, rear window open.

Brad reaches for the rear handle, then hesitates. The key phrase practically jumps from his lips. "Where are you going? Where have you been?"

The courier turns to regard him, dead eyes over lips like dried twigs and a chin scarred and sharp. Yet his voice is soft, almost mournful and poetic. "It's all over now, Baby Blue."

That's the response. They both nod. With a click, the rear door opens.

Inside, Brad finds the briefcase, another thing Nox had affirmed would be waiting. With two clicks, he opens it, revealing padding and cutouts, the contents instantly knotting in his stomach.

The courier adjusts the rearview mirror, eyeing Brad. "You know how to use those?"

"Some of it, yeah." Brad studies the gun, a Glock 34 with detached suppressor and a full magazine, shrink-wrapped with a tear-away tab. "What's with the plastic?"

"To preserve the fingerprints on the shell casings. It all traces back to a supporter of Sam Stephens, someone who's espoused anti-government sentiments. If you use it, drop it on scene."

There are other objects in the case. A knife and a tracking kit, a small clump of white putty labeled *DANGER! KEEP AWAY FROM FLAME.* He lets his fingers touch each object as if trying to anchor them into reality. Brad Lee, who has long suffered from a deep fear that he wasn't Foundation material, now finds a part of himself wishing his fears were correct.

"I'm told your target trusts you," the courier says. "So, a bit of advice from one button man to another. Get as close as you can and say little. The more you talk, the more you give away."

Brad nods. When did his mouth get so chalky?

The courier continues, "And if I were in your shoes, I'd go with one of the vials on the left."

Brad pries one free from the foam. The length of a cigar tube, it holds a stack of vials inside. Amber liquid clings to the glass.

"Is it uncomfortable or… What I mean is, will it hurt?"

The silence hangs heavy as the courier studies Brad. Then, "Someone always gets hurt."

[42]

WHITLEY COUNTY, KENTUCKY

THE RUMBLE STARTS BETWEEN THE ROAD AND THE TIRES AND ENDS IN his fingers. Michaels turns the steering wheel, guiding the car back onto the road. A deep yawn and a blink clears the dryness from his eyes. He glances at Caitlyn, still asleep in the passenger seat. Good.

With the Foundation probably pinging their last location, he's steering clear of the interstate. Good news: there's no shortage of rural roads here in the south. Bad news: they're as twisted as this investigation. And the summer bugs… He pities the poor kid who gets to clean this rental car.

Fishing out a Red Bull, Michaels rewinds the facts and lays them out in his mind.

First, the DNA, which tells him that Chase built something bigger than Clearwater. Something new. Something he tried to undo. That he's dead means he didn't finish.

Then, the GPS coordinates etched onto the aerogel. They point to a house south of San Francisco with no obvious connection. If Michaels had an asset out west, he'd call them, but he's already burned too many bridges.

And then Dr. Walker and the information Caitlyn squeezed out. Was the Foundation really pulling new subjects from death row? Sickening, and yet what better way to attain total compliance? Project Clearwater's undoing hadn't been the subjects' results. The ultimate liability was that one day the subjects had to leave the program, their minds weaponized and filled with the government's secrets.

Unless they were all legally dead.

Caitlyn mumbles, her eyes darting about beneath her lids. Sometimes, Michaels wishes he could step inside her mind, witness all that she has seen. From the cold crown of the world to the deepest lush forests and the endless blue seas.

And yet, it might break him, he thinks. This weight of all that she carries.

He yawns, clicks his jaw, and gives his sugar-free Red Bull a final chug. They pass a dark sign: four hundred miles to Atlanta. To intercept Walker. To track down a dead body that might still be breathing.

On the one hand, he doesn't care about Zade Holloway, Iliana Kennedy, Raymond Flay, and the others. He doesn't care about the newly departed, Georgia's own Aiden Sawyer. These are bad people, guilty of terrible crimes and judged by the courts.

And yet…

Michaels lets his left hand flap freely, tapping out primes on the wheel.

A year ago he might have been more certain about justice, more full of conviction. But Clearwater humbled him. Teddy Jensen—the God's Breath Killer—proved that justice wasn't always a straight line. That without closure, the past festers and rots and reaches into the present.

It also taught him the cost of ambition. How close the investigation came to repeating Dr. Chase's mistakes. Thinking such technology could be controlled.

Michaels shivers and turns on the heater. A curious taste clings to his tongue. The chill persists, ice sliding down his spine as the air takes on a charge.

A glance at Caitlyn, her eyes tight and a sheen of sweat on her skin. Her breathing is shallow and fast, a runner at marathon's end.

Slowly, he reaches up and adjusts the rearview mirror. Darkness behind him. The empty back seat. Two distant orbs flickering a mile back. Headlights perhaps.

At least that's what he tells himself when they don't reappear.

He turns on the dome light, amber filling the rear seat. Just their duffel bags, fast food wrappers and cans stuffed in a plastic bag. It must be the stress.

Caitlyn's eyes snap open and focus on him. Rusty tears leak down her cheeks as three words leave her lips in a whisper. "They found us."

It unfolds from the dark road before them, a thin man swaddled in fog. Two eyes like headlights, his face a concavity of jittering static.

But it's the mouth that spikes Michaels's adrenaline. A sickly Cheshire grin, jagged teeth and wormy lips, spreading from nothing.

He knows that grin. He saw it earlier, on the dossier of a man who died five months ago.

Harold Owens, age forty-two when the lethal injection supposedly hit his veins, smirks back from the middle of the dark road, from across time and memory. His fractured form races to meet the speeding hood of the car in a blink.

Michaels slams the brakes. Reaches his right hand to brace Caitlyn and swerves with his left. Too late. The front-wheel-drive sedan handles like a wet sled, fishtailing and spraying gravel. A bounce rattles his teeth. Then the headlights fall on the impossible form, that gaunt man, veins pulsing liquid silver.

The impact buckles the hood. The passenger mirror shatters. Then a *whoosh* and a chilling wind streams through the interior, a storm made for two. In a popping of glass and rattling stones, the hood rises, dips, rises.

Stars, Michaels thinks as the headlights go out and the summer sky expands before them. *Like stars on the boat and the pitch of the sea.*

IIe spins the wheel left, right, left, but it's too late. The tires leave the road. Then the hood drops, the dry grass and dirt rushes in, and all becomes a maddening fracture.

[43]

Five hundred years ago, Dirk Willems escaped his imprisonment by climbing down a tower on a rope of knotted rags. Skinny and weak from prison, he passed safely over the moat's thin winter ice.

The guard chasing him did not.

Turning back to save his drowning pursuer, Willems was recaptured, tortured, and burned at the stake. His death birthed a legend, a martyrdom, a symbol for the pious and kind centuries later.

Now, it is this vine-scratched statue of Willems that has the eye of Rodney Lawson, Big Rod to his friends in town. But Rodney isn't in town now; his friends are country miles away. Just him and old Dirk's statue, that sand-blasted gaze and decades of cracks giving the metal its dim luster. Rodney wipes the statue's face with a rag.

Then comes a flash in the night, cool brightness off Dirk's noble zinc features. Rodney turns and lets the polishing cloth rest on the ladder. He climbs down and walks out of his studio, the old, corrugated metal doors open wide for the midnight breeze.

A summer storm sweeping the hills, coming fast. He tells himself that's what it must be.

But why can he see stars bright above his metal workshop? And the moon, still low on the horizon? No, that's not lightning at all.

Another flash. With a click, the power goes out, leaving the hills in veiled stillness.

It takes Rodney five tries to start his old pickup. The check engine light and battery warnings blink. Not good, but not unexpected for this rust bucket. He lets out a whistle and Henrietta hops up in the bed, her tail smacking the metal, *thumpity thump*.

To preserve his night vision, he drives with the headlights off. To preserve his peace of mind, he keeps a hunting rifle across his lap. He knows these old roads. Not much here besides fallow hills, tornado sirens, and plenty of copper wire to be stolen.

On the horizon, a high-tension power line flashes, then darkens. Sparks drool from the conductors. No, not a thunderstorm, he realizes, more like a malfunction. Hell, it'll be days before the power company sends a truck.

So why does it feel like he's no longer alone?

Taking it slow over the hill, Rodney scans the shadows. His vision ain't what it was, but little of him is. Sixty's in the rearview and he'd be okay not to see seventy. The sooner he gets to take the big sleep, the sooner he gets to see his wife once again. Or maybe not. Either way is better'n waiting.

But Jolene needs feeding and care, and most days that wagging tail and his hobbies help him past these grim thoughts.

As he rounds the bend, another lights up the high-tension towers. Sparks dot the air like Roman candles. But it's not the falling embers that draw his gaze upward and bristle his spine.

It's the two shapes he just saw within them, a thin man and a woman. Two strobe-lit forms twisting and turning, all high off the ground.

"What'n the devil?"

Craning his neck, Rodney searches for another glimpse of the impossible. Just dim stars above now. Just those wobbling power lines cutting through the night sky.

And still that instinctual sense, that here in the middle of nowhere, Big Rod and his rust bucket are no longer alone.

He turns on the headlights just in time to see the wrecked car on its side, past the edge of the road. Next comes two shapes limping toward him, one of them weaving and waving. A young woman hobbles one step at a time. Her left arm's wrapped around a fellow, his head slumped, limbs loose and wobbly.

"Hold on, girl."

Rodney stomps the brakes, bringing the truck to a sliding stop on the loose dirt. In the bed, Jolene's paws scrape for traction.

Another bright pulse in the sky, farther away. A mile down the road, sparks fall from the power lines. Whatever that is, it's moving off fast.

So why does it feel like the storm's still overhead?

Because it's coming from the crashed car, Rodney thinks. *No, it's coming from her.*

A silly thought, he tells himself. *Just help these poor strangers.*

Fast as a bullet, Jolene is out of the pickup cab, her shaggy coat catching the moonlight. Rodney follows, cursing himself for leaving the rifle. If these two mean trouble, well, this old leatherneck will just have to think fast.

Ten feet and they're close enough to smell. Close enough to see. The man's slumped head, a gash above his left temple leaking blood. And the woman—dear God'n heaven—she's bleeding from her eyes.

"You've been in an accident, ma'am," Rodney says. "Here, let me help you."

His days of hunting and dragging dead bucks across miles are behind him. Still, his body finds familiar leverage and strength. With a grunt, he has the man's arm around his own neck, his shoulder supporting the weight.

"That's a pretty bad lump you got on your head, pal," Rodney says. "We'll need to get you to town, call Doc Crawford and wake him up—"

"No," the man slurs, head lolling to one side. "No doc... crawdad."

Then he drifts off, feet growing clumsy. The young woman hoists him from the other side. And damn, Rodney wouldn't have guessed from her thin frame, but she's pretty strong.

"No doctor? I'm not sure that's the best move, fella. Look, you're both in shock and—"

"Sir, what's your name?" the woman asks. And it's the oddest thing, like hearing her words a bit closer than they should be. Like they're coming from all around.

"Rodney, or just Big Rod."

"Big Rod," she repeats. "Can you take us somewhere to lay low? We can pay you. We have money."

"Lay low, huh?"

Rodney lets the question linger as they hobble to the pickup. Strangers offering money and refusing medical attention, not a good sign. And yet, there's something about them that piques his interest. Maybe it's the woman, her colorful arms and her accent. Maybe it's the man, his slurred words about foundations and trackers. Or maybe it's Jolene, how she circles them, her shaggy tail wagging, always the best judge of character.

Rodney lowers the tailgate. Light from the cab gives the wounded man a pasty glow, his eyes fluttering. It's a head wound, as Rodney can see, but far from life-threatening. Bad news: it'll need a few stitches. Good news: this old Boy Scout is always prepared.

He tells the woman to grab the first-aid kid beneath the passenger seat. Jolene follows, eager and excited. A curious thing as the woman makes her way around: her hand follows the edge of the truck.

Like she's feeling her way back.

"Mr. Big Rod," she says. "I don't mean to be ungrateful, but we should get going. I can dress his wound if you drive."

Her wet gaze drifts to the direction of the accident. To something beyond. Rodney can't shake the feeling that there's more to all this. The car crash. The flashes in the dark sky. And this woman with blood in her eyes.

So many questions, and yet each passing second thickens his dread. It's as if this dark stretch of road is—impossibly—becoming more crowded.

He says, "Yeah. Okay, I know a place."

Inside, Jolene rides shotgun, the old road sputtering up gravel, faster and faster. *What've you gotten yourself mixed up in, Big Rod?* No time to back out so he keeps driving forward. In the bed of the pickup, the woman holds tight to her friend.

A hill and a dip, and Rodney shivers, that same odd storm passing over him now, moving through the pickup. A flicker of the headlights, the dashboard, and some buzzing on the radio. Jolene lets out a howl and turns her eyes to the rear, tail curling between her legs.

"What is it, girl?"

At some level, Rodney knows the answer. The same nocturnal terrors that stalk children's closets. That same unnamable fear scraping at the edge of demented old minds. Something *was* coming; he had felt it earlier.

And now it's arrived.

A gaunt figure unfolds from the darkness behind them, visible only out the side of his eyes. Arms of crackling branches and fingers ending in hooked bone.

And a woman, skin glistening in sunset hues, her very edges woven by stars.

A woman who is also in the bed of his truck.

A concussive flash and they're gone, leaving the air charged and the windows fast fogging. Rodney reaches for Jolene, his hand falling on her shaggy fur. He thinks of Dirk Willems turning back to help his pursuer. He thinks, *To hell with that mess.* Whatever's behind them, it loosens Rodney's gut and tightens his bowels. A great and terrible storm he knows nothing about. Old Dirk can be the martyr. Big Rod just wants to see breakfast.

So he pushes his foot down on the accelerator, the needle

jumping, the old road rattling beneath them, and the storm crack-ling behind, angrier and colder and closer with each frantic breath.

[44]

DAY'S BANE, ALASKA

It's been a long dry spell, but now that it's over, Janet finds herself humming as she blowdries her hair. The date went as well as expected on an oil rig: a romantic stroll around the top deck, a little weed at sunset and a few beers while giggling at old movies, a highly aggressive romp in the sack.

Sore and happy, she steals a glance at Suresh, sleeping it off in her bed. His dark skin tangled with the sheets, a pleasant sight. Turns out their bodies speak the same language.

Then the lights flicker in an on-off, on-off pattern that narrows her eyes. A moment later, her tablet chirps: *MINOR CASCADE DETECTED!*

She does not wait for the circuit breakers to reset. She doesn't wait to towel-dry her hair. Tightening her robe and near-naked, she sprints the whole way: from deck three to Deck four, then down the secure stairs, blowing through the checkpoint and screaming at the guard, "Open it! Open it now, you idiot!"

She slides into the control room in time to see her worst fear before her. In the sterile lab, subject K29—Harold Owens—his torso twitching and spasming about in the suspension harness. His amputated legs, two knuckles running on nothing. His chest, rising and falling, rising and falling. His one remaining arm swings, a pinwheel of pain.

"God-fucking-dammit, Anders! Are you trying to kill us?"

Behind the central console, Anders and Bethany both frantically tap screens and turn dials. In the corner, Yuri is actually flipping breakers.

"It's not Anders, Janet. It's something else," Bethany says. "We can't pull the subject out."

"Because it's a hot connection, you fumbling monkey. Am I the only one who listened to Dr. Chase? Move over."

A grim look passes between the others. They wait for Anders to give the okay. He nods and Bethany clears space at the console.

Studying the wall of screens, Janet swipes and double-taps. Circulatory systems. Endocrine. Muscular and nervous. Half the boxes are flashing yellow or orange.

"Let me guess: you sent subject K29 into the field to handle your little problem and within minutes he was dancing this jig?"

Yuri hesitates. "Um…"

"Never mind what we were doing," Anders says.

"Oh grow up," Janet says. "You sent one decoherent to track down another without isolating the medical grid. That's like flushing your toilet with a firehose. Where do you think all that excess energy goes?"

"Can you fix this? Yes or no."

"Can you fix this?" Janet laughs, her fingers sliding across touchscreens and ticking off boxes. "Limitless funding and it's always fuck-around Friday. Can You Fix This should be my job title. And to answer that… I don't know. Probably not. But I can keep it from spreading. Yuri, put your PPE on, quick."

Yuri blinks. "What? Why?"

She points to the glass wall dividing the control room from the sterile lab. "Because you're going in. We need to disconnect the subject from the primary battery array."

Another flicker. This time it's not just the lights. It's the monitors. The centrifuges. The very machines keeping the subjects alive.

Janet grabs a Tyvek suit from the closet and shoves it into Yuri's arms. "We're going to lose this entire facility if we don't isolate the subject. Now suit up."

Anders gives him a nod: *Do it*.

Back at the console, Janet swipes, closing out boxes and redirecting power. In the sterile room beyond, four bodies hang in twilight suspension. Then, a series of clicks. Three subjects recede into their storage pods, like dry cleaning into a locker.

But not subject K29.

Anders asks, "What are you doing?"

"Saving your ass and the other subjects. Yuri, get in there, now!"

Zipping the last of the PPE and donning the connective oxygen line, Yuri waits in the anteroom until the door closes. Like hospital isolation rooms, the sterile lab is kept at negative pressure.

Which is why the fast-fogging windows have Janet's attention. "Wipe that off."

Yuri grabs a paper towel, wipes down the window. Just as fast as it's gone, more moisture appears.

"I… I don't get it," Bethany says. "Where's it coming from?"

"From each other," Janet says, swiping and typing. "Put a microphone and a speaker together and you get an infinitely amplifying loop. Do that with decoherents—who amplify through a dimension we know fuck all about—and you get this: a mental cascade."

"Okay, I'm inside," Yuri says over the comms.

The anteroom doors silently part. Like a child at the edge of a high dive, Yuri hesitates before the sterile lab.

There, in the suspension harness, subject K29 twists and turns. His medical restraints are soaked through. His pale skin glistens. A length of tubing hits the floor, orange fluids dribbling.

This is some sort of hell.

Janet's voice crackles over the speakers. "Okay, Yuri, on the subject's med-bay rack you'll see a plastic box beneath the fuses. Lowest tier, by your knees. Inside, there's two red switches. You find them?"

Yuri kneels at the stacked devices keeping the subject sedated and breathing. The ECMO, the ECG, the ICP monitor, and more. So many buttons and readouts. Then his gloved hands find the plastic box and flip it open.

"Good," Janet says. "Turn the two red switches to the terminate position. You'll have to do the left one first."

Anders hesitates. "Janet, is this the best course of action?"

"It's the only course of action."

Another spasm from the subject. Yuri leans right as an errant arm swings past, spattering his PPE with sweat. The windows grow hazier, hazier.

A sharp sucking of air from beside her. "Janet, I'm not—"

Janet wheels on Anders. "It's simple physics. That subject you sent into the field has the capacity of a nine-volt battery. Now he's funneling lightning. Look at his brain scans. Look!"

She taps her screen where purples and violets arc across every region of the subject's mind. New neural pathways forming, connecting, degrading, and erasing. A mental cataclysm.

"He's lobotomizing himself. Do you want it to spread?"

"Okay," Anders says. "Do it, Yuri."

In the sterile lab, Yuri flips the first switch. A silent click and then a warning flashes onscreen: *TERMINATE LIFE FUNCTIONS?* Yuri's helmet rises to take in the screen. "I… I don't think I can."

"Christ," Anders says. "You amputated his limbs but this is where you draw the line? Do it. That's an order."

Hands shaking, fingers twitching, sweat dripping down his face and burning his eyes, Yuri studies the subject convulsing in the suspension harness. His head moves so fast it's little more than a blur. And the sweat, Yuri can taste it through the Tyvek and charcoal respirator, a sour reek redolent of necrosis.

So Yuri says a little prayer and flips the second switch.

"Life functions terminating," says a neutral voice over the comms.

Behind their individual metal and glass containers, bathed in soothing blue lights, three test subjects hang in suspension, peaceful and silent.

But not out here.

Subject K29 writhes, shoulders stretching forward, back, forward. His hand—his only hand—shoots out, fingers clenching and grasping at Yuri's elbow.

With a cry, Yuri yanks his Tyvek suit free from the grip, stumbles, and goes spilling backward. A medical cart comes with him, sending vials clattering.

"Life functions terminated."

Like a nervous child checking a missing tooth, subject K29 raises his hand, fingers probing the goggles that cover his face. Then, with a sharp tug and a wet suck, off it comes. The goggles and respirator, the intubation and sensors, they all fall, peeling sterile dressing and opening sutures to reveal a visage of ruin.

With his final breath, subject K29's gray lips form a twisted sneer. A rattling warble leaves his dry throat, washing over Yuri, boring into his thoughts and chasing him to the door, where he pounds on the glass and shouts, "Let me out! Let me out! Let me out!"

ANDERS LEANS over the sink and splashes water on his face. Thirty minutes after they wheeled subject K29 to the morgue, he still tastes the reek. All the soap in the facility won't scrub it off.

A knock at the bathroom door. Janet pokes her head in. "You want to talk about it?" Behind her, the lights offer warm, steady light.

"If I wanted to talk, I would have found any one of you." He presses the hand dryer, lets the jet warm his fingers. "I know what went wrong. It won't happen again."

"It can't."

"Well, it won't."

"Anders, we don't have enough subjects for you to cowboy around."

"I wasn't…" It takes every ounce of his self-control to stop it. *Focus. Don't let a short-term loss cost the long game. There's more at stake here than anyone knows.* "They're already procuring another."

"And after that?"

"I don't know!" He finds his voice rising to a scream. So sudden it even startles him.

But not Janet. "God, you're petulant."

Anders sighs. "You're right. I was being foolish. Maybe we'll learn something from the autopsy."

Janet nods, but she's not buying it. And in that glance, he can see bumpy roads ahead. Without her support, he'll lose Yuri. Perhaps Bethany too.

And then he'll lose control of it all.

Another tap on the door, another head peeking in. Jason Freeman with a smirk and a phone in his hand.

"There you are." Freeman raises the phone to his ear. "Yes, sir, I've found him. I'll transfer the call now."

He lowers the phone and taps a few buttons. His smirk teeters on the edge of a grin.

"Anders, you should take this one in your office," he says. "The chief coordinator's waiting on the line."

Hands trembling, Anders lowers the secure phone and lets it rest in the cradle. He runs his palms over the steel desk. For ten months this was Dr. Chase's seat of power.

And Anders's for less than two weeks.

A fucking suspension.

He feels it now, the white-hot fury. His hands act on their own. In a violent swipe, he clears the desk, sends folders and papers fluttering. Sends the keyboard bouncing. That phone now—where Nox had ordered him to take a month's leave—he hoists it up and brings it down on the steel desk again and again.

It's not fair. He survived Clearwater. He should be thriving out here. They have everything they need: near-limitless funding and a staff worthy of the task. Every scrap of salvaged data from the Clearwater collapse. They have Teddy Jensen's body, his nerves, his very brain. And Caitlyn Grey's impossible scans.

How did those two find more strength and stability than this facility can produce?

Because they don't have the right data.

Because they don't have her.

And because Chase set him up for failure.

Anders flings a tablet across the room as the old man's words echo about. "A poor craftsman blames his tools."

He grabs the heavy filing cabinet and tilts it over. He takes Chase's potted plant and smashes it against the wall.

That old bastard was right, Anders realizes and sinks to the floor. It's so obvious now. He's not a fraction of the scientist Chase was. All he'd done is take shortcuts, again and again.

Now here, among the wreckage of his dead mentor—all these papers and folders—Anders realizes he's seeing things with clear eyes for the first time.

In a pile of old charts is a bundle of letters, all yellowed with age. The return address is redacted, but the sorting stamp says Iowa. Anders slides a finger into a folder, where a book comes loose.

No, not a book but a notebook, something once fancy and loved.

The binding crackles as Anders opens the cover. The pages come loose at the spine. He studies the handwriting and how it's degraded over the years. Sentences dance before his eyes.

He told me a secret…

The key is to build a house in my mind…

… and anchor it with good memories, the strongest I could find.

Carefully, reverently, Anders turns the pages, a smile crossing his face when he sees the evidence tag and the text written on the first page of the journal.

This Belongs to Theodore Jensen.

[PART 4]

"There are no secrets that time does not reveal."

—Jean Racine

[45]
WHITLEY COUNTY, KENTUCKY
NOON

CAITLYN IS PLEASED TO DISCOVER THAT BIG ROD HAS QUITE THE gentle hand.

After they arrived at his cabin, he phoned Doc Crawford, who walked him through stitching a wound step by step. Big Rod told the doc that he cut himself on one of his tools but couldn't make it into town because he was out at the lake. The second part was true.

After sleeping for hours beside Michaels, Caitlyn wakes to find her fingers probing the blurry shapes around her. An antique headboard of hand-carved walnut, little cherubs looking down. End tables laden with books. A window, where musty curtains frame a view of a cattail-wreathed lake, the noon sun sparkling upon it.

Caitlyn studies the window, taking in the hazy landscape. Among knee-high weeds and uncut grass, two forms stand staring back.

She ducks behind the curtain. Were those people? They were. And yet they had stood as still as—

Leaning against the window frame, Caitlyn cranes her neck around the curtain. Statues, right. Two metal figures, their defini-tion rendered into rusty smudges by her weary eyes.

She checks on Michaels. His head wound is dressed, his left cheek swollen and bruised. She puts her finger beneath his nose to feel that he's breathing. His nostrils expand and contract, a picture of slumbering exhaustion. *Let him rest.*

As she showers, her migraine beats a slinking retreat behind her eyes. This isn't the worst she's felt after tangoing with another mens corpus. But it's in the top three.

"For now," a cold voice whispers behind her.

Caitlyn spins, scouring the steamy bathroom but finds nothing.

Letting her hair air-dry, she follows the scent of bacon through the house. Dim flashes of several hours ago: dawn cresting the hills as the pickup truck followed trails so weed-swallowed they hardly existed, stumbling up to the door as Big Rod unlocked it, the discomforting sensation of being in two places at once.

In the hallway, a wall of framed photos greets her. One shows Big Rod, back when he was Little Rod, just a young Marine in a uniform. Beside it, a photo of a young woman, her hair up in a bun, fierce eyes behind horn-rimmed glasses. A third photo: the young couple together at the state fair, a stuffed bear in her arm.

Caitlyn follows their photographic journey down the hall, down the decades as hair turns from amber to gray, as wrinkles settle in and stretch out. Then the journey ends at a doorframe.

There he is beyond, Big Rod, sitting at the kitchen table, a cup of coffee before him and his nose in a well-worn Preston & Child paperback. At his feet, Jolene thumps her shaggy tail at Caitlyn's approach.

"G'afternoon," he says, voice like the weathered wood of this house. "There's bacon and some Jimmy Deans in the skillet. Scrambled eggs in the casserole pan. They've been sitting, so you'll have to nuke 'em if you like your heart attacks hot. Coffee…" He lifts the percolator and gives it a swirl. "Well, I guess I drank it all up. Here, I'll make a fresh pot."

"That's really not necessary," Caitlyn says.

"Nah, I insist. Need all the good juice I can get after the fireworks last night."

Caitlyn takes a piece of bacon straight from the skillet, chews and savors. Thick-cut, peppered, and with plenty of fat. Next thing she knows she's filling up her plate with a mountain of food, the aromas mouth-watering.

"This is delicious, thank you."

"Good. Go on and eat, please. Nothing makes me happier'n good food and interesting company."

Plate piled high, Caitlyn fills out the seat across from him. She does her best not to wolf it all down but soon finds herself failing. By her calculations, she burned a few thousand calories fighting off that gaunt man.

That man... Who was he? Like with Roger in Boston and Teddy Jensen, she caught flashes of his past when their mens corpuses entangled. A dark basement. An old furnace. Two children cuffed to a pipe. Blackened bones pulled from a furnace and stuffed in an old sack.

Was that Harold Owens, the Fort Gordon strangler?

Caitlyn shakes off the thought while Big Rod pours her coffee. Outside, the long road ends in the overgrown yard where metal statues stand. Big Rod follows her gaze.

"I would apologize about the state of the place. The truth is, it's always messy. My wife'd tolerate it, even take to cleaning from time to time. But it's a large patch of land for one man to handle."

"It's lovely." She chases the breakfast sausage with a sip of dark coffee. "I saw the other statues from the bedroom window."

"Ah, Kit Carson and Galileo. Kit came from the statehouse. Old Galileo, well, he was a restoration deal for a science museum in Houston that went belly up. I've got a soft spot for humanity's history in sculpture. Usually, I fix 'em up or sell 'em for scrap. A few make their way home with me. Used to drive my wife mad, seeing me pull up with some dinged-up Civil War commander or Cherokee chief that was going to be melted. We've all got our eccentricities, I suppose."

Sensing there's still food on the plate, Jolene lays her heavy head in Caitlyn's lap and stares up. Her tail thumps against the table leg.

"You can tell her to shoo if you prefer. Otherwise, she's gonna start demanding the tax."

"The tax?"

Jolene puts a floppy paw on Caitlyn's knee, her eyes two pools of love.

"The scratching tax," Big Rod says. "She may look like a sweetheart but that's part of the act. That dog is a garbage disposal with a stomach attached."

And then Caitlyn feels it, Jolene's paw on her thigh, so soft a moment ago, now flexing and bringing pressure to her claws. Yet she never breaks that affable gaze.

"She wants me to feed her?"

"She's not very subtle, is she? Probably best to oblige if you don't want your knee grooved like a record."

Caitlyn takes a piece of cold bacon and lowers it. Gently, Jolene retracts her paw, grips the bacon between her teeth, and ambles off, practically strutting.

"She always gets her tax." Big Rod takes Caitlyn's empty plate.

While he cleans up at the stove, Caitlyn drinks in the old place. The wallpaper, probably from the mid-seventies. The tiles, even older. There's a refrigerator in the pantry, magnets and curled pictures clinging to the metal. A wall of mason jars filled with beans and rice and preserves, labeled and dated on yellowed masking tape. It's the kind of house that was hipster chic long before that aesthetic made its way into pricey design catalogs and upcycled boutiques.

It looks like what it truly is: a home, dusty and messy and steeped in memories that never wash out.

Could she have such a future? Could Michaels and her? Perhaps…

Or perhaps they already had. That brief time on the *Dionysus,* like Big Rod with his wife. No happily ever after. Just happy for a while until reality caught up.

Closing her eyes, she can see it: her parents' years on the run, their secret, and how she's following their path. How long until the next traced internet query? How long until she puts Michaels in danger again? And how long until something worse happens?

No, she realizes. There will be no future unless the present is buried.

"Big Rod, I can't thank you enough for this," Caitlyn says. "You've been a great host. And I'm so sorry to do this but... I'm afraid I need to ask you for one more favor."

[46]

A FLASH OF THE DARK ROAD. A GAUNT, GRINNING FIGURE. CAITLYN'S eyes going vacant as a chill passes over his skin. Michaels reaches for her as the car rises and falls and the gaunt man blooms in the headlights and—

Now his hands fall on the empty bed space beside him. He blinks, and he is…

Where is he?

An old bedroom, the wallpaper patterned in orange and brown starbursts. The light comes in low and golden through the window. It's late afternoon. A distant voice drifts through the house, someone he knows yet a name he struggles to place.

Fingers probing his temple, he finds the bandage and gauze. A firm press and he feels the wound underneath. He steadies his thoughts and reviews his symptoms: the faint nausea, the hazy vision, the odd splices of the past day. He can see the moments like photos shuffled all wrong: a man with a dog and a rusty old pickup, fleeing the Candlelight Inn, a great burst of light where Caitlyn blinked out of her body and seized a gaunt man by his throat.

"Caitlyn?"

No answer from the bathroom or beyond. Just the sound of a

television and the low hum of amplified voices. Michaels finds his clothes on a chair. Still wobbly, he sits while dressing.

A concussion is a form of trauma when the gelatinous brain slides around the skull's cerebrospinal fluid. Sudden acceleration and deceleration are prime causes. Like when a decoherent makes your front-wheel-drive sedan fishtail on a rural road at seventy miles an hour.

Preventing sleep after a concussion is an outdated practice. For a wounded brain, rest is the best treatment. If his injuries were life-threatening, they would have presented in the first several hours. Judging by the angle and color of light in through the window, Michaels has been out for most of the day.

Which means they missed their chance to catch up with the dead man in Atlanta. Which means Dennis Walker has certainly gone underground.

Damn…

After gulping down water and washing his face, Michaels heads out into the halls, following the sound of the television until it brings him to a sunken living room with a shag carpet and over-stuffed leather couch the color of salmon. There, among a pile of blankets, his hand petting a sleeping dog, is the man from Michaels's fractured memory.

"Ronald?" Michaels asks.

"Rodney," the man says. "But you get credit for being in the right ballpark. How's the noggin?"

"Still working. I have you to thank for that, don't I?"

"Wait until you see my stitch work before you get too thankful. It's been thirty years since I did some sewing."

"Operation Desert Storm? I saw the photo in the hall."

Rodney gives him a nod.

Michaels clears his throat. "You know, I feel like I gave you a hard time about taking me to the doctor. I'm sorry."

The dog rolls over, her pink belly exposed. Rodney gives it a lazy scratch. "You had your opinions and your reasons why and I certainly respect them."

Your reasons, Michaels thinks. *Curious choice of words.*

All he has to work with are fractured memories stitched together more by motion and sound than cause and effect. The air charged by lightning. Cool wind in his hair. A hand squeezing his as a needle and thread drew close to his head.

And Caitlyn's eyes, at times shut and at times open. But that doesn't make sense.

"My partner—Myra," Michaels says. "I don't remember when she woke up."

"Myra," Rodney repeats. He raises the remote and mutes the TV, a Dave Drogan rally streaming live from Columbus, Ohio. "I don't know a Myra. But I do know a Caitlyn. Caitlyn and I had a nice brunch. Caitlyn and I followed that with a long talk. It's not often a fellow meets someone who can be in two places at once."

Michaels tenses. In the dark of this house, he suddenly realizes he knows nothing about this stranger. Or where they actually are. A glimpse out the window of a lake and hills, rural and remote. There was a rifle in Rodney's truck, wasn't there?

Rodney chuckles. "That came off more ominous than I intended. My apologies. What I meant was that her secret's safe with me. Yours too. Whatever y'all are wrapped up in—and Caitlyn gave me the CliffsNotes version—I ain't calling in the black choppers, so rest easy."

Michaels nods, still unable to shake the tension from his spine. People who say they can be trusted often can't. Yet if Caitlyn had told Rodney a fraction of the truth, and if he was going to turn them in, he would have done that hours ago, while Michaels was still sleeping.

The ominous feeling returns, crystalizing into fear. "Rodney, where is Caitlyn?"

Rodney sighs. "Yeah, like I said, we had a long talk and she asked me for a favor. She said you weren't going to like what I'm about to show you. In fact, she made me promise to wait until six. But seeing as it's ten till, I s'pose I can make an exception."

Rodney gropes around the old couch, probing the pillows and

blankets. Jolene rolls over, hops down off the cushion, and gives Michaels a sniff and a lick. There it is, an old phone almost a decade outdated. But it still works well enough to capture video and play it back.

"Yep, here you go," Rodney says. "I'll give you some privacy."

With a creak of old springs, he hoists himself off the couch. Jolene follows him out, leaving Michaels alone with the muted TV and the old phone.

At an instinctual level, he already knows what's on this video. He knows Rodney does too. No reason for a messenger to leave the room when the message is good.

He takes a deep breath, sits on the couch, and presses *play*.

Caitlyn's face fills the screen, hair whipping around as she rides shotgun in Rodney's truck. There's Jolene in the back. Beyond, a trail of dust as the pickup rattles and bounces down an old, gravelly road. The sun is much higher, perhaps just after one.

"Michaels, I keep doing this to you. Keep leaving or pushing you away. I'm sorry. I just… You know what I'm going to say. I'm dangerous. Something's changing in me and I can't explain it. Last night was proof. If I stay, I'm going to end up hurting you again… or worse."

A rattling thud and the pickup turns onto a new road, a highway, still rural but smoother. Michaels notes the on-ramp sign, the mile markers. He's already doing the math: how fast can he catch up?

"Big Rod doesn't know where I'm going, so please don't make this any harder. And please, know that I don't mean to hurt you. You told me that sometimes we don't get to choose between a good choice and a bad one. Sometimes, all options suck. And that it's how we meet tomorrow that matters. So, I'm choosing to keep you safe. If that means hurting you, well, please forgive me. We'll always have those months together at sea. Weren't they the best? Okay… Happy travels."

And then Caitlyn smiles and shuts off the video.

LEXINGTON, KENTUCKY

ONE HUNDRED MILES NORTH, WHERE THE HUM OF LEXINGTON'S BLUE Grass Airport shakes the walls of the Cozy Rest Motel, Caitlyn's finger hesitates over the in-room phone's dial pad. She committed the number Walker gave her to memory. Then, on the drive to the bus station, she threw her burner phone in a ditch with the Faraday pouch. One less way to be tracked.

She presses the dial pad, starting with an area code she'd never seen. The pickup is immediate.

"Thank you for calling Wong's Fine Chinese Dining. We are currently closed. Please leave a message."

She hesitates. Is this the right number? She double-checks the display. It is.

She speaks slowly. "My name is Caitlyn Grey. I'm the sole survivor of Project Clearwater. I understand you're looking for me. I'm alone, unarmed, and I'm willing to cooperate. I expect you to treat me with courtesy and dignity."

She swallows. What now? Nothing…

"Hello?"

A calm voice on the other end. "Leave this line open."

And that's it. She lays the receiver on the nightstand. One minute and fifteen seconds.

Caitlyn soaks in the quiet. From her left eye, the motel room is just another dreary way station in a long line stretching back to Kenya. No, she realizes. To the very day she left San Francisco and joined Michaels's investigation.

And from her right eye, she's outside her body. Looking back on her dim gaze and two open eyes. She squeezes her temple. No, not now. She needs to control this.

A low slosh and the *pitter-pat* of water against tile from inside the bathroom. Odd. She doesn't remember drawing a bath.

Nearing the door, she can sense it: someone is in there. She can feel their cold presence.

And yet, when she looks out from her left eye, she's ten feet back, still sitting at the edge of the bed.

A blink, and she's back at the door, crystal-clear definition through her right eye, the beige wood heavy and sharp. She is out of her body now yet her eyes are still open. How?

A wet voice whispers from beyond the door. "You've always known how." A voice she's yearned to hear for so long.

"Mom?"

No answer. A glimpse from her left eye back at the bed. The phone line still open. Six minutes and counting.

Now a glimpse from her right eye: the closed door. She was in the bathroom before; she knows what it looks like.

So she blinks. And now she is here.

Wherever the hell *here* truly is.

The walls shimmer beneath ribbons of light. The ceiling drips velvet shadows. Wet rivulets pour down the porcelain tub yet never touch the tile. Instead, they bend and rise in bubbling stings, pearls deep undersea.

Sitting here in the bathtub is her mother.

The linen dress bought in Greece and worn gracefully over so many years. Her hair, always so thick in those cinnamon-brown curls, flows down her shoulders. Her eyes, two pools of liquid green. Here is a woman who fled her home country, changed her name and buried her past.

She was Zara Eisler for the first twenty-four years of her life. Yet to Caitlyn, she has always been her mother, Terry. A woman from a different generation, indifferent to cellphones and new technology, born back when the world was less perplexing.

Or so Caitlyn believed.

Now, as her mother rises from the tub, it is her skin that has Caitlyn's attention. It's the very sand at the bottom of the sea.

"Do you think that's a wise choice, sweetie?" her mother's wet voice asks. "Calling the government and giving yourself in?"

"I don't know what else I can do."

Bubbles rising, her mother takes three sopping steps closer. Cracks form upon her sandy skin, sloughing off in tawny clouds. Everything hangs as if suspended in gel.

"You can fight back. Bring the battle to their door. Become what they've tried to stop us from becoming."

Eyes sparkling blue, her mother smiles that coy smile. Caitlyn could get lost in that face. She's wanted to see it for so long. Then a cold finger traces its way up her spine. Her mother's eyes were brown.

"Us," Caitlyn repeats. "Who are you, really?"

Another step closer. Another. "Oh, I think you know the answer."

That smile stretches across sandy cheeks, cracking and splitting and sending tendrils of dirt off in wet clouds. There, beneath the crumbling layers, is another face.

It is Caitlyn herself.

Gone are her tattoos and her dyed bangs. Gone is the undercut where her hair hangs swept to one side and shaved on the other. Gone is a decade, the treatments for her deteriorating vision, the fear of leaving her apartment, the weight of all she has learned since she climbed into Dr. Chase's damn pod.

This is her, standing here, younger and free with her whole life ahead.

"I'm the whisper that stands guard while you sleep. I'm the scream in Cairo that sends your enemies fleeing. When you were trapped in a broken boat and all was coming apart, who guided you through?"

Caitlyn shakes her head. "That was my dad."

Another smirk splits her reflection's face, inky shadows beneath it. "He was already gone. But you know who was on that radio, don't you?" Her voice deepens. "That's my girl. So much stronger than she thinks."

"You're a hallucination," Caitlyn whispers. "A side effect from blinking."

"Or maybe you're mine?" Her head tilts with a dry crack. "A girl goes into the sea and dreams up a new life. A god climbs out of the pod."

"No. I know what I am, and crazy isn't part of it."

"Then why are you here?"

"Because…" Caitlyn finds herself struggling for words. "Because I'm dangerous."

"Because we are strong. Because we're two halves of a whole. You're just afraid to embrace it."

And then, with a sharp snap, she's within inches of Caitlyn, the last of the sand drifting free from her young face in a wet cloud. "Think of all we've accomplished. We've scaled mountains together. Walked upon the very edge of volcanos. We reached across the country and turned a mother's gun on her son."

Caitlyn shakes her head. "No. I did that. I squeezed the trigger. I put Teddy down."

Her reflection tilts her head. "And whose strength did you borrow?"

Caitlyn can feel the memory whipping about inside her skull. The SWAT team breaching the house. Teddy's dhimoni falling away as he chased her across fifteen hundred miles in the blink of an eye. The thunderclap of her arrival in Iowa and the old woman's gun in her grip. A twist and the boom of thunder. Then Teddy's head leaking red in the water as his projection collapsed.

My God, Caitlyn thinks. Teddy and his dhimoni. The Clearwater cohort with their heads full of trauma. Some were hardly functioning when they got hauled in to get tested. *Now it's happening to me.*

"Happening?" Her youthful reflection smirks. "I would only question the tense."

Caitlyn tells herself to breathe. That wherever—or whenever—this is, she's in control. An inhale. Through her left eye, she can see the rise and fall of the motel room. She can feel the oxygen flooding her blood, anchoring her to this world.

Through her right, a rising bubble hangs in the air between them, Caitlyn and this dark partner. It might hang there forever.

"Remember this moment," her dark partner says. "You'll ask for my strength again soon; you might even beg. Until then..." She reaches out and pops the bubble. "Knock knock."

Two things happen simultaneously.

Caitlyn is yanked across a great distance—perhaps a great layer of time—and comes to on the bed, the phone reading forty-nine minutes.

Then the motel door explodes.

[48]

Rooney takes a deep breath and counts down from five.

After the debacle in Mombasa, she has to admit, she's been doubting her talents. The honeypot operation, a fumble. The extraction, no better. She's already deep in the red, spending discretionary funds on this whole operation. When she lost them again in Chicago, she was ready to give up the bounty.

But now, as the team makes their way to the motel door, she can almost taste the payout.

It tastes like det cord and flashbangs.

Taking a covering position by the neighboring room, Rooney reaches zero. Vee, on breach, taps his watch. She gives him a nod. When activated, pentrite det cord explodes at six thousand meters per second in a blast that cuts wood.

Rooney feels the explosion in her sinuses, a low-pressure boom that rings her ears and turns the air sulfuric. The room door wobbles, split but still clinging to the frame. Vee digs his fingers into the seam, yanks one way. Sepulveda twists the other. Two halves snap open.

Then Rooney's crisscrossing through the door with the rest of the Kevlar-clad team, shouting, "Clear! Clear! Eyes on the target!"

There she is by the bed, stunned by the concussion and speed of the entry. Rooney already has a phone up, confirming biometric matches.

"C'mon, c'mon," Hutchins says, his skull balaclava covering his mouth and giving him a demonic grin. "That has to be her."

Still scanning, Rooney says, "We need a fifty-point match and her partner pissed in the waters. It's not like unlocking your phone. Keep her face steady."

Hutchins's gloved hands grab the target's face, turning it straight into the lens. She blinks and winces, shell-shocked and spattered with wood chips.

"Are you Foundation—"

"Keep her steady means no talking," Rooney hisses.

Hutchins clamps the target's jaw like a dog at the vet. Rooney studies the biometric scan.

50%... 60%... 70%...

A hand smacks Rooney's armor. "Evac in thirty seconds," says team leader Ellison. "She stays or she goes. Make the call."

The woman squirms, her dim gaze darting about. Poor idiot, probably caught snoozing. Even now, as the shock of the explosive breach gives way to confusion, there's something about this woman Rooney finds unnerving. Like she's buzzing, a string plucked and vibrating at the edges.

80%... 90%... 100%.

MATCH: GREY, CAITLYN.

"Confirmed. Bag her and bug out."

The bag goes over her head fast, Hutchins a little too keen to get moving. Rooney can't blame him. It's one thing to pull an off-the-books extraction where the locals can be bribed. It's another thing entirely to do it in your backyard. Even with Felweather in mobile command monitoring police chatter, there's always risks. An off-duty cop or some yokel playing Jack Reacher. It's Kentucky after all. God help the well-meaning citizen that winds up in a shootout with her team.

And then there's the Foundation...

Outside now, they race along the second floor, passing the

target off to Sepulveda. He hoists her over his shoulder in a fireman's carry.

They hit the stairs, hit the parking lot, the humid night echoing with murmurs and the distant whine of a fire alarm. They're collapsing into evac formation.

Then Rooney spots the black SUV.

Wheels screeching, it turns off the boulevard and into the lot. Rooney notes the emptiness where a license plate should be. The tinted windows. The bulletproof doors.

Shit. They're here.

"Foundation!" someone shouts over the comms.

The gunfire comes from her team, staccato bursts from both flanks. The black SUV's windows whiten but don't shatter.

Another burst and she's on her knees, crawling across pavement.

Up ahead, Sepulveda squat-walks between parked cars, Caitlyn's legs banging off side mirrors and doors. Rooney shouts, "The truck! She's no good to us dead. Get her into the truck!"

A third round of gunshots, then sporadic return fire. Something explodes nearby, peppering Rooney with glass. She feels her heart thumping into her throat. Then comes the calm, the old familiarity of combat, instinct and bullet time lengthening each second.

She gophers her head from between the parked cars. Two black SUVs now, one blocking the exit, the other's hood pockmarked and hissing coolant.

Three doors open, Foundation agents returning fire. Far off, sirens whine louder and louder.

Rooney takes a second to visualize the lot from the briefing. The motel stairs back to her left. The parking lot to her right. The UPS truck idling and awaiting Caitlyn. The evac order once she's secure.

And to leave anyone else behind.

Time to check out. Seventy feet. Sixty feet. Fifty.

She blind fires over the hood of a Mercedes, a quick three-shot to keep Foundation agents from getting too brave. How the hell did she wind up near the end?

Behind her, Garret makes a break for it, body armor clattering. A strap catches on a side mirror. She's shouting at him to leave it when the bullets rip through the window and blow out his hips. Damn.

Ahead of her, the rest of the team hustles forward, trading fire with the black SUVs, pushing the agents into concealment. If she can just catch up with them…

"Rooney, I'm hit," Garret stammers and collapses, letting out a grunt as his ruined hip takes the impact.

With a rattle, the distant shutter of a UPS truck snaps open. A long burst of suppressing fire from her team's M4s. God, this op went sideways so fast.

Fifty feet to the UPS truck, where she can see Sepulveda passing off Caitlyn. The bounty, the long game, all the setbacks and frustrations. If Rooney can't cover that distance, all of this was for nothing.

"Rooney, help me… I think I can walk." Garret inches his way closer, another burst of gunfire shredding the windows above him. He leaves a red trail in his wake. "Rooney, I just need some support and I'm good."

Rooney can see it, how it'll play out if she falls back to retrieve him: the UPS truck with Caitlyn peeling out, the Foundation pushing in. In less than a minute, they'll be outflanked, outgunned, and she'll be all out of moves.

So she makes one of her own.

"Sorry, G-dog."

She squeezes off two shots, both catching Garret in his cheek, blowing out the back of his skull and leaving him teetering, as if he's about to sneeze. Then he slumps to the asphalt.

Rooney crosses fifty feet in seconds, wild-firing at the SUVs to push the assailants back into cover. Return fire plings off parked cars.

And then she is there, the UPS truck and the shutter crashing down as the bullets become a hailstorm.

"Is she okay?" Rooney scans the shadows for the target. There she is, wedged between Sepulveda and Felweather, the two men piling bulletproof armor atop her like burying treasure.

With a screech and a rattle, the UPS truck tilts and bounces. They just hopped the curb.

Rooney catches a glimpse of the video feeds: they're pulling onto the boulevard and the gunfire's receding.

Crawling her way over, Rooney lifts a bulletproof vest off Caitlyn. She finds the woman's hand and gives it a squeeze.

"Listen to me. We've got you, Ms. Grey. You're going to be safe."

49

LOCATION: REDACTED

IT'S AN ODD PATTERN OF SENSES. FIRST, A GENTLE PUSH IN THE SMALL of her back. Then, the clacking of boots on linoleum. When the bag comes off her head, sterile light overwhelms her.

Caitlyn shields her eyes as hazy details resolve. Potted plants. A wall-mounted TV. Three paintings, Kinkadesque pastorals, like those found lining hospital walls. Not a single window to the outside. She turns in time to see the door closing behind her.

This is some faux apartment. A bed and a stack of nondescript clothes folded and left beside bottles of water. A kitchenette, where fruit and energy bars sit on the counter near a bottle of Excedrin Migraine.

The first move she makes is for the door. Locked, damn.

She checks another door. Just a bathroom, tight and clinical. Everything in here is new.

So, what to do?

Her vision is spotty, but if she can mentally reconstruct enough of her surroundings, she can step out. Which means no locked doors can stop her.

Pacing, Caitlyn absorbs the sounds: the hum of cool central air, the clack of her shoes on the floor. She lets her fingers drift over surfaces, taking in the textures. The laminate countertops and brass faucets.

Okay, now time to step out.

Except she can't.

A rising hiss cleaves through her thoughts when she closes her eyes. She can see her mens corpus contained in her skin like light bending in liquid. She can see an infinite blizzard of static. God, how it hurts.

She wipes an orange tear from her left eye. That's when it hits her: she's inside a huge Faraday cage, just like at Clearwater. A way to keep the subjects from unauthorized decoherence. This clinic has its own built-in security.

Where the hell am I?

With a beep and several deep clicks, the door opens.

The first woman through is someone Caitlyn doesn't know. Her skin is caramel, her eyes a sharp hazel. Her hair is braided tight to her scalp. Angular shoulders and toned arms give hint of hours spent throwing punches.

Squinting, the second woman comes into focus. Caitlyn recognizes her. As do millions of others.

"Ms. Grey, it's so nice to finally meet you. I'm Indra Chatterjee." The congresswoman offers Caitlyn a tight smile and a firm handshake. "I'm sorry our paths haven't crossed sooner, but you are one challenging woman to track down. Please, let us sit."

She gestures to the chairs at the kitchenette counter. The other woman remains at the door.

"Are you hungry? Rooney here can call out for some food. You must be famished."

"I'm fine."

"Of course you are." The congresswoman places a reassuring hand on Caitlyn's wrist.

Whiplashed by the past several hours, Caitlyn finds herself struggling with the chain of events. One moment she was in a hotel room, talking to herself. Then those dark hours being moved like a horse in blinders, one truck to another. Now, here, talking to a woman who was debating Senator Drogan last week before an audience of millions.

Sensing this, Chatterjee nods. "This is a lot to take in. So, let's start with the simplest, what Maslow called the base needs. You are safe, Caitlyn. You are secure. Unfortunately, I can't provide more details because we both know they could be used to locate you. My security insists on these measures. If you've tried decohering—blinking, I believe you call it—I'm told you'll find it quite difficult. Forgive me. These terms are confusing."

Politics never interested Caitlyn. She never registered a party preference or kept track of who controlled the House or the Senate. When she finally moved to the U.S., she found she didn't identify with any political faction. Stuck outside yet again.

Yet she admits there's a gravity surrounding the congresswoman, a soothing power. The way she leans toward Caitlyn, her body open and tilted like an old friend stopping by for a visit. Her mother would be Chatterjee's age.

"I apologize for rushing you," Chatterjee says. "I just came from an event and I'm still in politician mode. You have questions."

"Yeah, number one: what the fuck?"

Wrinkles spread out from Chatterjee's eyes as her cheeks rise in a smile. "That's the ultimate question, isn't it? Let us start with what you know and work forward. Years ago, myself and others formed an agency you've become familiar with."

The name leaves Caitlyn's lips with a sigh. "The Foundation."

"Indeed. How much has your partner told you about his former employer?"

"Not much."

And it's the truth. During their time tracking the God's Breath Killer, Michaels remained tight-lipped on specifics. More so after. She'd pieced a few details together: tactics they'd employ, software they'd use, motivations. Still, getting the full picture was like assembling the plot of a movie through secondhand quotes.

Chatterjee says, "For a while, the Foundation did good work.

Saved lives and prevented unthinkable acts, both at home and abroad. Tell me, have you heard of the Iron Law of Bureaucracy?"

Caitlyn shakes her head, sensing an impending explanation.

"The Iron Law states that as an organization grows, its center of power shifts. Those who believe in the original goals are replaced by those who benefit from the organization's growth. It's why administrators—not teachers—run schools and why police unions protect crooked cops. Why Google got rid of "Don't Be Evil" as a company mandate. Evolution isn't just biological. It's sociological as well."

Caitlyn sips the water and considers it. The two groups at the motel, what she'd pieced together of the gunfight. Now it makes sense. "You're saying the Foundation strayed from its mandate."

Chatterjee nods. "Clearwater's potential could never be kept in a lab or contained to classified reports. It was only a matter of time before it evolved. That makes you a member of a rare group, someone with a skill worth billions. You are the focus of a great many forces."

"I don't want any of that. I just want to be left alone."

Chatterjee's brow creases. "Caitlyn, sweetie, we both know that's not going to happen."

Caitlyn tenses. These people. She's over it, over them, done with all these schemes beyond her understanding. She's tired, so damn tired of being a piece on someone else's game board. "Yeah? Why the hell not?"

"Because some of those forces following you have been my own." Chatterjee nods to the woman at the door. "Rooney over there, Michaels met her in Mombasa. I'm sure he filled you in."

Caitlyn glances at the woman. Those defined shoulders, that confident stare. Poor Michaels never stood a fighting chance. "You sent those men onto my boat. Men with weapons and a bounty—"

"That was someone else," Rooney says. "My team tracked Michaels, hoping to find you, but you'd gone separate ways. By the time the Kenyans hit your boat, my team was too far behind. You spooked, and we lost you. Until you called the Foundation."

"And we intercepted it," Chatterjee says. "A perk of being a founding member. Caitlyn, I understand how this looks; the optics are not lost on me. We should have tried a more direct approach. But try to understand, I'm betraying the very agency I helped create. Without a strategic exit, this all falls apart."

The names rattle around in Caitlyn's head, coming into sharp definition. "You mean like that judge, Maberry? And that Senator Meeks—"

"Marks," Chatterjee corrects. "You're well informed. And yes, that's what I mean. Here, I want you to see this."

Chatterjee points the remote at the TV and starts scrolling through channels. "I apologize if politics bores you, but it affects our futures. Yours especially. Tonight, while you were calling the Foundation, I was formalizing an alliance with Senator Drogan."

Onscreen, the commentary is muted, but the captions follow close behind. *BREAKING: Chatterjee Accepts VP Nomination; forming unity ticket; developing…*

The anchors are all nodding, perfect hair and bland suits. Behind them, footage of Drogan and Chatterjee strobed in flashes, holding hands and raising them high.

Caitlyn scoffs. "Isn't Drogan's platform against everything the Foundation represents? How's that going to work?"

The question has hardly left Caitlyn's lips when the answer forms in her mind. First, a vague impossibility. Then, a sharp inevitability. The congresswoman gives her a coy nod.

"Right, this is your exit strategy," Caitlyn says. "You're taking the Foundation down from inside."

"Dismantling." Chatterjee takes another sip of water while Caitlyn studies the woman's soft fingers. "Despite some ideological differences, Dave and I see eye to eye on key issues. We're pragmatists. He's up thirty points in every poll. Barring a major scandal, he'll sweep the election. And when he takes office, he'll clean house, just as he promised. It's like musical chairs."

"And you don't want to be left standing when the song's over."

Chatterjee plucks a piece of hair off her blazer. "For generations Americans have been told they are inherently exceptional. And yet, what do we have? They're out-innovating us in Asia. By every metric, the Europeans are living healthier, happier lives. Disinformation is flooding our news, using our love of free speech to unravel social cohesion. Americans are scared. When they're scared, they clamor for a strongman and simple ideas. Someone to tell them it's okay to be angry; it's not their fault. On an instinctual level, Drogan gets that."

"So this is politics," Caitlyn says. "You're saving your ass by riding his coattails."

"I'm saving all of our asses by working the system." Chatterjee stares deep into Caitlyn's eyes. "Look, I know about your parents. What happened to them at Clearwater was unconscionable. You have every right to distrust the government's words, I get that. But here are the facts: the Foundation has modernized the technology. They call it Day's Bane. Someone is leaking those findings onto the dark web. Someone is making their own exit plan. And that plan involves finding you."

"You people," Caitlyn seethes. "You learned everything from Clearwater except the right lesson."

"You people?" Rooney repeats from the door. "Two of my teammates died extracting you. Another two are wounded, one critically. The congresswoman had this facility built for your protection."

A pang of shame tightens Caitlyn's shoulders. She glances at Chatterjee. "Is that true?"

Chatterjee nods.

"I don't want any of this," Caitlyn says. "I never asked for it."

"This isn't about you, Caitlyn, but what you represent." Chatterjee lets the idea sink in before continuing. "Imagine North Korea with the power of a blind site. Or the Russians. Or non-state actors waging jihad with a cave full of decoherents. Civilization would crumble. We barely made it through a pandemic without tearing ourselves apart."

Caitlyn swallows. She's tired, tired of being the focus of so many eyes.

If she'd never been at that diner and seen the dhimoni…

If she'd never made that phone call to Michaels…

If she'd never gotten onto that plane…

And yet, those were hers, that long chain of decisions that brought her here, to this very moment. Frustrating as it is, she owns them, one choice at a time.

"What do you want from me?"

The congresswoman doesn't smile, but her eyes sparkle. "Your help, Caitlyn. We need you to lay low, stay safe. Whatever you need, we'll provide. When the time comes and not a moment before, we take out the Foundation with one surgical strike." She snaps her fingers.

Caitlyn considers it. She doesn't trust them, not entirely. But it might buy them some time. More importantly, it might buy Michaels some peace and protection. If she's no longer with him, he's no longer a target.

Or so she hopes.

Her answer comes in a small nod that draws a smile to Chatterjee's lips. "Good."

Rooney unlocks the door and Chatterjee pauses at the threshold. Caitlyn tries to steal a glance beyond, but all she can see are clinical halls.

Chatterjee says, "Three hundred million. That's what they've spent trying to replicate your skill. At the lab—at Day's Bane—they have a name for it. Can you guess what it is?"

Caitlyn waits. Chatterjee and Rooney, just two dim shadows she has to trust.

"They call it the Jensen-Grey Phenomenon," Chatterjee says.

Then the door closes and locks.

50

WHITLEY COUNTY, KENTUCKY

9:30 A.M. EST

BRAD SLAPS THE BUG ON HIS ARM AND GIVES THE WET MESS A FLICK. Nothing out here but insects and rolling hills and an old country road.

And this overturned rental car in the dirt.

Olivia scoots out of the passenger seat, her evidence bag full. She gestures: *Hand me another.*

Brad asks, "You really think this was them?"

Wiping sweat from her brow, she deposits a cracked tablet into evidence. "A burner iPad, a GoDark bag, and a rental without GPS. I'd say our odds are strong."

He looks up. "And the power lines. Kentucky Electric confirmed they had an event the night before last. Did Nox mention that?"

"No, of course not. Why would he?"

Brad slaps away another bug. Damn, they're eating him alive. He misses the tiny insects in Spain. "It's just that... Well, don't you ever wonder what part you're playing in all this?"

Olivia slides into the very back of the overturned car, her legs barely jutting out. "Of course I wonder, but I know better than to ask. And I wonder why you're bringing this up. Here, take this. If we're lucky, we can pull DNA."

She hands him a crumpled sugar-free Red Bull can that he bags and tags.

Brad says, "I'm just curious, you know? Michaels says one thing. The coordinator says another. I'm trying to triangulate the truth."

Olivia climbs out of the back and gets right in his face. It's the first time he's seen her truly angry since Cairo. "Our job isn't to triangulate anything. Our job is to follow orders and carry out our duties. If our job needs us to know something, we'll be told. Don't poison both our careers."

Brad winces. As the junior agent and the junior by age, he's grown used to being in Olivia's shadow. Even back in Korea when she was Dr. Dana Park, a professor at Busan University, he still struggled to keep up.

And recently…

No. She's right. Get your head back into the game.

"Forget it." He slaps another bug from his forearm and gives the remains a flick. "Silly thought."

Olivia blinks, studying him as he walks away from the wreck and back onto the road.

"So, Kentucky Electric was out here checking on the power lines, right?" he says. "Which means they'd be coming from the west, that way."

She follows his glance back the way they came. Just fallow fields and a country gas station long since out of business. "What's your point?"

He continues down the road until he's fifty feet from the wreck in the other direction. "Well, assuming there haven't been many cars, what's the chance someone would make a hard stop here, pull a three-point turn, then head back the way they came?"

He bends down, tracing the tire tracks and how hard they dug in. He can see the tracking and yaw marks where the tires started to go sideways. An older vehicle, no ABS, so the rear tires left thinner marks than the front. A pickup, perhaps.

Now that he's found that, he can see the rest: the paw prints from a dog, the faint footsteps still left from when the passengers walked back onto the road.

Not walked. Limped. One of them must have been carrying the other.

Until a third came to help.

He raises the phone to his ear and dials. Olivia asks, "Who are you calling?"

"Just following a hunch."

There is a pause while the line encrypts. Then, the voice: "Thank you for calling Wong's Fine Chinese Dining…"

"This is Associate Field Agent Lee, badge victor lima seven six zero. I need a full scan of all potential hospital and clinical admissions in the past forty-eight hours within fifty miles of my location."

"Copy that. Incoming."

Brad considers it: what Michaels might do. "And you know what? Check any house calls with registered physicians and nurses, flagging after-hours activity."

"Copy that, Associate Agent. Check your phone."

Brad does just that, reading the incoming list as it scrolls past. Twenty-one potential names and faces, photographs from the American Medical Association, from clinic or hospital websites, even the DMV. All local.

The algorithm highlights one in particular. An incoming call, 5:14 a.m., forty-eight minutes after the power went out on this lonely stretch of road.

"Dr. Thomas Crawford," Brad says, into the phone. "Run a full profile on that predawn caller. And give me the make and model of any vehicles registered to them."

Three minutes later and he's beaming.

"You look like you just won the lottery," Olivia says. "Explain."

"While you were plucking Funyuns out of the seat, I found a lead. Here, take a look."

He tilts his phone toward her. A 1996 Ford F-150, rust red and dusty. The tires on record: Goodyear Wrangler SR-A. The tire and a tread print fills the screen.

Then he bends down to touch the print in the dirt. A near-perfect match.

She says, "Looks like they met a Good Samaritan. You drive. I'll call it in." Pausing at the car, she almost smiles. "Nice job. Hopefully, we're not too far behind."

"Yeah, hopefully," Brad says and eyes the locked briefcase sitting in the back seat.

[51]

ALDER GLEN FOOTHILLS

SANTA CLARA COUNTY, CALIFORNIA

He has to admit, a leap of faith isn't like him. Still, that's what it took to step onto the plane: a deep faith in Robert Chase and the GPS coordinates etched into the aerogel. The only bread-crumbs he has left.

Now, driving southbound on Interstate 280, Michaels has no choice but to follow them.

Returning to the peninsula always feels like bumping into an old friend, one wrinkled and rutted by the years yet with familiar bones underneath. Here, bronze hills crest and fall, grassy waves dotted with oak and pine and redwood. A pair of Teslas blow past.

He never told Caitlyn that he lived here for most of high school, staying with a wealthy cousin while Alzheimer's chewed through his father. Those had been solitary years. Even now, he instinctively cringes, roaring past old off-ramps and memories of clumsy teenage fumblings. He rubs his temples, coaxing his thundering concussion to hush.

Thirty miles south and he takes Exit 22 to Alpine Road and follows it deep into Portola Valley, the shaded vales dampened by fog and redolent of the Pacific. This is where the tech money dwells, in estates tucked down unmarked roads, past old wooden fences that meander up scrubby ridges and down mossy hollows.

The GPS chirps. He's almost there.

According to his research, the coordinates Chase left are for a house recently transferred to a trust. Michaels procured a name and a brief biography courtesy of LinkedIn: Katherine Lopez, some junior product designer doing the VC shuffle from startup to startup.

He thinks of this as he pulls up the sloped driveway and the motion lights activate. Nice place. A little too nice for her job title. Solar panels and hard angles. Lots of concrete and glass. Muted colors, save for the warm glow coming from the interior.

A glow now cut by two shadows on the porch. First a woman. Then a German Shepard, its ears raised as deep barks echo off the trees.

Michaels leaves the car running—not because he intends to leave quickly but because turning it off might send an unfriendly message. How do you break the ice when a dead man's scavenger hunt brings you to a stranger's front door? He simulated multiple conversation starters on the drive. Now, like usual, they all feel heavy and fake.

So he waves at the shadow and says, "This probably sounds strange, but I was sent here by Robert Chase."

Which turns out to be the right thing.

The woman steps into the porch light and pats the dog. Its posture softens but it doesn't leave her side. "Yeah? What's your name?"

"Michaels. We worked together. Robert Chase and I, he gave me—"

"I know who you are, Michaels. My uncle said you were smart, that I should be expecting you. I have to say, it's a bit later than I thought. Uncle Bob's dead."

"I know."

He takes the steps up to the porch slow, listening for signs of movement, any other presence. Nothing. Just the burble of a fountain and the breeze through the branches, cool on his skin.

"I'm sorry about your uncle. He was—"

"He was complicated," she says. "Was that the word you were looking for?"

"Yes. Complicated. May I?"

He spots several security cameras, some high up and angled down, others at eye level. So much for not leaving a trail. If this meeting goes sideways, she'll have good shots of him. Another leap of faith.

"Yeah, come on inside." She leaves the door open. The dog follows, eyes never leaving Michaels.

The interior is spacious, minimal, and familiar. It takes him a moment to figure out why. He once stood in a place of similar design, back when he and Denise Carruthers first met Dr. Chase. "Your uncle designed this house, didn't he?"

"Uncle Bob designed a lot of things. Architecture was one of his quiet passions."

Michaels's footsteps echo. "It looks like it was just built yesterday."

"It practically was. He had the same firm that built Biotronika working twenty-four seven. Nine months ago this was an empty lot. The last great project of Robert Chase."

Michaels finds his eyes drawn to the chandeliers, smooth pipes forming ovals over mesh. Curious design. Like some retro antenna.

Katherine leads him to an open kitchen where floor-to-ceiling windows look out on a grove of redwoods. Fog blankets the hills, the ferns and brambles all soft at the edges. He thinks of Caitlyn's dimming vision and his heart starts to ache. If this wild goose chase will buy her a safe future, he'll see it through to the end.

Katherine passes him a steaming cup of hot water and a tray of teas. He settles on rooibos. "Uncle Bob spoke about you a lot recently. He said, and I quote, 'He reminds me of my younger self, if I made a few better choices.'"

Michaels takes in the earthy scent of the tea. Tries to take in the compliment but it fits strange, too fine for his skin. "Your uncle was quite the mind. Did they tell you how he passed?"

She raises an eyebrow, cups her tea, and blows on it. "C'mon, Michaels. *Secret Agent* Michaels, formerly of… What was it? The Institution?"

"Something like that."

"Uncle Bob had his secrets, but I filled in a few blanks. Especially toward the end when he became wistful and philosophical. You know what he said to me, here, at this very counter? He said he felt like he'd built the airplane, given humanity wings, and men went and strapped bombs underneath."

"That sounds about right."

Of course Chase would compare himself in such terms. Perhaps it was hubris or perhaps regret. But it didn't erase the fact that he'd partnered with the military to fund several endeavors.

And then the Foundation.

Outside, flood lights activate as two glowing eyes rise from the mist. The dog's bark breaks the pregnant silence. Michaels almost covers himself in hot tea.

"People think deer are cute," Katherine says. "Like Bambi. Not so cute when they devour your garden and drop ticks everywhere."

The dog is at the window now, barking its head off as the deer retreats into the fog. A moment later, the lights turn off.

"I'm envious. If you worked with Uncle Bob, you've seen some interesting things. I'm envious. Most of my time has been trying to make him proud. See, that's how I sensed something was off. He said he had one last project. Then he gave me the keys to this house."

Michaels's left hand twitches. He suspected Chase had contingencies. Still, how far out had he planned? The code they'd used to communicate had been put in place before Michaels left the Foundation. But this house…

She says, "I suppose you want to see it then."

"See what?"

Another curious tilt of her head. "See what Uncle Bob left for you."

Following Katherine downstairs, Michaels senses a change in air temperature and quality. The basement has its own HVAC. And the door they just passed, are those magnetic locks in its frame?

"Uncle Bob was very specific about his workshop. He said you could tell the quality of a craftsman by their organization. A place for everything—"

"And everything in its place. Ben Franklin."

Katherine smiles. "Yeah, you two are cut from the same cloth."

No surprise, the workshop is a study in minimalist design. What is surprising is the breadth of Chase's creations. Display cases hug the concrete walls, housing decades of biomedical devices Chase played a part in creating.

A gyroscopic cane that never tips over.

A full leg brace that fits to the contours of the muscle.

An exo-skeletal frame, from the shoulders down the back and out to the arms. Michaels has seen clips of soldiers with such exo-frames loading missiles onto drones.

And here it is. Where a dozen cords descend from the ceiling to a stainless-steel standing desk looms a simple desktop computer, beige and uninspiring. Yet there is a weight here, a sense that this may represent an end, an answer, or as close to either as Michaels will find.

"So, I type in my passkey," Katherine says. "And now you type in yours."

"Wait, my passkey? I don't know any passkey."

Too late now. She's already hit *ENTER*. The screen changes to the second user, *MICHAELS*, and a box with a blinking prompt.

"He didn't give you a passkey? That's odd. He made sure I memorized mine. Let's make distance."

Michaels blinks. "What did you say?"

"'Let's make distance.' That's what Uncle Bob made me memorize."

Michaels can see it clear in his memory. An old VHS tape stored in a safe. A humming VCR. The past playing out on the TV's warped glass, deep in the basement of Biotronika. Robert Chase, only thirty-three, asked by the man holding the camera to commemorate this moment.

"Let's make distance," Michaels says and then types out each letter. "… a thing of the past."

Then he hits *ENTER*.

"Challenge black," says a familiar voice over the workstation speakers. "Response omega. Challenge black. Response omega."

"Huh," Katherine says. "That's ominous."

"In my experience, it is."

A loud clang at the top of the stairs. Bolts slamming home in the door. Michaels rushes up, cursing himself the whole way. In his haste to unravel Chase's puzzle, he'd done the one thing years of experience warned him against.

He ignored his paranoia.

"It's locked. You have a key, right?"

"It's a smart home. Everything's on Wi-Fi." She swipes her phone, double-taps. Swipes and double-taps. Her scowl is unsettling him.

"What is it?"

"Huh. The, uh… Well, the Wi-Fi's not showing."

Michaels swipes open his phone, searches for the local networks. Nothing. "No Bluetooth or RFID either. Chase wanted those doors shut."

He paces the workshop, searching for errant signals. He has a dozen apps from the dark web that persistently scrape networks and find holes to exploit. But there's nothing here. Damn. He pushes on a few wall panels but the answer's clear: they're belowground, no other way out.

"What do these bars mean?" Katherine asks.

On the computer screen, a series of SFTP transfers, all outgoing. Gigs of data. Michaels studies the wires coming down from the ceiling, truly seeing them for the first time. "That's a fifty-micron connection."

"What's that?"

"It's a really fast network."

"Uncle Bob paid for the whole neighborhood to be hooked up. He said Comcast was too slow."

"Yeah, he's not wrong." Michaels follows the cable into the ceiling panel, twists it aside. Just a pipe and concrete. No way out up there.

A blip on the screen and several new windows open up. More outgoing uploads, files too fast to be named and no way to stop them. It's all automated, some script executing final commands.

The screen organizes into a grid of security feeds across the house. The top row, from the outside: above the garage, the porch, the back garden with its redwood grove. The bottom row, from the inside: the living room, the open kitchen, the halls.

And one outside the door that leads down to this basement.

Now comes a voice and a face in the last window. A man who stood at this workstation not long ago.

Catherine's eyes moisten. "Uncle Bob?"

"If you're watching this, what I've feared has come to pass," Robert Chase says, staring out from a bed of bright pixels. "I've made many mistakes in my life. My greatest was not knowing when to stop. First at Clearwater, and now Day's Bane. Michaels, my creation has been taken from me. It's now a matter of time before it's fully twisted."

Katherine asks, "What's he talking about?"

Michaels holds up a finger.

Onscreen, Chase checks his watch. "At this point, my dead man's switch should be uploading the evidence I smuggled off Day's Bane over the past year. Videos. Audio. Bank transfers. It's all being emailed to friendly parties now. I take full responsibility for my failings. My reach truly exceeded my grasp."

A cold pang traces Michaels's spine. If Chase's script is firing off evidence en masse, then there's a few screens at Kray Mesa lighting up about now. And emergency protocols being enacted.

"No doubt my employer, Mr. Nox, and the Day's Bane facility are tracing this data. I've included red-list files to trigger their systems. I'm afraid that in such a leak, the procedures are quite brutal. Any moment now, several decoherents will be arriving. I've made sure to prime their minds with this blind site."

"Uh, what's a decoherent?" Katherine asks. "Is that some sort of hitman?"

"Yeah, like a hitman. Except we can't see them and they can move through walls."

Katherine scoffs. "That's impossible."

"*Was* impossible. Your uncle made it very possible."

Movement on camera three, the backyard. Something just set off the motion light. A curious distortion, a thin ribbon of light stretching and crawling through the ferns and the mist.

Now a bloom on camera two, the front porch. The video quality stutters, downgrades. Dark spots form on the wood door —Lichtenberg figures, branching fractals created by electron discharge. A hunched form pours forth from nothing.

"Are… Are those footprints?" Katherine asks.

"Yeah. And handprints on camera five."

The glass door that leads into the kitchen silently shatters. A second later, a deep groan comes from above the workshop.

"The first law of thermodynamics," Chase says, "stipulates that energy can neither increase nor decrease in a closed system. We built Day's Bane to be perfectly enclosed, hidden from maps and curious eyes. Yet there is one weakness inherent to its design. Quantum entanglement means this system has a secret entrance."

Heavy footsteps rattle upstairs. Cameras two and four show blooming beams of light stretching across the glass-spattered kitchen. Camera three shows a hulking shadow flipping over the dining room table. Camera five shows the door to the basement, where a sinuous shape rises.

Katherine whispers, "What did you get me into?"

"Hopefully nothing we can't get out of," Michaels says. Privately, it's feeling like all options are fast closing down. This isn't a workshop. It's a survival shelter.

Chase's video changes to a blueprint of the house. "My final invention. Built within these walls is a fully functioning Marx generator, ready to discharge a single electromagnetic pulse. Katherine, dear, I'm afraid it's going to fry the appliances. But you'll be shielded in this workshop. Day's Bane will be less fortunate. You need to hit them, Michaels. These coordinates are for your eyes only. Memorize them. Expose the program. Undo my mistakes. I know this cannot buy absolution, but perhaps it will buy you some time. I guess these may be my final words." He takes off his glasses, looks into the lens and out through time and distance. "Some doors should never be opened."

With the stretch of a hand, Robert Chase ends the video.

A new prompt appears: *DISCHARGE MARX GENERATOR?*

The dog is barking now, going nuts at the shaking basement door.

"C'mon," Katherine says. "Press the button."

Michaels, studying the video feeds. Three decoherent forms in the house.

One large and dark tearing the living room apart.

One sinuous and gray crawling along the hallway's ceiling.

And one twisting itself in impossible configurations, a tesseract of limbs and eyes, vibrating hands chipping concrete and shattering glass. The workshop door bends and buckles and—

"Cover your ears," Michaels says.

Then he presses the button.

A Marx generator uses stacked capacitors to convert low-voltage DC sources into high-voltage pulses. They can stress-test the energy grid against lightning or simulate fusion reactions in thermonuclear bombs. Sandia National Labs has thirty-six in a bank configuration.

Robert Chase's invention is more modest. Fed by multiple PowerWall batteries, the chandeliers empty a full 13.5-kilowatt charge in a series of earsplitting clicks.

The pulse raises every hair on Michaels's and Katherine's skin, every strand of the dog's fur. It fries every non-shielded electronic device within the walls of the house—as well as the rental car outside, the cameras, the decorative yard lamps. In the garden, the fountain pump spews water skyward. A bathing blue jay keels over.

The pulse hits Iliana Kennedy, Zade Holloway, and Raymond Flay. None of them know what to make of the static-laced waves, visible only to their eyes for a fraction of a second.

Then it's in their consciousness—a mental contagion that rides their thoughts up into a higher dimension where time flows in impossible eddies and distance bends against a curtain of static, all places at once.

Amplified, the charge descends across nineteen hundred miles. It exits their physical bodies and enters the Day's Bane circuitry like a collision of stars. In this moment, the three subjects in the sterile lab are fortunate—their bodies simply pass off the message.

Dr. Janet O'Farrell, less so.

She is studying a slice of the late Teddy Jensen's brain when the electronic microscope pressed to her eye vibrates white hot. It takes off like a rocket—takes her face off with it—and sends her body pirouetting across the lab.

In the gym, Dr. Jason Freeman—who had tendered his resignation and then backed out—finds the metal shower head buzzing as the water turns from tepid to scalding. In seconds the moist air crackles with electricity, crackles louder than his screams as his skin blisters and steams.

In the rec room on level two, Dr. Baker is inserting a disc into the Blu-ray player—no streaming services here—when the player and the TV above it blow out in a wave of superheated glass substrate. He makes it to the hall on adrenaline alone before collapsing, the remote now melted to his smoldering hand.

It goes on across the platform: deep vibrations and detonations, the whine of fire alarms and sputtering lights, these now-shadowed halls fast thickening with screams.

[52]

DEEP INTO WESTERN OKLAHOMA, A CONVOY OF VEHICLES STRETCHES nearly a half mile down I-40. There are Japanese hybrids, German electrics, and gas-guzzling domestics. There are motorcycles flying pride flags and lifted pickups stickered with Veterans for the 2nd Amendment. There are old Volkswagen busses from the sixties, rebuilt and painted in psychedelic pastels, followed by the occasional Tesla running in self-driving mode. There is even a 1930 Rolls-Royce Phantom, its body painted red, white, and blue, a digital sign in the rear window flashing *TAX ME HARDER DADDY!*

Near the head of the convoy, nestled between security vehicles and unamused state troopers, looms a large bus. Glenn Beck rode this bus back when book tours were a thing. Billy Ray Cyrus brought his family along, touring from Alaska to Mexico. Its interior is stylish, granite tabletops and marble floors, mood lighting and climate-controlled rooms.

It is the master bedroom that the senior campaign manager stops before. She knocks and waits and listens. She knows that after rallies and major announcements, her boss likes to unwind with some constituents. She's even joined in occasionally.

But tonight, campaign business comes first. Time is working against them already. She knocks again.

"C'mon in, don't be shy," the candidate calls out in his playful drawl.

She enters.

Drogan sits on the floor, cross-legged and loose tied, a bottle of CBD kombucha in his lap. To both sides sit young women. The one on the left, a doctoral student from Alder Glen University writing her thesis on rhetoric and populism. On the right in the beanbag, the chairwoman for the Midwest chapter of Young Republicans. She lobbed a few loaded questions at Drogan back in Omaha, hoping to bait him. Instead, Drogan invited her for the ride out to Las Vegas, promising a long-form conversation.

So here they sit: the PhD candidate on her tablet, the Young Republican with her eyes on him. And Drogan, focused on the TV. His fingers work the controller where colorful combatants fire off lasers and lob plasma grenades onscreen. He's one of the last players standing.

"So what I'm trying to understand is this," the young chair-woman says, making sure the video is centered. "How can you claim to be for fiscal responsibility while supporting universal basic income?"

"It all comes down to priorities, Rita," he says. "So, the real question is, who do we prioritize? Our citizens, many of whom are just struggling to get by? Or the wasteful spending of the entrenched special interests? Forty cents of every dollar, that's the cost of our bombs and rockets. That's what we all pay with no choice. When I was deployed, the government had us dig pits and fill them with everything from old tires to medical waste. We used jet fuel to torch 'em. I even stirred a few. No one asks about those fiscal atrocities. All those small government hypocrites, you watch them start speaking in tongues when you point to their corn or fossil fuel subsidies. They say they support the troops, but the minute our boys and girls in uniform cost us a thing, it's 'Thank you for your service. Now kindly be quiet.' And it's not just the military either. It's—"

The campaign manager clears her throat. "Dave, sorry to interrupt, but there's something—"

"Hold up, Cindy. I'm coming up on a new record here. Fifteen kills in a row."

Dave repositions his controller so his left hand moves the joystick, his right fingers tapping the buttons. He rolls up his sleeves. Cindy tries not to stare at the mottled flesh that knots his left arm. Like an old, axe-scarred tree, rutted and ruined yet still standing strong.

"Dave, you really need to see this."

"And you really need to say hello to the audience." Drogan points to the camera atop the TV. "They keep begging you to play and I keep telling them you think video games are unbecoming. Wait… Now there's a good fundraiser. You auction off an hour of *Fortnite*, we could raise a million for the, uh… What do you like? The Humane Society, right?"

"Dave, listen—"

Onscreen, a flash of green light and an explosion of plasma. Drogan's character takes a rocket grenade to the face. "Shucks. You distracted me."

"Holy shit," the doctoral student says, brushing a blonde lock from her face. Her fingers quickly swipe and scroll down the tablet.

"Dave," Cindy says, gesturing, "we need to talk… off camera."

"Okay, let me wind down." With a few taps on the controller, the screen reads *END SESSION?* "All right, folks, it's getting late, so thanks for tuning in for another round of Dave Plays. Remember, go register to vote. And bring a friend. Heck, bring a dozen. Democracy dies in the darkness, so let's be the light."

Cindy knows where this is going. A minute of endorsements for grassroots organizations. Another minute for down-ballot candidates. She fields dozens of inquiries a day, begging for a shout-out at the end of his stream. She even suggested monetizing it, but he found it distasteful.

Still, she does what she must. She walks over and disconnects the camera.

"Cindy, what the heck?"

A chirp on the Young Republican's phone. Then, two more. Whatever it is, it's brought the same curious squint to her face as the doctoral candidate.

"Dave, we need to talk, privately. This is..." The word "huge" doesn't seem to do it justice. "Cataclysmic," perhaps.

And perhaps an opportunity.

As if sensing the weight of her incoming words, Drogan nods. "Okay. Brief me."

But it's the doctoral candidate who speaks first. "Are you guys reading this? Something called Project Day's Bane just hit the news."

Cindy passes Drogan her tablet. His eyes scour the emails. Hundreds of new messages, all in the past thirty minutes and filled with attachments. And they're still coming.

There, at the bottom, the name of one man, a name he recognizes: Dr. Robert Chase.

Drogan swallows. "I need to make some calls."

In Kray Mesa, every screen in the bullpen is now flashing the news. The lines are overwhelmed. Diego takes it all in, frozen, like it's some sort of a drill.

Twitter is already trending a new hashtag: #SamStephensWas-Right. On YouTube, a video is purporting to show a young man with red hair crushing a parakeet with his mind. *The New York Times* is fact-checking the claims. A few fringe networks are already running the story.

"What the hell do we do?" asks an agent-trainee from the next cubicle over. It's the first time Diego has tasted fear in the air. He wants to crawl beneath his workstation, curl up, and stuff his fingers into his ears. He wants to wake up from this dream.

"Christ, it's gone international," someone says and changes one of the screens to Russian, where a pretty newscaster stands before a picture of a brain charged with electricity. The subtitle translation reads *Strange Claim of American Mind-Weapon*.

Is it true what is being put out there? Was the government responsible for creating the God's Breath Killer? And is the Foundation weaponizing that research?

Propaganda, of course. The opening wave of another Russian psyops campaign.

And yet…

Diego's thoughts rattle around, loud, louder. But not loud enough to drown out the ringing phone on his desk.

It is the name that hastens him, snaps him out of his stupor and into fast action. He answers the phone.

"Yes, Head Coordinator."

Then he listens. While the bullpen around him devolves into chaos, Diego's own world shrinks to this silent island.

The head coordinator does not ask any questions. Instead, he spells out his vision, his strategy, his plan.

One so bold it will probably work.

In Washington, D.C., amid down comforters and two snoring pugs, Indra Chatterjee is just descending into REM sleep. Exhausted after a day of tense maneuverings—political and otherwise—she dreams of the Oval Office and the Resolute Desk. If she plays her hand wisely, she'll soon be behind it.

Then her phone rings.

The voice on the other end chills her bones and straightens her spine. He knows. He has to. Why else would he be calling but to tell her goodbye? To press the button and send in the decoherents.

Instead, Nox says, "Turn on the news."

Ten minutes, five channels, and one cup of coffee later, and her heart rate settles at 120. She is safe for the moment. But her plans have now shifted. What was supposed to take months will now be a matter of days.

But okay, she can probably pivot.

"Drogan's a pit bull and he's already pouncing," she says, checking the latest from the candidate's internal message board. "Once he's bitten, he'll never let go. The message they're running with is this is bigger than Snowden. He's coordinating an emergency hearing."

"Good," Nox says. "See that he has help."

[53]

THREE HUNDRED AND TWENTY-ONE MILES AWAY FROM WASHINGTON, D.C., near the industrial parks and rail yards of northwest Columbus, Ohio, Caitlyn wakes to gray curtains and a loud knock at her door.

She pulls on a hoodie and wipes sleep from her eyes. Three days here, and she's been given everything she asked for. Except for the freedom to step outside her windowless suite.

She finds Rooney at the door, two cups of coffee in hand and a face scrunched in worry. "We need to talk about your partner, Michaels."

Five minutes and twice as many browser tabs later, and Caitlyn is still squinting at the screen, still struggling to unravel what she sees. On *The Washington Post*, a video of Robert Chase auto-plays. "If you're watching this, it means I'm already dead…"

Another click over to Reddit, where a forum is discussing a digitized video from thirty years ago. They've already identified several of the key Clearwater researchers, all dead.

More clicks to CNN, Fox News, *The New York Times*, all showing a variation of the same story: *Trove of Whistleblower Documents Hits the Web; Allegations of Secret Weapons Lab Rife with Human Experimentation; Still Developing.*

"Drogan's team called us at dawn," Rooney says. "They're furious. You can see how this complicates things for the congresswoman, if she's to be his VP pick and this gets connected to her."

Another tab. Sam Stephens's site, *The Straight Shot*, still going strong. The morning's top story: *EXPOSED! Deep State Mind Weapons; Sam Stephens's Lawyer Claims Vindication; Press Conference at Noon.*

"Your partner and Chase blew the doors off this operation before it was ready," Rooney says. "We've lost the element of surprise."

Words fail Caitlyn. It's everything the Foundation tried to prevent, all happening at once.

She steadies her mind. "You didn't come here to whine. There's a play to be made or you wouldn't have knocked. So, what is it?"

Three minutes and one loud conversation with the security guard later and Rooney is leading Caitlyn by the elbow, down a long narrow hall. The color of paint, the width of the hall, even the echo of their feet, it all feels somewhat off to Caitlyn's senses. Somehow hollow.

"What's back that other way?" she asks.

Rooney ignores her.

They cross through frosted doors, the hallway opening to a wide atrium washed out with lights. A faint vibration raises the hair on her arms. When her vision settles, what she finds herself looking at knots her stomach and brings a sigh to her lips. The workstations, the geodesic dome that makes up the Faraday cage, the staff in their clinical white coats.

"No, you didn't," Caitlyn whispers. "You shouldn't have."

In the center of the chamber, like a half-opened Christmas present, is a stainless-steel object, egg-shaped and smooth. A sensory deprivation pod. Judging by the dents and scuffs, it's the last pod from Clearwater.

The one she used to fight Teddy.

"The Foundation isn't the only one with skin in the game,"

Rooney says. "This was the best we've been able to cobble together. Hopefully it's enough for you to work with."

"I'm not getting into that."

"You'll need to. We've never calibrated the systems."

"Well that's too fucking bad."

A technician connecting cables casts a sidelong glance their way. A nurse drawing up a nutrient IV hesitates. Caitlyn can feel the eyes upon her, a half dozen pairs. Suddenly, the atrium feels cramped.

Rooney's nostrils flare. "Ms. Grey, I don't think you understand what's unfolding. We have a chance to stop this, to end Day's Bane. But to do that, we need a two-part attack. The congresswoman will be doing her part in D.C. Our strike team is heading to Alaska. But without you, they're going in blind."

Caitlyn feels the expectation leaving its sour taste on her tongue. And yet, hadn't she used similar words against Michaels once? Didn't she give him such an ultimatum?

"Take a look around the room," Rooney says. "These doctors and support clinicians, even these machines, they were flown in this morning. All of this here is for you. The congresswoman is sticking her neck out."

"I didn't ask for this."

"No, you didn't. Yet here it is just the same."

Caitlyn walks around the sensory deprivation pod. There's the sound-dampening interior, the float membrane that cushions her body and matches her temperature. They even added video screens inside to assist with visualization.

As she traces the pod's sensual curves, that bicameral perspective washes over her. She is running her hands down the smooth metal, fingers warped by its reflection. She is looking out at herself from inside the pod's silent shadows.

A girl goes into the sea and dreams up a new life. A god climbs out of the pod.

"There's something else you should know," Rooney says, and now Caitlyn's back beside her, the metal cool against her palm.

She passes her a tablet. Caitlyn can make out the airport security video onscreen, today's date, less than one hour ago. And a man pausing to glance back up at the camera.

"Michaels is also heading there," Rooney says. "He's alone. And without our help, he won't stand a chance."

[PART 5]

"None but those who have experienced them can conceive of the enticements of science."

—Mary Shelley,
Frankenstein

[54]

IN THE ENDLESS BLACK DEPTHS, THE CORAL SCRAPES AT HIS THOUGHTS
and rattles his bones. He twists and he tumbles and he struggles
to swim. Yet his body does not obey. Limbless, he sinks. No direction. No sense of time. Bathed in aching regret of what he'd made
of his life. All gummed up, each day worse than the last.

So why does he stay? Some weight keeps him tethered here,
yes. Some name.

Mariangela.

Then, the strangest of things.

Another name follows. Aiden Sawyer. *Yes, that's who I am.*

Next comes the light, a single cool bulb in this sea of dark
glass. Something to swim toward among the ebony depths. Something he's drawn to on instinct.

Moving now, faster and faster. He is form without figure, a
body without boundaries. Hard to tell if he's falling or rising. All
he knows is that the light is calling him, and he must answer it.
Yes, he *must* swim closer.

The solitary bulb multiplies into a dozen, then a field. Rows
upon rows sprout from liquid silver. It overwhelms him. He is
blinking now—yes, he can blink—and he is batting at the blinding

light. Fingers and hands form against the white haze. He gasps for air like a newborn, yet the air is thick and hitches in his mouth.

Gagging, picking at his lips, he pulls a root from deep in his throat, tugging until wet rubber and plastic rise. Past his tonsils and his tongue. Past his lips and his teeth. The tube hits the floor beside him, wet and glistening.

Aiden Sawyer coughs and spits, blinking off this odd chemical haze. That thing on the floor, it was stuffed down his throat. But why?

Another dozen blinks, and he realizes there's something else on the floor.

Five feet away lies a body. A man in hospital scrubs. A red puddle behind his head that makes Sawyer think of dropped strawberries.

"Hey… Hey, you." The words leave Sawyer's lips, feeble and hoarse.

The body does not answer.

He gives the fallen man a nudge with his toes. Living skin shouldn't settle like that.

Another touch, this time with his left hand just to be sure. Nothing. The scientist or doctor or whoever this is, he'll never move again.

And what's the dead man holding in his hand? It's been years, but Sawyer recognizes the shape of a tattoo gun, the power cord singed and melted.

Sawyer's right hand instinctively touches his left wrist. A surge of pain, that rattling and scratching that tugged him from the void. Etched here in his flesh is an odd swirl, like a barcode with unfinished alphanumerics: G2.

What'n the hell?

The room crowds in from the edge of his vision, Sawyer truly seeing it for the first time. Bright lights over two doors with no windows. Stainless-steel cabinets and sinks. Glass cases stocked with medical vials and ointments and more sharp tools than he's seen in a decade. This is some kind of hospital room.

Head pounding, Sawyer rubs his eyes, trying to blink himself back to sleep, back to wherever he came from.

Then he notices the distant alarms. Like prison.

It hits him, a series of flashes like light off polished metal, each brighter than the last. There had been a group watching him strapped to a gurney. A chaplain offering last-minute salvation.

But why?

Because it was the big sleep, the most important nap of your life.

A low rumble and the distant beep of a security sensor. Another sound he recognizes from prison: the clang of heavy doors and movement beyond.

A second beep, closer. Someone's coming into this room.

Sawyer inventories his situation. The corpse on the floor. His violent history. He didn't kill this man, of course, but that hardly matters. They'll find him alive and he'll have to explain.

Explain what?

Doesn't matter. Just find a hidey place and round up your thoughts.

A third beep and the murmuring voices near the door. They're right outside.

So Sawyer finds the closest place he can hide: the stainless-steel closet.

Inside, it's bigger than expected and colder as well. No emergency lighting. He closes the door, presses his ear against the metal. Listens as the muffled voices grow closer.

"Damn, looks like Tim took a blast."

"Yeah, he's not getting up anytime soon."

"Jesus, what a clusterfuck—*wait.*"

A pause. Sawyer can sense that whoever these two men are, they're whispering now. Maybe they're leaving. Mere inches of metal separate the two rooms. If he could just see beyond, he could—

"Hey, mister!" one of the voices shouts. "Mister... shit, what's his name? Mr. Subject, sir, uh, if you're in here, come on out, okay? We're... We're here to help."

Like hell you are. It doesn't take a good liar to spot a bad one.

Especially when the liar is nervously shouting and opening up doors.

Which means they're coming in here.

When Sawyer hid, he thought this was a closet. Now that his eyes are adjusted, he sees the room for what it is: a place to store cadavers.

There are two gurneys like the one he woke up on. The left one is empty. The right one is not.

The bag upon it is lumpy and misshapen, as if the body within is some sort of reduction, more torso than limbs. Printed upon a patch of white plastic, that same spiral barcode and an alphanumeric: K29.

"Sir, if you're in there, we just want to help. We're coming in."

Nice of them to broadcast their plans. Sawyer climbs under the gurney. Hoists himself up into the lattice between the legs and the wheels. Just enough space to tuck in and curl up and not an inch more.

A glance back. He's dragged his IV behind him, the port still in his arm. With a quick snap, he yanks the IV into the shadows.

Then the door opens.

Light, and the outline of two legs at the threshold. Then another pair join.

"Jesus, is that him? That is, isn't it?"

A pause. The two shapes step into the small room.

"I've never seen one in person. Just the videos and the measurements."

"Watch the door. Make sure it doesn't lock."

A chuckle. "You think?"

The squeak of rubber shoes on the cool tiles and the scent of coffee and sweat. They're near the other gurney now, on both sides. One's wearing hospital scrubs, like the dead man on the floor. The other's wearing jeans and running shoes. So close Sawyer could touch them both.

And Sawyer's limbs. With each breath, his muscles tremble

and twitch. He wants to relax, to let go and fall to the floor. But if he does, they'll see him from that angle.

So he bites his lips and clutches the gurney's legs. Keeps himself wedged below while they gather above.

A slow unzipping. The crinkle of plastic above as the body bag is opened. "God damn, they really took him apart."

The smell assaults Sawyer, a stinging wave of putrefaction that dampens his eyes and roils his gut. It takes every ounce of restraint not to vomit.

Mr. Running Shoes isn't as resilient.

A gag from above and then a wet splat. The man buckles at his knees, clutching his stomach. Another gag and the rest of his lunch hits the floor.

Mr. Scrubs lets out a low chuckle. "Ya, they stink when they're alive, too. Here, wipe up."

A crinkling and the buzz of a closing zipper. Paper towels hit the floor, followed by hands and a sweaty face wiping wet lips.

Mr. Running Shoes is just a kid, really, some scruffy gumdrop more comfortable at a keyboard than down on his knees and cleaning up puke.

It is his eyes, however, that catch Sawyer's attention. Even in the shadows, he can read the surprise widening his eyes.

He's looking at Sawyer.

"Uh, Yuri? So, I just found the missing sub—"

The kick catches Mr. Running Shoes square in the face, splitting his lips and sending him crashing back into the gurney. The bagged body tumbles onto him.

Mr. Scrubs bends down, finds Sawyer reaching out and seizing him by the collar. A quick shake, like a terrier thrashing a rat, and Sawyer slams the man's head off the gurney's legs. Mr. Scrubs lets out a low grunt and falls to his chest, limp-boned and moaning.

Most days, Sawyer would be ashamed at how prison hardened him. The skills he developed to stave off beatings and shower room rape.

Today, he's grateful.

His hands moved on instinct. Now his feet do the same. A quick twist of limbs and he's out from under the gurney, closing the distance to the open door, then grabbing the metal handle and pivoting back into the lab.

A quick glance back into the cadaver closet. Mr. Scrubs rubbing his head. Mr. Running Shoes cups his dripping lips, screaming, "Dun clothes tha thoor!"

Which is exactly what Sawyer does.

With a heavy clang, the stainless-steel door slams shut, dampening the cool air and the smell of rot and ruin, sealing the horror inside. Sawyer finds the lock and engages it. A second later, hands hammer the door, little more than soft thunder and muffled shouts from within.

Sawyer lets the moment wash over him, this little victory among a sea of defeat. Prison also taught him to listen and think. Those two men had given him some answers without knowing. Yet many questions remain.

He needs to get out, quietly. Wherever this is, he must get away. And maybe, if he plays his cards right, he can get back to Mariangela. He can tell her he's sorry. He's made so many mistakes.

But first, he needs to know what he's up against.

His gaze drifts back to those surgical tools in their glass case, all shiny and sharp. He promised himself he was done killing. He promised he'd start making amends.

But that doesn't mean he has to play nice.

TED STEVENS INTERNATIONAL AIRPORT

ANCHORAGE, ALASKA

OVER THE YEARS MICHAELS CULTIVATED A ROTATION OF ALIASES, each planted at key locations near airports and train stations and interstate bus depots. He used social media bots and random subscriptions to build credible presences. Jeremey Vedder, his preferred alias, is now heading to Texas, booked on an Amtrak e-ticket, Los Angeles to San Antonio.

Here, in Alaska, he is Marvin Greenwald, a blogger from San Diego with a credit score of 670 and a penchant for anime on a Crunchyroll subscription. Another overworked millennial visiting the Last Frontier on a last-minute discount.

In San Francisco, Marvin passed through security without incident. Marvin spent half the flight using the Wi-Fi to stream the latest news from D.C. Marvin registered for a C-SPAN account for when the joint hearing begins. He used VPNs in a chain arrangement to cover his tracks.

Which is why when he exits the plane and finds several Anchorage Airport Police and a jumpy K9, he senses the impossible: somehow, they found him.

"Mr. Greenwald, a.k.a. Gideon Michaels," one of the deputies says. "Come with us."

"I'm sorry, this has to be a mistake."

The airport police glare. No mistake.

Two long corridors, one security checkpoint bypassed, and the cool air of Alaska hits his face. They're on the apron now, luggage carts being towed about as bored handlers chat. Far off, an A380 screams down the runway.

They lead him to a white van. A good sign, he tells himself as the van drives across the vast airport. That he's wedged in the center but not cuffed is another decent signal. And the warehouse they're taking him toward, he's worked it out now; they're couriers, not captors.

They begin removing their uniforms. First the Velcro name tags. Then the belts. The driver unbuttons his collar as the front passenger steers.

"So, you're in too good of shape to be cops," Michaels says. "And I see too many tattoos for Foundation undercover. Let me guess: private military contractors."

A chuckle from the man to Michaels's right, a big fellow. No answer. Still, the less they say, the more they show.

There are over a dozen major private military companies in the U.S. At one time or another, the Foundation has broken bread with them all. As the wars in the Middle East dragged on, PMCs filled in by the thousands. But those jobs didn't go away after drawdown. They just hit the gray market. Still, the question remains: how'd they find Michaels?

A helicopter idles outside the warehouse, men in dark tactical gear removing tie-downs. The warehouse doors open and the van drives inside.

"Out," the man to his left says, so that's where Michaels goes.

He finds himself looking at a halfway house for lost artifacts and mislabeled packages. A depot of forsaken luggage turned operational staging ground. Weapons on delivery and check. Curious body armor laid out on tables. It looks, Michaels realizes, like the moments before a SWAT deploys on call out.

And maybe that's what this is.

One of the contractors chuckles. "Over there, 'Marvin,'"

There is where a laptop sits, and a young technician opening a folding chair. Amid the bustle of snapping buckles and loaded duty bags, familiar icons blink onscreen, confirming the highest-security connection. Shit.

Then comes a face, one of the last faces he was expecting to see.

"Congresswoman Chatterjee," Michaels says, leaning in until the whole screen has his focus.

"Hello, Michaels. It's been a few laps, hasn't it?"

"Better part of a year by my count."

"I hope you'll forgive me for our previous chat, but it's like you said: 'Every hearing needs a villain.'"

The last time he met the congresswoman had been during the disciplinary review that punctuated his resignation from the Foundation. Chatterjee, like the others, had come to a truce with Michaels. He was faulted for some of the mishandling surrounding the God's Breath Killer. But far less than the Foundation had tried to pin on him.

She says, "We did what we thought best at the time. But the times change. You have proven to be a slippery man to catch up with."

"Well, I learned from the best."

"And surpassed them. Lucky for us, your partner saw fit to assist us."

Chatterjee nods offscreen. A moment later, a new window opens up and a new face joins the video call: Caitlyn. "Hey, Michaels."

Michaels scoots closer. "Cait, where are you?"

"Relax. I'm fine."

His back stiffens and his shoulders tense. His eyes drink in the clues onscreen. Chatterjee and Caitlyn, both at different locations based upon the angle and color of light. Or at least staged to look separate.

"So that's how you found me," he says. "What are you offering her? A consultancy if she assists?"

Chatterjee shakes her head. "Caitlyn came in on her own. We intercepted her moments before the Foundation swarmed her motel. She's safe and well protected."

He hesitates. Before the Foundation arrived? Perhaps she misspoke.

"And she's agreed to use her skill to assist our operation. We hope you will as well."

"Our" operation, no longer his. Now it starts to make sense. The PMCs gearing up. The helicopter being fueled. And the fact that she mentioned intercepting Caitlyn *before* an extraction team got to her… *Holy shit.*

"You're going after Day's Bane as well."

A tiny smile tugs on Chatterjee's lips. "The men and women around you are, yes. My attack will take a different approach. In ninety minutes I'll be co-chairing the emergency joint hearing here at the Capitol. I'm sure you've kept up on news. Dr. Chase lit a fire that exposed some dark places. Senator Drogan intends to carry that torch."

"And you're using us to hide what it brings to light."

"I want Day's Bane extinguished before it becomes our Chernobyl. Coordinator Nox has been playing a dangerous game. No doubt he believes it's for the safety of our nation, but this is too much for one man to control. It ends now."

"Then what? You sweep it under the rug, your running mate gets his campaign boost, and no one's the wiser?"

She sighs and leans forward. "Michaels, take a deep look at your options. You're in Alaska, headed to a classified facility like a one-man circus. Marvin Greenwald? We found the helicopter and the pilot you booked. What was your plan? Force him to fly into restricted airspace at gunpoint and hope for the best?"

Not exactly. Still, when he hears part of the plan read back, it feels like a stretch. If only he had more time.

"You need us," Chatterjee says. "And we need you, on-site, helping my team figure out what we're up against. You're the only one with experience."

So there it is, the pitch. Time to kick the fence. "You said Caitlyn's safe?"

"Safe and secure and getting the very best medical treatment. She's lost a lot of weight. Our doctors have her on IV nutrition. I'll step away."

The congresswoman gives another motion off camera. Her connection ends. Now it's just Caitlyn taking up the whole screen, her eyes two dim jewels reflecting the screen's glare.

Michaels hesitates. What to say? Where to start? *Tell her, you idiot. Tell her what you've felt ever since that night in Boston.*

The warmth of her skin.

The comfort of her smile.

The strength of her pain.

Yet his words catch in his throat, rigid and dry. "You left me. Again."

"I did. And I'm sorry. Again."

She tells him about the motel, the shootout, the escape. He fills her in on Chase's dead man's switch. The pieces mostly fit.

And yet, he senses other plots in motion, details just past his understanding. It's not what you know or what you sense that's deadly. It's what you don't even suspect, the *unknown* unknowns that riddle this case.

"Cait, you remember the codeword, right? If you're not safe—"

"I would have used it."

He nods. "No, you're right. It's just—"

"You care about me."

For a while now, he thinks. *And somewhere along the way, I fell in love.*

What he says is, "I wouldn't be here if I didn't."

"I know. I don't think I deserve it."

"You deserve it. You always have." He takes a deep breath. "Caitlyn, I—"

An airhorn pierces the conversation. PMCs snap their heads as the team leader waves them over to a pallet of plastic containers. "Suit up, you monkeys!"

Michaels finds his clumsy words retreating back into his throat. *She never needed me. It's the other way around.*

"I have to go," she says. "We're getting ready on this end. I'll see you soon."

She reaches out and touches the screen.

And then she's gone.

[56]

OVER THIRTY MINUTES MICHAELS IS STRIPPED DOWN, SHOWERED, AND fitted into a tight body suit, a thing of flexible fabric and integrated wires. Like the biosuits at Clearwater, but denser. He squeezes a gloved hand as a technician named Felweather clips a battery pack to his waist.

"You're wearing the best protection whipped up on short notice," Felweather says. He's just a kid, probably poached from MIT or some promising startup. "It's essentially copper, aluminum, and polyethylene fibers woven into the shape of your body, like—"

"Like a Faraday cage," Michaels says, adjusting the arms. It's a curious sensation, something between yoga pants and motorcycle leathers.

"Exactly. Thank God for us geeks, amirite? So much easier to brief than the bullet catchers."

"It's clever." Michaels checks the battery. A hundred percent. "And this powers it?"

"Bingo. Ideally, the attenuator dampens decoherent contact."

"Ideally?"

"It's not armor, okay? More like a deterrent."

"Like an electric fence."

"Hey, that's good. I'm gonna borrow that. In theory, it'll buy a few deflections, so don't get into a wrestling match." He cinches a few straps and zips up the legs. Michaels catches a glance of the others suiting up, a few laughs and back slaps before game time. "Look, the truth is y'all are beta testing this. I mean, it should work."

"In theory."

Felweather grins. "Theory is all we're working with here, amigo." The kid zips up Michaels in the back, gives a sharp tug and the whole suit snaps into place like a tight rubber glove. "Okay, you're good. You'll get your loadout at briefing. You've used NODs before?"

Night observation devices—NODs to the military—strike Michaels as an odd choice. Even if they rush, the sun will be up soon. "Yeah, I have."

"Solid. One less thing to explain. Okay, Ellison's giving me the stink eye, which means the briefing's about to begin."

Across the warehouse, a broad-shouldered man wheels a set of monitors before a stack of Pelican crates. The team gathers around, neck and wrist tattoos poking out from the suits. There's a tightness here. The way they tuck in each other's straps and pass out gum. A friendship forged in combat.

What the hell has he gotten pulled into?

"All right, kids, gather around for the powwow," Ellison shouts. "We've got a choppy flight ahead, so we're front-loading logistics." He opens a crate, gives it a shove forward with his boot. "You know the drill, phones in the box. Don't make Sepulveda check cavities cause you couldn't stay off TikTok."

Chuckles from the team. Someone says, "Yah, I bet he volunteered."

"Damn right I did," Sepulveda says, winking. He's a big man, linebacker wide in the chest and all veins at the neck. War horses, the whole crew. Probably a dozen busted elbows and blown knees.

The phones clatter as they're placed in the crate. A few eyes on Michaels as he swipes, powers down, and places his inside.

"Thank you," Ellison says. "So, you're wondering who our guests are. Spoiler alert: you're going to keep wondering. You don't need to know his name or his backstory or any bullshit about how he wound up here. His name is Mr. Nobody, because when this is over, nobody will remember he was here. Clear?"

A couple of taps on hard surfaces and grunts of approval. "Who was here, sir?"

"Exactly. Mr. Nobody holds the rare honor of being the only one in this crew to have direct contact with a decoherent. He's our resident expert. Now, Dr. Chase may have kicked Day's Bane in the teeth, but Mr. Nobody is here to help us put her down like Old Yeller."

A few heads turn in Michaels's direction. Stony faces and sharp glances. Eyes that have seen things that chip away at humanity. Funny, he never thought of himself as a veteran of this new future, yet here he is.

"And there's another who'll be assisting. She should be arriving"—Ellison checks his wrist display, and there's a flash on the screen: *DECOHERENCE DETECTED*—"any second now."

The pulse hits low and cool, dimming a few lights. It's hard to tell if the sun-threaded figure has been there the whole time. Or if she just snapped into existence, static warping the TV screens and charging the air.

"Say hello for us, would ya?"

"Hello for us." Caitlyn's voice booms from all edges of reality. From the back, Michaels has a perfect view as the shiver moves down the team. Mercenaries of tactical cool, their backs straightening and shoulders going rigid. Somebody makes the sign of the cross.

After all this time, Caitlyn's ability still fills Michaels with wonder. There she is, luminous strands rising from her silhouette. Vibrant one second. The next, just an afterglow, like headlights in rain. He wants to rub his eyes and wipe the impossible from his vision.

Yet he doesn't want to see her leave.

"Yeah, it creeps me out too," Ellison says. "You read about it, but seeing is believing. Meet our ghost. You'll refer to her as such. Once we're on-site at Day's Bane, Ghost and Nobody will be our eyes and ears, our intel and everything else. There's an air-gapped server on the fourth level, the dirty heart of this project. That's our target. We get in, alpha and bravo teams evac all personnel from the platform. Felweather and Nobody delete every trace of the program."

A hand shoots up, scarred knuckles rising above a mane of braided mohawk and balaclava with a skull. The kind of merc who really leans into the warrior persona.

"What is it, Hutchins?"

"What about armaments?" Hutchins asks, adding, "Besides these leotards and that human hologram, I'm guessing jacketed hollow points won't cut it."

"Felweather has some new toys for you."

"Yes, that's right, *toys*." The young technician groans and hoists something out of a case that tilts half the heads. "Our friends at DARPA would love to hear their directed energy weapons called toys. But nonetheless, Santa is here."

He slides the cart down the row, one case per person. Clasps pop as curious fingers dig in. What Michaels finds himself looking at is remarkable, if not uncanny. It has the same basic shape as a submachine gun, yet the handguard is brick-like and the barrel ends in a flat grid of diodes. Metal and plastic intertwine down the stock and end at an angled screen that reads *DEW STANDBY - POWER 100%*.

"You've heard of Havana syndrome, so you know about those attacks on our diplomats in Cuba. We tracked similar events in Beijing and Moscow and Hanoi, all friendly places, mind you. Intel suggested GRU and MSS were testing directed energy weapons capable of penetrating bone and superheating water in cells. These are similar. Do not be downrange unless you want to feel like a microwave pizza."

Michaels knows about DEW systems. For years, the Foundation shadowed the reports of Havana syndrome, even embedding an asset in the DoD investigation. Felweather is right: these aren't toys in the slightest.

But he's wrong about the intel.

The attacks weren't just GRU or MSS, but also rogue American operatives sewing confusion and selling results to the highest bidders. Like all technology, it's been rapidly miniaturized. What was crammed in a van a few years ago now fits in a case.

Felweather continues, "By generating pulsed millimeter waves, the DEW temporarily interrupts entanglement necessary to sustain a decoherent's mens corpus—their mental body."

He gestures to Caitlyn, who seems to flicker brighter for a moment as she studies them, her stare blooming chills on their skin.

"Yeah, *temporarily*," the man with a red beard says, the tag *MARCO, M.* on his case. "So basically it's like fanning a fart."

"More like blowdrying one," Felweather says. "Basically."

"Let me throw another question at you, Quartermaster," says a muscular woman with a scar from her ear to her neck. "How do we plug 'em if they're doing that invisible thing?"

"Yes, well, I suppose that's why they pay me the big bucks, Chanchanni. In the second layer of your swag bag, you'll find tuned NODs. As our Ghost will demonstrate, decoherents can adjust their luminosity or vanish entirely. At least to our eyes. But they cannot change the beta particles they emit."

The NODs fit snug on Michaels's head. He practices raising and lowering them. Bulky and cumbersome, they narrow his field of view to a thin tunnel.

"The switch on the left tube cycles the modes. Look for the deep purple filter. Then give our Ghost your attention."

The first click of the tube ring turns the world green. Another click and the emerald haze falls to thermal. Michaels holds out his hand, warm yellows and oranges and a fleeting web of greens between his fingers.

A third click, and it's a field of dim violet. He turns to Caitlyn, vertigo devouring him. Seeing her full form is like being launched from a cannon into a kaleidoscopic cosmos. Next comes the awe as black static gives dark contour to a woman's nude shape. Threads flare and arc, radiating from her edges. Two eyes flicker and burn, binary pulsars atop a body of shadow-wrapped stars.

A memory from childhood, his first solar eclipse. The darkening sky. The crickets at noon. The understanding of how vast the cosmos truly is.

"*Dios mío*, that's really something," Sepulveda says. "Like looking at God."

"Nah, it's looking at the future," Chanchanni says. "Our jobs just became obsolete."

[57]

WASHINGTON, D.C.

Few rooms have heard more grandiose proclamations than the marbled walls here in the Hart Senate Office Building's Hearing Room 216. From four-star generals and tech CEOs to investigations into failed incursions abroad and disrupted elections at home. Praise has been uttered here. And endless threats between squabbling political factions.

Today, it is an emergency arena, the Joint Committee Hearing on Undisclosed Research and Review.

Convened in record time, the venue has twice been moved, a fact that irks several members of Congress, members who have pledged to get to the bottom of this, knowing neither what this is nor where the bottom truly lies. They know only that there is blood in the water and an opportunity for posturing that will pay dividends come November.

To the C-SPAN camera crew setting up, it's business as usual. They've seen it all: the loud outrage, the pledges for reform, the D.C. elite salivating for a meaty clip, something they can use to fire up their constituents.

To the man with the turquoise eyes and the gray suit, today is a performance. No more an authentic display of true power than pornography is true passion. Yet a display many buy into.

Nox gives his lawyer a nod and takes a seat beside him. There are boxes at the table, places for water and internet plug-ins. Nox stashed a few energy bars in his jacket. There will be much bloviating from the dais today; Nox is no stranger to long hearings.

He turns and studies the aides setting up. The room's at half capacity now and filling. More than Nox hoped for. Chase did unprecedented damage but there's plenty left to salvage.

So, work to be done.

Privately, Nox retreats inward and slows his breathing. Lets the chatter become distant and mute. He is in the courtyard of his mind, a place of great defenses. Today is just another assignment, another surprise mission like all those before. A chance to preserve security, to save American lives.

A clang of the gavel and Nox opens his eyes. Ten minutes have passed.

There's Dave Drogan, sliding into the far right, folders stacked like a kid at his first high school debate. Nox feels pity. The man's career is already over and he doesn't yet know it.

Another clang of wood against wood. Congresswoman Chatterjee lets the gavel rest and studies Nox, her eyes moving through him, past him, beyond.

"Let's bring this hearing to order," she says. "Mr. Holland Nox, thank you for agreeing to join us on short notice."

Nox leans into the microphone. "My pleasure, Congresswoman. Whenever you're ready to begin."

The Airbus H175 is a favored helicopter for wealthy hedge fund managers and the offshore oil and gas industry. With twelve passengers, its radius of action is a full 218 nautical miles. More than enough to fly to Day's Bane and back. Most comforting of all: its cabin is spacious and muffled, a fact Michaels appreciates as it pitches in the misty winds off the Gulf of Alaska.

Out the left window, a pod of humpbacks breaks the gray waters. Out the right, columns rise from the haze, blades in the fog. *A wind farm*, Michaels realizes. *So that's how Day's Bane stayed off the grid.*

The pilot's voice crackles over the comms. "Platform drop-off coming up in five."

The squad checks their gear one final time. Loose straps are tucked in, battery packs activated. Beneath the Kevlar and Faraday mesh, they're an odd combination: a SEAL team and a surf team, DEWs humming and NODs blinking.

Ellison's voice booms. "Remember: Day's Bane is an old oil rig, tight halls and sharp turns. Secure your sectors and clear down, floor by floor. Our Ghost took a peek and the word of the day is chaos. That's good, but no reason to get sloppy. Any civvies act tough, you break their index finger, show them how fierce they are when they can't pick their nose."

A boulder of a man named Vee asks what everyone else is thinking. "What about the decoherents? Are they…?"

"No sign so far. Save the DEWs but keep them ready. All right, folks, show time!"

The helicopter banks, swinging low and close to the wind farm. Two towers are smoldering, the nacelles scarred by fire and still burping smoke.

"Jesus," Sepulveda says. "Their map says it's all empty."

But there it is, glistening against the predawn haze: Day's Bane.

Pylons rise to the layered platform where metal and glass merge in cold lattices. Michaels squeezes his hands. Tries to count his comforting primes but can hardly think straight. Here it is, a place that does not exist, now coming into view like a mirage. A place never meant to be found.

With a jaw-rattling thump, the helicopter touches down. Voices on the comms shout, "Go! Go! Go!"

IN THE DARKNESS of the pod, Caitlyn Grey lies upon a soft membrane of float gas matched to her body's temperature. A curved display streams a live feed of Day's Bane along with platform schematics and maps of the nearby island. With a swipe, she darkens the screen and settles in. She floats among silence.

Rooney's voice comes in over the speakers. "Faraday cage dropping in three, two, one."

Now Caitlyn floats among the fabric of existence.

All space unfolds before her, an endless tapestry of blind sites rendered as static upon curtains. The hissing song of the universe, this blizzard of whispering ash. Her senses take over.

In her earpiece, Michaels says, "We're clearing the landing deck now. Ghost, we could use your eyes below."

So that's what she does. Two thousand seven hundred and eleven miles in a blink.

The gridded farms of North Dakota rush past, blurring into southern Manitoba and Saskatchewan. The great forests and endless lakes of Alberta rise into the Rockies, cold spikes piercing lavender skies. Out now, over Alaska's fractured valleys, glacial blues clawing at the continent's edge.

Caitlyn can see it screaming in from the west in the predawn glow, the platform and the pylons and the teams upon it, weapons pointed. When she hits the top deck, they jump.

"Weapons down," Michaels says. "That's her."

A pause as they eye her, adjusting their NODs.

"How you feeling?"

"Fine," she says. "Good. Great, actually."

"Everything stable?"

Stable where? she wonders. Not back at the pod.

Your mind, that dark voice whispers. *The old attic of one.*

The lie leaves Caitlyn's lips smoothly. "Perfectly stable."

Felweather comes to a stop at the loading shafts. He toggles the button. "Elevators are offline."

"Copy that," Ellison says. "Teams, take position."

Wind whipping their faces, the squad splits. Alpha team hits the east stairwell where the sun is a tangerine hint. Bravo team heads west, to the primary stairs. All quiet on the comms as they stack by the doors. All eyes turn to Michaels as he thumbs his mic.

"Ghost, can you give us eyes inside?"

In a blur of metal and piping, Caitlyn blinks her way into the stairwell. Dark walls and flashing emergency lights. Another blink and she checks to the east. Back out now, through the door and up onto the windy platform.

"Stairwells are clear," she says, arriving beside Ellison. "First up are offices, food storage, dining. There's a few people in the kitchen."

"Copy that. Breachers, hit your doors on my count. We'll clear and contain, then connect in the middle. Keep at least two with NODs scanning for decoherents. Here we go."

Vee, on breach, presses his tablet against the door's key reader. Nothing, no signal. Out comes the Halligan and the metal chocks. Vee's a big guy but this is a marine-rated inward-swinging door. Time for a deep breath.

Vee slides the Halligan's leveled fork tips up the door's jamb and edge. He braces it and nods to Chanchanni, who strikes the adze end with her hammer. Even against the thundering waves, the hammer clangs loud.

Two more strikes, and there's enough of a gap to wedge the metal chock between the jamb and the edge. Vee grunts, digs the Halligan in deep and rocks it back and forth, back and forth, and—

The door swings inward on its own.

Caitlyn flickers on the other side. "Thought I'd buy you some time."

At the east end of the platform, the other door opens just as fast.

"She's handy, that one," Felweather says. "Rest of you better start earning your ride home."

Ellison points into the cool shadows, the platform creaking with the might of the sea. "Everyone in!"

[58]

In Washington, D.C., Holland Nox is nearing the end of his opening remarks. His posture is straight. His palms are dry. His heart rate has not gone over sixty. Not even when that exhausting congressman from San Diego played a clip of Robert Chase claiming the God's Breath Killer was made in a lab. Nox held his cool then, just like he holds it now: all flat smiles and polite nods.

"If it pleases the committee, I'd like to get to the heart of this hearing," says the presidential candidate from Kentucky. "Mr. Nox, I'd like to play a game. Do you enjoy games?"

Nox nods. He can see where this is going. Drogan, scoring points for the social media crowd. They'll retweet and hit *LIKE* but will they cut checks and show up to vote? Nox has his doubts.

"Are you ready, Mr. Nox? Have I got your attention?"

"My undivided attention, Senator Drogan," Nox says. "We both enjoy games."

Is that a blush on Drogan's freshly shaved cheeks? Pre-hearing, Nox took a peek around Drogan's iCloud photo account. Nothing damning, but a few photos of Dave and his babes at a Vegas weed lounge. Why are politicians so allergic to encryption?

Drogan clears his throat. "I'll read a statement and you'll answer 'confirm' or 'deny.' Pretty simple, right?"

"Confirm."

Laughter from the audience. Nox abhors half the people in this room, but he has to admit, there's an element of pleasure in swaying them. A liar's club, all peddling their bent version of the truth.

"You've heard of the late Sam Stephens, correct?"

"Sadly, confirm."

"And you've heard his conspiracy theories. Among them, that vaccines contain tracking chips or a cabal runs our government from bunkers beneath the Lincoln Memorial? To the best of your knowledge, do you confirm or deny his allegations?"

"Deny, Senator. Government is too clumsy to be run by a cabal."

More laughter. The cold room is beginning to warm up.

"And I believe you've met Dr. Robert Chase?"

"Confirm. I know *of* Dr. Chase."

"And you've heard that Dr. Chase—a man who founded and advised multiple biotech companies—has corroborated every word of Mr. Stephens's previously released testimony?"

"I can confirm he believes as much, Senator. It's why we're gathered inside, on this beautiful day. Instead of out golfing or—"

"For the sake of time, Mr. Nox, a simple 'confirm' or 'deny' will suffice."

"Confirm."

"According to my records, both you and your brother were Army Rangers. You were recruited into Delta Force, and then the CIA's Directorate of Operations, correct?"

"Confirm."

"Well, as one veteran to another, I thank you both for your service. In your work, a security clearance is vital, correct?"

"Confirm."

Nox can see it coming a mile away. Drogan is lulling him into patterned answers, getting him comfortable with the truth before he tries to catch him in a lie. Not a bad tactic. Certainly better than the blunt tools of lesser politicians. But Nox has decades of experience.

And a few friends on the panel.

When the meaty question finally arrives, he does what he knows will sew confusion: he speaks the truth.

Or a close enough version to knock Drogan off script.

"And Mr. Nox, have you ever heard of something called Project Day's Bane?"

Nox leans in. "Confirm."

Drogan shuffles his papers, then pauses and looks up. "I'm… I'm sorry, sir. You said—"

"Confirm. Day's Bane is my project."

Silence fills the chamber. The creaking of chairs as committee members lean forward. Only one person, still and stoic. Chatterjee. A smirk tugs one side of her face.

Then the room erupts in a dozen voices and a dozen questions, all frantic and overlapping.

FLASHLIGHTS ILLUMINATING THE STAIRWELLS, alpha and bravo teams descend into Day's Bane in synchronized waves.

First, they hit the offices, where half the lights are under repair, ladders and tools scattered about. When five armed figures emerge from the shadows, the platform technician freezes in his tracks, pliers falling from his hand as he mutters, "Ah fuck."

Then he's flex-cuffed and sat by a coffee machine while Felweather tags his location with a GPS tracker.

The kitchen staff come next, hands raised. Ellison restrains and tags them. Marco checks their IDs with a retinal scanner. Now they're marked on the team's map, five labeled red dots.

"First floor clear," Ellison says. "Move on to second."

It goes on as such: Caitlyn scouting ahead, her sun-threaded form vanishing in a low pulse and reappearing with an ear-popping hum; the teams rounding up scientists, technicians, security.

On the second floor, they surround a group of electricians and two doctors in lab coats. The flex-cuffs go on fast.

On three, they meet resistance: Foundation-trained guards who draw their guns and shout for backup. Michaels recognizes the one in the rear, Barnes, a big fellow last seen at Clearwater. He must have earned a promotion.

"Barnes, lower your gun," Michaels says, tasting the adrenaline tang of being sighted down barrel. "No one's going to hurt you. Just stand down."

Barnes's eyes narrow. Recognition, then anger. "You… *You* sold us out."

His forearm tenses. *Shit.* He's working up the courage to take the shot over the security desk.

A blur of golden light and a twisting of limbs. Caitlyn rises through the floor and seizes their arms. Dumbstruck and wincing, the guards can only stumble back as the weapons are wrenched from their grasp by a shimmering woman—here for a heartbeat, gone for the next.

Then come the cuffs and the tags. Michaels gives Barnes a pat on the shoulder.

The fourth floor now, where the servers and batteries loom, monoliths of cold data science. Even in low-power mode, the halls twinkle with blinking hard drives. Dimmed emergency lighting hangs above a humming generator, diesel-powered and burping.

"There." Michaels points to one server separate from the others. "I'll bet my life on it. That's what Nox doesn't want getting out."

"You're sure?" Hutchins asks.

"He's right," Felweather says. "The other servers are on different circuits to avoid wild currents. This one's silo'd, see? Totally isolated. This is where the gold's buried."

"How long do you need?" Ellison asks.

"As long as it takes and not a second more. I'll have to scope the keypad and see what I'm up against. Ask me once I'm drilled in."

"You've got twenty minutes."

"Asshole," Felweather mutters.

He pulls a large case from his rucksack. The Innervate Porta-Charge provides five kilowatts of continuous power, more than enough to juice the server and wipe it.

Michaels connects power cables as Felweather lays out his drilling equipment. Behind them, the two squads split up to reverse-clear and track down stragglers.

"Good morning, Day's Bane," Felweather says, and the server lights cycle from amber to green. He connects a drill bit and fastens the motor to a weak point in the panel. Using the magnets to inch up the metal, he aligns the drill bit. The camera overlays the safe's internal schematics. "Okay, looks simple enough."

He squeezes the trigger.

In Washington, D.C., Nox ignores his vibrating phone and scoots closer to the mic. He has the chamber's attention, every set of eyes, especially Drogan's. Time to squeeze.

"Day's Bane is the code name for a covert government telecommunications project," Nox says. "Two hundred and ninety-five million dollars, all aimed at reducing our reliance on foreign technology. These cell towers that carry our conversations? These Wi-Fi hotspots we're all using right now? Little thought is given to the chips and signals that carry our secrets. And yet, most of our hardware is foreign, pieced together by countries whose interests do not align with our own. Day's Bane means to remediate this."

"Pump the brakes for a moment, son," says a voice from the far left of the dais. The congressman from Nevada's sixth district. "You're saying Day's Bane is, what, some infrastructure project?"

"A highly classified counter-espionage infrastructure project. At least it was, until Senator Drogan insisted this meeting be public. Our legal team has all the information that's been cleared for release."

His attorney rises, gesturing to a handcart stacked with boxes. "If the committee could spare a few aides, we can have these packets distributed."

The staffers unbox and distribute sealed folders to the committee. A ten-minute recess is called. Enough time for Nox to duck into the men's room.

There, where the urinals burble and feet hurry back to the chamber, Nox calmly finds an empty stall and checks his phone. What he sees drains the color from his face. His flat heart rate, about to be broken.

>SITE CZ-93 BREACH: SECURE SERVER DATA ACCESS IN PROGRESS

Chatterjee, he realizes. This is her way of neutering Day's Bane while covering her ass. A stealthy divorce. The hearing is just one more scheme nested within others.

No matter. He has safeguards in place.

Nox gives the toilet a courtesy flush. He swipes and taps on his phone, thinking today is not the end of the world, not for him.

But for the others, it's about to get messy.

[59]

IT BEGINS DEEP IN THE FIFTH LEVEL OF DAY'S BANE, WHERE overworked fans push cooled air past tissue and brain. Here, on its own circuit, its own system entirely, is a fail-safe tested only once. When the man who created decoherence threatened the man whose funding made this facility possible.

Nox's signal arrives, rousing isolated generators and beginning a process of second awakenings. Processes not fully understood yet feared, like the nervous men who first split the atom.

In the sterile lab, dark dreams end as three slumbering minds come online. Digital signals are converted to electrical impulses, then fed into optical nerves. Their blind site arrives: a place they've never been able to visit by design.

Until now.

One floor above, Michaels senses ice and the charged air of a storm. His eyes rise to the security cameras. They should be offline. They said they would be.

Then why weren't the IR illuminators glowing before?

He lowers his goggles. "Everyone, check your NODs. We've got company."

Five rooms over, where the air ducts drip with salty condensation, Vee and Sepulveda round up the last of the server floor technicians. Wrists are flex-cuffed. Orders to stay put are barked. Alpha team slaps GPS trackers onto the workers and marks them for evac. Bravo team confirms the pickup.

Then comes a low hiss and the popping of sparks to Sepulveda's right. Out the corner of his eye: an arm stretching toward him, gone when he turns. Just a pulse of blue light and the scent of burnt metal.

"I… I think something just touched me."

Felweather speaks over the comms: "Check your battery."

"Sixty-four percent."

Another hiss and a pop down the hall behind Vee. For the space of one breath, it's there beside him: a flowing shape, wraith-like fingers and jutting muscle. The afterimage of lightning with two smoldering eyes.

"Fuck, that stings," Vee grunts. "Fifty-eight percent. Felweather, I thought you said these would protect us."

"They just did." Felweather's voice crackles. "I didn't say for how long. You want a guarantee, go to Home Depot. My team had to whip this up in a day."

Another crackling hiss and a pop to Sepulveda's left. The cool breath of winter and the taste of charged air.

Vee spins, sighting down the DEW and lowering his NOD. The hall blooms violet.

And there it is. Where the doors open to a small kitchen, a dark shape unfolds from nothing. Wires and wet flesh and vaporous arms like branches. Cracked lips split into a cruel grin.

"Decoherents in the field!"

To Vee, what follows is a quick prayer and a question: *Will this weapon really work?*

It turns out that it does.

There is no kickback, no muzzle flash when Vee presses the trigger. Just a haptic vibration and a flicker of static. The decoherent form simply bursts, cindering the air like a dying sparkler.

"I… Holy shit, I got one," Vee says. "Hot damn, I killed it good."

"You didn't kill it," Felweather says. "You just stunned it. Keep your head on a swivel. There's more on the way."

"Yeah, fucking bring 'em," Vee says.

So they do.

The first blow hits his right leg, yanking him forward, into the floor, and shattering his kneecap. He cries out at the impossible: blooming arms wrapped around his legs, a dark body rising from the ground.

The second blow comes from above. Impossibly, the ceiling collapses onto him. No, he realizes, he's being thrown *into* the ceiling. Now he's falling, his world receding to fireworks and screams, fractured metal and bone.

Sepulveda rounds the corner and stops in his tracks. There, where the break room meets the hall, he sees what makes little sense. Vee, throttled against the ceiling like a fish against rocks.

Down come the NODs and there they are, two shadowy assailants. A furious woman, crawling along the ceiling with too many fingers. A broad-shouldered man, floating off the ground.

Sepulveda fires the DEW again and again and again. It all blurs together: the haptic feedback and blooming colors on his NODs, the bursting shapes and crackling static. Vee cries as he tumbles from the ceiling.

Through the tablet, Michaels catches flip-book glimpses from the body cams: the squad convening, falling back, and dropping to cover each other in high low. The warping of post-human forms. People that no longer move but pulse and vanish in spastic blasts.

A server rack collapses in a crumple of metal.

Ceiling tiles jostle and snap.

Far off, where the windows meet the gray haze of dawn, cracks expand down the glass.

The decoherents are flanking them from multiple angles.

Michaels spots a colorful blur by the south stairs. Aims and—

"Careful," Caitlyn says. "Every time you guys graze me, it makes it harder to find my way back. How much longer?"

"I'm wiping the server now," Felweather says. "Evac team should be heading up top. Five minutes, max."

"We'll hold off the hostiles," Michaels says. "I'll be right beside you…" He almost says her name.

"No, you'll be behind me." Caitlyn's luminous form unfolds before him. "I'm not letting them near any of you."

"Well, you might not have much choice," Felweather says. "Here they come."

To Michaels's natural vision, the broken man is limping like a puppet on strings. A twist of the NOD and the truth clicks into view. Zade Holloway, hoisting the battered frame of Hutchins, making his legs walk with a *clackity clack*.

"Catch," Zade cackles into the groaning soldier's ears.

Then the moaning body is sailing through the server farm and into Michaels and Felweather.

But not into Caitlyn.

Fifty feet in a blink and she hits Zade with enough force to blow out the glass of every rack in the row. Enough speed to sweep him up like a child.

One floor up, in the recreation wing, Sepulveda drags a wounded Vee while Ellison scans for Iliana. The goggles have narrowed his view to a dim tube. He pushes them up, scanning, sensing, but not seeing Iliana as she materializes behind him, her arms two rising scythes.

But Caitlyn sees her.

The flash blows out Ellison's eardrums and knocks him flat on his ass. Caitlyn embraces Iliana, a silver mens corpus held tight in her arms. Then they're gone.

Second floor, the west stairs, where Chanchanni is squeezing off pulse after pulse at Raymond Flay and missing each time. He's adapted fast to these new weapons. Hard to hit a target that moves one-fifth the speed of light.

"C'mon… C'mon!" she screams at Flay's hulking form, bending and weaving, long fingers reaching out as he worms his way closer and closer.

Then the flash hits him, knocks the breath from Chanchanni's lungs and leaves her alone in this hall.

On that lonely Kentucky highway, Caitlyn tasted one of their powers. Now, she feels the full brunt of three minds as fast as her own. Three mental bodies less bound to this world.

She rips their mental forms from place to place, sending them spinning and tumbling through a confusion of locations. The amber sands where Namibia meets the Atlantic. The stormy fjords of Norway. A Venetian hotel drawn from her time in high school. It's all here, her memories and places and landscapes without end, each merging into each other again and again.

New memories assault her. She is in a throne room pockmarked with bullets. Then an army base at dawn. A labyrinthian basement where Raymond Flay once kept those he first worked on, those whose perfect shapes he hoped to subsume.

Caitlyn senses a great fracturing occurring. A schism in memory, in place, in time. She can see Day's Bane among the fog. Can see her dark pod and her dead parents inside crawling toward her. Can see her old landlady, Mrs. Bakshi, and the San Francisco apartment crumbling to sand upon blue Kenyan beaches.

She can see it all. Can see too much happening at once.

[60]

In Washington, D.C., the committee pores over the documents while Nox pours himself some water. So many confident voices, now muted. So many sets of reading glasses, low on noses. This hour's new soundtrack: ballpoint pens scratching out notes.

"Mr. Nox, if you could just be patient with the committee," the senior senator from Montana says, his bushy eyebrow rising. "This is a lot to chew on at once."

"Take your time, Senator. If you have any questions, I'm happy to answer them."

Nox glances down at his phone. Already the hashtag #Drogan-Chokes is out in the wild. A new headline is trending: *Sen. Drogan accidentally reveals classified counter-intel operation. Developing...* The good boys and girls at Kray Mesa are on time.

A few grumbles from the dais and turning pages. Nox's attorney gives him a satisfied nod. Nox smiles, not outwardly.

But inside, he has to admit, this was a close one. He's had to call in dozens of favors. And he had to include some leverage in the documents, custom-tailored to each reader.

The first twenty pages of the brief are identical, an overview of how American telecommunications are vulnerable to attack. A prospectus outlines what the Foundation is upgrading. The next five pages are personalized, for the eyes of key politicians on the dais.

Two senators who took fracking bribes find themselves staring at their campaign receipts.

Three committee members who tried to deny a fair election find themselves staring at Russian *kompromat* they presumed deleted.

On the far right, another loud and proud family values Christian with a secret penchant for young men. Seems like there's a new one each week.

As for the rest, the Day's Bane dossiers Nox provided are far from definitive. But they don't need to be. Cast enough doubt on today and political interest wanes. Sew enough distrust and the committee loses its teeth. Dave Drogan's big reveal, now a public fumble.

And that's all that Nox needs.

So here he sits. Counting the click of his mechanical watch. Counting on those in his pocket to declare this session worth ending. To turn off the cameras, tap the gavel, and adjourn this silly committee.

Nox's thoughts drift to Alaska. A pity the research will need to be moved. Day's Bane had a certain rustic charm with its damp metal and wind.

The late Robert Chase had even surprised Nox with his dead man's switch. Yet Chase never saw the bigger picture. Day's Bane was never just a research facility, not really. It was a proof of concept, a mobile weapons platform. One that could be deployed to destroyer ships, to submarines, to coordinate with low-orbit satellites, globally strike-ready within minutes.

But that's tomorrow.

For now, the facility will need to be purged.

Nox considers risking a peek at his phone. He's curious how the intruders are faring. And how the weapons are testing.

It's a pity he can't see it live, he muses. A pity he can't be in two places at once.

Someday soon, perhaps.

LIMPING, Ellison and bravo team push the Day's Bane crew onto the top deck and into the lifeboats. It's a two-hundred-foot drop to the cold waters below. Half the crew are wishing they'd listened during evacuation drills. The other half are glad to have guns out of their backs.

The lifeboats are orange TEMPSC—totally enclosed motor-propelled survival craft—more plastic tube than open raft. The windows fill fast with nervous faces, the crew looking back as doors are slammed shut.

With a thundering clang, Marco pulls the winch, deploying the first vessel. A rumble and a rattling *whoosh* as the orange lifeboat's rollers release. Then comes the acceleration.

Thirty minutes ago the crew were swapping out fried GPUs and refilling generators. Now, their teeth are chattering as the boat slides down the ramp and into free fall. The seat straps dig in, belts squeezing as the layers of Day's Bane rush past.

The lifeboat hits nose-first, water drumming every inch of plastic. Inside, heads rock and bodies heave and the Alaskan gulf spits the lifeboat back up.

High above, Ellison watches the orange vessel bob in the water. One down, two to go. He confirms the head count, fills the second lifeboat with the remaining crew. Another slammed door, another pulled winch. Out it goes.

Rattling down the ramp, the lifeboat windows fill with eyes watching their work recede. Eyes widening as they see the impossible: a woman of starlit skin locked in a furious dance with three vaporous figures that had once lain upon surgical tables.

Figures that are tearing each other apart.

Then Day's Bane slides past, the platform and the windows, the catwalks and the pylons. A great spray of water, and the sea swallows and spits the lifeboat back up.

Ellison and the secondary team launch the final lifeboat empty. Good. Now the only way off this rig is the ride they came in on.

"Ready for evac," Ellison tells the pilot. "Pulling teams out, five minutes."

"Copy that."

"Felweather, time to roll."

IN THE HUMID warmth of the server room, Michaels covers Felweather while Caitlyn covers them both. Arms shaking, Michaels tracks the decoherent forms, sinuous limbs and shadow-wrapped legs. The cold eyes of Zade or Iliana or Raymond Flay, warping like leaves in the wind. He aims, bracing for the DEW's haptic feedback.

But it's Caitlyn there, her form heaving and swimming in starlight. He raises his NODs to give his eyes some relief.

"You know, we make quite a good team."

She says, "We always have."

He smirks. "Thank you."

"Don't thank me yet. We're not out of this mess."

"Yeah, but you've got us to the home stretch."

He raises and fires to the left of a filing cabinet, catching Iliana as she scampers across the floor. A burst of dark violet and the taste of ozone.

"That's it," Felweather shouts, yanking wires and unplugging his tablet. "The server's wiped. Ghost, can you cover our exit?"

"Already on it."

A loud crash to their left where three forms thrash at each other. A hulking shadow and a shrieking banshee. And Caitlyn, weaving like ribbons in the wind, then gone.

"Careful." Michaels pulls Felweather into a nook as the fight tumbles past. An errant limb sends Felweather's tablet sliding from his kit to the floor.

"Is it always like this?" Felweather asks. "Just crossing your fingers and hoping for the best?"

"Welcome to obsolescence." Michaels picks up the tablet. He holds it out to give to Felweather.

Then he sees what's onscreen.

>100% DATA EXTRACTION COMPLETE.

The Taser catches Michaels in the base of his neck, a half million volts surging through his nervous system and clamping his bowels. The pain doesn't hit—not yet—just the odd awareness that he is dropping, bouncing off the floor, and curling into a tight ball.

"Nothing personal, Mr. Nobody," Felweather says. "You seem like a nice guy, but orders are orders."

Felweather steps over him and takes back the tablet. A throbbing band wracks Michaels's temples, his forehead. He forces his flapping hand to rise, to snatch at Felweather's boot.

Down comes the Taser and the white heat explodes. The server room retreats to a thin point as Michaels spasms and contracts. From a dim tunnel, he hears Felweather shout, "Give the locals our best."

Minutes whirl past. An entire shadowed battle. *Breathe, Michaels. Move your toes. Now move your fingers and hands and hoist yourself up. Good.*

Dripping sweat, Michaels rises, rises, and comes to a wobbling lean against the wall. He feels… what? Pins and needles piercing deep muscle and bone. His hand flaps so fast he has to clamp it under his armpit.

And he feels lighter. His weapons are gone.

Three floors above, a golden rectangle casts dawn onto the stairs where Marco holds the door open. Felweather shields his eyes and hands Ellison the extra DEW. "Poor bastard never saw it coming. Where's the Ghost?"

"Contained." Ellison slides a chain through the door's plated handle. "Get to the bird. We're skids up in thirty."

Under cover of DEWs, they race for the chopper.

Three floors below, Michaels bats away the humming blackness. His hobbles become patterned, and his limp turns to a clumsy sprint, nervous system all out of synch. He thumbs his earpiece. "Ghost, do you copy? Ghost?" A glance at the transmitter: *BROADCAST ID DISABLED.* These bastards knocked him offline.

Forty-five adrenalized seconds later and he's at the first-floor landing bay. He runs past the wreckage crates and folded cargo nets.

There, the platform stairwell. Teeth chattering, he hobbles up. There's the door, the frame still dented from the Halligan, the sunlight beyond. Thirty feet. Twenty. Ten. It takes all his strength to push the door open.

But it only gives him an inch.

Through the chained gap, he can see the platform and a rising shadow. There it goes, the helicopter, lifting off into the amber fog.

Michaels thumbs the comms, tries all the buttons. "Ghost? Do you copy? Ghost?"

Nothing. Only hissing silence, the whistling wind through the chained gap, and the yawning shadows below, these dark halls rattling and angry.

[61]

With a crackling rush, shadows congeal and devour the rosy dawn of Alaska. Caitlyn winces, the world before her a muted deep blue. Here are the dim lines of the pod, the float membrane beneath her. She traces the warm monitor, trying to activate the visual feed. In the corner, blurry text reads *OFFLINE*.

She's been pulled out. But why?

"Rooney, something's wrong." She wipes blood from her eyes, pushes the pod door open. "I got pulled out. Someone activated the Faraday cage."

Rooney hands her a towel. "For your face."

"Are you listening? I said I'm not finished." Then Caitlyn realizes she is. In the silence, she understands. The dim form of the Taser in Rooney's hand. The bulge of the holster on her waist. "Michaels is still there."

Rooney says nothing. Just studies her. With the world swirling and the curtains edging in, it's hard to see. Is she smiling?

Caitlyn swallows, her throat salty and dry. "Why are you doing this?"

"They'll be expecting to find a few bodies at Day's Bane. And a story about an ex-field agent motivated by payback... Well, that plays better than the truth."

"The truth? What, that you're all covering your asses. Is that it?"

"Way of the world, Ms. Grey. But you'll be in good hands, soon enough."

Crimson fury boils up inside Caitlyn. *These people*. She closes her eyes, visualizes…

Visualizes nothing. Just a gray haze of static, endless and electric. She blinks away coppery tears and tries again.

"Ms. Grey, c'mon. Do you really think we'd give you Dr. Chase's amplification without protection?"

Caitlyn seethes as her world tilts behind that endless curtain. Damn, she's done a number on herself. Can't even stand without swaying. Can't see more than Rooney's vague shape.

"Sit. Hydrate. You've burned thousands of calories; you're probably ketotic." Rooney holds out a blurry something. A water bottle? Hard to tell with halos pushing in.

"I trusted you people."

"And you'll come to trust us again, in time. Or maybe you won't. It really doesn't matter to me."

Caitlyn reaches for the water, then rushes forward. Runs straight at the woman.

Or, rather, where she thought the woman was standing. Like a mirage, Rooney's somehow not there, not quite. Caitlyn hits the floor, knees scraping the concrete.

Then she rises. Another surge forward but Rooney sidesteps. Caitlyn can smell the woman's lotion. So close.

"C'mon, Ms. Grey…"

Caitlyn focuses on Rooney, who shifts into a fighting stance, left foot back, hands raised palms out. If Caitlyn could just get close, she could get back to Day's Bane and Michaels.

A third try, and the dim shape of Rooney pivots.

The punch catches Caitlyn in her stomach and drives the air from her lungs. She's on the ground, gasping for breath before she knows it. Rooney looms, a shadow past her grasp.

"You really don't get it, do you? I've killed with these fists. But you, without your little trick, you're just half blind and grasping at shadows."

She's right, the cold voice whispers deep inside. *You're not strong. Not strong enough… yet.*

Caitlyn closes her eyes. Instead of envisioning a place some far distance away, she envisions the world within herself. She can see her memories laid out on a dim stage, split by a static-laced curtain.

The shape of her father, backlit by the sunset.

Her mother, smiling as she lifts the silver medallion.

Caitlyn, sixteen and sleeping, the boat darkening around her.

The flickering lights. The fogging windows. The clock starting to crack.

Mmm, there you are, her dark partner whispers. Smoldering fingers probe the stage's black curtain from beyond. *You can't blink here, Caitlyn. You know that. You cannot step out.*

"No," Caitlyn whispers. "But maybe you can."

A sharp tug at the curtain. Oily fingers and glistening nails and eyes of furious silver. *We are strong. Stronger… together.*

And she's right, Caitlyn realizes. She's always been there, just past the edge of perception. Whispering. Encouraging. Helping Caitlyn past the impossible.

Just ask for my help.

Rooney has had enough. First that debacle in Mombasa. Then missing them by hours in Chicago. And the shootout and the good operators they lost. Now, here she is, watching this woman —this mewling *freak*—reach out to trace the empty space between them. Her dim eyes focused on nothing. The bloody tears streaking her cheeks. It'd be grotesque if it wasn't so pathetic.

But that's why the bounty's so high, Rooney supposes. Time to earn her fee.

"C'mon, Ms. Grey, we're done here. Don't make me drag you back to the room."

Then Caitlyn brushes something aside. A damp wind skitters past Rooney.

"Yes," Caitlyn whispers. "I need your help."

You need a cage, Rooney thinks. *But first, you need to be delivered intact.*

Rooney has the flex-cuffs out when she feels the cold fingers settle upon her neck. She spins away from the blind girl, checking the emptiness behind her.

She finds it no longer empty.

Impossible. Caitlyn is there. Her eyes are open and the safeguard's engaged.

And yet Caitlyn is here, too, a visage of dark splendor. Eyes of winter frost and lips like twin leeches. Shadowed skin crackles with black static.

Rooney Amaranth, a mercenary of no religious conviction, finds herself struck by awe as she beholds a glimpse of this new future. Then she is struck by frigid fingers and her world falls to the darkness Caitlyn knows so terribly well.

[62]

In the creaking depths of Day's Bane, Michaels steadies his heart and tries to rewind his dizzy thoughts. He can see the platform's blueprints and schematics, all rising from the haze of memory. The map from the tactical briefing. Their evac called for lifeboats and the helicopter. The lifeboats are gone.

And so is the helicopter.

There is a third way, however. One never discussed yet mentally bookmarked. An errant fact his mind now greedily paws at.

Beneath the fifth level hangs a series of maintenance catwalks and ladders. No lifeboats below, but there's a good chance of life preservers and vests.

Now, to make his way back down.

On the second floor, he senses it, a mad giggle that sets every hair on end. He crouches beneath a table as Iliana's mens corpus crawls along the wall.

On the third floor, he catches a glimpse through his NODs: Raymond Flay lumbering along a parallel hall.

Quietly, slowly, Michaels turns a dark corner.

And comes face to face with a man who is legally dead.

Aiden Sawyer, a fire axe in his hand, now raises it and—

"No, wait!" Michaels says, flinching and putting a finger to his lips. "Sawyer. Aiden Sawyer, wait!"

Something softens in those frantic eyes. The axe hesitates. Sawyer's dressed only in a medical gown and trailing an IV still ported to his arm. It takes Michaels less than a second to unravel this dead man's trajectory. Executed less than a week ago. Written off. Now he's waking up here where all hell's breaking loose.

"You... You know my name."

Michaels whispers, "We tried to track you down after that fake execution in Georgia."

"Fake? I don't... What'n the hell is happening?"

A clang down the dark hall. Michaels pulls Sawyer into a storage room. Keeps his finger to his lips. Thirty seconds pass, heavy and tense. Michaels can smell the man's sweat, the odor of chemicals and sterilized skin. They shaved his head, even started tattooing a number onto his forearm.

When the clanging passes, Michaels whispers, "You sold your body for medical use, right? Dr. Walker, he faked your execution and transferred you here, to a secret facility off the coast of Alaska. You were going to be experimented on and turned into a weapon. Complications ensued."

"Complications?" Sawyer takes it all in, teeth pressed so tight it looks like they might snap. Then he scoffs. "That doctor, I fuckin' knew it was too good to be true."

And that's that. Michaels gives the man his windbreaker and gestures to the hall. "Keep quiet and follow me."

He lowers his NODs and hits the hall fast and smooth. With no shoes, Sawyer is as silent as the wind.

They stop at a maintenance room, Sawyer trading out the medical gown for overalls and all-weather boots. He says, "If you're part of my imagination, well, this is one hell of a dying dream."

"I might prefer that. Okay, here we go."

Out into the hall now, where a low-frequency boom rattles their teeth and bristles their spines. Rising out of the floor like mist off a lake: two furious eyes and a broad body. Blue roots unfurl to form shimmering skin. Zade Holloway's mens corpus.

Michaels covers Sawyer's mouth and drags him down the stairs, to the fifth floor. Sawyer sputters, "What'n the fresh hell was that?"

"That weapon I said they were going to turn you into? You just met one."

Sawyer shivers. Michaels might even pity the man if they had enough time.

On the fifth floor, they blow through an unmanned security checkpoint and come to a halt. There's the door far away, daylight through salt-spattered glass. A sign reads:

Emergency Exit
DANGER! HIGH WIND!
NO UNAUTHORIZED ACCESS

From his mind's schematic, he can see the metal catwalks beyond, zigzagging and dropping below the fifth deck. Orange pylons and churning gray waters and an island too distant to reach. Grim odds, and yet better outside than in here.

Then his stomach drops.

Unfolding between them and the door: three decoherent forms, so bright and angry he doesn't need his NODs to spot them.

This is bad. As bad as it gets.

Feet pounding, heart pumping, legs like spent pistons, Michaels pushes Sawyer back the way they came, shouting, "Run!"

He makes it as far as the medical bay before they're upon him.

The first blow knocks him sideways—hard against a gurney—but he catches his balance. The second sends him spinning, cold pressure on his hip. Now he's limping past windows and labs, focused on a far corner of the hall. His concussed brain throbs with each pounding step. If he can just make it, he could double back and—

No. The hands squeeze him, the shimmers surround him, furious and consuming. The fabric on his thigh dimples. The skin on his wrist bruises. This is it.

Desperate calculations stampede through his concussed mind, alternatives and deft maneuvers and feats of brute force, each screaming for attention and not a single one plausible. Frantic, he tries to dig his left hand beneath their spectral grip. Then his fingers break with a pop.

Blinded by pain, Michaels is hoisted up. Faces close in, surrounding him, arms pressing him against the cool glass of the lab. For one terrible second, he realizes that this is it. He's had a good run, but here's where it ends.

He doesn't think of his calming prime numbers.

Nor his closet full of identical suits.

Nor his precious order.

He thinks of Caitlyn, wishing he could see her once more. To tell her what she truly meant to him. All those words he struggled with and no more breath to say them.

"Hey!" Sawyer swings the axe hard but it passes through Zade in a glistening whorl. Iliana seizes him and squeezes.

And yet, something is changing.

It begins with Zade's face and those cold, flickering eyes. Just a squint and the tilt of his blurry head. Iliana follows, releasing Sawyer. Raymond Flay's gaze shifts from Michaels to a crackling sound behind him. That's the sound of breaking glass.

"I'm not… your enemy," Michaels coughs as the crushing vise loosens. "I'm not…"

The floor rises up fast, rolling his ankles and buckling his knees. He's been released.

Because they're no longer focused on him. Because they're

staring, transfixed, at something beyond. Sawyer rubs his arm, a bruise already forming above that unfinished tattoo.

Raymond Flay raises a hand and tenderly presses it against the cracked glass. The shattering is instant, white shards dusting the control room.

Then they're gone, stepping through the partition and into the lab.

Shaking, Michaels buries his left hand beneath his right armpit. Presses his right hand against his left elbow and twists. Two fingers pop back into their sockets. Another jerk, and the third one follows.

On an instinctual level, he knows what is beyond the broken glass. He caught a glimpse while running; his mind filed it away. It's only now that he sees the full horror.

Three flickering forms stand where a control room meets a sterile medical suite. Clean lines lit by the low-energy glow of stacked devices. Machines that spin and circulate blood. Machines that hiss and click and breathe. Machines that cover faces and encapsulate brains. Acrylic-fused chests give glimpses of pumping hearts and lungs inflating and deflating within transparent sacks. Iliana's hand rises to her mens corpus, feeling her chest heave in time with those exposed lungs. Raymond Flay's eyes follow the nerve fibers spindled into sensors and chips.

There is little left of these bodies hanging here in their perpetual twilight. Little left to call human.

But enough left to recognize.

"That's my arm," Zade says. Sure enough, a faded tattoo runs from his body's bicep and ends where his left arm has been amputated above the elbow. On his right: that curious spiral code and the alphanumeric tattoo.

Zade studies his mens corpus. Two arms, liminal and strong, his irezumi tattoos almost vibrant. Those same alphanumerics: D22.

Another violent shattering, and now the three decoherents are inside the sterile lab, staring at their ruined husks as glass pebbles the floor.

"Sterile breach!" cries the alarm. "Warning: subjects exposed to contamination."

"Subjects," Zade says and crushes the speaker with a squeeze.

One by one, the shimmering projections stop at their bodies. They say nothing. No dimensional echoes or furious screams. Just the hum of air purifiers, the clicking and beeping machines that give their bodies rhythm and life.

With a vibrating finger, Iliana traces the contours of broken flesh.

Mr. Flay—all swollen muscles—kneels to behold his true form. Just a torso opened like a dollhouse, a single limp arm below an emaciated neck rising to a mask and a brain laden with tumors.

With slow fingers, he begins undoing the mask and goggles.

"Don't," Iliana says.

"I have to know."

The turn of delicate nobs and the twisting of surgical screws. Then it comes loose, the wires still clinging to the respirator. Just a raw, hollow beyond, all nerves and circuits.

"There's… there's hardly anything left," he whispers.

One by one, the others do the same. Detaching clips and pulling clamps from skin. Peeling back dark goggles. Peering at their unrecognizable reflections.

In their own ways, they each thought they were dreaming.

They were wrong.

"I'm sorry," Michaels says. And he means it. These are bad people here, monsters in life.

And yet they paid their debt. Or they were told that they had. He doesn't know what he should feel, only that he pities them. No one deserves such a fate.

"I remember it," Zade says. "They made me an offer. A way to help out my sister."

"And you did," Michaels says. "I met Beverly. She told me she loves you, despite what you did. That she was proud, too, because you got to leave the Gardens."

"Leave the Gardens," Zade repeats, wistfully. "And see so very far."

It comes first as a whisper, then rises like a kettle to a near shriek. Iliana's voice, piped right into Michaels's senses.

"Who did this to us?"

[63]

In the Hart Senate Office Hearing Room 216, beneath vaulted ceilings inspired by ancient Greece—that most sacred cradle of democracy—the committee is nearly finished with their dossiers.

The only man not blushing, sweating, or nervously turning pages sits behind a desk, his turquoise eyes set in a face that's a statue of calm.

"For years the Chinese have been forcing American companies to turn over technological secrets," Nox says. "In essence, the price of their market access has been the keys to our nation's security. Day's Bane is—well, was—a way to retain control of our vital communications so the Chinese can't just flip a switch and brick half our systems."

"And this, uh, exposure today," says the congresswoman from Milwaukee. "On a scale of one to ten, how much damage did Senator Drogan's circus create?"

"Congresswoman, I'm not sure I can answer that. Senator Drogan isn't the first to be fooled by the media's misreporting—"

"On a scale of one to ten."

"About a thirteen."

Deep murmurings from the dais and the audience behind Nox. He takes a moment to sip some water and let that number sink in.

There, at the edge, Dave Drogan clicks his pen and studies Nox, boring holes to his very core.

And what will Drogan find? Another man of ambition, Nox muses. One who saw the whole chessboard and not just a few pieces. A man not smarter, just better informed.

And Chatterjee... He'll have to do something about her too, he supposes. Trying to end run the Foundation while simultaneously torching her running mate's campaign from within. Typical politician, trying to juggle too much at once.

"Mr. Nox," the Mississippi senator says. "You've been the picture of patience here today, and more'n generous with your time. I'm hoping this here committee is in agreement we start putting this hoopla behind us, before our, uh, esteemed junior senator from Kentucky exposes any further national secrets."

Grim chuckles in the chamber. "As do I, Senator."

A squeak of microphone feedback. Yes, the cracks are forming, and with them, others will follow. Nox can see it. The committee members don't all have skeletons in their closets. But the ones that do now understand how thin that door really is.

And how quickly it can be opened.

"Well, you're a busy man, Mr. Nox, and the committee is just spinning its wheels at this point. What say we motion to adjourn?"

Nox tries to speak but an odd tickle rises in his throat. He reaches for the water. His hand stops midway.

Ice clings to the glass. Little frozen beads sliding down to the table, *clinkity clink.*

At the dais, Dave Drogan leans in and squints.

At the bank of audio-visual equipment, a C-SPAN cameraman checks the monitor.

To Nox's right, his lawyer's laptop flickers and blooms vibrant white before shutting down.

And Holland Nox feels that tickle give way to something worse. A curious tug down his left arm. A red ribbon opens from his elbow to his watch. Rubies bloom from the seam. He slaps his splitting skin and cries out.

The arrival hits the committee, a concussive rumble that shakes heavy bladders and rattles whitened teeth. The audience find their eyes rising to the chandelier, the lights twinkling like stars.

No, not here, Nox thinks. *Not now*. He still has so much to accomplish.

The arm seizes Holland Nox from behind. The body unfolds. First in a kaleidoscope of iridescent flesh, then bones and nerves and glowing red veins. Two smoldering eyes turn to behold this chamber of laws and government order.

Zade Holloway floats, tugging Nox upward, up, where legs dance a spastic jig, scattering papers and shattering the water pitcher. It takes all of Zade's focus—every last neuron—to make himself fully seen to the chamber.

And he's not alone.

In luminous splendor, two more shapes unfold from thin air: Iliana and the thunderous Raymond Flay.

The gasps come loud now, the panic rising. Two officers raise guns while people duck in their seats. Not a single person goes for the door.

Holland Nox, face reddening, fingers prying at the unbreakable tightness, is hoisted higher where all can see him.

Where he can meet the faces of the supposedly dead and their furious stare.

They do not blink. Not when their fingers dig in and squeeze. Not when they pull and tear. And not when Nox's scream hits their ears—ears they no longer possess beyond vestigial memories.

They do not stop. Not until this man who sat here and lied to the country now lies everywhere, in pieces.

[64]

THE LIVE FOOTAGE ON C-SPAN SHOWS THE IMPOSSIBLE: THREE floating figures and the dripping red mist. Then comes the stampede. The toppled chairs. The rush to the door. Hardly anyone is watching when the figures simply fade from the chamber.

But the camera is. And Michaels as well.

He closes the livestream and turns away from the computer. He waits in the control room for their return. Here they come, windswept vengeance beside ruined bodies.

Iliana says, "You promise you'll end it."

"I do," Michaels answers.

"Make it quick," Zade says.

"I will."

"Wait." Mr. Flay's eyes narrow as he studies the lab. These brutal machines. These medical utensils turned to cruel purpose. "All of it burns."

The fires begin simultaneously in separate locations.

With a twist, the kitchen gas lines rupture, propane hissing from tanks that split like frayed rope. Then the labs, with their vast chemical closets and disinfectant, their industrial hand sanitizers and Bunsen burners. And the battery floor, where towering white monoliths house lithium cells, each crumpling and flaring as shimmering fingers rend metal.

It goes on as such. The cindering electronics, the whoosh of a loose acetylene hose, the deep boom of a generator or gas tank or battery.

As they promised, Michaels and Sawyer find the red switches beneath the life support machines. They wait with them as their bodies spasm and twitch and their lungs breathe their last.

They hold their hands as they die.

In less than fifteen minutes, the structure is a blazing pyre, windows superheating, blowing out to suck in the wind. In thirty minutes, the first support beams begin to sag.

Structural steel melts at twenty-eight hundred degrees but it loses half its strength just past one thousand. The battery banks alone hit twelve-fifty.

From the distant lifeboats, Day's Bane burns bright, a pyre in the morning haze. It takes an hour at full blaze before the platform collapses. The smoke is visible for miles and the heat follows the breeze, driving off the fog.

The first helicopters arrive within the hour, rescue swimmers descending on ropes. From the lifeboats, the Day's Bane staff look out, squinting faces filling the windows. In the smoke, a rescue swimmer embraces two wet shapes.

Then they ascend into the haze.

Several thousand miles away, at another facility under lockdown, another furious purge is occurring.

It happens in a control room where a technician mashes buttons and shouts, "I don't understand. Containment's engaged!"

It happens at a security checkpoint, where stunned guards study the monitors while a shadowy young woman flickers in multiple locations at once.

And it happens in the lab, where a doctor taps a screen that shows Caitlyn's brain producing neural patterns never before seen.

At least not by these eyes.

Three decades ago, Robert Chase witnessed such a moment in his prized pupil's scans.

Then Clearwater was closed down.

Thirteen months ago, he glimpsed it again when Caitlyn met Teddy.

Then the facility came apart.

Now there is no one to perceive these sought-after measurements. No one to behold the great apex of Chase's invention.

It happens everywhere, all at once, a furious tempest that breaks lab equipment and shatters glass and sends tables flipping end over end.

At the storm's edge, the fleeing staff glimpse something that will haunt them for years: a young woman, her inky skin an ocean of stars, somehow everywhere at once.

At the storm's center, Caitlyn calmly walks, crimson streaking her cheeks, eyes unblinking and open.

Dizzy and bitter, Rooney pulls herself up off the floor and nurses her jaw. That damn freak did her trick, but how? Everything in the brief said she needed quiet and closed eyes and no Faraday cage.

But that's bullshit, Rooney realizes. They don't know what they're dealing with, not really.

Which means she doesn't either.

As the room spins in chaos and sharpened dark forms, Rooney spots the one thing not coming apart.

Caitlyn.

She fumbles for her Taser, raises it.

Then it's simply snatched away by a murky gust of wind.

Rooney thinks of the bounty. All that money, useless if she's not alive to spend it. *To hell with this job.*

She retreats, pushing aside stumbling technicians and

confused guards. She blows past them all until the door flies open and the rail yard greets her.

There, where the containers wait and old bulldozers slumber, is a landing pad and a helicopter setting down upon it and kicking up dust.

The client is early.

The helicopter doors open. The team fans out, guns drawn, squinting at the warehouse and the storm within.

The client follows them, a pasty man she recognizes by voice. "Ms. Grey, tell me she's still inside."

Rooney holds up a hand against the downwash. "Yeah, but she's pretty pissed off. Send everyone you've got. The rest of us, we should get out of here."

The client pauses. "Actually, you should stick around."

It's just a quick glance on the client's face and a nod. Not to her but beyond. Rooney understands the meaning a half second too late.

"No, wait—"

The gunshot is a near-noiseless *plap* beneath the helicopter's engine. The bullet enters her temple and exits her crown. It drags with it her ruined mind, the shattered ambition and bounties, taking all that she could buy and be and see and reducing it to nothing.

$$[\ 65\ ]$$

Caitlyn opens her eyes. Or rather, she thinks that she has. Her fingers probe the oozing shadows until the light overwhelms her.

She feels… What does she feel? Is this an overturned table? Is that a sputtering computer? She is distantly aware of whining alarms and a taste on her tongue, burnt circuits and dust.

She is back. But she's uncertain where she went or how long she was gone. Only that she was on a platform, in a boat, and then —somehow—she was *everywhere* at once.

She takes several tenuous steps, body aching like she just ran a marathon. Her crumbling vision doesn't help.

I cleared the way out, says that cold voice from the depths of her mind. *Now you need to walk it.*

"If I can," Caitlyn says, shuffling forward one step at a time.

She is aware that she is talking to herself; she knows how it looks. And yet, she also knows she is no longer alone.

Something has awoken. Grown. Emerged within her.

Something so strong she no longer worries about the familiar darkness.

Or this unfamiliar quiet that suffuses her ears.

And the numb touch of her fingers.

"Where's Rooney?"

No longer a problem. But first, you might want to change our pants.

So that's what Caitlyn does. She showers off and dumps the soiled garments in the trash. She finds fresh sweatpants and a hoodie. It takes her shaking fingers minutes to tie off the drawstring. Can't even see where the string ends. Her sense of touch is unraveling, the other senses as well.

As she dresses, she catches a glimpse of her dark partner. "You're still here?"

An inky-black smile. *Always have been. We're binary stars, the pair of us. And I've been waiting a long time.*

"Waiting for what?"

A tilt of her head and two cindering eyes. *For what we're meant to become.*

Caitlyn drinks two glasses of water, devours three bowls of Special K with strawberries, and chases it all with a can of Coke. No matter what, she is still hungry. She can hardly taste the sugar or hear the crunch of cereal or feel the cold spoon in her mouth.

It is fifteen paces across the suite's kitchenette. Twenty-five paces down the hall to the double doors. Where a guard should be stationed, there is only silence and broken glass. The handle opens to her touch.

From her left eye, the hall's a dim tube that ends at a bright door and the shape of her dark partner. From her right eye, she's looking back on a blind girl, hand carefully tracing the wall, edging closer, closer…

One hundred paces. Fifty. Twenty-five.

Then the wall changes. Her fingers scrape at… What is this? She pulls a piece of blue tape from her finger and holds it close to her nose. Written in pencil: *END WILD WALL 17.*

The wall joins an intersecting hall to her right that—impossibly—leads into a wide-open space. There are power cords here, blue tape holding them to the floor. Open electrical panels and swaying loose lights. Her muffled footsteps echo off cavernous space.

It doesn't make any sense. Unless…

It's a set, she realizes. Like a film production, staged here in some massive warehouse.

You really thought Chatterjee would build you a blind site? her dark partner asks.

Caitlyn doesn't answer. Just follows the quiet wind. Past empty carts and break stations. Past toppled chairs like the ones in her suite.

Then she sees them.

The guards and the technicians, the doctors and assistants, the entire team that kept her here for the past several days. They're sitting in a line on the cement. Their wrists are bound behind their backs. Black bags are over their heads.

A shadow breaks from the group, a hand to his ear. He's wearing body armor, fabric of sleek efficiency and low visibility, like the team on the rig. He keeps a gun slung at the ready.

"Ms. Grey, you're safe now."

"Safe?"

The shape nods. "We'll handle the cleanup. Go on. He's waiting outside."

The man gestures to that looming door lit by the afternoon glare. Pausing, Caitlyn looks back. She can see the wrecked contours of the clinic, the amplification chamber, the halls. From the inside, it had all seemed so thick, so strong.

Here, from behind, they're just nothing but drywall facades. Just more lies.

Outside, the wind whips cool across old railways where rusty warehouses moan in the breeze. Caitlyn shields her wet eyes from the sun. A dozen shadows linger at the edge of her vision.

"Caitlyn Grey." One of the shadows breaks away from the band, growing larger on approach. "We've been searching for you. Please, don't be alarmed."

It takes her great effort to see the *we* that he mentioned. More forms in the dark band. Men and women in tactical garb and heavily armed.

The nearest man says something but Caitlyn shakes her head and motions to her ears. "You need to speak up."

"I said we met at Clearwater," the man says. "You don't remember me, Caitlyn. But I remember *you*. I've never forgotten you."

"You're here to kill me?"

His tone shifts. "No, no, oh goodness, of course not."

"Good. 'Cause I've had a rough sort of day."

"Yes, I… I can see that."

She falters, stumbles to the right. Several shadows collapse upon her, arms reaching out. She should feel them helping her, lifting her back up.

Instead, she feels nothing.

"I have something to show you," the man shouts. "May I approach?"

He sounds skittish, a nervous kid, valentine card in hand and doubts gumming his tongue. Caitlyn nods.

"We pulled it from your brain scans, from the data in Clearwater. It's not perfect, but… Well, we worked with what we had. I think we can help."

His pale shape ambles toward her until he's close enough that she can smell his sweat. He holds out something bright—a tablet. Beneath the afternoon sun, it's a smear of featureless light.

"See, I've been studying your mind for the past year. When you were decoherent—when you and Teddy Jensen were entangled—you thought back to your past. There was a moment where your vitals were in perfect alignment. I used an algorithm to reconstruct that memory. Here…"

"You looked inside my head?"

He swallows. "I've been looking inside for a long time now. Sometimes I get lost. It's the most remarkable place."

She squints at the tablet. It's impossible to see, just pixelated crimsons and blues. She shakes her head. "My vision, it's—"

"Cortical blindness, right. You're probably legally blind again, maybe worse. Here, if I hold it for you, maybe you can do your thing. Step out. Blink, as you call it."

She sighs. "Look, whoever you are, I have to tell you, I'm pretty much spent."

"I understand, but I think you'll like what you see." He steps closer, holding out the blurry tablet, its colors vibrant and fiery and familiar.

"And it's Anders," he says. "My name, it's Morgan Anders."

[PART 6]

"You never change things by fighting the existing reality. To change something, build a new model that makes the existing model obsolete."

—Buckminster Fuller

[66]

The most viewed video on YouTube is a children's song about a family of sharks. The second is a banger by two Puerto Rican singers.

Until a day in late July, the third was a dancehall-infused pop song by a ginger-haired English singer-songwriter.

It is knocked off by a video titled "C-SPAN JOINT COMMITTEE HEARING ON UNDISCLOSED RESEARCH AND REVIEW."

Despite a warning that the video contains graphic content, it is viewed and emailed and analyzed down to the pixel. Global news hosts on all points of the political spectrum inch the footage forward frame by frame, narrating the impossible: three figures materializing out of thin air. Three people declared legally dead. Three furious shapes that tear a man to pieces before a stunned committee, before the impassive cameras, and now before the eyes of billions.

The top comment on YouTube simply reads, *So, how do I unsubscribe from THIS future?*

It has nearly one million likes.

Holland Nox, a man with minimal public record yet access to intelligence that landed before the Joint Chiefs of Staff. A man whom agencies are fast scrubbing from their logs. A man who—minutes before his demise—leaned into the microphone and said, "I can assure the committee, nothing would be more exciting than a little excitement in my life. However, I'm sad to inform this room that there is no covert program, no secret lab, no death ray or quantum weapon. Clearwater and now Day's Bane, these are catchy names the PR team comes up with. Far stickier than Project Upgrade the Wi-Fi."

Holland Nox, a man known as the first victim of this new technology.

The first *acknowledged* victim.

No public statements are made in these early days. Not by American agencies. Nor by congresswoman Chatterjee, who abruptly resigns, citing family matters, and hires a team of attorneys specializing in criminal and constitutional law. And nor Dr. Dennis Walker, who was last seen in Atlanta, stepping into a van labeled *Wong's Fine Chinese Dining*.

Privately, the scramble has already begun. Every agency applies maximum pressure to seize the keys. From the satellites that rented bandwidth to the redacted energy grants, phones ring endlessly across Washington and offices stay lit through the night.

Pivoting, Dave Drogan embraces the betrayal and rebrands his campaign slogan: *The Truth Must Be Freed.* The hats go for fifty dollars and come in Angry Red, Bitter Blue, Tinfoil Silver, and Redacted Black.

They sell out within minutes.

At a brief public appearance at an unmarked airfield, a man stands beside the lone senator from Kentucky. A man who died in Georgia one week ago. Legal scholars are already debating the case law of what comes next.

No agreements are reached.

In New York City, the UN convenes an emergency session. Russia threatens retaliation if this new weapon is not immediately disclosed. China summons the American ambassador, vowing to halt the manufacturing of chips and technology used in decoherence. The United Kingdom declares the experiments to be in violation of Rule 92 of the Geneva Convention.

Privately, they reach out to remind the U.S. of their long-standing alliance.

"Faraday Cage" becomes Google's most searched phrase of all time when Elon Musk tweets that he's installed them in all of his houses.

The price of mesh shielding skyrockets.

Quantum Consciousness.

Non-Local Telekinesis.

Dimensional Abridgment.

The names come in an endless stream, pundits and talk show hosts offering their own spin on this confusing new concept: that from thousands of miles away, someone could kill with a thought.

ELMENDORF AIR FORCE BASE, ALASKA
7:30 A.M., AST

FORTY-EIGHT HOURS AFTER HE LEAPT FROM A COLLAPSING PLATFORM and hit the frigid waters of the Alaskan gulf—driving his tibia up through his knee and splitting his femur like a dry log—Michaels blinks away the fog of anesthesia. There are eleven pins holding his left leg together. He counts them on instinct, finding comfort in their prime number.

"Careful now," says a voice from the corner of the hospital room. A voice that brings him back to a warm Cairo night. "They said you'd be coming out soon, and to make sure you didn't do anything dumb."

Another blink. There is a tablet in the man's hand and a medical chart on his lap.

"And I already told them you'd done enough stupid for the whole world to see."

Backlit, the visitor's features are hard to make out. Good training, Michaels thinks. They've made a fine field agent out of Brad Lee.

"Nice to see you too." Sitting up, Michaels winces. "How's your fiancée? I hope she's not too mad about Egypt."

"We're working on our trust issues and communication."

"Yeah, I hear you there."

Michaels takes stock of the room. Bare-bones medical equipment, last generation. Little barcodes to keep track of every device. This is a military facility. He's not in handcuffs, so that's one positive sign.

"I don't suppose you're here on friendly terms," Michaels says. "Have you already switched out my medical chart?"

Brad taps the folder beneath his clipboard. "My last directive was to stop you at all costs. Succinylcholine, via your IV."

Michaels runs a finger up his left arm. Sure enough, taped to his elbow ditch is the IV, the port, and the plastic tube. At the side of his bed hangs the pouch going *drip, drip, drip.*

"It's pretty neat stuff, succinylcholine," Brad says. "I had to look up how to pronounce it. In high doses, it causes total paralysis, including the lungs. Coroners call it the perfect poison because the body metabolizes it so fast. I was told the best time to administer it is a few minutes before the target wakes up."

Brad places the vial on the bedside table. Michaels just studies that smooth face of the young agent, like looking back on his own past. He might have told Brad not to do it. Might have offered him alternatives. But he's tired, so damn tired of all the endless deception.

"And I believe I told them to go fuck themselves," Brad says. "They'd have to send a whole unit with the security I've set up."

A deep sigh settles inside Michaels, like a warm blanket. His eyes moisten and a weak smile tugs at his chapped lips.

"Don't get too misty-eyed, okay? You're a national hero. Well, you would be, I mean…"

"Nobody knows my name," Michaels says.

Brad nods. "You know how it goes."

He does. There's some comfort in that.

"So, what has this all cost you?" he asks.

"Nothing. Everything. The Foundation collapsed hours after the platform."

"Collapsed?" Michaels winces, scooting forward too fast.

"Full burn. Every phone number, all of our devices remote-wiped. There were cleaning teams scrubbing the sanctorums. Then cleaning teams for the cleaners. Conspiracies within conspiracies until the whole thing doesn't exist. Which means I am now gloriously unemployed."

"Something will come after. It always does."

A nurse enters, nodding at Brad and checking out Michaels's vitals. It's a quiet affair until the nurse reaches for the chart at the foot of the bed and finds the slot empty. Grumbling, she takes it from Brad, who watches every swipe of her pen.

"Mr. Michaels," the nurse says, "I've dealt with you black-ops types before. But none with a partner as stubbornly protective as Mr. Lee here. You've got a real sheepdog watching over you."

"He's not my partner," Michaels says, stretching his bruised leg out so the nurse can inspect the stitches and pins. "He's my friend."

THE HOSPITAL COURTYARD is a thing of military inspiration: scrubby bushes swallow an androgynous statue and concrete benches offer a meager view of the base. A few recuperating soldiers suck down cigarettes and grind them in ashtrays.

Michaels grips the armrests as Brad pushes the wheelchair down the ramp. They find a quiet spot by a dry fountain.

"So, how much do you remember?" Brad asks.

Michaels considers it. There was the fire, the scramble down the catwalks. After that, mostly flashes out of order. "I remember the fall, but I don't remember the jump. And the rest..." He shrugs.

After a moment, Brad says, "I spoke to the rescue diver that fished you and that Sawyer guy out. He was convinced there was a third. Some woman keeping the two of you afloat. When he went back down..." Brad shakes his head.

Michaels smiles. Perhaps it's the concussion, but he doesn't remember that either. Nor does he doubt it.

"Tell me she's safe."

Brad hesitates. "This is where the good news concludes. Caitlyn was taken."

"Taken? By who?"

"Someone was selling Day's Bane out piecemeal on the black market. Chase or Nox were the prime suspects. Turns out it was just some lab rat. You recognize him?"

Brad passes his tablet to Michaels. The face on the screen is a distinct tickle. He has to reach back into the hazy weeks at Clearwater to dredge up the name.

"Anders," Michaels says. "He was one of the technicians."

"Good memory. He survived the massacre. Nox made him Chase's number two. He was running the whole Frankenstein unit you found. Anders got Nox to start tracking Caitlyn and you. Chatterjee's team got there first."

"Chatterjee." Michaels struggles to put it together. His gaze falls upon the base and the creamy morning beyond. "Her team turned on me."

"Yeah, it's five kinds of twisted. Chatterjee double-crossed Nox in the run-up to Drogan's hearing. Anders used that confusion to double-cross her. He's been pre-selling the findings from Clearwater on the dark web, using that to buy out Chatterjee's team and go rogue. Nox called it a Russian doll scheme, plots within plots. Only problem was, Nox was one of the dolls nested inside. While you were storming the oil rig, Anders's second team hit Caitlyn's safe house outside Columbus."

"How'd they find it?"

"A mole. You had the pleasure of meeting her in Mombasa."

A flash of a woman smiling down the bar. Another flash and she's throwing punch after punch. "Nandipha?"

Brad shrugs. "Her real name was Rooney Amaranth, a bounty hunter out of Pretoria. She was shot at close range along with a dozen support staff. What was it you taught me about conspiracies? The more people involved, the faster the collapse."

"Yeah, that's about right."

"Once they had Caitlyn, Rooney was another loose end. That's when they all vanished. Anders. Chatterjee's team. Even some trainee named Diego who'd been feeding them intel from inside Kray Mesa."

"We need to start sweeping." Michaels grips the wheelchair, tries to turn it but ends up rattling the whole thing. "Here, help me back inside."

"Hold up a second."

But Michaels doesn't want to hold up. He winces, trying to rise from the chair and hobble back toward the door. He has to get to his room, has to get his clothes and his shoes, get the hell out of here and start looking.

Brad says, "C'mon, we've got every possible resource searching for her."

Michaels makes it three hops on a wobbly leg before his knee buckles. He reaches for the door but finds the courtyard rising up. Stars bloom in his eyes as he hits the concrete.

"I have to find her. We have to."

"And we will. Just… c'mere." Brad digs a hand beneath Michaels's shoulders, hoists him up and back into the wheelchair. "Sit before you re-break your leg, okay? Thank you. Now listen, there's another reason I'm here. You were right about the Foundation; something is coming after it. They want you involved."

"Me?" Sweat beads his skin, his left leg all needles and glass. "Why me?"

"Because the powers that be trust you," Brad says. "Because you knew the Foundation and where it went wrong. Mostly, because you did the right thing once: you walked away."

$$[\ 68\ ]$$

Descending through dense morning mist, the Gulfstream G200 lands and taxis to a hangar at the far edge of the base.

Officially, this is a fuel stop. A brief interlude on a revitalized campaign tour overseeing off-shore wind farms built with legislation he sponsored. He will shake hands and take questions and pose before a giant turbine, his war-hero smile gleaming white like the fresh-painted blades.

Unofficially, he is here to pick up a man who legally died. And to talk to another man whose agency never existed.

With the help of a cane and a leg brace courtesy of Lovelace Biotronika, Michaels limps up the stairs and boards the jet. He gives himself decent odds that he will walk out. Despite the Secret Service agents and the weapons under their coats. Despite the knowledge he possesses.

The senator nods and gestures to an empty seat in the cabin. His eyes are on the TV. CNN is looping footage of the smoldering oil rig. A panel of experts on Fox News has labeled this the dawn of mental warfare. CNBC shows Chatterjee, flanked by attorneys, ignoring a horde of reporters and scurrying into her limo.

Politics. It's all a bit much for Michaels.

Drogan mutes the TV. "Feels weird, doesn't it? All that's

changed. Like one day we'll wake up, and we won't even recognize the world that we've built. Like we're already there."

This is where he wants Michaels to nod, or say something, or fill in the silence. Instead, Michaels just sits and listens. Dave Drogan, smaller in person than he appears on TV. They always are.

Drogan drums a finger down his armrest. "You are not a popular man, my friend. You've exposed our nation's deepest secret while destroying the very organization my former running mate had a hand in creating. Dr. Chase's tech has gone rogue. I've heard the word *treason* more times in the past three days than I've heard in my life."

Michaels keeps his eyes on the senator. Squeezes his hand between his sore knees to keep it from twitching.

A long beat as Drogan holds his stare. Only the distant chatter of the ground crew refueling the jet. Then Drogan grins. With his loose tie and his five o'clock shadow, his silver-fox hair and muscular arms, he looks less like a politician or a war hero. Just another nervous man trying to understand a future that's suddenly present.

"You know what I respect about you, Gideon? Can I call you—"

"Absolutely not. Michaels is fine."

"Fair enough. Where was I? Right, what I respect about you is you're a survivor. I know that because I'm a survivor. When that IED blew up my convoy, I spent three days in a drainpipe. Three days while insurgents executed my friends, burned their bodies, and stole off with every weapon we had. They awarded me the Purple Heart but I never deserved it. My brothers and sisters in arms, they did. But the thing is, people need a chest to pin a medal on. Otherwise, it's just one tragedy after the next. People need hope. So from that desert and that drainpipe I built a new life."

He taps his left arm, more mottled flesh and burnt scars than smooth skin.

"I'm up forty points in the polls. Four months from now, there'll be an election. Two months after that, I'll be sworn in. That's the future, Michaels. But Day's Bane, decoherence, that's now. It's loose in the world and people are scared. We've got the momentum and the political capital, but it needs to be spent, fast."

The chair squeaks as Drogan leans forward. The cabin constricts. All at once, Michaels is aware just how very far off the map he's wandered.

The slow roll of Caitlyn's boat in the sea.

The two of them swimming in the teal waters.

That warm Cairo night.

And then waking up in that Kentucky cabin, the empty bed beside him.

"This is your desert ambush, Michaels, your chance to build something from the ashes of this mess. So, what I need to know is, are you with me? Will you help me build something new to keep America safe?"

Michaels lets the moment wash over him. This morning, a nurse helped him clean his metal-studded leg. Now here he is, so close to the presidential front-runner he can smell Drogan's cologne.

Holland Nox was neither mentor nor friend, and yet he taught Michaels a great many things. When the world tilts and teeters and accelerates too fast, that's when you retreat inward and use the patterns of this moment to plan your next move. He does this, taking a page from Caitlyn's book and closing his eyes.

So, what does Michaels see?

War. Neither cold nor hot but waged in shadows and sharpened with algorithms and renegade science. He sees a global hoarding of data. Distrust on eight billion lips.

He sees dark facilities in silos where missiles once slept. Endless rows of bodies in twilight consciousness, waiting like the terracotta warriors of antiquity, to rise and serve new emperors, new masters.

He sees society retreating inward, trading safety for paranoia and a dream of protection. One where enemies lurk unseen yet are always felt, always strike-ready.

And at the end of that path, he sees civilization's collapse.

"No," Michaels says, the word leaving his lips effortlessly, the sum total of his mental simulations if he is to accept this offer.

"What do you mean?" Drogan doesn't quite know what to say. This wasn't the expected answer to such an offer.

Which is why it feels right.

"No to what part?"

"No to all of it." Michaels tries to read the senator's face but he's never been good with such skills. Is that anger or shock creasing his brow? Perhaps both.

"Whatever we build with this—no matter how well-intentioned—it will ultimately become our own monster. The world doesn't need another Clearwater, nor another Foundation."

"You could head this agency, choose the direction it goes. Total control."

"With what I know, what you've told me, I can do that already. But there's only one direction we're going. We're going to find Caitlyn. Then we're going to burn and bury this technology, every last server and scrap. That's the goal. That's the *only* goal."

"So that's your answer? You're refusing my offer?"

The senator draws a long, steady breath. Dave Drogan, Purple Heart recipient, author, two-term junior senator, and one hell of a survivor. His eyes blaze in the sterile light of the plane. That's a predator's gaze. Michaels felt it from Nox.

He meets that gaze and does not break it.

"Yes, I am refusing. But I'm giving you a chance to be part of mine."

Drogan blinks first. "I can see why you gave your former agency such frustration." Then he smiles. The politician outplayed. "And I'm glad we understand each other."

It was never an offer but a test. A friendly wink from Drogan tells him he passed.

For now, Michaels thinks.

"I look forward to helping you," Drogan says. "Whatever you need."

Rising, Michaels takes a wobbling moment to steady his nerves.

"Oh, and something to consider, now that we're in alignment." Drogan swipes and taps his tablet, streams a video to the cabin's TV. "We pulled video from that safe house in Columbus."

Michaels studies the screen. The angle is high and poorly lit, just some interior security feed.

First comes a furious wind down a long hall. Then the shaking of lights, the rattling of doors. The air grows thick with dust and debris.

What he thought was smoke and shadow resolves into the outer edge of a flickering vortex, a storm swallowing the hall. A storm made of racing shapes. Arms that stretch and fingers that peel the very paint from the walls.

And Caitlyn, in the center, walking one step at a time.

A whirling piece of debris hits the camera and knocks it offline.

The video picks up outside, where the noon sun glows off the warehouses and shipping containers. The shadows of a dozen armed mercenaries in tactical black.

There, in the center, where the biometric software highlights their faces and analyzes their voices, is a squat man with long, greasy hair.

Anders.

And limping toward him, Caitlyn.

She falls to her right but several mercenaries catch her. She looks totally spent. It kills Michaels to see that.

"What's he giving her?" he asks, leaning close to the TV.

"He's not giving her anything," Drogan says. "He's showing her something."

Closer now, so close that the pixels merge into a grid of endless colors. Michaels can feel the screen's warmth.

There's Caitlyn, her thin form, hair blowing in the wind. The video feed flickers, and now it's like there's two of her. One, in soft colors and tan skin. Another, in dark shades.

But that's impossible; her eyes are still open.

And then it's just Caitlyn. She's holding the tablet, studying the screen as a tired smile tugs at her lips.

She passes it back to Anders, says something too soft for the mic to pick up. The caption reads *INAUDIBLE*.

Then, the two of them walk off toward a helicopter. Anders opens the door and Caitlyn steps in. That's where it ends.

Drogan clears his throat. "So you see, Michaels. Caitlyn wasn't taken, not exactly. She went with them on her own."

Michaels says nothing, simply rewinds the video. Back to the handoff, the tablet. Back to Caitlyn's face leaning in—blinking—so she can see the screen.

Closer, closer, and now the TV is all he can see. Then the tablet Caitlyn's holding, a screen within a screen. Those are deep crimsons and amber, blues turning to black when dusk overtakes the day on far-distant waters. Those are the colors of the coast they once sailed, colors he could never forget.

And on that screen she holds, two faces turn, looking back, a soft focus hardening as they come into frame.

Those are Caitlyn's parents there, smiling and sun-kissed and looking out across time.

THERE IS A BOAT AT ANCHOR IN A SUN-SPECKLED BAY WHERE THE shorebirds fly in the tropical breeze. The boat is forty feet long and packed with trinkets from every port it has touched. The rattan basket and placemats from Denpasar, Bali. The Kampot pepper grown in Cambodia's red soil. The black pearls from Seychelles, and how they dance iridescent around her mother's wrist.

And the Ganesha medallion that now hangs from her neck.

It is this figure—her mother, Terry—that blooms into view against the nautical twilight. Her fingers pluck ice from the cooler and drop three cubes into a glass. Then comes the sugar and lime and the Dzama rum from Madagascar.

"Ah, she's awake," Terry says and hands the cool glass to her husband. "I was wondering when you'd climb out of the shadows."

With wobbly legs, Caitlyn hoists herself out of the cabin and into the eventide glow. It takes her eyes a moment to adjust to the cockpit, to the light. The darkening sky above her, the splash of crimson and amber to the west. Blue-black to the far east, where the first stars are beginning to blink. And the sea, a mirrored bed that reflects towering clouds. A perfect glass marble where all boundaries merge.

"You were gone for a while there." Terry's fingers dip into the cooler and pluck out more ice. "Here, something to cool yourself down."

Caitlyn reaches for the glass, but something stops her fingers. Her arm. Where teenage flesh should be colorful, tattoos swim within skin.

"Caitlyn, sweetie, is everything all right?"

Caitlyn takes the cold glass from her mother. Her grateful fingers soak up the chill on this warm evening, wherever the sea has brought them.

"Yeah, Mom," Caitlyn says. "Everything's all right."

She tilts the glass, sipping the cocktail. A cool salve for her throat and a warm fire for her gut. And she smiles, realizing this is the first time she's had a drink with her parents.

"What is it, sweetie?"

"Nothing," Caitlyn says. "It's just… It's good to see you. Both of you."

Atop the cabin, her father is setting up the boat's new weather station. The wind whips his black hair against his face. How long has it been since she's seen his eyes?

"Cait, do me a favor and throw the breaker," he says. "Should be the second from the top."

"Down below?"

He looks at her. "Of course. You know where it is. Heck, you know this boat blind."

And she does. It's just… It's been a while, hasn't it? So many miles.

Below deck, she finds the breaker box and flips the black switch. Her father calls out that it's all good. Everything is working as intended.

But is it?

Because there's an odd sound now from the depths of the boat.

Caitlyn stretches out, peering below the breaker box, into the narrow berth that leads into the heart of this craft.

There, where all lines should tighten and space should

compress, stands the impossible: a door that has no business being here on this boat.

Behind its clinical whiteness, its metal knob and solid frame, there is a hissing rise and a click, as steady as clockwork. There is a machine-like beeping, as precise as the tides. And a chorus of voices, whispers and words stretched and distorted, like sound through a curtain.

There is no engine there, behind that door that doesn't belong. Caitlyn senses that if she were to reach out and open this door, if she were to look past the very heart of this moment, all that is important and good would cease to exist.

So she doesn't.

She turns and shimmies out and climbs up the stairs, into a view of this gleaming bay against great jungled rocks and endless white beaches. Gulls cry out to the south. To the north, storm clouds rumble.

"All done," she says and finds her cocktail. She savors the sweet and the bitter, how perfectly they mix on her tongue.

Her father speaks, not from the top of the cabin but from everywhere, his words a booming thunder born deep in her mind and echoing forever.

"Caitlyn, are you listening?"

"Yes. I'm listening."

"Good. Now it's time to begin."

ACKNOWLEDGMENTS

Each novel is its own monster built from scavenged parts and influences and given shape along the way. I'm fortunate to have had some truly great help in imbuing *Refraction* with life.

Clay Stafford and the team at Killer Nashville connected me with law enforcement and medical professionals that shaped *Blind Site* and now *Refraction*. Plus, they put on one hell of a conference. You'd be surprised how effective a good mock crime scene is at analyzing violence and blood spatter patterns. Thanks to them for nurturing these books when they were in their larval stage. And thanks as well to the FBI's IPPAU, who entertained some truly ridiculous questions and helped me understand investigative procedure at the federal level. Additional thanks to the San Jose State University Department of Justice Studies and the men and women of law enforcement who gave their time generously to answer this writer's far-fetched questions. Jan Stevens and Todd "Raid Leader" Kawasaki, thanks for answering my firearm questions and patiently, kindly explaining why a silencer doesn't work on a .38 Special. And my sincere thanks to my doppelgänger brother from another mother, Texas badass Andy van Wey, who always offers excellent suggestions on SWAT tactics and procedure.

Some of Michaels's paranoia and practice was formed by Kevin Mitnick and Robert Vamosi's excellent book *The Art of Invisibility: The World's Most Famous Hacker Teaches You How to Be Safe in the Age of Big Brother and Big Data*. Additionally, Judy Melinek and T.J. Mitchell's book *Working Stiff: 2 Years, 262 Bodies and the Making of a Medical Examiner* is a gruesomely beautiful work and a must-read for anyone curious about what happens in the autopsy suite. For an insightful trip into the brain's inner workings, be sure to pick up Michael Pollan's wonderful book *How to Change Your Mind: What the New Science of Psychedelics Teaches Us About Consciousness, Dying, Addiction, Depression, and Transcendence*. For anyone else struggling with looped thinking, check out Dr. Jeffrey M. Schwartz's book *Brain Lock*. And for another perspective on consciousness, cognition, and the beautiful horror of our own minds, check out Barbara Lipska and Elaine McArdle's excellent memoir *The Neuroscientist Who Lost Her Mind: My Tale of Madness and Recovery*.

On the creative front, my deepest gratitude to my beta team, who helped in the checking of facts and the hunting of stray prose. Thanks to Bodie Dykstra for suffering my malapropisms and comma splices with patience and grace. On the audio front, Tom Jordan did another bang-up job with the performance. It's truly a delight to hear him read my words.

All that I got right is due to the fine people above. All that I fumbled is on me.

Refraction is speculative, but you know what isn't?

In 2019, Yale researchers kept pig brains alive for up to thirty-six hours after death, allowing cells to restart their metabolic processes. Also in 2019, researchers used deep neural networks (DNN) in tandem with functional magnetic resonance imaging (fMRI) to reconstruct images from brain wave activity. Neuralink, Elon Musk's company focused on cutting-edge brain interfaces, is already running clinical trials of its embedded system-on-chips, on both pigs and monkeys. Human trials are planned to begin soon.

While the Foundation is fictional, some maintain that there are over twenty-one *trillion* dollars missing from defense funds. Since independent audits began in 2017, the Department of Defense has failed every one.

As always, my thanks and love to Marissa, my wife, my best friend, my partner through this crazy adventure of life. Writers are needy folk, and she puts up with a lot of my insane ideas and questions. If you read something you enjoyed, it probably started as a what-if on one of our walks.

And you, dear reader, who made it here to the end. In an age of infinite distraction, you've chosen to spend some time with my words and in my worlds. Thank you, truly.

Andrew Van Wey
March 2022

Novels

Forsaken: A Novel of Art, Evil, and Insanity

Head Like a Hole: A Novel of Horror

Blind Site: The Clearwater Conspiracies (Book One)

Refraction: The Clearwater Conspiracies (Book Two)

The Last Shadow: The Clearwater Conspiracies (Book Three)

Collections

Grim Horizons: Tales of Dark Fiction

ABOUT THE AUTHOR

A child of the eighties, Andrew Van Wey was born in Palo Alto, California, came of age in New England, and lived as an expatriate abroad for nearly a decade. He currently resides in Northern California with his wife and their Old English Sheepdog, Daeny.

When he's not writing Andrew can probably be found mountain biking, hunting for rare fountain pens, or geeking out about D&D and new technology.

For special offers, new releases, and a free starter book, please visit andrewvanwey.com

instagram.com/heydrew

facebook.com/andrewvanwey

goodreads.com/andrewvanwey

bookbub.com/authors/andrew-van-wey

amazon.com/author/andrewvanwey

twitter.com/andrewvanwey